Kilo

M Y Alam

route

M Y Alam

M Y Alam was born in Bradford and has lived there all his life. He currently works as a researcher and part time lecturer at the University of Bradford, a bastion of enlightenment which pays enough to stop him from resorting to criminal acts in order to survive. He is currently working on writing a third book as well as considering growing a neat but thick Magnum P.I.-style moustache. As yet, however, he is not thinking about growing a beard and blowing himself up in a busy shopping mall although he might just do that in order to boost the sales of this book.

First Published in 2002 by Route
School Lane, Glasshoughton, West Yorks, WF10 4QH
e-mail: books@route-online.com

ISBN: 1 901927 09 1

Cover Design: Andy Campbell

Editor: Ian Daley

Thanks to
Anthony Cropper, Isabel Daley, Maria Garcia,
Lorna Hey, James Dean Garside

A tip of the hat to
Martin Scorsese and Nicolas Pillegi

Printed by Bookmarque Ltd, Croydon, Surrey

A catalogue for this book is available from the British Library

Full details of the Route programme of books
can be found on our website
www.route-online.com

Route is the fiction imprint of YAC, a registered charity No 1007443

YAC is supported by
Yorkshire Arts, Wakefield MDC, West Yorkshire Grants

For Parents

'The man who views the world at fifty the same as he did at twenty has wasted thirty years of his life'

Muhammad Ali

'You talkin' to me?'

Robert De Niro, *Taxi Driver*, 1976

dil walla dhukra

I ended up doing the deal with old Satnam Singh. So here I am, standing where destiny should have put me in the first place. I used to dream about this. I wanted this more than anything in the world. And now that it's mine, it's such a disappointment, such an anti-climax. All that fuss for nothing. A shop? Running a shop? Am I being serious? A pissy little convenience store? I sell everything from condoms to cigarettes; carpet cleaner to coke. Why would a guy like me, with my background, even consider something so mundane, something so dull and so boring? Truth is, I needed to know if I could do it – if it was still a part of me – and that's all there is to it. So now I know that I can't, that this life is not for me after all. Better a doleite, a mugger or even a low life drug dealer than this. Keeping a shop is no job; more like a life sentence. Call it an error of judgement but let's not start nit picking. It's not the first mistake me or mine ever made.

Satnam Singh: the man who sold me my birthright. He said he understood how I felt and wished me well as he handed the keys over.

Meanwhile Satnam Singh's bought himself another shop. Must be in his blood, I reckon. For now, me and him aren't too different, though. Like him, I exist independently, without history, without a significant past. One of the many little people. Most of my customers don't even look at me as my ever smiling mouth thanks them for their purchases of sweets, cigarettes and daily dose of truth. Punters are the same no matter what they buy because the only thing they're interested in is what's in it for them; what they get out of the deal. So as I stand here, smiling at all these people who I don't know and, in all probability never will, a little piece of me dies. I'm so much more than what they see. The life I lived, the one no one will ever know about now, or even suspect a humble shopkeeper could have possibly lived, is over and although that's a good thing, I still find myself – from time to time – grieving the loss.

Still, considering how things have turned out I should feel good about myself. Never had to buy into that rat-race dictated lifestyle and it looks like I never will. The shop? This shop is the end result but it's not forever. The shop's nothing, really – just a front which helps justify me, my money and my place in the world. I hate it but I can't seem to let it go.

It's like a drug: the highs are good but never last long enough and the lows, well, the lows – like now – they speak for themselves.

Price visits now and then, checking up on me, like he does. Eager to know how things now go for the man all but Price would call Kilo. Price needs to be sure I'm still on the same side as him, which, so he reminds me, happens to be the winning side. Price is something else, really. He hasn't changed one bit and why should he? There are some people who are born to be what they are and that's just how it is with him. Always been a copper and always been happy being that. For Price there is order and sense in the world. There's so much more to him than simply catching the bad guys. Price is a rare beast in that he still allows his mind and his morality to dictate his life. For Price the law of men is only a guide, a very rough one at that. Why else would I be here, standing behind a counter instead of spending most of my day behind a heavy, metal door? That's right, Solomon Price – a copper no less – is my saviour. But the man himself doesn't buy that theory. Prison and even death were always possibilities for a guy like me but he reckons the chances got slimmer, not fatter, as time went by.

'I didn't save you,' he told me. 'You did that on your own, Khalil.'

I didn't respond. I find it difficult to talk to Price because he makes me nervous. He makes me nervous because he knows me. He knows me because… well, because he knows me. Knows me as well as I know myself.

'So this is you, then?'

'For now,' I said, after a moment's hesitation.

'Are you okay, Khalil? You seem a little… preoccupied. Nervous.'

'Headache,' I lied. 'Just this headache I got.'

'I see,' he pondered. 'But is this you? Is this what you want? It doesn't seem you, somehow.'

I was about to ask him how he would know *what seemed to be me* but I decided against that. Price just knew. Always had and always would. I hate people who not only know things about others, but also know they know as opposed to only thinking or believing they know. There's a difference.

'Trying it for a while. See how it goes.'

'Turning a profit are you?'

Profit. One hell of a word. It's what we live for. We all want to maximise our earnings be they the fruits of labour or that most exploitative of concepts that we call profit. In the modern world there's good profit and there's bad profit but it's all the same shit. In one way or another, profit means death. Multi-national corporations kill just as many people as the more illicit of entrepreneurs. Myself, I know people who have killed and died in its pursuit. Hell, I was one of them.

'Enough. I make enough,' I said.

'Good. That's good.'

Price paused and moped around for a few seconds. Something was on his mind. I could tell. Maybe him and me had some weird telepathy shit going on.

'I was wondering,' he said, pausing to clear his throat. 'Wondering if you'd like to come over some time.'

I didn't get it.

'What? Come over where?'

'To my house. For a meal. Just you, me and my wife. I'm inviting you for a meal.'

I could have pissed myself laughing but I didn't even crack a smile. Being treated like this – as a friend and equal – was an absurd thought considering who I was and what I'd done. But that's Price for you. Who else but him would treat me that way? And where else but here, in the most culturally diverse, equally opportune and economically active of cities called Bradford would a copper be so human?

'So what do you think?'

'I'll think about it,' I said. 'Maybe we could do that.'

'Well, anyway,' he smiled. 'I've some other good news for you.'

Price's other job must have been the angel of the lord or something; bringing me tidings of peace and joy and whatever else he could muster.

'Oh?'

'You'll be pleased to know that the press should be getting a hold of the dirt in a day or so.'

'Dirt?'

Price beamed at the rack of newspapers.

'It'll be leaked, no doubt,' he said, and then added: 'The truth, I mean.'

'The truth? What truth?'

'About him, his double life. His real life.'

I nodded and for a moment thought the same could be applied to myself. I dismissed the thought quickly. Didn't want to go back there again.'

'Yeah? And who'll do the leaking?'

'Who do you think, Khalil?' he said, coming over all pleased and satisfied with himself. 'Don't worry, you'll be kept out of it.'

I nodded.

'You forget,' I reminded him. 'I am out of it. I'm a shopkeeper now.'

1. witness

dream a lie

Near enough four hours I'd been there. Since six that evening. Like every other day, my dad had been up and at it since dawn, non stop, without a break. He looked tired, but he always looked that way. My dad: the shopkeeper, the husband, the smiler, the moaner and yes, the perpetual yawner. Seemed as if just those things made him that person but it wasn't like that at all. So much about him that I never knew, not because he kept his personal life personal, but because his professional life, if that's the right term, happened to take over every other part of his existence. He worked in a shop which made him a shopkeeper. That's just what he became to me and to the people he served. And he served them well. I discovered, perhaps too late, that the shopkeeper part of him functioned as the superficial, the least important component that made the actual measure of him. So much more than he appeared to be.

I got such a kick working in the shop. One day, when I eventually grew into an adult, I'd be in his place, serving customers but without him watching over me. He'd remind me of the good times to come and I'd yearn just a little bit more, just a little bit harder. Believe it or not I wanted that – a shopkeeper – more than anything else in the world. And then, one night, the dream died and the nightmares began.

We rarely got someone so late but still, you never could tell who'd walk in next. This one time, a customer walked in and bought a whole case of Tennents Super lager, two bottles of rum and a dozen packs of smokes. Customers like that were few and far between but still, we lived in hope. Like I said, you never could tell.

Missus Ross. Knocking on a bit but she deceived any young potential lovers of her true age by applying ample layers and varieties of potted rejuvenation. Blue eyelids, rosy red cheeks, pink lips and hair which always seemed to turn out wrong: that night, a curious mixture of yellow, gold and brown. A bit of a slapper but always nice and pleasant enough. She bought *The Sun* and on Saturdays she'd collect *2000AD* comic for her 29 year old son, Gavin. Without doubt Gavin was the most miserable bastard I knew. At the time, I had no idea as to his problem but I realise now that Gavin's misery stemmed from his lack of experience with the opposite sex: bought top shelf wank mags as if he had a couple of voices in his head insisting on such purchases.

She didn't look too well that night, Missus Ross.

'Gammy tummy,' she moaned. 'Y'got summat to help settle it?'

Although a mere convenience store owner, my old man happened to be versed with remedies for all manner of ailment and condition: *Beecham's Hot Lemon* for cold and flu-like symptoms, *Nurse Harvey's Gripe Water* for the child with trapped wind or colic, *Savlon Antiseptic Spray* for minor burns and then there were all the stomach/indigestion lines: *Remegel*, *Alka Seltzer* and, of course, good old sticks of *Rennie*, one of which Missus Ross bought, then promptly left.

A couple of minutes remained before locking up time, long enough for the final ritual: cashing up. One of the high points of any day involved watching him count the takings. One note sliding over the next, his fingers and thumbs moving with the precision and exacting rhythm of a set of German pistons.

Next, off came his grey, nylon, never-crease shop coat. Another honest day's work done and soon time for rest. It felt good, now that we were all but done. I couldn't wait to get some food down me. Food always tasted better when I worked in the shop. I could smell it cooking, on the wind almost. According to my dad, good, honest, honourable and above all halal work had a way of giving any man a healthy appetite.

'O-right,' he said. 'Home time here now, son.'

I never worked that one out. In the shop he spoke that halfway English as if it was the only language he knew. At home, however, English seemed to lose all value due to it being rarely uttered by any of us. Over time, this non-use of English became an unspoken rule. I had no idea why, and although he never said anything about it explicitly, it felt like a rule simply because no one in our house ever broke it.

I walked around to the front of the counter, jangling the keys while he had his usual last minute glance around the shop. I felt a slight draft hit the back of my neck as the door opened. I turned around to look, hoping the one who bought the lager, rum and cigs had decided to pay us another visit.

I recognised them. Not the big spenders we stayed open for. These were the most undesirable of customers. The white bloke had short, closely shaven hair, a gold earring, tatty jeans and out of his T-shirt protruded two of the most veiny, muscly and tattooed arms I'd seen in my young life. And the other one? A huge Pakistani with a pony tail and bags of bad attitude. Still, I couldn't stop myself from gawping at the main man, the one who looked a little crazed. I was a kid but I'd heard stories about him, mostly from other kids like me. Charlie Boy.

'Evenin',' he said. 'Bet you didn't think we'd be back.'

Charlie Boy looked at his mate, Pony Tail.

'Bet you he gives us a hard time.'

Pony Tail looked my old man up and down, nodded and then replied:

'Nah. Bet he don't.'

'Alright,' said Charlie Boy, 'You're on. How much?'

Pony tail thought for a moment and said:

'Tenner.'

'Tenner? Make it worthwhile at least. Make it fifty.'

Pony Tail mulled over the proposition some more and finally replied.

'Right then, fifty it is.'

Meanwhile, I could sense my old man's growing mystification at all this talk. He stepped forward, only a half step mind.

'What you want you? Why you trouble give me?'

Charlie Boy smiled and then held his hand out. Pony Tail shook his head, cursed then pulled out a wad of notes and peeled off five.

'Nice doing business with you,' said Charlie Boy.

'Jammy,' replied Pony Tail.

Charlie Boy cracked his knuckles loudly and stepped further into the shop, only a foot or two away behind me now. I wanted, needed to move but I couldn't even lift my feet. Charlie Boy, like last time, grinned confidently and then stepped closer still, the sole of his shoe bending to creaking point.

'See you got yer bodyguard again,' he sneered, flicking his head my way.

'Khalil,' my dad gently called.

I looked up at him and opened my mouth to say *Jee*. Nothing, not even a breath came out.

'Here come, Khalil, son. Here come.'

Eyes closed, I took a step but moved no more when the heavy hand of Charlie Boy placed itself on, and then held, my shoulder. A shiver ran through me.

'Now where the fuck d'you think you're going?'

I carried on looking at my old man, tears welling up, clouding my vision. We shouldn't have been there. Should have been in the comfort and safety of the old banger of a family car, on our way home, hungry but looking forward to the only real meal of the day.

'Dad?'

I started sobbing. I felt so ashamed; tears were fine in front of my mother but not my father, not other men. Charlie Boy didn't give a shit. My dad? He looked ready to start crying himself but that couldn't have been true. Inconceivable for any father or any man to cry. It's not what they do.

'Khalil?' he sighed, then shuffled around, not sure whether to come around the front of the counter to save me or to stay there, where he wanted me to be.

'You wouldn't have it, though. Would you?'

'You bloody bashtur you!'

I'd heard him lose his temper before but not like this. Strange, but as he cursed, he sounded unsure of himself, scared even. Charlie Boy chuckled, my dad's accent and pronunciation a source of amusement. I tried to stop myself from sobbing.

'Be o-right, Son,' he assured, although he convinced no one, not even me, really. 'Be o-right.'

'Sure it will,' chuckled Charlie Boy.

He shook his head at the room, as lost as his son.

'My son alone you leave you bloody bashtur.'

I felt light enough to float when Charlie Boy moved his hand away. I sniffed, wiped my nose on the sleeve of my coat and then slowly took another step. I closed my eyes, squeezing out tears, watching them fall to the floor. I could swear I heard them land one by one.

'O-right, Son,' he said gently, but surely, pushing me behind him once I got around the counter, back to relative safety. 'No worry now.'

'So, feller,' said Charlie Boy, sniffing snot up his nose. 'You thought about my little offer or what?'

'Pen-chode bashtur! Out my shop now!'

Charlie Boy sniggered while Pony Tail walked over to the porn mags.

'You fucking pakis,' said Charlie Boy, moaning at us now. 'You think you're fucking everything.'

'You no paki me! You bashtur you!' he yelled, hitting the counter with his pointing finger. '*You* bashtur! *You* pen-chode rammee.'

Kids, ones who'd come from Pakistan, would swear like that all the time but I'd never heard anything like it from my old man.

'Maa-chode!'

Charlie Boy shook his head again. Pony Tail laughed while flicking through a magazine with a tattooed and naked woman on the cover.

'You, you big pen-chode,' my dad called to Pony Tail and then, in that hotch-potch of a tongue with many names, but little value, asked him: 'What are you doing wandering around with a maa-chode like this?'

Pony Tail walked over to Charlie Boy and gave him a nudge.

'Yeah, what *am* I doing running with a motherfucker like you?'

Charlie Boy shrugged then cracked up laughing. I didn't get the joke. Neither did my dad.

'Can't even speak the fuckin' language proper.'

'I know you language you bashtur you,' my dad said, pointing at one then the other.

Pony Tail didn't seem bothered by any of it and he should have been, that's what really bugged me. Like us, and yet, so against us. Did not make sense. But then, neither did the rest of that night.

'Guess we're gonna have to teach this old puhdooh a lesson, then,' said Pony Tail.

The urge to shit and piss started about then. Within seconds it had taken over me, my whole body a constant tremble. I heard myself whine.

'I think you're right,' said Charlie Boy. 'Let the lesson begin.'

Like a gunslinger drawing guns from side holsters, Pony Tail pulled out two baseball bats, one from either side of his long, black leather coat. He then walked up to the chocolate unit, soles of his trainers squeaking against the lino, while me and my dad watched, an audience waiting for a magician to reveal his next great illusion. He tossed a bat through a few yards of air, over to Charlie Boy and then, as one, they began to smash the shit out of everything before them.

I sneaked around in front of my dad and looked up at his face. A tear in his eye but he stayed a silent bystander, only watching as the teachers administered their knowledge. Everything he'd worked and strived for was there one second, still valuable, still worth something and in the next, useless. Unsaleable, spoilt, damaged beyond salvage.

He looked down at me, pushed me behind his back again and that got me hopeful. For a moment, I thought he'd fight back but he did nothing except watch. Scared, like me, but at the same time transfixed.

'Dad!'

My protest only seemed to egg them on. Charlie Boy started laughing like a demented hyena. My old man went for the phone but Charlie Boy spotted him, swung, shattered the handset and his hand in one go. I heard my dad let out a scream and me, I did the same. I began to cry as I watched the blurring figure of my dad clutching his broken fingers. Another swing of the bat, another crack of noise. An invisible hand turned my head and made me watch. Through my tears, I could see Charlie Boy, as clear as day, displaying what power he had over people like us.

'You fuckin' pakis,' he grinned, punctuating every subsequent word with a swing of his bat. 'It's – thanks – to – people – like – me – that – you're – fuckin' – here – in – the – first – fuckin' – place.'

His words frightened me more than the bat. He really did hate us, whatever he thought we were. I remember my old man telling my mother what life used to be like when he first got here, in this country, when he was alone. National Front people, all called Enoch Powell according to him, would march past his shop and throw abuse, eggs and rotten veg while he stayed behind his counter, praying for the trouble to stay outside and to pass sooner rather than later. He got shit through the post and once, he actually got a death threat, just because. Up 'til then, I thought he made those stories sound worse than they really were. That night confirmed it all.

Without warning Charlie Boy's bat came to a sudden rest. Pony Tail carried on. Seemed to be in a world of his own, that crazy bastard. Only when Charlie Boy gave the signal, did the sidekick stop. The lesson, however, had to run its course. In a single bound, Charlie Boy landed on the counter and then stood, towering above us both. He crouched so that his eyes became level with my dad's but they didn't share the gaze for more than a second at the most. Instead, Charlie Boy shifted his attention to me, peering into the windows to my soul. My universe shrank so small it became a void, save for the pounding of two hearts.

'You scared, little man?'

My dad edged in front of me while pushing me further behind him, my back hitting the medicines unit, knocking over a row of aspirins: rattle and roll.

'Leave him lone,' he said, no strength at all in his voice now. 'You leave him lone.'

That's when I knew he could never do enough, a man like my father. Didn't have what it took to stop Charlie Boy from getting to me and doing God knows what. I wished for more than being at home. Unborn seemed the best place.

'You bashtur,' he said, half-sighing, half-sobbing.

Charlie Boy jumped down off the counter, displaying a grin that became etched into my memory. He rolled something around in his mouth and then spat it on my dad's face, who, by way of response, did nothing. His presence, however, just him being there mattered to me more than he'd ever know. Still there, still my dad and still doing his best to provide some kind of safety. A wall, fragile and crumbling, but a barrier all the same. A tear ran down his cheek, mixing with another man's spit.

'Now,' said Charlie Boy, cracking his knuckles then pausing for a smile.

He didn't say any more words. Instead of speaking, he stepped up close, face to face with my old man, while his arm reached for me. Without searching or even feeling, his hand grabbed my face, startling a breath out of me. Thumb under my chin, fingers gripping the top of my head, I continued to gasp for air. I tried squirming out but no use. Well and truly clamped in his grip, the thought of which still makes me wince to this day. No way out… too young to die… stale cigarette stink from his hand… what a smell to die with. He pulled his arm towards himself, reeled me in: me powerless, him powerful. My old man didn't stop to think. At long last it seemed that instinct had kicked in. He grabbed my shoulders but he could never match Charlie Boy's strength. So instead of playing tug of war, with my neck as the rope, he let go: let go or risk a son being torn apart. I let out a wail. I thought I'd spend the rest of my life like that, in the middle of two people, in pain, in limbo, in between. That tightening, pulling and tearing of my muscles, veins and sinews would remain with me until I died but that would not matter. As long as my dad held on to me, it would still be okay.

'Gerroffme! Gerroffme!'

Charlie Boy laughed. Pony Tail joined in.

'Dad! Da-ad!'

Charlie Boy's hand slipped over my mouth, his fingers pushing up and against my nostrils.

'Shut the fuck up y'little cunt.'

Out of breath within seconds, eyes rolling, head spinning and thoughts of a slow, painful death flooding into my mind. No matter how much I squirmed, no matter how hard I tried working free of him, I got nowhere. Held me there without effort and with every spasm I energised, his hold seemed to grow tighter. My crotch, then my legs, felt warm, then cold and finally, wetness trickled down to my ankles.

I could still hear it all going on but I didn't want to. Better if I'd been born deaf than this. Anything seemed better than hearing his pleas and cries for mercy. And then, like the dream I've had so many times since, I found myself drifting away from them. My dad's voice becoming distant as Charlie Boy's hand grew lighter.

It must have been terrible, what he endured that night. Watching the demise of one son and the birth of another must be a sufferance for any father.

I woke up thinking I'd died.

The old wooden wardrobe by the wall, the mirror opposite, the pattern of the curtains, the polystyrene tiled ceiling above me.

Home, tucked up safe in bed.

To my side, sat my mother, The Qur'an in her hand.

'Mum?'

Head still bowed, she glanced off the page and smiled at me and then came the tears. She put the book to one side and then kissed me on alternate cheeks, over and over again, calling me her beautiful son.

She stood, went to the door and in a breaking voice called to my dad, telling him I'd woken. A few seconds later, he'd entered the room. As usual a smile on his face.

'Son,' he said, speaking in his perfect home tongue. 'You're alright?'

'How can he be?' my mother answered for me. 'Look at him. The boy's whole appearance has changed. What have they done to him?'

They hadn't done any damage to me, at least not physically. I did feel a bit ill, though. Cold inside. Shaky and a little tired, still. Maybe my mother, prone to exaggerate in the first place, saw traces of shock on my young, tender and still innocent face.

'He's lost all colour. So white.'

'It's nothing,' he said. 'I'll straighten things out with these people.'

He'd been to the hospital while I'd slept. Had his hand potted up but apart from that, he looked okay.

'You sleep some more,' he told me. 'You need the rest. Don't you worry about anything. Day off tomorrow for you.'

'What time is it?'

'It's very late, son of mine,' my mum smiled, gently running a hand through my hair. 'Nearly two in the morning.'

They each kissed my cheeks before leaving me to wonder about the shop and the violence I'd been a part of. God knows what happened after I passed out.

Half an hour later, I got out of bed and headed for the toilet. I stopped and listened when I heard raised voices coming from their bedroom.

'You have to sell the shop. You have to. After this night, how can you not?'

'No,' he insisted. 'They only want fifty pounds a week. It's not a lot for peace of mind.'

'Fifty now, a hundred later and then God knows what. These people, once they smell weakness, then they never leave you.'

'We'll see,' he said quietly, but still trying to sound confident. 'Things will work out.'

He got that wrong and he knew it. I couldn't see his face from behind the door, but I could see through his brave words. The weakness of voice, that on its own gave the game away.

'Can't you see this is a mistake?' my mum said, almost pleading with him. 'Why don't you listen to me? Look at what they did to you. Look what they did to our *son*.'

'We'll see.'

As I turned away, the door opened.

'Son? What is this? What are you doing up?'

I shrugged, my back to him.

'Son?' my mum called from inside. 'What is it, Son? Is something wrong? Are you in pain somewhere?'

'No, it's nothing.'

He touched me on the shoulder and then spun me around, forcing me to face him.

'What's the matter?'

'When I'm big,' I said. 'When I get to be big, I'll kill those men.'

He shook his head. Might have been difficult, trying or even impossible times but he didn't want to hear that from his only nipper, all nine years of me.

As he tucked me into bed, he told me what he thought he, and therefore me, were both about.

'You sleep now,' he whispered. 'And no more of this gunda talk. That's not what we do. We're good and honest people, not like those people. You understand?'

I turned over, closed my eyes and thought about his words. I didn't understand what he said and I hoped I never would. It made no sense to me, even then. Someone else could be bad, a *gunda*, but why not us?

26

What made us so special?

'You'll understand better when you're grown up,' he said on his way out.

Every Friday night, ten minutes before closing up time, Pony Tail, whose name turned out to be Tahir, would stroll in and collect his master's dues: fifty pounds dead.

'Taxes!' he'd call, his collection time catchphrase.

My old man, his lesson well learnt, would raid the till and hand it over without complaining like he did the first few times. And so, a new ritual became gradually established. He'd put the money on the counter and then get on with his business. Being extorted was just a *thing* he had to endure every Friday night. Never greeted him, never offered him farewell. Silence sufficed more than adequately. Even when Pony Tail came out with his snide little comments, my dad would play deaf and dumb. As for me, well, not a lot I could say.

For two years, give or take the odd month, I managed to understand why he put up with it. It was better, common sense dictated, to lose a few pounds than a limb, an eye or perhaps the rest of an existence. And it's not like they'd singled us out alone. It got to be that paying protection money became a fact of life for all shopkeepers on that little parade. When Pony Tail came a-calling, they'd all cough up. It didn't make it any easier although it always seemed like reason enough for my dad.

'This thing, it's not for you to worry about, Son.'

'But…'

'It's like this,' he explained on the way home one night. 'It's like trying to play football without a ball. We're just not equipped to deal with these sorts.'

'Can't we just say *no*?'

'Son,' he told me. 'Life's all about making deals. Some work to your advantage and others don't. Remember these words of mine.'

I couldn't have been more than twelve when things changed for the worse. The fee suddenly doubled. Cost of living? Ridiculous, so Pony Tail made out. My dad put up a half-hearted fight, but that's all it would ever be - a gesture - if anything. After his little protest, Pony Tail nodded and then held out his hand.

'Taxes!'

So once again, my old man paid up on time, perhaps hating himself a little bit more with every week and wad of notes that passed. Those men with power were slowly killing him and they knew it. Maybe it worked out to be an added bonus for them.

We made do, but the joy of running a shop had gone for my dad. Not his own man like he'd been for so long. That's why he became a shopkeeper: got sick of being told what to do by people who had neither respect nor understanding for a man like him. But the shop had now turned out to be the same as working in a mill. The shop was now a job, and with it came a master. Might have carried on smiling, might have appeared to be the happiest person in the world but that simply wasn't true, not any more. Anyone could see that if they cared to look. And if they didn't care to look at his face, then they could smell his breath. I caught a whiff of it one evening and it made me gag. Hated the smell of booze since.

'Dad? What's the stink?'

My old man, all offended to hell and back, looked at me with disgust and then gave me a good and quick back-hand slap. Of course, he regretted it instantly. I didn't mind. He had the right to teach me in any way he saw fit. I never said anything about his drinking again, not ever. I did wonder how long he'd been sneaking it. Could have been months. I thought about mentioning it to my mum but that would not have made things any easier. So I let things lie. Like father like son.

Maybe I should have said something when I had the chance but I doubt if he'd have paid a blind bit of notice from his teenage son. He took to the old firewater like a new born to a mother's tit. I only realised how far he'd gone when I noticed how we appeared to be doing a roaring trade in Bell's Finest Scotch Whiskey but the till roll said different. A few months down the line, he'd become an expert alcoholic who knew all the lies, tricks and excuses to help hold his head up in public, but not always behind closed doors. For all of that, I tried thinking of him as he used to be. Him the dad, me the son, neither with any conditions attached. Not the same for my mum. Arguments, rants and slanging matches became common. No more family meals. No more comfort, no more happiness and at times, not much of a family, neither.

As I got older, I found myself resenting him for what he'd become. Not only were the profits being drunk away, he'd become an embarrassment. Customers would come in and I could tell they were aching to laugh their heads off at him, with the way he swayed around, slurring his speech and all the rest of the pisshead shopkeeper routine; a novelty in itself. I didn't hate him. How could I?

School remained my only escape. A few years earlier, I'd wanted to be in the shop for the rest of my life but that dream had crashed and burned. Anywhere beat the shop, even school.

I didn't play truant, didn't shout abuse at teachers and didn't really make any waves. By the same token, I didn't fit into the *quiet one who gets the shit kicked out of him once or twice a day* role, either. An average school kid who knew a few other kids but overall, pretty much kept himself to himself. Neither recluse, jock, brain nor stud.

During lunch time and breaks, I'd play footy on the tennis courts with some of the other kids. At one end of the courts, about a dozen thickies would meet and snog their birds, peppering each other's necks with love-bites which would, some said, eventually lead to cancer. That didn't concern me but the cigarettes did. They were always begging cigs off each other, not because they were skint, but because there were no shops nearby and also because the smokers were known and therefore routinely frisked by members of school staff.

On any given day, I'd sell at least twenty single cigarettes and make a tidy little profit. Okay, so not ICI, but better than nothing. It took a while but I became well known and well liked by most of my peers. So not only did school become my refuge from the shop, it became a place where I made a few quid and got to be appreciated into the bargain.

Selling loose cigs in the school yard might not have been the best introduction to the world of commerce but it helped me understand the basics. The idea of business appealed to me for lots of reasons. A businessman like my dad, only better. Even then I knew business offered so much more potential than any other kind of work. Capitalism. Sounds ugly, even now, but that's where it's at. Why bother being labour when you can actually own it?

School is how I got into drugs. I must have been about fifteen years old the first time. A sixth former owed me some money for at least a dozen cigarettes and I refused to give him a match, let alone a cig, until he started making a dent in his bill. Instead of money, he slipped me a joint. Although a little reluctant, I accepted it eventually, thinking it was better than nothing. But that presented a new problem: what the hell was I supposed to do with it? If I smoked it, then who knew where it would end? I'd probably become addicted to the stuff and the next thing I knew, I'd be mugging people all over town just to keep my newest habit alive. If I gave it away, then I'd lose out. Simple, then. Only left with one choice: it had to be sold which is what I did.

So I sold that joint for a quid. Lucky for me, my customer happened to be a first timer who didn't know his arse from a hole in the ground. Could have sold him rolled tea leaves for all the difference it made. That's all they were, those sixth former pricks, just kids who liked blagging about sex and drugs. They'd cover rock n roll next term in humanities.

The first few deals were nervous, rather hurried affairs but gradually, the more I sold, the less tension seemed to surface. No big thing after a while, certainly no more dangerous or thrilling than selling single cigs. Could have been selling Mars Bars, really. Just business, just transactions. Product for money, even then.

Still a boy, still way too young to be thinking what I wanted to do with my life but my future concerned me. I wanted an easier way than the ones on offer after I left school. The dole, or worse still, working twenty years and then feeling dissatisfied after it all. Made no sense. So damned pathetic. So weak and yet millions did it all the time. Surely it drove them insane, knowing they could never be happy. So many people wasted their lives doing something they hated. How could they *do* that to themselves? Not me, not ever. Fuck that. Why bother with a sure fire road to misery? Wiser, more sensible to learn from the mistakes of others, especially from all those gigantic fuck-ups my old man made in his time.

And so, as I grew, so did my business. I stepped up a gear by cutting the *small time middleman* out of the loop. I bought the raw materials from a *slightly bigger time middleman* called Vinny who gave me the bullshit *very big time middleman* routine the first time I met him. Ten pound deals didn't sound big time to me but he proved to be a step in the right direction. I bought the weed, made the joints myself, at home in my bedroom, and then I sold, more than doubling my outlay with every deal. Proper little entrepreneur. I had no idea about real deals and real dealers, though. In time, I'd get introduced to all that.

rock bottom

I watched a gangster flick for half price on account of Tuesday's being lousy for the box office receipts. Got a taxi back to the shop where I'd help my dad lock up. Can't say I looked forward to it. He'd been getting worse as those months and years had worn on. Didn't take much for him to jump down my throat. Some days it was my clothes, other days my hair, general appearance, even tone of voice. Pretty much anything and everything about me could start him off. After a couple of years of his incessant bickering and moaning I'd stopped trying to please him. I realised he couldn't be pleased, not any more. I didn't get all suicidal but I won't deny it did piss me off.

Opened the door, took one step inside and I froze. My eyes remained fixed on the floor, where he lay, stretched out like a boxer down for the count: spread-eagled and well and truly out of it. I knew what had happened. I could see it all in my head and like the movie I'd just watched, everything felt so clear, so brutally violent and just like that slick bit of cinematic history, not one bit of it seemed to be real nor in any particular or even logical order.

Custom had died down to nothing. Even the girls who worked the kerbs called it a night and had gone home, to the ever waiting, ever itching, money grabbing hands of their pimps. He had four or five hundred pounds worth of takings in his back pocket, barely enough for the following day's stock, let alone the bills. But it had been a good day, considering. Just the kind of day that called for a celebration.

Half way through his bottle, they entered. He should have known better than to have refused Pony Tail the Friday before. Doing so was not an option, he said, and now, as I stood there, it seemed this had been proved. That bastard, that pony tailed traitor to all that was decent, had warned him:

'I'll be back. Charlie might wanna come along for the ride.'

Charlie Boy had stopped being the front man ages ago. I actually thought he'd left the scene but inside I knew he was still the man, still in charge. And when I heard Pony Tail mention his name, my heart missed a beat. Charlie Boy. This was no boy but a man. The only man who had scared the shit out of me and that's how he remained for the longest time. I don't know whether it's a good thing or a bad thing, but he scared a lot of people in his time and just knowing that made me feel a little better, like I wasn't alone in the world.

So that night, while I sat in the cheap seats, laughing when a certain Mr Marcellus Wallace (who perhaps did or did not throw someone out of a 14th storey window for giving his wife, a certain Mrs Marcellus Wallace, a foot massage) got fucked in the arse by a redneck, Pony Tail and his boss walked into my old man's shop, again, betting on the outcome, a ritual they had. My old man ignored them. Too loaded to give a shit. Charlie Boy, still the same working class grunt with the same petty biases, prejudices and attitudes he'd always had, didn't like the feel of a cold shoulder, not a drunk old paki's at any rate. And that drunk old paki continued to ignore them both, a combination of alcohol and long standing resentment making a fight out of nothing. Wrong time to have been doing that, really. Big mistake.

They beat him senseless. Took the takings, the keys and then loaded the back of the old banger with all the cigarettes and spirits it would carry. Teach that drunk old paki to ignore people.

'Sign of the times,' he told the coppers the next morning, while lying in a hospital bed.

A sign of the fucking *times*? I didn't think so. Had me stumped, he really did. Something must have been playing with his mind. Not rational. Maybe not even sane any more.

'You put him on anything?' I asked the junior doctor who, up 'til then, had been passing through the ward like a whirlwind.

'Just painkillers.'

'I think they're making him delirious.'

The doctor, who didn't look any older or any more experienced than me, concentrated and then furrowed his forehead not with concern but annoyance.

'There's nothing wrong with the gentleman's mind. He's not delirious. Sustained a few cuts, bruises. One minor fracture, but he'll live.'

'You've not put him on any drugs, then?'

'No. I don't think he needs anything except painkillers. They don't cause any such side-effects.'

The coppers knew damned well what happened but he, the victim, didn't want to play. He told them a bunch of ruffians he'd never seen before entered the shop and attacked him. And even if he did care to spill the beans, what would happen? At best, Charlie Boy and his faithful dog would get off with a suspended sentence, a fine or perhaps both. Not worth the hassle, considering the repercussions.

One of the coppers pulled out a book of mug shots and asked him to look at them carefully. He'd been around for a good few years. In his forties, experienced but he seemed sincere enough, a copper who believed in right and wrong as well as the rule of law.

But my dad shook his head. I couldn't believe it but then, I lacked the life experience he'd accumulated over the years. I might have thought I knew the way crooks worked but I didn't know shit about the real world. Criminals had this tendency to get free. And when at large they visited the people who helped put them away in the first place. From where my dad lay, it was infinitely wiser to shut up and live to tell the tale.

'Are you sure, sir?' said the copper.

'Very sure. Everything O-right now.'

The copper looked at me sadly and then pulled out a notepad onto which he started scribbling.

'If your father changes his mind…if anything comes to him, then give me a call.'

A strange one, this copper. Sounded too cool, too considerate and perhaps even too intelligent to be an ordinary PC.

'We'll see what happens.'

I looked at the paper he passed over.

'You can leave a message if I'm not in. Call any time you like.'

I told him not to hold his breath. He seemed to understand.

'You can do something about these people, you know,' he said as he and his mate got up. 'Can't let them get away with this kind of business.'

Wrong. We could and we did. My dad got the shit beaten out of him, got mugged and humiliated but not only that, his kidneys got fucked into the bargain. For the rest of his days he'd chase his scotch with a pill cocktail courtesy of some consultant called Mr Jackson.

After they discharged him change came wholesale. Three times a week an ambulance would park up outside the house, wheel him in and then take him into the dialysis ward where machines did the job of his kidneys. In a matter of months he'd put on perhaps three, maybe four stones. Nothing to worry about, just a side-effect of the dialysis, according to Jackson. He should have been grateful. Jackson told me once:

'Wouldn't get this level of treatment in Pakistan, of course.'

Meanwhile, the shop remained closed, my dad dreading the thought of going back because he didn't know where to begin. He couldn't claim on the insurance because he'd forgotten, been too pissed or simply hadn't been arsed to renew the policy. Of course, that only made him feel worse about himself, life and the world in general. He'd sit in the dark and blame himself for our misfortunes. Totally defeated and that's why, perhaps, beginning again never really happened for him, nor me, in that way. It might have been the straw that broke the camel's back, but in truth, his back and his spirit started splintering the moment he became a shopkeeper. That's when it dawned on me. That's when I realised that running a shop could never be just a *job*.

After a year on the market, the shop got sold, almost given away to a Sikh guy, one of my dad's new drinking buddies. My new future became sealed. Not a shopkeeper but something not so different. Certain parts of life's path, my mum told me, weren't even on the map.

'Perhaps something better will come along. What's meant to be, is meant to be.'

I could live with that but not my dad. He'd chopped off and sold a part of his own body by selling that shop. Made him angrier and sicker than ever and that caused my mum just as much pain. The five hour sessions on the dialysis machine were one thing, she could handle them all day long, but when he got really bad, when she thought the throes of death were upon him, she'd wail over his weak, prematurely aged and broken body. And it drove me up the wall, all of it. Weak of me, I know, to run from rather than confront life's problems but that's what I did. I stayed out more often, all the time, really. Couldn't stand being home with him always at the ready to start ranting about whatever took his fancy.

I'd go down the local youth club and when that was closed, I'd wander over to one of the amusement arcades. Those places sufficed as they occupied my mind, distracted me from home life shit. Whilst there, I'd sell a few bits and bats but it meant more to me than money. Didn't qualify as work in terms of effort, either. Might sound like a boast but selling drugs, at whatever level, is easy. No wonder it's so tempting, no wonder there's so many at it. Buy, pack and sell. Sure beats being a shopkeeper or working a nine-to-five. Didn't have to smile, did as *I* pleased. My customers valued me more than I valued them and that felt just great. Big fish in a small pond. So small it felt more like a puddle in the beginning.

Home life aside, destiny allowed me to steer the course for a while. Maybe it was an illusion but unlike most people, I felt in control of my young life. I'd see men who'd get up with their kids for school and off to work they'd go, returning once they got their clock cards stamped, eight or ten hours later. Wage slaves but slaves all the same. Bought into the system wholesale by desiring what they were told to desire, watching what they were told to watch and working to the rules and specifications that controlled their whole lives. Everywhere I looked, I saw Ikea, C & A and Woolworth's zombies who were too brainwashed to even think about rebelling, too conditioned to even realise rebelling was an option. Class might have been dead but I couldn't say the same for compliance. I wasn't like them. Not ordinary, not duped and certainly not prepared to accept the same shit my old man had so readily accepted. Not any more. Not me. People, far too many people, did jobs they hated, worked for employers who didn't even know their names, worked with colleagues they detested but *not me*. Not in line for that future any more. I'd do the things that would please me. I'd deal with people I'd want to deal with and as for bosses, I'd never stoop so low as to have one of those head and soul fucks.

My parents, meanwhile, oblivious to my secret life, believed my story about working in a warehouse. Anything as long as I avoided the dole, they said. I'd become a part-time, somewhat amateurish dealer, lowest of the low, mostly dealing from safe environments where only the younger, still experimenting punters would feel confident about frequenting. Even car, café and back alley deals remained out of my reach, thankfully. At that tender age, messing with those who dared tread the deepest of inner-city routes might not have been such a good idea and besides, I seemed to be doing fine as things were.

However, there were moments when the temptation to turn full time would creep up on me. More risk than dealing kiddie bags of corrupted resin, but more money. I argued with myself, eventually deciding to stick to what I knew. Not such a bad place, I occupied. Seemed like nothing could go wrong if I stuck to my patch and kept that low profile low. My parents didn't know, I didn't use and what's more, the coppers never gave me a second look. Maybe they thought I had an innocence about me or something.

Usually, I got home for about midnight (late shifts paid better, I told them at home). More to life than money, my mum would complain but at least her son was fortunate enough to work in a climate when most did nothing but laze around. That pretty much covered the home end of things, so I thought.

I got in one night, knowing my dad would be waiting for me in the front, like always, ready to ask me how work had been, my reply a lied formality I'd grown so accustomed to that it no longer registered as deceit.

He'd just got out of the bath. Hot baths eased his pain. Hair slicked back with BrylCreem, no stubble on his face, the smell of Imperial Leather aftershave wafting along and hitting me. He looked worse than ever, though. Tired, in pain and, as usual, fed up to the back teeth with something or other. Only that night, it seemed more so.

Along with the dodgy kidneys, he'd developed a few more conditions that slowly squeezed the life out of him: blood pressure, heart, stomach, arms, legs... The ambulance still came to take him into hospital three times a week. At least he didn't have the hassle of Charlie Boy and Pony Tail any more, but them bastards, they'd done enough damage already.

Weak, in pain or not, he remained strong enough to give me a load of grief, the source of which I knew nothing. A disgrace, he called me as soon as I offered my salaam. A blight on the family name, an embarrassment. Without decency, honour and respect. Usually, he didn't get past the decency bit without stopping for breath.

'Khalil,' he said, looking at the floor. 'You're a deep disappointment to us.'

'What have I done now?'

About a year before, some spiteful bastard grassed me up after seeing me with this slapper I knew. Not as if I'd done anything other than talked to her, but for some, being seen with a female is tantamount to devil worship.

'Words have come to me.'

'Words? What words?'

'About you. About what you're doing. About where you get your money from.'

Rumbled, but denying it felt like the right thing to do.

'I didn't bring you up to be this way. You should be ashamed.'

'Dad, I don't know what you're talking…'

His hand came up, stopping me midstream.

'You're polluting our graves with this work of yours.'

I shouldn't have thought it, but he had no room to talk. He sold booze and what's more, he drank like a fish, too. Same shit, different name.

'This is wrong, Son,' he said, only sadly now. '*All* wrong.'

'But…'

'I can't live with this shame.'

The source of my shame, the disappointment that I had made mattered more than his vice. He could live with his sins, but not his son's. My wrongs had a greater effect on the universe. As a second and better version of him, the next prototype, I'd taken a wrong turn somewhere. As far as he could tell, I seemed to be a step backwards, a regression.

'Dad…'

Up came the hand again.

'You say nothing. You've lied enough already.'

I bowed my head.

'Well?' he demanded. 'What have you got to say for yourself?'

'This thing,' I managed. 'It's all out of proportion.'

'Everyone else is a liar but you, then?' my dad accused, eyes half open, head rocking wisely.

Even talking took a lot out of him. The treatment made him weak, that's what the doctors said but no, more to it than that. He'd lost a lot of will and right then, what remained, was seeping out of his pores. I felt bad, not because of anything I said, but because I actually pitied him.

'You'll be the death of me.'

Unfair, hitting below the belt like that. I had good intentions, had them both on my mind all the time.

'Dad…' I began, not knowing what to add.

Head still bowed, full of respect, I decided to speak quietly. Perhaps that'd make a difference.

'People exaggerate, always make things sound worse than they are.'

He tried to frown but when he realised he couldn't, he bit his lip instead. He didn't want to hear it which worked out fine as I had nothing more to offer.

'Where there's smoke there's fire,' he threw back.

After considering my options, I chose to maintain a polite but defensive diplomacy. He had enough worries on his mind without me becoming a source of more. Besides, not in my nature to kick a man when he hit rock bottom. That was the trouble. He'd always been down. If only he fought back. If only he'd been a cunt all his life and fucked people up the way they fucked him up. If he'd done that and failed, then we both could have lived with it, knowing he'd tried. Could have been proud of such an effort.

'It's a mistake. It won't happen again,' I lied.

legalise it

I avoided him for a few days. Then, late one night, just as I got in, I caught him staring into space, chasing down the wrong turns of his own past, perhaps seeing into the future, trying to foresee mine. How he wanted things to be so different when they were only potential things, when they were only ideas, dreams and desires. I wanted to tell him everything would be alright. I needed him to know that I understood how hard his life had been and how much of it he'd lived for me, for my sake. Before I could say a word, he dropped it on me:

'Your mother has the forms. Fill them in properly. You understand?'

'Forms?'

'Fill them in and send them off.'

It had been mentioned before. All came out when I got seen with the slapper: marriage. At the first sign of trouble, the one word that gets mentioned is marriage. No shit, it really is the quickest fix going. *Your son turning to petty crime? Want to stop him mixing with white women? Think he's a serial killer? Then get him wed. If marriage won't sort him out, nothing will.* Marriage, the answer to everything. Strictly a short term thing but they never saw it that way, people like my parents. For some reason, they thought irresponsible, immature and sometimes idiotic offspring would suddenly reverse any and all negative traits as soon as the ceremony ended.

'Make sure you use registered post.'

Had all the potential of becoming two death sentences in one, those immigration forms. I knew a girl from school who'd filled in similar sheets of paper and months later, the person she used to be had all but disappeared. These things have a tendency to kill spirits, in some cases, even the shells that hold them.

I stood there for a moment or two, just taking in his presence. Forty years on this planet but looking like he'd been around for more than sixty. The belly of a pregnant woman on him because of all the booze and, to be fair, because of the knackered innards. Hair thinning, and gone from black to white, not even bothering to pause at grey. As for his complexion, well, just one shade away from the hue of death.

I tried to present a voice of reason but no, he wouldn't have it. Where he came from, those who went against the wishes of their elders, the ones who knew better, were as good as heretics.

'If you have the desire to do right by me and by God, then you'll marry her without question.'

All a matter of duty and keeping the culture alive, so he said. I didn't see it quite like that. His duty, simply put, was to find me some bride and mine was to marry her. As a result, his culture would live on through the kids we'd have. I didn't appreciate it at the time but someone like me marrying someone from the home country strengthened a weakened bridge to an otherwise dying culture. Still, the way he tried selling the whole deal, using religion, duty and izzat as further justifications should have bugged me but it didn't. I'd grown used to all that shit by then. Moral blackmail, plain and simple.

Me and my old man were different, but not totally. Neither of us could get rid of our skin, ancestry, genes, blood and bone. I used to think he and I were so far apart but there's a big difference between the me of then and the me of now. Maybe I have changed, gone back to what my old man wanted me to be but that doesn't mean I have to like it. That doesn't mean he was right.

So, in a last ditch bid to salvage the situation, I told him how I felt. I could not go through with it, no matter what the cost or whose daughter he had in mind. Even if she turned out to be Miss Pakistan, even if she turned out to be the original Pakistani Princess, Benazir Bhutto herself, my answer would remain firmly in the negative. It had nothing to do with looks, money, intelligence and it wasn't even about personality. At the simplest level, I just wanted the freedom to choose.

But the proposal was God's Will as much as his. He got pretty skilful at picking and choosing the bits of Islam he deemed relevant and just as good at forgetting or overlooking the bits that didn't tie into his needs. When it came to having a say in who I'd marry, then my input went out the window.

My mum came into the room, very meek about it all. When I needed her to be strong and to support my cause, she let me down. My mum, so much wiser than my dad, always had been right about a lot of things when he'd been wrong. To her credit, she'd been tactful about setting

41

him right for as long as I could remember. She didn't want to hurt his pride, dent his ego and sap his already weakened spirit. When it came to important things she might have disagreed with him, but it made more sense to let him think he knew best. An act of kindness on her part.

With this marriage business, she simply couldn't bring herself to carry out her veto. How could she give me the life I wanted, but, at the same time, inflict pain on her husband by opposing him? It took two hands to clap, but as my marriage negotiations proved, only one to slap. When it came to my future, she went along with him but she never actually said a word. At the time, her silence functioned as approval enough.

He got up and went to the kitchen, leaving my mum and me to iron out the details. I told her there and then I couldn't go through with it which is when she started trying to talk me into it, telling me it made sense, that it was the only way. Eighteen and soon enough I'd be twenty, then twenty-five and then, in a flash, I'd be over thirty and therefore, over the hill. Practically unmarriageable. Such opportunities had to be seized, embraced and loved when they presented themselves. But she missed the point. Me choosing my own bride was not a sinful act but what they were proposing couldn't have been any more wrong. They knew as well as I did that without consent, a marriage didn't exist, was null and void. My mum bowed her head, frowned and walked the prayer beads through her hands for a while. As I got up, she held onto my arm and told me to sit.

'Son, parents aren't the enemies of their children.'

'I know that.'

'No you don't. You won't know until you have your own.'

Children. If marriage didn't do the trick, then children did. If a couple had kids, then bingo: instant family, stability and reason for living. That's why the marriage thing got peddled as such a hot-shit solution. Fucked up idiots got married, had kids and then had no choice but to be fathers, husbands and above all, responsible human beings. Kids were hope personified and people like my parents, they knew it.

'Now this girl… you should know that she was born to be your bride.'

I looked away as a smirk drew itself on my face.

'If it's her looks that concern you, then that's nothing to worry about. She's very beautiful,' my mum declared.

I held strong but I listened anyway. The least I could do for my mum.

'This girl, she's a good, homely kind of girl but don't think she's one of those simple girls who doesn't know anything of the wider world.'

'What is she? Don't tell me…she's an air hostess. No…she's an international model.'

'Big badmaash!' my mum chastised, and then continued, in her own, semi-proud way. 'She's been educated.'

'Educated?'

'She can read and write, English and Urdu. She's just finished a degree in maths at a college for girls.'

Trying to impress me that way didn't seem to be working out. She had me all wrong, my mum. Needed more than a few dud qualifications to ring my bell, and besides, Pakistani degrees weren't worth shit. So long as you could write your name on the dotted line and hand over a nice fat wad of rupees, you could have as many degrees as you wanted.

'If she wants, she can go into teaching.'

What the hell did such a young, talented, clever and all round wonderful person want with a no-hoper like me? Sounded like she deserved something a hell of a lot better than an unwilling soul mate who also happened to be peddling drugs for a living.

'She's perfect for you, Son.'

Thing is, that girl from Pakistan probably didn't want to know me at all. Two people, her and me both, were being squeezed here. In all likelihood, she hated the idea of marrying a stranger possessing some strange culture as much as I did. That's what it came down to, this cross fertilisation of people, this bridging of the culture gap by force. I could imagine her parents trying to force me on her, and while I had the liberty to bitch about it, she'd be sitting there, head bowed, ready to accept it, silently praying for a husband who treated her okay. Love, happiness and even something like respect would, if ever realised, be extras.

A couple of months younger than me but nevertheless, a *jawaan*: a young adult. I found it funny, the way my mum insisted on giving me all those details even though I didn't ask once.

'She's made for you. A better match won't be found on this earth.'

'I don't think so, Mum.'

In a desperate attempt to win me over, my mum pulled out a photograph that had come through the post a few months before. Like some kind of secret weapon, she'd been saving it for the time when all else seemed lost.

'Look,' she said.

I looked at the figure in the cheap frame, sitting on a cheap wooden chair, in some cheap photographer's studio, cheap purple curtain behind her, head covered, the gaze not quite catching the camera's lens. Henna-covered hands resting on silky salwar clad thighs. Her face touched up and made to look whiter. Pretty enough, though. Looked the way all girls from Pakistan seem to look before they get here and consequently get wise. Strangely decent. Way too decent for the likes of me.

'See? What do you think?'

I shook my head.

'I think no.'

This concerned two futures and with me being the male, the one with relatively more power, I felt obliged to stop this tragedy in the making.

'Don't say that, Son.'

'Think about it, Mum,' I told her.

My mum stared at me.

'We have. We've been thinking about this for a long time.'

'Not properly.'

I told her how things would turn out if this girl from Pakistan got to be my wife. She'd be confined to misery for the rest of her days. Seven out of seven, I'd leave her home, alone, with only daytime TV and Hindi feature films on video for company. I'd be out all day, busy spending my time on any old slag and I'd only come home when my batteries needed recharging. I'd crash in my own single bed, sometime way past midnight, and I'd ignore her. She'd take it for a while, thinking I'd come around to the idea of marriage, kids and then love in my own time. But I wouldn't do that. I'd keep that protest alive for the rest of my days not because of her but because of her parents and because of my parents, the ones who'd done us this wrong.

'Son,' my mum began.

Things would get worse. She, that wife I'd never know, would write sorrowful letters to her parents in Pakistan, in response they'd write angry ones to mine in England and everyone would fall out over it. Consequently, my parents would be seen as bad people to all the clan in Pakistan. My parents, the ones without morals, shame or even respect for their own kind. My parents, being the way they were, would never live it down. To add insult, pain and guilt to my own misery, they'd blame it all on me, this farce of a marriage. I might have looked it, at times I might even have acted it, but I wasn't such a kid any more.

'Oh Khalil, son,' my mum said again, trying but failing to make my dark projection stop.

But at least we'd never divorce, the decent girl from Pakistan and me. We'd never have a marriage in the real sense of the word but so what? We'd still have that front, enough for some, but not me. So sad, we'd become, but her more than me. She'd suffer so much, her life ruined and dead. One day she'd notice how shit it had all become. She'd rummage around and find a length of rope kicking around in the drawer under the kitchen sink. She'd tie a noose around her neck, just to see how it felt… What *was* the point of all this shit? Damned if I could see one.

'Your father,' she said. 'You know this will kill him.'

My dad and me, we said we wanted different things but we were the same. We'd been deluding ourselves, that's all. As a child, I thought he was something special, when in fact, he'd been anything but. I thought life would turn out better for me than it had for him, and for years, he thought the exact same thing. All my life he prayed for his only son to be a mirror: obedient, loving and of course, like him, hard working beyond belief. I had all that to prove, to myself as much as anyone else, but marriage would leave me shackled. Didn't need or want that kind of responsibility. I needed my business, my mind and my body to be free of these constraints.

'Your father, you know he has problems with his health, and some-times his mind.'

I knew that all too well, lived with it for nearly ten years. By eighteen, I'd figured the root cause of his melancholy. His problems stemmed from the fact that he'd been such a loser all his life. A terrible thing to have thought but by then, my whole outlook had changed. I could justify anything I wanted. I could be honest about him, what he did and what he meant. A nice man, the nicest man in the whole world and that's what fucked him up so much. Nice meant weak, susceptible and naïve. But not with me, not with his son. In the end, I came to know the truth and it was simple. My father couldn't control his own life and so, to make up for that shortfall, he needed to control mine.

After nearly two decades of bringing me up, it all ended in failure, something he should have been used to by then. Once my mum got through with me, my dad walked in and just like that, without even asking my mum about my decision, laid it all out.

'Say no to marriage if you want. But it means there's no place for you here.'

I can't say I didn't expect it.

'If you refuse this, then you're not my son.'

Fine. If anything, getting thrown out saved me from looking like the villain of the piece.

'Understand?'

'It's okay,' I said without thinking about it for too long. 'I understand.'

My dad looked at me with a mixture of resignation and disgust. For once in his life, he showed strength and I welcomed it, I really did. I looked him up and down, at his greased hair, the flowing lines of his salwar kameez and then, I ended up looking into his eyes, trying to find some trace of life, perhaps love or even hate would have done. He shook his head and then slapped me. Thing is, it didn't hurt.

'That's it?'

He slapped me again, tempting me to smile because just the effort alone forced a film of sweat to form on his worry lined forehead. He didn't have the strength, the actual energy needed to inflict physical pain. At that moment, I left my childhood behind, but he still struggled to be a man.

'This is what you've become.'

'What have I become?'

'Disrespectful of your parents,' he said, keeping his voice calm and steady.

I shrugged it off. Saying something would only piss him off more. I didn't want to hurt him, never had been my intention. No matter how weak, no matter how many mistakes he'd made, he'd always be my dad. My dad: the best shopkeeper in the world. I'd always love him for that, what he and I had both been.

'You're a disgrace. God will forgive you but I won't.'

There he went again, bringing God into it. I sighed but stuck with plan A, the one which involved me keeping my mouth shut. Money talks and bullshit walks, I told myself as he yelled at me to get out of his sight. Not the end, though. Merely another beginning. One day I'd return and set things right. All would be forgiven once I showed him I had the skills he'd lacked all his life.

After packing a bag, gathering my money and dope, I calmly walked out of the house I'd grown up in. My mum followed me to the door-step, while my dad continued to rant to himself in the living room. I kissed my mum on the cheek and she kissed me back, a smacker on each side. I heard her crying as I walked off. I wanted to but I couldn't bring myself to look back.

2. glengarry glen ross

A sense of aimlessness accompanied me as I wandered further away from home. The world had a darker tint to it but I kept thinking about them, about going back. Couldn't do that. He'd win and I'd lose. Had to prove this point alone, whatever it turned out to be.

The more I walked and the further I got away, the more hopeful I became. Lots of people made it on their own. How hard could independence really be? No big secrets to be discovered. I had to go native, that's all. Be like all those white kids who flew the nest when they thought they were old enough. If they could do it, then so would I. Surely it couldn't be that hard.

Whilst I might have grown hopeful about making it on my own, the further I left home behind, the more the idea of living on my own began to feel like an alien act. Like eating bacon sarnies or having my first drink in the pub with my old man as soon as I hit sixteen, this simply wasn't a done thing. Such rites of passage had never made me jealous. If anything, not taking part in such rituals secured my feelings of difference: people like me, we didn't go out drinking with our fathers and one thing for sure, we didn't bring home girlfriends for our mothers to meet. As for leaving home, well, that had never been on the cards because I never grew up with total independence as a realistic part of my future. I'd never fly the nest, only build my own which would always remain linked to theirs, my parents'. Leaving seemed symbolic of me going against everything, and perhaps of being more white than black.

Vinny, my dealer, introduced me to a landlord called Ahmed. Ahmed was not a tidy man. One of those people who didn't like the sensation of a razor blade against his cheeks too often nor did he welcome the practice of soap against his skin. Short, fat and middle aged. He wore a white lace prayer cap, black plastic framed glasses and an off-white salwar kameez, which, upon closer inspection proved to be unwashed white. A scruffy, dirty and unhygienic man was one thing but a man who felt proud of being that way was another. Ahmed told me, as soon as I met him almost, that washing and being clean made him ill. In fact, the whole thing about hygiene and cleanliness was a myth dreamt up and then perpetuated by the soap, toothpaste and cosmetics industries.

When it came to doing business with him, however, he seemed okay enough. Once the conspiracy theory was over and done with, he wasted no time in showing me a shitty little flat in Manningham. Nothing wonderful but it had running water, some furniture, carpet, heat and light. The bare essentials but cheap. It would do, for now.

I paid Ahmed a month in advance and got cracking that very night. The usual haunts where I dealt were dead. I took a risk and wandered further into the heart of the Manningham drugs zone. A mad scene, I discovered. Another world almost. Hectic but at the same time ordered; running smoothly to some big, well laid plan. There weren't that many of them, maybe a dozen people at any given time including dealers, pimps, prostitutes and respective punters. Scattered all over the place, but mobile, constantly on the move, either going or coming back. Cars of all shapes and sizes, owned by people of all backgrounds pulling up outside the pub, the cafe and the bookie's, then speeding off as soon as the transfers of goods for money were made. An eye-opener not to mention a buzz, watching it all go off. An education, watching the various forms of business take place.

Every now and then, when dealers were busy doing their thing, someone would approach me with the intention of making a score. One old fart said he'd give me twenty quid if I sucked his dick. I told him no and then he switched, saying he'd give me twenty to suck mine. Right then, temptation spoke to me. I'd never made twenty quid with one throw of the dice. Still, didn't plan on being a rent boy so I told him to go fuck himself. He smiled and told me he wouldn't be there, wasting time talking to me, if he could do that.

The first real deal I knocked off wasn't too difficult.

He looked like a remnant from the seventies, real scruffy with it. Flared jeans with embroidered flowers on the pockets, baggy Indian shirt and of course, he just had to wear a pair of blue tint Lennon glasses. He didn't look dangerous or anything, just odd.

'What you got?'

I looked around, side to side. No one watching.

'Nowt but sensi right now, mate.'

He nodded slowly, listening to some Fleetwood Mac hippy shit in his head.

'Bit young for this, aren't you, man?'

'Erm,' I said. 'Nearly twenty, me.'

'Yeah?' he smiled. 'Well if you're twenty, my man, then I must be about ready to draw my pension.'

I looked away from him, trying to be all casual, nonchalant, like I got this shit all the time.

'Do you want anything? Cos if you don't, you can bugger off.'

'Only messing with you,' he winked. 'Just trying to make you feel welcome, man. As a new face, you know.'

'What if I am new?'

'Relax, my man. Just better watch yourself, you know?'

He sounded genuine, like he gave a shit. Just a good actor, I told myself. Nobody gave a shit about anything around here.

'Oh yeah?'

'Just watch yourself. They,' he said, flicking his head at the two dealers working down the road, 'they don't like seeing their profits in someone else's pockets.'

'And what are they gonna do? Not as if they can sue me or call the coppers.'

He smiled.

'Coppers? Them,' he said, flicking his head once again, 'they got their own way of doing things.'

'Thanks for the advice,' I said, cocky as hell. 'But I'll be okay.'

He nodded to himself.

'Just deal me an eighth for now, my man.'

'An eighth?'

'Yeah, an eighth.'

Now an eighth of an ounce sounds like nothing but by my lowly standards, we were talking about serious shit: another three deals like this, and I'd be empty. No problem, though. Soon get a top up from Vinny.

'Eighth it is.'

'Might see you later on,' he said.

As I watched him walk off, his flared jeans flapping around, I told myself I'd now become a part of the scene. The threat the other dealers presented didn't exist. If they really didn't like the idea of me being there, then one or all of them could have told me. It seemed like they hadn't even noticed me, the new guy. I felt confident and safe.

As the night wore on, my deals grew more authentic, my manner more controlled with every transaction. It felt so natural to me. Dealing drugs for real? A cinch. By four o'clock in the morning, I'd bought over from Vinny about nine times, grossing three hundred and some quid, about half of which were real earnings, my profit. That's when I decided on calling it a night. Thoughts of hitting a manky looking bed sustained my walk home, to my manky little flat. I'd sleep like a log, even though the place had this damp, mouldy musk to it. Tomorrow night, I'd make even more money and consequently, I'd sleep better than a dead person.

I carried on daydreaming like that until I heard the sound of a few cars creeping up behind me. I skipped onto the pavement, ignoring them, thinking they were some late night cruisers, looking for sex, drugs or both. Two of those nippy little Toyota 'Twinny' Corollas speeded up, got in front of me and then slammed on the brakes, one of them still on the road, the other mounted onto the footpath, blocking me in. I actually thought they were wanting to deal off me. Maybe I'd impressed the right people.

One by one, the doors opened. The occupants got out, sizing me up, some looking at me as if I'd just fucked their mothers, castrated their brothers or even killed their fathers. I checked them out and realised that amongst them were some of the same faces I'd seen dealing. Those I hadn't seen were mostly white guys but a couple of them Asian and black. No such thing as Reverse Discrimination or Positive Action in those days. Just a bunch of dealers and this, I figured, would be some kind of formal introduction to their world.

A skinny one, buck teeth, shoulders hunched up close together like he felt the cold more than anyone else, made his way to the front. Asian, dog ugly and a little unwell looking to boot. Didn't look like much at all and his dress sense didn't impress me, neither: cheesy leather coat that went down to his hips, those stupid fucking combat trousers flapping around his bony little legs and a huge pair of black *Caterpillar* Boots on his feet. This guy, I told myself, he wasn't a dealer. More like a cartoon.

'Alright, guy?' he asked.

Damn, this prick made me laugh. Sounded so slick and easy. So cool about this, whatever it would turn out to be.

'What do you want?'

'You got some fucking balls, you know that, guy?' he smiled.

'What?'

'What?' he mocked, cocking his head and making his eyeballs bulge, the others laughing at his little visual gag. 'You a fuckin' parrot or what, guy?'

Confused, I shook my head.

'What?'

'Fuckin' must be a parrot, Tony,' one of the others commented.

Tony as in Montana, no doubt.

'Pretty fucking polly,' one of them called.

I got it. Tony and his band of merry dealers were just pissing me around. Having a laugh with the new lad kind of thing.

'Oh, I get it,' I said, allowing myself a smile.

'You fucking well will,' said Tony. 'Gonna have to sort you out, then.'

Where did this guy get off? I looked him up and down. Surely, he couldn't be serious. What did he say again? He'd sort *me* out? How the hell would he manage that? Although a gang of them surrounded me, he made it sound like a personal matter. It would be his fight and his fight alone, so it seemed. Why he wanted to *sort me out* in the first place didn't matter. Seemed enough that he thought he could do it. Naïvety seemed to be my strongest suit in the early days.

Now me, I'd been brought up thinking that people fought fair. If someone wanted to fight you, then they did. That's just not how it works with drug dealers. That's simply not a part of their ideology nor is their creed based on fairness. I've since learnt that a whole bunch of them will join in some other prick's fight like it's the right and perhaps the only thing to do. Sure, strength in numbers, hitting hard and making sure might sound like good tactics but they're all pussy ways to operate. As far as I'm concerned, there's simply no honour in getting others to fight your battles.

I didn't know what to expect, the way they started closing in. I convinced myself that they were still pissing around, just a thing they did with new guys on the block. They were confronting one of their own, a dealer, so how come we had a problem? Well, apparently, I wasn't a dealer. More like a cheeky little fuck who only thought he'd made it to dealer status. Least, that's how I'd remain until they made me a member of their exclusive club.

Tony, being the head bitch spokesman, started dancing around like Muhammad Ali. I thought he looked ridiculous, myself. I even smiled.

'You think this is some fucking joke, cunt?!'

He threw a punch that felt as lame as his voice. I allowed it to land on my shoulder; all the impact of a feather.

'Sort you out, cunt! Sort you out!'

His eyes were wild, his mind crazed with crack or smack or fuck knows what. That's when I realised I had to do something about this. This shit was serious and if I just stood there, smiling like some out of place village idiot, I'd be feeling pain.

So I swung, got him one in the face, then swung again and finished off the combination with a kick to his balls. I don't know when it happened, but there must have been a split second where my mind just went into frenzy mode. Just could not stop myself from lashing out at him.

'Come on then, bitch. Come on!'

I could take pricks like Tony all day long. But the others, his insurance policies, were nothing like him. Tall, short, fat, thin, all frames but none so lame as that boney fuck. Even then, I didn't expect them to participate.

Being hit over the head with a metal implement is unlike any pain you can ever feel. In your own head, the first thing you acknowledge is the sound and not the pain from the impact. Not quite a clang and not a thud, neither. A combination of the two is perhaps more like it. And there isn't any pain...not immediately, but it's more of a feeling, a certain disruption of the reality you're used to being immersed in takes place. Partly, there's the shock of the experience itself. It actually feels unbeliev-able: people do *not* hit other people on the head with hammers; cartoons do that. What next? An anvil? But that is what happened. One of them, I never worked out which, hit me over the head with a hammer. A fucking hammer. Can you believe that shit? I know I didn't. The logic of it had me stumped. Ten of them and one of me and yet, one of the yellow bastards still felt the need to use a hammer? Why not make sure and use a gun, or better still a rocket launcher?

The strange thing about being beaten is how time seems to become elastic. Now, in my experience, the only other occasion where time stretches is when you're waiting. When you're being beaten up, however, time gets stretched, shrinks back and gets pulled in every way imaginable. Time takes on the properties of a rubber band in the hands of a nutter with a real bad case of the nerves. That night, while I lay on the pavement, I experienced moments which would never end and yet, there were also moments, thoughts and feelings which were barely given life. The air continually punctuated with the sound of my lungs expelling breath under duress, whilst absorbing the sound of shoe leather crunching into bone and flesh. A veritable symphony it must have been to those playing me, the instrument.

I think I got hit on the head two or three times before I went down. And when I did hit the pavement, those boys got busier still, booting into my head, ribs and arms. I did what I could to protect myself. I could feel the impact, but again, no pain. I'd fallen into one of those bailing machines you see on farms only it didn't bail, it beat the shit out of whatever it swallowed. It would be, I thought as they pummelled me into the ground, a moment that would never end. And as such, I began to feel strangely calm and then, due to this calmness more than anything else, I felt obliged to make some kind of noise. And that's what I did. I moaned and I carried on moaning until I couldn't do anything any more. Until I wasn't even there any more.

When I did come around, sometime after daylight had broken that morning, I saw this ugly ginger cat sitting on my chest, licking itself, the way cats do. Occasionally staring at me, looking me straight in the eye, the little bastard had made itself right at home. I told it to fuck off. It carried on staring but jumped off as if it understood. I watched as it stalked away to find itself another beaten chest to chill on.

I sat up, looked around and worked out my whereabouts and how I'd got there. After they beat the shit out of me, they picked me up and dumped me in the nearest back street, amongst a load of overflowing refuse sacks which turned out to be pretty comfortable, but stank to high heaven. The money I made that night, along with my watch, had gone. I'd done all the work and they reaped the rewards. Still, they had the decency to have left me clothed which was some consolation.

My face, gut, sides and back ached like never before. My nose bust and bleeding, eyes blinkered with swelling, both ears caked with blood, I must have looked a sight. When I lifted my top and looked at myself, I winced. Not a totally brown body any longer, but complemented with shades of blue, purple and even yellow. Various sized patches of powder paint covered me, a human colour card. I got to my feet and started the long, slow and painful trudge to the flat. All the while people stared, wondering what would possess anyone to go ten rounds with a sledgehammer.

That beating turned out to be a good thing, though. Through adversity and through that trial by violence, I did find strength as well as direction. Like the last time I'd been made a victim, something happened to my mind, to the way I thought about and then saw the world. As I got into the flat and crashed on that stinking bed, I realised that if I wanted to work alongside those people, then I had to be like them. Use their rules to gain entry and then succeed in their world. Only use those rules, though. Not live and die by them.

journey

Anyone else might have entertained thoughts of giving up, perhaps even returning home with a keenness to start living the quiet and simple life once again, but not me. During that week I spent recovering, doubts did come now and then but I'd soon put those to bed. I'd show those pussy bastards who they were dealing with. Not a pushover, not any more. If I gave up so soon, then I'd go through life getting shat on by everyone. And those pussies, I just had to get my own back on them. Felt compelled to teach them all, every one of them, a lesson.

Above all, it was the thought of going back home as a failure that kept me in. If I went home, tail between my legs, then there could be no hope and I'd deserve everything I got, including a bride I'd never know, a job I'd always hate and a destiny that would remain unfulfilled. The way I saw it, there was no choice.

I made a plan. Not too complicated, as plans go. I'd tool up and go for Tony, the skinny fuck that he was. Me and him, mano a mano. Not that I'd ever done anything so violent, not that I had that kind of experience. I'd lived a sheltered life, by and large, but deviating from a straight path wasn't difficult, almost a natural thing to do, given the circles I had to move in. You had to fight violence with more violence. The alternative? Be a victim once again and that, I simply didn't find appealing.

I had time to kill while my body healed. Those days dragged on and on. Sometimes, I'd sit and count to sixty, mark a line on the wall, then start over. Over the course of that week, my walls had hundreds, maybe even thousands of these little scratches, so much so that they looked like part of the décor.

Alone is such a cold way to be. No one to talk to, no one to see or simply be around. I wouldn't say it's boring. Solitude is fine in small measures but after a while it gets to be so dull, so disheartening. To pick myself up, I went out and bought a two quid tranny radio which I listened to all the time. A poor substitute for the real thing.

I had no trouble admitting it. I missed their presence. Living at home, there were times towards the end when we hardly communicated as a family but I still found comfort, a sense of security, knowing my own were close by, if not in heart or mind, then at least in body.

My mum, I missed her so much. I didn't wash my clothes because I could still smell the faintest fragrance of her cooking on them. I'd sit there, on the floor by the manky old wall heater, a shirt or a jumper in my hands, recalling the array of her specialities: keema, gosht, saag cholay, puree, halwa, chaat, stuffed kerala, lassi saag and on the mental list went, with me reliving and salivating over the mere thought of any one of her meals, thinking about the care she took over them, the pleasure I took in eating them. Even something simple like a roti she prayed over as she slapped off the excess flour, both hands working as one, stretching, spreading and caressing the dough into a perfect circle every time.

Towards the end, just her and me took part in the one ritual we both needed. She'd join me once she'd done loading the table with food, ready to be consumed. We'd eat in silence but I'd be thinking all the time, about her, about my old man and their lives. Sometimes, it was difficult not to think about just the food as the flavours, the textures and the fragrances would themselves fuse into one sense and more often than not, stimulate and evoke new but always pleasant thoughts. I longed for it to come back, for me to go back but no. Out of the question until…until the right time, whenever that came. Had to carry on working. Had to make a mark, carve a niche and do it fast before I succumbed to the thought of being where I really belonged.

I had about three hundred quid stashed in my flat. A cautious man, a prudent man, a man like my dad, would invest a portion and save the rest, just in case things didn't pan out. I didn't think that way. Didn't have a *just in case* scenario. All or nothing, that's the approach a real business animal would take. Buy bulk which meant buy cheap and then sell cheap, too. Undercutting the others would piss them off no end and that's exactly what I wanted. I actually wanted their attention now. I wanted them to confront me again because when they did I wouldn't come off like some nervous kid without a clue. When they hit me next, I'd respond in kind only I'd give far better than I got. This time it'd be Tony, and maybe one or two others on the pavement, not me.

Seven days after the beating, the swelling had gone but I still ached. I went to see Vinny for some cannabis resin. I wanted a big block: four, maybe even six ounces, depending on his mood. It'd rush me most of my savings but so what? Higher risk paid higher dividends. Retailing at a tenner an eighth, five pounds less than the going rate, I'd see a net return of between three and five hundred quid. And with that, I'd buy another six ounces, maybe half a pound and then knock that out too. Before I did a thing, however, I had to get myself prepared. Tooled up.

Around certain parts of town, there were people who sold all sorts of shit. Drugs, hi-fis, tvs, throwing stars, high-power catapults, knives and guns, you could get the lot if you knew where to look. I asked a few questions, got a few names and I bought myself a switchblade. Ready to go make Tony that offer:

'You and me, right here, right now,' I'd say, 'and no fucking around.'

Whatever he'd decide, I'd show no mercy because such concepts, as well as honour, integrity and decency were meaningless to these people.

Vinny lived fairly close to me, about ten minutes on foot. A flat in one of those big old houses by the park. His motor, parked outside on the road, looked a bit rough around the edges. Yet another little Japanese job with the go faster stripes, the alloys and the spoilers but it did nothing for me. In front of it I saw another car. Tasty looking German wheels for a change. Gti tag on the boot, KEFF speakers on the parcel shelf, ultra-lo-pro rubber banded over polished rims, lowered suspension and a double barrel chrome plated exhaust poking out from beneath a colour coded bumper. A professional job that cost serious money, you could tell just by looking. It gave out the same sort of vibes as Vinny's Twinny but only more so. On another level which meant whoever owned it did big business. Bigger than people like me and Vinny, at any rate.

Vinny smiled as he let me in.

'I heard you met the others,' he said, sniggering to himself. 'You don't look that bad.'

I followed him into his main living room. Nothing special. Pretty much like my own pad: crap but you can live with it.

'You want some gear, then?'

'What do you think I want?'

I heard the toilet flush and then the sound of someone slamming the bathroom door.

'You got a guest?'

'Aye, summat like that.'

The first time I saw him he seemed so out of place in Vinny's pad. Suit, tie and nice comfortable looking shoes. My old man told me you could tell a lot by a man's shoes. *All* this guy's gear looked like expensive, designer shit. I could smell aftershave, the classy kind, rich but not over-powering. The kind that didn't have advertisements because it didn't need them.

'How about you cleaning that crapper of yours, Vinny? Place is a sty,' he said, and then, looking at me asked. 'Who's this, then?'

'Just one of my runners.'

Runner? As far as I was concerned, I ran for no one. No one owned me, neither. I bought off this guy, but that didn't make me his.

'Khalil,' I said. 'My name's Khalil.'

The suit didn't respond much, just sniffed and then went over to look out the window, leaving us to get on with business.

'Give us a couple of minutes, yeah, King?'

King? So this is how he looked? I'd heard about this guy. One of the few higher ups. Supposed to be something of a professional, a busi-nessman. With a name like that, I expected some twat with a chip on his shoulder but he didn't seem to be like that at all. Down to earth, al-though a bit on the flash side.

'So you okay?' asked Vinny.

'I'm sound,' I told him.

'You should know,' he said. 'That what happened, it was nothing. Just a thing.'

'A thing?'

'Yeah,' said Vinny. 'It's a thing they do. Nothing personal.'

He gave me some cock and bull about new faces getting laced like some rite of passage, some initiation they had to endure. Didn't register that way in my book. For me, it was simply a way to make easy money and rid yourself of some new competition in one go.

'Well,' I sighed. 'That fucker Tony…I'm gonna kick his head in first chance I get.'

'Wouldn't do that if I were you,' said King, still looking out of the window.

'Oh yeah? Why's that, then?'

'It could create more problems for you and for me. I'm not happy when I have problems.'

'Really?' I reflected. 'That's supposed to scare me?'

Vinny gave me a look and then cleared his throat, his way of telling me to shut the fuck up.

'I don't need to scare you,' said King, sounding as if I meant nothing to him, which, I suppose, must have been pretty close to the mark. 'Besides, he only did what you'll do the next time some new kid turns up out of the blue and starts dealing.'

I shook my head but said nothing. King continued.

'You think what happened to you had anything to do with you? You think it was personal?'

I suppose he had a point. It might have been pussy shit but it really wasn't personal at all. Like Vinny said, it was a *thing* these idiots did. I left it open. That way neither King nor I lost face.

'So,' said Vinny. 'How much you need? Ounce to start with again, is it?'

I decided on four. I'd be left with a few quid's worth of walking around money. Better to play it safe after all, just in case.

'Four.'

'Four what?'

'Four ounces. You know, one ounce times four?'

'Quarter fucking pound? Are you mad?'

'I can move it. I got the money to pay for it, so where's the problem?'

'Listen: you get caught with that kind of weight and it's a stretch, man. That's possession with intent, serious intent at that.'

King turned to watch. Arms folded, contemplating our situation, almost like he wanted to help clear things up.

'Just deal me it,' I told Vinny, and then dug into my pocket. 'Here's the money.'

'No way I can deal you a quarter pound.'

'And why's the fuck not?'

'Cos I haven't fuckin'gorrit. Got two ounces at the most, maybe.'

A couple of ounces? Chicken feed. A guy like Vinny, although only a step up from me, he should have at least been handling quarter pounders. Should have had loads of shit kicking about.

63

'I'm running low' said Vinny, as if it was obvious.

King cleared his throat.

'I think we need to talk,' he said, a glint in his eye.

'About what?' asked Vinny. 'Said I'd sort you the balance out in a day or so, man.'

'Not you,' said King. 'Your runner, here.'

'I'm no runner. Self-employed, call it.'

King smiled and indicated agreement with a nod.

'Okay. Self-employed it is, then.'

'Him? What you wanna talk to him about, man?'

King walked over, watching me watching him.

'Just a small matter about weights and measures.'

'I can handle this, King,' said Vinny. 'I mean this is one of my fuckin' runners, man.'

'I'm not your anything, Vinny. You're my supplier, not my boss.'

'I deal to you, therefore you run for me. Got that?'

'Fuck you, man. I run for me and I buy from you.'

All three of us remained motionless. A Chinese stand off without the guns. I looked at Vinny and told him the thing that perhaps King wanted to hear:

'I used to buy from you.'

As expected, Vinny didn't take it lightly.

'You ungrateful little shit. After all I've done for you!'

'Done for me? What have you done for me that hasn't cost me?'

'I got you a pad for a start. Treated you like one of my own.'

'Don't gimme that shit. For all I know, you get bunged a commission from fat boy Ahmed.'

'That's bullshit. Who told you that?'

Not that I asked, but sounded as good as a confession to me.

'And as for product, you been dealing me shit since day one. If anyone owes, it's you who owes me.'

'You cheeky bastard!'

I reached for the blade as Vinny came for me. King got in the way.

'That's enough,' said King. 'I haven't got the time to piss around listening to you two bitching.'

He took out a set of car keys and handed them over.

'Those wheels outside. Get in and wait.'

I could feel Vinny's eyes burning into the back of my head as I walked out. I had a pretty good idea that King wanted me to work through him. I'd do it so long as he knew I belonged to no one. Well, that's what I told myself.

When King got in his car, he started it up and without a single word of explanation he set off, to where, I didn't know. I thought he said we needed to talk.

'What you say to Vinny, then?'

'Told him he should stick to dealing kiddie bags. A guy like you, you're too much business for people like Vinny.'

That sounded reasonable. I'd wondered about Vinny. A dealer or just a user who did small time deals from time to time? Didn't matter. Not any more, not now that King had expressed an interest in me.

'So what do you want with me?'

'Me? It's not what I want from you. Not that at all. It's what you want from me that matters. Quarter pound, remember?'

Holme Wood. Rough as anything, but not his pad. We walked in and all I could see was a shit load of primo gear including one of those smooth Bang and Olufsen TVs, a Bose hi-fi and furniture made of real wood and real leather. None of that cheap MFI shit for King. The room smelt nice, of real flowers, not chemical air freshener like the Jones's next door. He grabbed a remote control and pointed it at his hi-fi. Coolio started rapping on about some made up Gangster's Paradise.

'You wanna coffee, tea or you want something else?'

'Okay, tea'll do.'

'Make yourself at home.'

I sank into his soft leather sofa, a pleasing, calming shade of cream.

'Damn,' I said to myself. 'This place is nice.'

Crisp, tidy and what's more, organised to hell. Not only did he have money, this guy had taste. A few minimalist paintings positioned in the right places, varnished hardwood floor, Indian rug in the middle but best of all were his fish. A section of wall had a huge built in tank, a load of colourful little critters swimming around, not a care in the world.

'I put you two sugars in,' said King, walking in from his kitchen. 'Same as me.'

Apart from the car, he didn't look like no drug dealer. In those days, when you heard the words *drug* and *dealer* running together a certain image would pop into your head. Male, seedy-looking, ruthless, dangerous and more often than not he'd be covered in designer sports wear, gold chains and sovereigns. King wasn't like that at all. Clean shaven, well dressed, polite and in a fucked up way, the guy looked and behaved like a professional. He had a good frame on him. A big man but not all tight and rigid like some steroid popping bodybuilding freak. To all intents and purposes, he could have been another nice, happy-go-lucky kind of white guy who worked in an office, paid his bills, occasionally scored some pussy and went to the footy with his mates every other Saturday. Normal, I guess, is what he looked like.

'That's just how I like it,' I said, taking the cup.

'So,' said King, sitting down opposite me. 'You're the new guy, then. What's your name again?'

'Erm, Khalil,' I told him, and then, for reasons that are still unknown to me to this day, said: 'But my mates call me Kilo.'

A lie but Kilo sounded right. More appropriate than Khalil, for a start. Didn't seem to make much of a difference to him, though.

'Okay, Kilo. So you wanna make some money?'

'Don't we all?'

He raised his eyebrows, perhaps agreeing, perhaps not.

'You living at home?'

'No. I'm living…not at home.'

'How come?'

I shrugged.

'So you got your own pad? Live alone?'

'Yeah.'

'That's good. Better that you've no one else to worry about. How old are you anyway, Kilo?'

'Eighteen, nearly nineteen.'

'That's cool. Maturity's a good thing to have in this game.'

'Maybe.'

'So how come you're not living at home?'

'Personal.'

'Only asking, man. See, thing is, most pakis I know, they stay at home forever, with their parents and that. Family makes them weak. Holds them back.'

'Not me. I'm on my own. One man band.'

'Good,' he said again. 'You using anything? Drugs wise?'

I shook my head.

'So you're not into anything? No bad habits I should know about.'

'Apart from talking with food in my mouth, no.'

King smiled and then flipped open his cigarette packet, offering me one. I declined. No bad habits meant no bad habits. He continued with what I took to be an interview, waving an un-lit cig around as he talked.

'What about selling? How you get into that?'

'Dunno…just drifted into it.'

He sparked up.

'Okay, Kilo. Here's what we'll do. I'll give you some shit, you sell it, pay me what you owe and we'll take it from there. How's that sound?'

A bit sudden and a bit vague, that's how it sounded.

'Sounds okay…but what sort of earnings are we talking about?'

King took a long pull on his cigarette, hissing an exhalation.

'Don't worry, you'll do good with me. Gimme a sec though. Got a call to make before we take this thing any further.'

From his jacket, he pulled out a mobile phone. He looked up, recalling the number before punching it in.

'Slim? It's me, King. How you doing these days?'

King made some more chit chat before getting to the point.

'I got this guy called Kilo with me. The one that got initiated last week. No more of that. He's in and he's with me.'

I didn't dwell on the relationships between King, Tony and whoever this Slim was supposed to be. They were vetting me. I didn't mind. As for Tony, I *would* sort that fucker out sometime in the future.

The way I saw it then, I couldn't lose. I'd be supplied by my former supplier's supplier which meant I'd get the same product but I'd get it cheaper. That wasn't the only advantage. In one step, I'd been officially planted on the scene and better still, I had King to protect me. Seemed to be a secure situation but I couldn't stop myself from making one thing clear:

'You don't own me, though.'

'Scuse me?'

'I'm not your runner.'

King stared at me for a couple of seconds.

'Let me get something straight,' he began. 'I don't care who you think you are. I'm not bothered about what you hope to accomplish in your life. I don't give a shit about politics, race, religion, family, life, death, sin. All that shit means nothing to me. All I'm bothered about is one thing and that's me. As for you being my runner, you're doing it again.'

'What?'

'Flattering yourself. I'm giving you a chance, but that's only because I know I stand to gain.'

'As long as we're clear,' I said. 'I'm in this for me, not you.'

'Touche,' said King. 'Tou-fucking-che.'

He reached over, extended his hand and we shook on it.

'Yeah, here's to me.'

Felt like I'd been a part of the whole thing all along, like I'd been peddling drugs for years, an old hand now. A couple of them even apologised about the beating but they'd all been through it, some of them
more than once, so they said. A test, nothing more, that so called initiation. I suppose it might well have been effective as a vetting procedure,
kicking the shit out of people, I mean. If a new guy didn't show up after
a first beating, then he'd last two minutes with the coppers. Just as well
he went back to stacking shelves or whatever he did before he had a bash
at pushing weight. If a new guy came back empty handed and took
more subsequent beatings, then that was just as bad. Such an example
could be a different kind of liability but a liability all the same. It paid not
to allow fools into this line of work. A new guy who prepared to fight
back, however, he got clearance before his first blow landed.

Most new dealers don't start the way I did. Youngsters are almost
forced into dealing, especially the ones you might happen upon these
days. Perhaps coerced is a better word than forced. I've seen how it works
and I can't say I like it. It's too blunt, too selfish and just too convenient
an option, the way it is now. An eagle eyed dealer spies some young
hopeful, offers him a mobile phone, some dope, a line of credit and a
shit-hot income. What's a young on-the-dole kid to do? Refuse good
money, prestige and all those other perks or stay on the dole? Thing is,
a lot of these new kids don't fully realise why they're approached by these
hot-shit paper gangster dealers in the first place. New blood is needed in
any industry but when it comes to the drugs world, new blood is needed
for the sake of appearances as well as economics. It's about having a
ready supply of street people and it's also about having big teams. New
recruits are also useful because they're the first to be given up when the
need arises. I've seen it happen but kids being kids, they'll continue to
fall for the bullshit lines, thinking they won't go down like the others,
thinking they're different.

During the early days, I worked foot patrol. Hung around pubs,
cafes, bookies or sometimes I'd go out on a night, with a couple of
others, and we'd deal it large into club-land. Three months into working
foot patrol, I started taking driving lessons. I learnt the basics and then,

after very little deliberation, I bought myself one of those humble little Nissan Micras. The next thing I knew, business had gone mobile.

I got on okay with only a few dealers in particular. Most were full-time users themselves, getting high on their own supply, kicking their legs around better than junkies when doing without. Their perception of the world got skewered to hell and back thanks to any and all manner of chemicals. And then there were those who formulated often illogical theories which they thought explained the fucked up situations they found themselves in. Some of them were even convinced I messed up their ventures just because I happened to be clean which, I suppose, had a weird logic to it: they did badly not because they were junkies, but because I did well.

And then there were those who professed to hold an ideology. I'd come across ignorant racists in my time and the ones on the drugs scene sounded no different. For these people, pakis took their jobs, their women, their shops, their homes, and now, pakis were in on their criminal activities. Us pakis, we had this habit of taking one liberty after another. And if that wasn't bad enough, the whole world had suddenly gone mad giving pakis, chinks and niggers every conceivable opportunity. PowerSkin, they called it. Taking, thieving and cheating had become the paki's purposes in life. Fucking losers couldn't even work out why they were so shit at what they did. They were a dying breed in lots of senses and I had no sympathy for them at all. Matter of fact, I felt good about being resented by those pricks.

Business had become pretty brisk. With the car, profits were healthier, and turnover grew to a respectable level. Friendly banter wasn't necessary because unlike my dad, I didn't need to kiss arse. No one ever complained about me not greeting them, telling them goodbye and coming out with all that false, happy, customer friendly, arse-kissing bollocks because I did all the favours and what's more, they knew it, something my dad's punters never even realised, let alone appreciated.

Thanks to King I sold quality. Mainly Mary Jane in her various guises, but from time to time he'd off-load something different just to see how I'd make out. Ecstasy, Brown, Coke, LSD...Anything he'd have trouble getting rid of he'd shove my way and nine times out of ten, I moved it on without breaking sweat.

For a while, a huge fuss about so-called designer drugs got made, maybe even designed. Interesting choice of words, really. Designer drugs? Not like some advertising twat sits in his office and comes up with some wonderful product concept and then markets the shit out of it. From what I recall, no one, not a single soul ever actually came up to me and asked for a designer drug. A pure media myth, in truth. The only real designer drugs I ever saw were freely available in off-licences, pubs and supermarkets.

Anyway, I never carried a great deal of anything because that generated too great a risk. Instead, I organised a couple of hides which were close enough to be convenient but far enough to be beyond suspicion. If it all fell down due to some well elaborate and expensive police sting operation, then maybe I'd done one on a possession count but not with the intent to supply. Most guys I knew didn't bother weighing up the risks and then reading the cards. Like I said, they were too busy getting themselves up and loaded to worry about getting caught.

My conscience, in the form of my dad's voice, would try messing with me, but usually I got it to shut up simply by dreaming of the riches yet to come. Not such a bad thing, this drugs business, not evil like he made it out to be. And at least I didn't lie. How many car salesmen told the whole truth when selling their motors? How many life insurance spiels contained porky pies? How many cigarette companies told the truth about cigarettes and how many governments lied as a matter of business. With me, lying wasn't a part of the equation. A punter got what I said he got. I sold illegal substances, most of which were addictive, not to mention harmful to the human body. On the plus side, drugs made you feel good, for a while at least.

I felt responsible in the way I conducted myself. I also thought I had the risks all but eliminated. I dealt with those who knew what they were doing. On King's advice, although I didn't need it, I stopped even looking at kids, cut them out of the loop altogether. Sure, there were kids using all kinds of shit, but not thanks to me, not any more. Matter of fact, any time I saw some idiot pushing weight onto a youngster, then words were exchanged.

As time wore on, I became a face and yes, I admit, it did feel good. Gave me a sense of belonging. At the bottom, still the newest member of this family, still growing, still getting to know the other relatives and how they did things. Those were my formative years. Might have been competitive, but we were all on the same side. As a street dealer, I knocked out over three zeros a week when things were going good. Sounds like a lot of drugs but it's next to nothing, really. One junky with a decent habit, even some idiot who needs a tenner's worth of product a day, then that's seventy quid a week. Get ten of them on your books and you're rocking. As long as you don't start selling your punters poison, they'll keep coming back for more.

There were all sorts of people dealing. I heard a guy in his 70s supplemented his pension by dealing a few pills to some of his neighbours. Then there were these brothers with an Indian take-away, over in Eccleshill, doing close to twenty grand a week. There were a few respectable sorts with jobs, mortgages and families who did it part-time but most dealers were like myself in some respects. Young, not particularly well educated but there were far too many arseholes kicking around for comfort. Big bad dudes who carried weapons not for self defence, but for show. A few of these jokers walked around with guns shoved down the back of their waistbands. Not me. Much preferred the quieter life. If some idiot had a beef with me, then I tried making peace. My business concerned money, not war. However, if things looked impossible, then I had no other choice but to fight back. It was either that or be a victim. Kill or be killed.

Above people like me, the rank and file, there were a few middle men, men like King. Above them, right at the top there were a load of bigger, much more powerful players. These people had pretty good relations with each other as it made more sense. Asians, whites, blacks but they weren't about that. Skin colour, and even nationality had stopped mattering a shit years before. It was all about the money.

My boss, although he was never my boss in those days, was a guy called Saleem Choudhuri. While he drove around town in his stretch Merc, a goon kept any danger, real or imagined, well at bay. Now the local press portrayed Choudhuri as the local Asian done well, a pillar of the community, a philanthropic businessman and all that shit. Now close to his fifties, he'd been in and around the drugs scene for years but neither the police nor anyone else had ever managed to prove a thing. I suppose untouchable is a word that springs to mind. So, he was an old hand, knew the game inside out which is another reason why he remained an elusive suspect. In terms of business, he preferred words over violence but if he had to kill you then he would do that, or at least have someone do it on his behalf. Considered himself the archetypal *The Man* when in fact he was nothing special at all.

Guys like Choudhuri at the top, me at the bottom and middle men like King…in the middle, wholesalers. However, it was fairly early on in my career when word spread about an exception to this rule. I never saw him at the time but I do recall rumour surrounding a wholesaler who'd fallen out with Choudhuri. His name was Sweet. Sweet because the girls said he was. A real Mister Lover Man with a deep voice, a pretty face and a dick that could go on all night. This guy was everything Choudhuri was not, which meant he was young, slick, fast moving and ruthless. A new breed, a highly ambitious drugs professional. Like I said, I didn't know much about him. Certainly not hard and fast facts. I only heard the man's rep that covered his real self. Nothing real, just rumours.

According to the dealing community, Sweet had left Choudhuri's stable of large scale buyers and started working with his woman, a foxy blonde *biatch*. They'd been together years, romantically speaking. To all intents and purposes, they could have been married. Glamorous, hard and vicious, the pair of them. His woman used a blade better than Zorro, shot straighter than Robin Hood and, word had it, she made like Bruce Lee when it came to a bit of the old Kung-Fu/Ju-Jitsu/Fujitsu bullshit. Sweet, so they said, used to be like me a few short years before, nothing more than a lowly street pusher who just sort of stumbled his way along until he found himself in a position of some clout. Which is when things went wrong between him and Choudhuri. No one ever knew exactly what happened but that didn't stop them from gossiping. Rumour had it, once again, that Choudhuri tried 'dealing' with Sweet once and for all but Sweet came through without even a scratch. Sweet being the bad bastard that he was came close to 'dealing' with Choudhuri in return. Of course, this couldn't go on and so they had a little sit down, came to a compromise and agreed to put it all behind them. Even so, Sweet remained a thorn in Choudhuri's side. A crazed, lone wolf who really didn't give a fuck about anything or anyone, least of all fat fuck Choudhuri. Exactly how much of this was true and how much had been made up was anyone's guess. Still, people seemed prepared to believe it. Maybe it was all bullshit, even the stuff about Choudhuri, the compromise and the reputations. Not important, any of that stuff, not to me, but still relevant. King worked for Choudhuri which meant I worked for Choudhuri. Reminded me of the relationship I had with my grandparents in Pakistan. I knew they were there but I'd never get to meet them.

Sweet and I, in many ways, appeared to be the same. Same colour, culture, generation and we did the same things to make ends meet. On the inside, however, nothing really tied us. Sweet and me? Two different beasts altogether. Sweet, to me, seemed to be in control of everything but I couldn't say the same thing for myself, least not always. And, of course, there were moments when I would begin to think I had some morals, a conscience, even. We had to be different. I never used but Sweet was like a kid in a sweet shop, sampling the lot. That might have been a weakness if he thought of himself as a junky but he didn't think that at all. Think about it…a user only becomes a junky when using becomes problematic. A user, even an addict, is still only a *user* because there is no problem. If junkies have access to whatever they're into, then they wouldn't have to do junky things in order to get off. There'd be no innocent people getting mugged and robbed, no young kids selling every hole going just to get good and loaded and last, perhaps least, there'd be no guys like me, priding ourselves on a job well done, maintaining as many junkies as possible.

The thing about Sweet was you could never be sure because stories, myths and bogeyman tales clothed and protected him better than armour plating. Rumours. The man was one huge rumour machine and towards the end, no day went by when something new wasn't being banded around. Sweet killed a sixteen year old kid for double crossing him when he was starting out; Sweet used to mug beggars when he was struggling; Sweet battered some night crawler into the realms of brain damage for holding out; Sweet had just silenced a witness; Sweet killed his own father because his father looked at him funny; Sweet had kidnapped a copper because he was bored. And on and on it had gone and continued to go. Sweet dealt in kiddy porn; ate babies alive after raping old age pensioners; fucked his own mother while his father watched and wanked. Rumours, nothing real, made Sweet the man he was which is why, I suppose, people started sweating by the very mention of his name.

Guys like me, however, we were only one step away from punters so therefore, individually, we were largely insignificant pieces of shit that hardly ever floated up the ranks. When it came to those above us, however, we were talking about big money with the egos to match. King, so he told me, pushed over fifty grand every week and that was when things were quiet.

The town itself wasn't split into designated retail pitches or anything. Most of us were mobile operators who moved around in order to shift product. The coppers were okay mostly but now and then, they'd pick up half a dozen dealers, and get all happy about themselves. A publicity exercise so the good and law abiding masses got lulled into thinking drugs were being dealt with, still on the agenda when in fact drugs were a lost cause in Bradford. The coppers didn't exactly condone drug dealing, but they might as well have. Instead of targeting crimes within drug-ridden areas, they left them be and instead, concentrated on keeping the more important, the more wealthy and the more hooked victims happy.

And, with varying degrees of comfort, discomfort and numbness, I passed through. My waking moments were sound, easy and sometimes even enjoyable. Nights were shit because nights I spent alone. Unoccupied and left to my own devices, I'd end up thinking about my childhood and almost every night, I'd relive that episode with Charlie Boy and that pony tailed fuck called Tahir. Haunted me but it also spurred me on. Hatred might be unhealthy, but it can be one hell of a motivator.

I fucked off Ahmed's pad and instead got myself a newer, much better place to call home. I had plenty of money, plenty of *friends* and life didn't seem all that bad on the surface. I'd tell myself that I'd give the game up when I hit a decent bank balance, and for a while, the lie would work. That's when my dad would visit my head.

I'd have these little dialogues with him and they were nearly always the same. He'd tell me I'd done wrong. I'd tell him I'd quit soon. He'd say that kind of justification didn't wash. Then he'd preach on and on about morality, sin, life, death…the whole works he'd give me. Sometimes, he'd actually reduce me to tears. That's how real his voice had become. More significant than when I'd heard it for real.

I went to see them about a year and a half after I started working through King. It would have been the second Eid-ul-Fitr I'd spent away from home, had I not gone. I had a nice set of wheels by then and I wore some decent clothes. Made the effort especially. I didn't set out to impress them, though. Just thought I'd show them things were alright with me. That their son didn't have to doss down on park benches with the tramps every night. I owed them an appearance.

The street hadn't changed. I mean not one little bit. Our house, my parents house, hadn't even been decorated. I could have done that, if I'd still been there but no use thinking that way. Water under the bridge.

My mum opened the door. She didn't speak, didn't say a word but started sobbing which made me feel like shit. I got a lump in my throat, trying to find a word to say. For ages, she just stood there, looking at me, tears in her eyes, sobbing away. When I stepped into the house, she closed her eyes and put her arms around me.

'Oh son of mine,' she sobbed.

She said it as if she'd heard of my death. Gently, she held my face with both hands and kissed me on the cheeks, over and over again, like she used to when I was a kid. That's what I was to her, still.

We walked into the living room.

'Where's Dad?'

'Gone,' she said. 'Gone to pray.'

That's why I'd come to see them, in a way, because of Eid. First thing in the morning, we'd go to mosque to offer Eid prayers. I should have been there with him. Maybe next year it would be different.

'Eid Mubarrak, Mum.'

She returned the salutation and again, kissed me on the cheeks. I felt happy, glad that she seemed glad. As I sat there, I remembered how I used to love everything about Eid, even the month of fasting that preceded it, something my non-Muslim school mates could never comprehend. For thirty days, from dawn through to sunset, we'd go without anything, not even a drop of water. A time of abstinence, inner reflection and devotion. I don't know which part I liked best, the waking up for an early breakfast or the evening times, when the fast opened. Evenings were probably better in terms of food but the mornings, they were good in terms of experience. Sleepy eyed, bumping into furniture, not even knowing what I'd eaten until after, by which time I'd finally come round a bit. Two whole cycles of fasts I'd missed and I felt like shit for forgetting, or not bothering to care.

Eid-Ul-Fitr, usually the day after the thirtieth fast, a different experience altogether. One of the two days in the whole year when my old man seemed not to give a shit about the shop. We'd get up early, crack of dawn, bathe, put some fresh or new clothes on to which my mum would dab a spot of this rich, sweet smelling rose-perfume called *athur*. As we drew closer to the mosque, we'd see the others who'd be smiling, greeting each other. Most of them in traditional togs, white prayer caps on their heads, a few with something more ornate. We'd walk in, take off our shoes, enter the prayer rooms and we'd wait for the Mullah to begin. As soon as they were read, my old man would give me a hug.

'Eid Mubarrak, son of mine,' he'd say, before shaking my hand, the way grown men did.

So many things I missed about home. The chintzy wallpaper, the spotless furniture, the photographs of people I'd never seen and never would, the fragrance of spices present throughout the house.

'What are you thinking, Son?'

'Just,' I said. 'Just thinking, Mum.'

'Food,' she smiled. 'Been a long time since I've fed my son.'

She came back a couple of minutes later, loaded up with trays and dishes of everything I dreamt of during my lonely nights.

'Eat,' she said. 'And don't leave anything.'

Like the good son I used to be, I did as she asked. All the way through, she watched me intently but not in silence. I ate while she talked about anything that came to mind. We had new neighbours. Very nice people, apparently. My dad's health? More or less the same. He had good days and bad but at least he could still drive and do everything that needed doing.

I expected her to fire a load of questions at me. Like where I'd been, what I'd been doing, where and how I lived, all that sort of stuff. But she didn't. Maybe she felt good just seeing me. Then again, maybe she thought I'd come back to stay and these mysteries would be explained later.

I helped her clear the stuff away and then wash up. While we were doing that, I heard the sharp zip of a Yale key ramming into its lock. I swallowed, knowing he stood on the other side of the door. I prayed he'd be pleased to see me.

'Son, your father's here,' my mum said, turning around, and staring down the hall.

He walked in slowly. Hadn't changed that much. Perhaps a couple of pounds lighter, perhaps heavier, difficult to tell. What hair he had left, slicked back, kept in place. My old man, the perennial BrylCreem Man. White salwar kameez, brown Nehru jacket, black Jinnah hat in his hands and a pair of black leather loafers; this was his standard Eid gear since forever. I'd seen him in worse condition, but then, he always seemed to shine on Eid, the high points of the year. I waited anxiously for him to see me, to notice the stranger.

At first, he screwed up his eyes, not sure of what he saw. Then he walked closer, his head tilting, recognising my face but still not absolutely convinced.

'Khalil?'

'Dad?'

We embraced. A good, hardy clasping of bodies, chests and cheeks touching. Just like he would before I went away, he shook my hand once we parted.

'Eid mubarrak,' I offered.

'Khair mubarrak.'

He put his hand on my shoulder and led me into the living room, my mum following us eagerly.

As I'd been half expecting, he dispensed with the pleasantries early on. First, he asked me where I got the car that occupied his parking spot.

'Bought it, Dad.'

'Bought it? With what?'

'Money.'

I turned away from his cold stare. That's why him and all the others came here, wasn't it? Money. He came to make a better life through work and that's all he ever did for as long as he could. I had the same ethics, but I had one big edge over him. I knew things automatically. I knew things by virtue of being born here. Knew things he had no idea about.

'You're working?'

'Yes.'

'What kind of work?'

'I'm a salesman.'

My dad shook his head.

'Leave the boy alone,' my mum said. 'Been so long since I've seen him. I don't want you to drive him out again.'

Silence. There, she'd said it. I could see the pain on his face. God knows how many times she'd said it while I'd been away. For the life of me, I couldn't leave him hanging there, taking it all by himself.

'Nobody drove me out, Mum. I left.'

My mum didn't answer. Best not to.

'It's okay,' I said. 'Doesn't matter any more.'

'Doesn't matter?' my dad asked. 'You abandon us for drugs and it doesn't matter? What kind of joke is this?'

He threw *me* out, as I recalled. Couldn't defend myself because by doing that, I'd be offending him. Some things never change, I told myself. Same as last time silence felt like the better option to take. I'd only come to say hello, anyway.

'I better go,' I said.

'No, Son. Not yet. Stay a while?'

'I've got things to do, Mum,' I said, walking out into the hall, my mum following me.

'Son, please don't go. He's not himself any more.'

'I know that. But I should go. I'll come again.'

I scribbled down my phone number on the address book in the hall and then opened the front door. My mum kissed me and that was it. Out I walked, never to see him again.

negotiation limerick

King and I, we were never friends but he never failed to interest me. He changed so much over the time I knew him. Sharpest son of a bitch around when I first made his acquaintance. But then, slowly but surely, I started to see a man who'd become his own worst enemy. Used more than he sold but I figured what the hell, each to his own. He still looked the part, his pad still cool, but his face, his features had altered almost beyond recognition, like he'd weathered one storm too many. There were moments when he felt generous enough to pass down the wisdom he'd acquired over the years. In the beginning, when I saw him as a role model, his words had value, clout. Later, as his slide into nothing became obvious, he sounded a bit on the hollow side.

'There's lots of ways to survive in this business.'

'I suppose there must be.'

'Surviving's alright but if you want more than that, then there's only one thing for it,' he told me.

'Like what? Sell for more than you buy?'

He dismissed my flippancy with a smile. Almost twenty-three but still a kid with an occasionally immature, wise cracking mouth. He had absolutely no room to talk, practically living up there, with the birds, the kites and the clouds.

'You got to lose yourself and in a way, you have to become someone else,' he said, still pondering the thought.

'Yeah?'

'I wasn't always like this,' he said, looking himself up and down, brushing some fluff off his togs. 'Comes a time when you got to change yourself totally. Be the one thing you thought impossible.'

I nodded. I didn't like to admit it, but it had happened to me already, that changing. At some point a metamorphosis had taken place, resulting in the simple son known as Khalil mutating into a devious little dealer called Kilo.

'I getcha.'

Khalil and Kilo looked pretty much the same on the outside, but between us, a gulf of difference sat. Khalil was okay. A bit of a pussy but polite, gracious, and at times even honourable. A kid with the heart in the right place, decency by the bucket load, do anything for his parents, his friends and his fellow men and what's more, the sucker would do it all for nothing, without question. Kilo? Different in lots of ways, that fucker. Both of us had goals but Kilo's could only be achieved by forgetting about the life he'd known as a child, as Khalil. Kilo made money and nothing else mattered. He dismissed the thoughts that Khalil allowed to plague him. Kilo could be anyone's associate, but no one's friend. Sure, he'd help, but only if the price made the right kind of noise.

According to King, I had no choice but to be the opposite of what I used to be. At the time, it didn't sound too ludicrous. For a while at least, he'd been living proof that it worked. As for where he'd gone wrong, that didn't warrant much thinking. Casual sampling of product became a regular thing and when it comes to drugs, it's only a matter of time before a regular thing gets to be a necessary thing.

Twenty-three years of age and I'd made more money than my dad had earned thoughout his life. The work wasn't even hard, and for a while at least, nothing about it disturbed me. I'd moved on a bit, I suppose. Started selling a bit of brown, sometimes crack, coke, whatever came along. Idiots got busted and bigger idiots got themselves hurt. Every now and then, some stupid twat did too much and ended up in hospital or even dead. Nothing to do with me. I mean, come on. How the hell could I be responsible for what other people did? What did I look like? Mary Poppins? What did people want from me? To hold their hands while they jacked up? I didn't put a gun to no one's head. I didn't make anyone do anything they didn't want to do. My conscience, believe it or not, was clean.

There were times when King got really touchy about stuff, a couple of delusions away from paranoia. I remember asking him about his family. The guy nearly bit my head off.

'I have no fucking family, you idiot! Don't fucking need it! Got that?!'

Me, on the other hand, I had a family but it felt like I'd misplaced it, or it had lost *me*, somewhere, sometime during a lapse in concentration. I felt bad about not going back to see my mum after that Eid experience. Always kidded myself by thinking I'd go some other time, once the dust had well and truly settled. Besides, I did keep in touch with her…sort of.

My mum, she'd ring and leave messages on the machine. I never had the courage to ring back, in case my dad answered. I'd get in on a night, hit the play button and listen to her voice. Her voice. It was the only thing I had to remind me of me, that looped lullabye that never failed to send me to a sound and pleasant sleep. Inside, I knew there'd come a time when I'd have to go back but for a long time, I actually thought I'd do it on my own terms. When I did return, it'd be for good and because I wanted to, not because things went wrong. Didn't pan out like that.

I saw a fight between a couple of dealers that day. But so much more than a fight. Two idiots punching, grappling, kicking and cursing on each other like nobody's business. And all because one of them had finger fucked the other's woman. That's right. One little finger going in and out of one not so little hole. They'd been gasping on crack fumes in a little den called The Spinner for half a day before they eventually decided to step outside, where they'd poison their bodies with the same noxious air everyone else had to make do with.

Sat there, watching these two junk fiends beating the shit out of each other, minding my own business, my mind, as it often did, began to wander into the future. Before I started seeing myself rolling in money, one of the two junkies pulled out a piece of steel. A cut throat, a lethal weapon in any hands. He started slicing at the air while the other one kept on jumping back from it. Ridiculous, really. These two idiots, risking life and limb over some woman who had a habit of getting fucked and finger fucked by anyone who was bored or desperate enough to bother. No shit, but this one, she'd red rocket a dog for a fifty pence.

As I watched the crackheads dance their waltz of death, I thought about calling the coppers but before I could hit the first nine, the one with the blade hit home, or rather, slit home straight across the throat. The poor fucker on the receiving end, he just crumbled to the ground, hands around his neck, trying to stop the flow. The blood kept on gushing, through his fingers, down his arms and then dripping off the top of his elbows. The one with the blade shat his pants and then ran like crazy. With the exception of a dead junky who seemed to be floating in an ever expanding pool of blood, the scene had become deserted within seconds. Myself, I didn't think hanging around would do me any favours.

Just as well that happened because otherwise, I'd have stayed out there, perhaps dealing for another twelve hours. I really needed some time off as I'd been working since the night before, one of my many marathon sessions, catching a few winks in the car only when I could.

I hit the play button on the machine as I got in. My mum's voice came on.

'Son? Khalil? I'm your mother speaking.'

She cried, but tried real hard not to. I knew what had happened but until she actually said it, I'd continue denying it.

'If you're there, then come home. Come now. Straight away. Hurry, Khalil. It's your father…'

I checked the message. Turned out to be almost a day and a half old. No time to think about that and no time to sit there, wallowing in my own pity or perhaps blaming myself for not being there, answering her call in person when she made it. Blame, regret and pity I could do later.

I ran out, got in the car and raced over to my mum's, jumping red lights, breaking the hell out of speed limits and ignoring as many give-ways the fear of my own life would permit. One of those journeys that I didn't even think about. Don't even know how I got there.

Maybe a dozen cars and a couple of Toyota Hiace mini-buses lined the street. The vans, a red one and a blue one, had these little curtains in the windows which signalled only one type of driver to me: Pakistani, most likely an import. I knew what had happened back in the flat when I heard my mum's recording. Seeing all these vehicles confirmed it.

As custom dictated, the front door remained unlocked for those who'd come in with the desire to express whatever degree of sympathy the relationship between them and the deceased merited. I picked my way through the hall, littered with shoes, adding mine to the mass as I got closer to the front room. From the back, in the dining room, I could hear women wailing like a load of banshees: standard practice when someone dies. I opened the door to the front room. Sitting there, on the floor, were a load of strangers, most of them looking grim while a few nattered away about any old shit they cared to mention.

'Nawaz Sharif,' an old goat with a beard said. 'He's a proper bastard.'

'And what about the other one – Bhutto – that prostitute's good, then is she?'

'I'm not saying that at all,' the old goat protested. 'They're all proper bastards. It would be good if we had another Zia. Then we'd see. Put a noose around all the politicians and get an army man in. Then we'd see. Yes, then we would really see.'

A bloke sat in the corner must have cottoned on as to my identity. He got up and guided me back out, into the hall, while the others carried on listening to old men argue about the state of Pakistan's economy, society and fucked up reality.

He didn't look too good to me. To me, it looked like he'd been crying with those eyes all bloodshot red, face a haggard bag of skin, voice sounding tired, hoarse and pissed off.

'Khalil?'

'Yes.'

'I'm sorry,' he said, shaking his head. 'About your father...God's Will.'

'What happened? Do you know? I mean...how?'

'He'd fallen ill and had to be taken to the hospital.'

'Oh...'

'There was a nurse. She put a tube into his lungs instead of his stomach.'

He took his time and died in pain, drowned, by all accounts. Just his luck to go out like that. My dad, only forty-five and dead. Not that I'd ever seen him really alive but how come, I asked myself, how come all the bastards got to live to a hundred while the good ones died young?

A relative of mine, this guy with the news. Karamat, he called himself, and then explained that he was one of my dad's first cousins. I'd never seen him before but he said he remembered me as a kid. Didn't even know the man and here he was, telling me the most important news of my life.

'Your mother... she said you'd come.'

My mother. What she must have been going through, only God and her knew. In an ideal world, I'd have been there with her when she found out but it's never been an ideal world. After that point, it never would be.

'My mum? Where is she?'

'Gone, they've gone.'

'Gone? Gone where?'

'Airport. Where else?' he said, looking at his watch.

'Airport? When? When's the flight?'

He shook his head again.

'Six o'clock.'

I looked at my watch. It had just gone five.

'Manchester. If you hurry you might…'

I put my shoes on and ran to the car. I had sixty minutes. More than enough time in normal circumstances but during rush hour, even getting on the M62 took twenty minutes at least. I drove like a maniac. Endangered countless lives by going on the pavement when confronted with queues. A similar story on the motorway where hard shoulder became my personal property. I had to get there before she left. I'd never forgive myself otherwise.

Throughout the journey, I lost and found my composure countless times. Not right, my dad dying on me. Not fair. He deserved a chance to see me doing good and I deserved reconciliation. I'd been such a bastard for falling out with him but…but I didn't kill him. Some nurse took care of that but even that wasn't true. Lots of people shared in his murder. I played a part, as did his customers. Who could forget his life-sucking creditors and of course, Charlie Boy and his loyal pony tailed fuck-dog, Tahir? They'd started my dad's dying process and now they'd completed their handiwork. Made me feel even worse, realising that.

As I drove on, I remembered the night we got attacked. Pissed in my pants that night. Watched in terror as Charlie Boy broke my dad's hand with a baseball bat. Ever since, my dad had a problem gripping things. Told my dad how I'd kill those men when I got older and my dad told me how we didn't do that kind of thing, people like us. And what happened to that vow I made? Gone, erased from history. As a kid, I actually believed I'd right that one big wrong once I achieved adulthood. I felt ashamed of myself for dismissing it, for hiding it away from myself.

In the car, I began mourning my dad's passing silently, in private. I just sat there like a machine, watching the road ahead, ignoring the mobile every time it rang, thinking about all those times I worked in the shop with my dad watching over me. It, being in the shop, being around my dad, used to feel so good. He'd tell me what to do and I'd do it, most times without even asking because it made sense. He'd always be proud of me. I showed so much willing, so much promise, I guess. Life would have been so different if things had gone to plan.

I found her fretting in the queue, a small bunch of cousins reassuring her, telling her she'd be fine, God's Will, came to us all, this thing called human, bodily death. She looked at me, started crying, and then she put her arms around my shoulders, the tears coming thick and fast.

'I knew you'd come,' she said. 'I knew you'd come to see me.'

'Mum,' I managed. 'I didn't know. I only just found out.'

She shook her head.

'That doesn't matter. What can you do for him, now? He's dead and nothing can bring him back.'

The other relatives looked at me with disgust. I'd brought all that shame and now I had the nerve to come back? At a time like this. Fuck them and what they thought. I knew about them and I knew how they felt about my old man. Half of them he couldn't stand because they always went on about him selling, and then later drinking the demon nectar. And yet there they were, making out like he meant everything to them, their all and all.

I waited with my mum until she had to leave. She smiled at me and then handed me a carrier bag holding two items.

'Don't forget this thing,' she said. 'Don't ever forget it.'

I watched as she got to the end of the last corridor, expecting her to turn back to me before rounding the corner. She didn't.

3. how to get ahead in advertising

magic's wand

I'd been listening to some DJ verbally masturbate for ages. I sighed with relief when they locked him up and put the news on instead. I turned the volume up in case something interesting, or important, happened to be going off in the world. As usual there was, and as usual there wasn't.

First up, Middle East news: a cell of Palestinians had killed a wail of Jews. Believed to be an act of retaliation for the three Palestinians shot by Israeli military personnel the night before. The American President condemned the violence and added that this was not good for the stability of the area. Next, death sentence news: an American redneck hillbilly crack-whore was only hours away from getting fried because she'd been refused clemency for killing her redneck hillbilly man and her own redneck hillbilly kid in the making. Russia: in some part ending in -*stan* or -*nya*, a war raged and old women, no doubt with few teeth and checked headscarves, screamed red murder to the small army of reporters who'd been drafted in to keep the story stoked up. French news: three Algerian people burnt to death and authorities were treating the matter avec le grande suspicion. Financial news: in Japan, a lack of confidence in the economy translated as bad news for us in the rest of the world. The correspondent said: 'When America sneezes, the rest of the world catches a cold, but when Japan sneezes, the rest of the world sends a get well card.' It seemed like an attempt at humour. I attempted to laugh.

This was followed by a look at home news. Some smarmy Blairite bastard came on and started bitching on about how 'this' government needed more time to deliver promises to the people of this country. In Essex, a ten-year-old boy was missing for a week. His parents cried at the press conference while a copper urged anyone knowing anything about the boy's whereabouts to come forward without delay. Petrol was going up by a penny a litre: the RAC said it was a terrible blow for the average motorist as well as hauliers, farmers and I imagined, for Buddhists who protested through self-inflammation. Trivial world record news: some woman called Irene from some place in Wales broke the world record for staying still. I figured she must be a blast at parties.

An hour later, after the big stories repeated, I encountered a change in format. Some wanker MP, speaking in the House of Commons, started harping on about the inevitable corruption of society if drugs were allowed to remain a part of it.

'Believe me, we intend to hound these people into submission,' he said, waiting for the House to finish murmuring its approval. 'No longer are decent, moral and law abiding citizens prepared to stand by and watch this country be driven to its knees…'

So, Inspector Morse, drugs were responsible for all the shit in the world, then, were they? Society might have been getting a right royal fucking but not by the likes of me, but by those with the capacity to fuck it, by the ones who tried to control it. The same people who made speeches attacking the symptoms of society's malady were the ones who made it ill in the first place. The state of the nation has nothing to do with dope, of whatever description, but it might just be linked with politicians doing what they do best: promising wonders and yet, delivering great big domes full of shit.

'This government will pursue all legitimate avenues in order to eradicate this evil menace once and for all.'

I'd spent over a month inside the house. I didn't go out once. I'd spend my time sat in silence, in the dark, just thinking and doing little else. Every now and then, I'd turn on the radio and spend some time listening to tossers talk their shit but I'd grow tired of them and sink back into nothingness. I didn't take any calls and I stopped wanting to deal. It was a down time but not without reason. My old man was dead and I needed to mourn him, which I did through doing nothing. Of course, it had to stop at some point. Had it not been for King, it might have gone on for a lot longer.

It took him a long time for King – going on six weeks – to figure something was wrong. By then he'd been on the ropes for a long while – a year at least – and it seemed as if he got more wrecked, more strung out with every passing day until his addiction and his madness had achieved a strange but harmonious rhythm: the more he used, the more paranoid he got and the more paranoid he got, the more he used. Somehow business managed to remain a priority for King. Not that he was the happiest bunny in the field at the best of times, but when he got wind of my prolonged absence, he took it as a personal insult.

'What the fuck's going on, man?'

I walked back into the house, King following me in. He didn't seem too concerned about my pad being a mess, but then, it looked a lot like his place looked of late.

'You want a coffee or something?' I half-heartedly asked.

'I just wanna know why the fuck you've not been working,' he said, pausing to sniff. 'Do we – you and me – have a problem or something?'

'No but,' I began. 'But I've had some problems.'

He looked at me and then stepped up, grabbing my wrist, looking along my arm for any signs of weakness. Kilo's forearm? Cleaner than King's had ever been. If I rolled his sleeve up, I'd find more tracks than a double album but this wasn't about that. King still had to play the part, be the big bad boss man who thought he could discipline those he sold to, people like me.

'Thank fuck for that,' he said and let go. 'So what's these big problems you're having?'

'Family. Had a death in the family.'

King smiled, revealing an incomplete top row of gammy looking teeth.

'Thank fuck for that. Thought it was something serious for a sec.'

'My dad,' I told him. 'My dad died.'

King looked at me blankly, shrugged and said:

'And? What's your point?'

I didn't want his sympathy but he didn't have to be like this, didn't have to be such a cold bastard about it.

'What?'

'Remember what I told you, Kilo? About changing yourself? Remember what I said about becoming someone else?'

'Yeah. I remember. But this is my dad we're talking about.'

Could have been talking about a goldfish for all the difference it made to King.

'You're missing the point. My own parents? Losers, both of them. When they did finally croak, I didn't find out about it until a good three months after. Didn't mean anything to me then and doesn't mean anything now. You got to get something into your thick fucking head, Kilo.'

'And what's that?'

'In this business, there's just you and every one else is a bastard. You got that?'

I told him I did. Before he walked out, he turned to face me with one last bit of advice:

'Get your shit together. Got money to make out there. People are screaming for shit and here's you, being a bitch.'

He might have been a junky, but he could still think straight when he needed to. Life went on. I'd had long enough to get over it. And like my mum told me, my dad would not come back, no matter how many more tears I shed for him.

Less than an hour later, I found myself sat in the car, making calls, telling my regulars I was back in business, ready to cut them in on better than usual deals. A couple of them offered me their sympathies but it felt rehearsed, not genuine and not sincere like cousin Karamat's few but choice words. And why should it have been? They didn't know me and they weren't a part of me, either. Punters, of whatever description, are only interested in what they want, not who's giving it.

Ordinarily, not too many surprises came up for an average dealer like myself. Sure, the law not to mention the rest of the world, had this thing about fighting me and my kind but that kind of grief I could handle all day long.

Neither the coppers nor the government really figured in my world. Sure, they said they were trying to kerb the rise in The Epidemic with a few awareness campaigns here and there, greater powers for the coppers and the judges but all these things amounted to very little. People will always want drugs and you can't stop that demand by telling them drugs are evil, immoral, a health hazard or whatever. That's why dealers are here to stay. Think about the options we have. I mean, what *is* a dealer to do? Give it up just because some dodgy-dealing, expenses-screwing, mistress-keeping, QUANGO-sitting MP says it's the right thing to do?

Now I'm not boasting, but with a dealer there is no dishonesty, no lying, no advertising and none of that special introductory offer, buy one get one free shit. There's just the truth which is this and it's great big letters in case people miss it:

YOU CAN BE ADDICTED TO THIS SHIT SO YOU BETTER WATCH YOUR FUCKING STEP

Make your own mind up if you want it or not, only don't come crying to me when you've no money, no possessions and no mind left. You have been warned.

I watched a potential punter approach my car. Never dealt with him before but I could tell the nature of his addiction was severe. He crouched and then tapped on my car window. I wound it down.

'Listen,' he said. 'Beg a favour off yer, chief.'

The poor bastard looked to be in need, a lot of it at that.

'Yeah?'

Said he wanted something – anything – to see him through until his woman scored some dick. I realised I had seen him around. An especially low life form. A junky pimp, mugger and thief. Not being judgemental but frankly I saw nothing redeeming about this fuck.

'Yeah, my friend. A favour.'

No way a friend of mine, let alone customer. And now, all of a sudden, he decided to come along to ask *me* for a handout?

'I don't know you, man,' I said flatly.

'You gotta help me out,' he moaned, like he had it worse than any other junky on a forced fast. 'I mean come on, man.'

I gotta? Since when did I gotta do *anything*?

'I don't know you,' I told him again. 'Go see your man. Maybe he can help you out.'

'Aah,' he moaned. 'Can't do that, chief. Owe the man some shit already and that.'

He looked around suspiciously but no one cared about him or me.

'And you want me to lend you some? You must think I'm some fool, man.'

'Come on, man. I need some.'

'I got bills to pay, you know. Overheads and shit. Take a hike.'

'Come *on*, man. Help me. Fuckin' *help* me.'

'Bitch, make your own help. What I look like? Some kind of charity shop here? It say Oxfam on my head?'

Quick as a flash, he pulled out a blade. One blink later he had it held to my neck. I wasn't scared because I had a handle on these people. Usually, they were that fucked up, they didn't even know where they were, let alone know what they were doing. This bastard in particular must have been in really bad shape to pull this kind of shit. A good dozen ticks beyond desperate.

'Take it easy,' I said, reaching into my pocket. 'I got something for you.'

'That's more like it, man. Hurry the fuck up or I'll cut your fucking neck.'

I pulled out three rocks wrapped in cling-film, a fifty note deal, and held it out the window for him. He moved the knife away, already slavering like a dog, ready to pounce on the package then run like a bastard down the nearest alley way. I dropped the wrap, he went down to pick it up and I opened the door, slamming into his head, fast and hard. I stepped out, tempted to kick ten balls of shit out him but decided not to. The way he moaned already started to do my head in.

'Fucking idiot,' I said and picked my shit up. 'Try that again and I'll kill you.'

Well, at least I had a talking point, I told myself, as I watched him scurry off like a wounded animal. I got back in the car and waited.

A cop car drove by. The driver eyeballed me and I looked away. Paid not to beg for attention. Coppers are only a problem when they want to be, which usually happens when you rub them up wrong. Having said that, there's coppers, and there's coppers. Some of them don't really give a shit about people like me which I think is cool enough. But then you get some right whackos who take your existence and way of life as a personal attack on them and their way of life. Grizzly Adams, for example. Big fat, ugly fucker with a thing about my 'lot' – pakis – which to him means anyone of Asian origins. I never gave a shit that he was as racist as they got but I did mind people like him making out dealing to be strictly a *paki* and a *blackie* thing. For every one of my *lot*, at least one of his *lot* pushed.

I've always thought it stems from a lack of communication and understanding, myself. The trouble with a copper like Grizzly is that he didn't realise I needed air to breathe, food to eat and a place to sleep.

Never realised I was just like everyone else, just one more body taking up a little room on the face of this planet, that's all. I wasn't evil and I certainly wasn't out to ruin all that was good and holy in the world. I was a regular guy, just another regular Joe Blow, except I sold drugs for a living. To the police, I was the visible enemy, and to make things right, I just had to reciprocate such sentiments. So we got a balance – a state of equilibrium – they hated me, I hated them, and in a fucked up kind of way, we were all happy with that little unspoken understanding.

slave driver

I sat behind the wheel, waiting for the needy to come asking, maybe begging. But no, nothing seemed to be happening, other than the world continuing its eternal movement through space. The sun going down, a warm breeze on my face complimented a sky tinted with red and orange, whilst a few streaks of yellow but dying sunshine reached and gently caressed the clouds. The ludicrous tune my mobile emitted ruined that beautiful, unique moment forever.

'Yeah?' I said, half sighing, half groaning.

'Kilo?' the voice asked.

'Yeah?'

'It's me. It's Tony, man.'

Tony. That's right, the same fuck who, with the help of a few of his buddies, beat the shit out of me a few years before. Only now, I knew him better and as a result, hated him even more. Tony the pussy, Tony the king of bullshit. An out and out liar, all front and very little substance. Still, had to hand it to him as he did the business, did Tony. Sold to anyone and everyone. Always packing and always ready to make profit. A funny guy, a fucked up guy more than funny guy but why nit pick?

His real name turned out to be Ilyas. He only called himself *Tony* as he thought it sounded cooler or some lame shit like that. Most of us actually called him Tony Montana – as in Scarface – but he'd never make it beyond the realms of tissue gangster-dom (single-ply Kleenex, if that). I had him sussed out. A mouth. Talked the talk but the sorry bastard couldn't even crawl the walk. One of those guys you could smell coming a mile off.

'So what's happening?'

'You know,' said Tony, like everyone knew. 'Boom time in a small town.'

For this fuck, every day happened to be *boom time*. For the rest of us, however, a working day never made it past the status of being business as usual.

'You don't say.'

'I'm sending someone to see you, K.'

Always bugged me the way he messed with people's names, calling them initials like that. Must have thought of this as really quite an original and revolutionary thing to do, this new system of address. Kilo became K, Fred translated to F, Ned N and Zed... Well, Zed remained Z. No system's perfect.

'Yeah?'

'Yeah. People wanting.'

He'd given me, and others, runarounds plenty of times before. Promised punters but they'd never quite managed to materialise. Either got themselves held up or ran into some other last second hitch. Clearly, Tony had problems of the attention seeking kind. The kind of guy who never got to suck on his mother's tits as a nipper.

'They're coming over to see you now,' he said.

Alarm bells started ringing about then. He dealt drugs and yet, big money punters he wanted to send my way? Did that sound a little odd or was it just me, jumping to conclusions?

'How come?'

Tony paused, probably thinking I was too busy salivating to stop and actually analyse this.

'My shelves are a little empty, K,' he told me after a second too many.

Tony's shelves were rarely empty. Selling drugs is not hard but this guy, he had it down to a tee, an exact science. People who approached him with the intention of buying an eighth of sensi would walk away with that and a free half gramme of coke. You can lead a horse to water but you can't make it drink...but there's nothing to stop you from sprinkling plenty of salt in its oats. And that's just what Tony did. He made people thirsty for his product and all the while, they thought he was doing them a favour.

The man knew how to move shit and he also had his stock priorities nailed down to near perfection. Held aloft the first rule of dealing like an Olympic torch. Even thoughts of using made the guy feel ill. Having said all that, even the best of us are bound to run out sooner or later. Still, that didn't mean these people of Tony's would actually show up. Tony's people never showed up.

'Right,' I said. 'Well, you know where I am.'

Tony, sensing that I really didn't give a shit, pushed the point home.

'They want serious weight off you, though.'

'Right,' I said. 'That's good.'

Something else, something rotten, about this. What was stopping Tony from seeing our mutual supplier, King, for a top up? Then I remembered. King and Tony weren't seeing eye to eye. King reckoned Tony, one of the best street guys around, lusted after his spot and Tony reckoned King lusted after his business. Myself, I reckoned there might have been something to both sides but even so, I really didn't give a shit. Pair of them could go fuck themselves, or each other, for all I cared.

'You still not on terms with King?'

'Not really,' Tony said quietly. 'You know what he's like. Can't talk sense with the man no more. Always juiced up, always itching for a beef.'

'He can be a bit out of it,' I agreed.

'Fuck him, anyway,' said Tony. 'But I'm not kidding about this deal, K-man. You are fixed, right?'

'Don't worry about that,' I whispered back. 'I'm fluid enough.'

'It's just that they've got some serious dunzai on them.'

'This isn't some I O U deal or nothing, right?'

'It's real money. I'll send them down with Rose.'

Rose. Tony's piece. Nice looking. Classy. Not the usual crack slapper who'd suck your dick in the hope of getting a second hand hit. Relatively new to the scene but she seemed clean veined and clear headed. I wondered what made her hang around with a guy like Tony because, well…I could see more reasons not to hang around with such an ugly, boring and chickenshit tit. He did have dope, however. Enough of the old white stuff to keep a soap opera cast happy for a month.

'Okay. I can handle it,' I said. 'Don't sweat a thing. You know me.'

'Cool,' Tony said, sounding relieved. 'Black Lexus. With you in five, ten at the most.'

'Right,' I said, checking my watch.

'Check you laters, K.'

So I waited and I waited. Half an hour after Tony had started this shit, I thought about calling it a night. Gone eight and I had thirty-five quid for my day's endeavours. You got those days sometimes, though. It's the nature of the retail business. My old man used to tell me how there's two things in the world that you can never be sure about: death and customers. They both come eventually but when is anyone's guess.

Finally, and to my surprise, I saw a Lexus pull up behind me. Black. Any other colour just wouldn't cut it. For me a Lexus is not the same thing it is for millions of low to middle rank corporate execs. To them, a Lexus is an aspiration that means prestige, security, safety, build quality and other such nonsense those *Top Gear* wankers habitually rave about. For the gangstas of the world, a Lexus motor vehicle can hold a different kind of potential. Sure, still a symbol of class, style and ex-fucking-cess but there's a big difference between an ordinary factory vehicle and a car that falls into the hands of a gangsta. In most cases, a gangsta, even a wannabe, will modify his vehicle according to the guidelines set out in a little known publication called: *How to Gangstarise a Motor Car The Easy Way*. Easy? Sure. Expensive? Definitely. That's the whole kick. The more you get done, the more it costs and the more it costs, the more it shows and the more *it* shows, the more *you* (the gangsta) shows. So much you could do… where to begin? Drop the suspension, glue slim rubber onto the fattest and most polished metal going, dress the body in absurdly wide skirts, clamp a whale tail spoiler on the boot, tint the screens as black as night, coat on enough paint to double the whole thing up as a huge, car shaped mirror. And that's without taking security, entertainment and personal number plates into consideration. Do even half of that shit with a Lexus and you end up with something that's sexier than a supermodel and a hundred times more intelligent.

I looked into my rear view mirror, still half dreaming of owning my very own Lexus within a year, two at the most and saw a couple of white boys get out. Nodding to each other and cocking their heads like a pair of pigeons, taking measure of the environment, it seemed these boys had been around a bit. One of them opened the back door for Rose but they were no gents. Dangerous and a little too sure of themselves, in these alien surroundings, to be gentleman addicts or even users.

Rose stepped out and looked herself up and down, sort of checking her skirt for creases and what not. She looked okay, I guess. Cool, casual but hip with it. She moved towards my car and like a couple of dogs on patrol, the two pigeon necked punters followed.

The taller one opened the passenger door and popped the seat down. I knocked the volume off the stereo so it became little more than light, background music. The men jumped in the back leaving Rose to take the passenger seat, next to me. One by one, I nodded at them all.

'How you people doing?'

'Fine,' said Rose, staring straight ahead, not even looking at me.

But I found myself looking at her. Brown eyes, not glazed but bright, alive and intelligent. Not a user, not this one, no doubt about it. A full, round kind of face but not chubby. No scabs, no patches of dry, uncared for skin. Tall and strong postured. Full lips, perfect teeth and a button nose. She seemed out of place, running around with pushers and their punters. Still, I figured her to be mature enough to look after herself.

'And you? You're busy?' she asked.

'I'm doing okay,' I told her.

I glanced in the back and gave the two guys a little nod.

'This is Kilo,' Rose said to them, still looking through the windscreen. 'An associate of Tony's.'

'That's me,' I agreed, as if admitting to something bad.

'Tony says you're okay,' said one of the voices from the back.

I turned and looked at them properly. The one on the right, dead ringer for Dustin Hoffman with his nose all big and generally fucked up. The other guy, however, he had one of those pixie little noses which girls with big noses would kill their own mothers for. He reminded me of that weird and violent little singer with the funny name and the squeaky voice from some place cold, except the bloke in the back of the car happened to be male and that singer woman, well, she was a woman.

I looked at my wristwatch, the way people do when trying to ascertain time elapsed, as opposed to hour of day.

'You're late,' I stated.

I had all I needed to know about the two punters. On the left, a tick over six foot and weighing in at maybe fifteen stone, sat Bjork. The scars on his knuckles could only belong to a fighter. His face, more or less untouched, indicated a contender. To his right, perhaps the same height but much lighter, sat Dustin. Unlike Bjork, Dustin dressed better and had a much cleaner image. Soft, clean and unmarked hands which suggested a peace lover. His nose said otherwise. Bent, probably broken which implied he'd been used as a punch bag, maybe more than once. He should really have got that thing seen to.

'What can I do for you fellers, anyway?'

'Gear,' Dustin said, like I didn't need to know anything else.

'Any particular kind?' I asked, like we were discussing potato crisps.

'Charlie,' said Bjork.

'Charlie,' I mused. 'How much?'

'How much you got?'

Suddenly Bjork lost what little credibility I'd given him. Why people insist on asking the most ridiculous questions when trying to score I'll never know. Enquiries about price, quality and even discount I can understand but what am I supposed to say when some bozo asks me *how much I got*? What *I got* and what *they want* are two different, unrelated things. Why can't people keep things simple and tell me how much they want instead of all that *how much action you got* bullshit?

'Why don't we start again?'

Through the rear-view mirror I saw Dustin smile. I looked to Rose who was now staring back but with nothing to say.

'How much do you people want?'

Bjork pulled out a wad.

'I got a grand on me.'

I frowned. What a wanker.

'Looks like you have.'

Heavy duty notage made me uncomfortable. Too heavy to start flashing around all over the place. Not unless you were looking for trouble.

'I can't handle that kind of business,' I said.

'Fuckinell, man,' Bjork scoffed. 'Tony said you could.'

'Yeah? And how would he know?'

Bjork grumbled something to himself.

'Anyway, how come he's not dealing you himself? Not like him, turning good money away.'

'He said he was out,' Bjork replied, confidently enough. 'Had a run earlier on or summat.'

'Tony? Out of stock? Never thought I'd hear that one.'

'Tony's been having a few problems with his line of supply,' said Rose.

I nodded, not wanting to bring King into the conversation. On top of everything else, King had some pretty sizeable debt problems of his own, and they weren't the kind that came with the banks.

'Okay. Seeing as we're here…'

Before Bjork could finish, Dustin butted in with his big fat nose:

'How much *can* you handle, then?'

'Maybe six,' I said. 'At a stretch I suppose I could go to seven hundred. Twelve, fourteen, maybe even fifteen grammes.'

Bjork made *a what do you think?* face for Dustin who responded with a *what difference does it make?* shrug.

'Okay,' sighed Bjork. 'I suppose that'll have to do us for now.'

'Yeah,' Dustin chimed in, grinning. 'Enough to keep us going for a while.'

Bjork licked his fingertips and started counting out the notes. Amateurs.

'Hold on a second.'

He stopped counting immediately, lifting his head to face me as if he'd just been caught playing with himself.

'What's up?'

'I've got to get a hold of it before we can walk away from each other.'

Bjork, miserable bitch, sighed again. Dustin muttered something under his breath.

'If you don't like it, you can always go somewhere else.'

'It's not that,' Bjork said, raising his hands and shaking his head. 'We've not got a lot of time, that's all.'

'Well, things like this take time.'

Dustin tried sucking his teeth, black man style, but instead, pushed a line of spit onto his chin.

'I suppose we can wait,' Bjork shrugged.

It took us, just Rose and me, ten minutes getting over to King's place. On the tape, a song about roller skates played. Rose didn't seem to like the song much.

As we pulled up outside King's gaff, I noticed King's bedroom window wide open. King might have been mostly wrecked but as usual, the energy and sense to trade stayed with him. In his kitchen, wearing nothing but a pair of shorts, my supplier stooped over his production table, coughing his guts out, a cigarette dangling between his lips, busying away with the packaging end of the business. In front of him, the tools of the trade: a set of small electronic scales, some tiny plastic self seal bags, a spoon for weighing out cocaine which had no doubt been cut with a big fat volume of odourless talc.

'I'm in a rush.'

He stopped coughing, grunted and then resumed his work. The loaded Golf, the Versace suits, the rich Aramis after shave and the swanky pad, long gone, just memories now. If ever the drugs business needed a deterrent, then it would find it in the shape of this guy, King.

'Everyone's in a fucking rush,' he bitched. 'You're in a rush, and guess what? I'm in a rush too. I should open a club for cunts who are in a rush.'

His latest shag thing, a young, and barely legal, scrubber called Stella came into the kitchen in her undies and gave me a smile. I thought about them, King and her. Old enough to be her father but age differences are a thing of the past, I guess. As for Stella, I'd seen her around, here and there. Pretty young thing, but cheap. Young, very young, but already travelled around the block a couple of times.

'Where the fuck's that coffee?' King growled at her.

She made a face at him but only because he had his back to her.

'In the coffee maker,' she said, scratching a dry, begging to be itched, forearm.

Only a kid but she had her ways set, ready to screw the fullest life she could. Couldn't blame her. Like a lot of hangers on, she had this habit of sponging off everyone she met, and right then, King still managed to pass as a meal ticket. I didn't really give a shit. King had it coming to him with the way he'd been letting himself go.

'Bitch,' King said.

'I come at a bad time?' I asked Stella.

King stopped with the bags and looked up at me and then Rose.

'I know you,' he said to her.

Rose shrugged.

'You're,' he began, his eyes narrowed, his spoon doing the pointing. 'You're Tony's piece, right?'

Rose looked at him, appearing disgusted by what she saw.

'I'm no one's anything,' she said. 'I'm my own person.'

King smiled.

'I used to think the same thing about me but it's not true. Just a matter of time before you realise it, but we're all owned by some fucker or other.'

'Well,' she said. 'Speak for yourself. I'll make my own mind up about me.'

'You do that,' said King, nodding to himself surely. 'It's good that you think that.'

Rose turned to me.

'Can we speed things up? I've got other things to do.'

I nodded and then addressed King:

'I got to get going, man. We can do the philosophy bollocks another time.'

'You blind?' said King. 'I got things to do myself...but seeing it's you...'

King held his hand out. I passed him three hundred notes which he counted out. Twice.

'This a one hit deal you got?' King asked.

'Yeah,' I said. 'Seems some guys wanna get happy.'

Stella went into the bathroom, pulled a bag of good shit out from the cistern and then came back into the kitchen, dumping it on the table, right in front of King. He weighed me two bags: one containing reasonably shit quality cocaine, the other something a lot less illegal.

On the way back, Rose asked me about the other bag. No big deal, I told her, a precaution I took with people I didn't know. She shook her head.

'You're taking the piss.'

'Deadly serious, this. A potential life saver, this bag.'

I stopped off at a paper shop and bought a packet of chewing gum. I left one of the bags with the owner and told him I'd be back within one hour but he knew that it could stretch to twenty-four if things went wrong. I had a few places like that in different parts of town: my own little stash holes, just in case.

Still there, the black Lexus patiently waiting for us when we got back. The longer I thought about it, the more out of place it seemed. Something about those two guys and something about the car I didn't like, but for the life of me, something I couldn't put my finger on.

'You know these guys, then?'

She shook her head.

'Not really.'

'Not really?'

'Tony says they're okay.'

'Something about them,' I mused.

They got out of their car and joined us.

'Fellers.'

'You get the gear?' Bjork asked immediately.

'Course I got it. Where do you think we've been?'

He pulled out his wad and began counting.

'There you go,' he said. 'Bang on seven.'

I took his money and gave it a quick count myself, just like my dad would when doing the daily takings. In the drugs game, every penny needs counting just like every eighth of an ounce needs weighing. If some sensitive prick feels all insulted just because someone questions his integrity, then tough shit. Business, any business in the world, centres around money, not feelings.

'All here,' I said, trying not to sound too surprised.

'What did you think we were going to do?' Dustin piped up. 'Short change you or something?'

I opened the glove box and took out the bag.

'Now it's your turn.'

Bjork grabbed a hold of the bag and felt its weight in his palm, as if estimating the weight of a stone before flinging it at someone. With a small pen-knife hanging from his key ring, and without saying a word, he made a slit in the bag. Carefully, he dabbed his pointing finger-tip in the powder…

It all seemed so convoluted, like a film and I could have easily cracked up laughing. Who were these guys and just who did they think they were kidding? And when he licked his finger, then rubbed his gums, I half expected some cheap 1980s movie maker to yell 'Cut!' First time I ever saw a guy do that dabbing fingers thing in real life. Every other time I sold, coke just got lined up and swiftly snorted to the back of the head. The rubbing the gums thing, pure Hollywood B Movie stuff. This shit, the gums, the spiel, strictly for the birds. I was ready for them from that moment onwards.

'Done deal,' he mumbled.

A scam, a set up, then. So be it but I had myself protected. Nothing to worry about in the least.

'We should do this again sometime,' I smiled.

Which is when something solid touched the back of my head. I turned to look at Rose but the barrel got pushed harder still, forcing me to keep looking ahead.

'I don't think so,' Dustin said. 'Don't move.'

Bjork leant forwards, shoving his warrant card in front of my face then hers.

'I'm arresting you…'

I glanced at Rose.

'You bastards,' she said. 'You bastards!'

'Shut the fuck up you stupid bitch!' spat Dustin.

'Hook, line and sinker,' said Bjork, before asking. 'Where was I, again?'

'You guys,' I said. 'You're making a mistake.'

'A mistake?' said Rose, almost accusing me. 'A mistake? Is that all you can say?'

'Hey,' I said. 'Take a chill pill, love.'

'Love? Who you calling *love* you stupid wanker?'

'Shut the fuck up, pair of you. Or else.'

'Or else? Or else what?' said Rose. 'Or else you'll nick us twice?'

I smiled. A good one, that.

'Funny bitch,' complained Bjork.

'Guess what?' asked Dustin. 'You're under arrest.'

'So you've said.'

Dustin cleared his throat.

'I'm arresting you…'

'Spare me,' I said. 'I know how the rest of that shit goes.'

let the music play

There's a first time for everything. For most people, getting nicked must be a serious sort of business. But if you got yourself an escape route lined up, then it's almost fun.

I lay there, on a cold, uncomfortable wooden bunk, thinking: cool, I can handle this shit for as long as it takes. Completely unconcerned about the future. They had nothing but they didn't know. That's why it was funny. I couldn't wait for some smarty pants copper to come in and give me his best shot.

I wondered about Rose, about the shit they were putting her through. Didn't worry too much about her because she seemed sensible enough, although a little cold. She must have realised why the both of us were there, celled up, waiting for plod to give us the whole nine yards about drugs, dealing and the threat of fuck knows how many years inside. Tony. Stood to reason. Could be no one else.

Still. Getting nicked is not something to be proud of. My dad must have been spinning in his grave. If my mum found out, she'd probably keel over. But she would never know about this little episode. I saw no need to tell her. Being nicked might be a laugh if you've got your back covered, but it's not something you boast about to those who love you.

Someone unlocked the door about an hour into my detention. In he walked, his shoes hitting and scratching against the cold, hard surface of the floor. At first glance, he seemed too old to be a copper but I could have been wrong. I'd seen most of the drugs squad faces driving around town. Young, well built and they would have been hip looking blokes had it been ten years ago. Streetwise, so they thought.

'Khalil Khan,' he said, with a slowly spreading smile, as if we were a couple of old friends, meeting after years and years.

My solicitor, I figured. As someone who made big money for drawing up a few contracts, writing a few wills and, every now and then, being arsed enough to make a few courtroom appearances, he didn't look like much. The man had no taste in clothes for one thing, I mean stuff from BHS and Marks and Spencers, even. He did have a decent, not to mention spotless, pair of shoes, though. Black, polished but not new, just really well cared for.

'Quality never goes out of style,' he said to me, winking.

I looked at him and sniggered.

'Sure,' I said.

'I've noticed you've been admiring my attire. Clothes maketh the man, they say, but I'm not convinced, myself.'

'What?'

'It's what's inside us that makes us what we are. Don't you think, Khalil?'

I shrugged and then told him that I:

'Never really thought about it much.'

'Perhaps you should,' he said and then, with the friendliest smile he could muster, pulled out a warrant card. 'Drugs Squad.'

A copper? Well there was a thing.

'Drugs dealer,' I told him and then laughed. 'But sorry, I'm out of business cards.'

He gave a little laugh before proceeding.

'My name's Price. Detective Inspector Price.'

Price. Now that I had a name, the face suddenly rang a bell. Price. Where had I heard that before?

'Have we met before?'

He smiled.

'Yes, we've met before, Khalil.'

Can't say I liked that, the way he called me Khalil as if he knew me.

'And where was that, then?'

'Some years ago now, I believe it was,' he began. 'In the hospital. Your father, I recall. He'd been attacked.'

He hadn't aged too well but as I looked closer, I realised it was him alright. How long had it been? Must have been years since I met this Price bloke last. He seemed to be the wrong kind of material for a copper then and he seemed just as unsuited to that work now. Coppers, as a rule of thumb, need to be a strange brew. Thick as shit, as sensitive as John Wayne and ten times as arrogant. Could have been wrong, but this man seemed to be the opposite.

'So you're working drugs, now?'

'I move around from department to department. Keeps me from seizing up,' he said, tapping his temple with his finger.

'I see,' I nodded.

Any other copper would have been jumping up and down on my chest by now, giving me some tough-cop-on-the-edge routine. This one, making polite conversation, continued to throw the hell out of me. He really did seem too nice a copper to be real. Not hardened to the ways of society, numbed through decades of witnessing all manner of human misery, pain and grief. For what it's worth, I can understand coppers being a right bunch of miserable bastards with all the crap they see, hear and experience. Must drive some to despair while others cope by becoming insensitive, arrogant, unhinged…by becoming normal coppers. Whatever the reality, Price had me nervous.

'So, Khalil,' he smiled.

'People call me Kilo. I prefer Kilo.'

'Hmm, Kilo,' Price muttered. 'Kilo.'

He looked up, at the ceiling.

'Don't wear it out,' I said, smiling.

'Kilo,' he said, facing me now. 'Is that a corruption of Khalil or does it have something to do with your line of work?'

I couldn't help but to look into his eyes. Warm, understanding and above all, kind. Couldn't have been the case. Coppers don't do kind.

'A bit of both,' I said, and forced myself to look away from him.

'Which bit goes where?'

'Don't you worry about that. I know where I'm at. That's all that matters.'

He seemed impressed about something. Damned if I could make the same connection. He licked his lips, nodding to himself, smiling, wise about something.

'Who we're *supposed* to be and who we *are* aren't always the same things, are they, Khalil?'

'If you say so.'

'I do say so. Within you – within us all – there's a greater and more real entity.'

'Come again?'

'The soul,' Price said, 'I'm talking about a man's soul. Do you believe in souls, Khalil?'

I scratched my head, wondering about this line of questioning. Who was he? Copper and preacher rolled into one? People like me, we weren't suitable nor had we earned the right to be asked about the soul. I heard this kind of spiel in the middle of town, when the loony religion freaks did their thing with innocent and not so innocent shoppers. Sometimes, however, I did wander down similar paths of inquiry but only in my head. In my head things worked out fine. In my head, no one else but me could hear.

'Well?' Price asked, jerking me out of my thought.

'What?'

'The soul, remember?'

'Do I believe in it? I suppose I do, yeah.'

Price nodded to himself.

'That's interesting.'

He sat down on the bunk, right next to me, not minding me.

'I suppose,' he sighed. 'I suppose you think you're pretty smart, Khalil.'

'Depends how you look at it,' I said. 'Your guys are a bit thicker than me, that's all. It's all relative.'

'Not the brightest duo in the world, are they?' he admitted with a smile.

'Hey,' I shrugged. 'You pay peanuts and you get monkeys.'

'Your accomplice…'

'My what?'

'The girl.'

'You mean Rose. She's got nothing to do with anything. I was just giving her a lift, that's all.'

'Funny,' he chuckled, smile spreading. 'That's just what she said.'

'You know you're gonna have to let us go. You know you've got nothing.'

His expression seemed to agree.

'She's been released already.'

He dipped into his pocket and pulled out a packet of cigarettes, offering me one.

'Don't smoke.'

'Very wise,' he said, as he lit up. 'These things are killers.'

He took a deep pull. As he exhaled, the room slowly tinted blue.

'So?' he asked. 'How exactly did you know they were working under-cover?'

'Is *that* what they were doing?'

Price tossed his head back and laughed.

'You should have been a comedian,' he said. 'But seriously…how?'

'I dunno, just had a feeling.'

That bag of talc never worked for me before, but then, I'd never been set up before. An easy enough procedure, but sadly, it only worked well with cocaine because of the physical match. When it came to heroin and especially crack, it could be done but you had to mess around for ages getting the substitutes to appear authentic. This is how it worked: if you were dealing with a genuine punter, then he'd spot the difference but no big deal as you'd give him the real shit, maybe something on top as an apology after you sussed him out. But if your dodgy punter happened to be a copper, then so what? What would he charge you with? Possession with intent to supply skin care products? You couldn't lose.

'You must feel good about yourself, getting away with money and the drugs.'

'I don't know what you're talking about. What money? What drugs?'

'There's no need for that. We're talking…we're talking as friends, not enemies, Khalil.'

This had me stumped. Friends? He should have been threatening me with everything under the sun, not telling me he and I were mates. He copper, me pusher. Where and how did the word *friend* enter into it?

'So,' I said. 'You letting me go or what?'

'You're free to go but I thought it might be nice if we had a little chat. Got to know each other.'

Price pulled on his cigarette, long and hard. Savouring every particle of smoke as it passed over this tongue.

'You're in a complicated situation,' Price said, as if he'd pondered over this moment countless times.

'I am?'

'I think so,' he said. 'Complicated is about the right word.'

'Listen, I really don't have time for this. I got things to do.'

'I understand you're a busy man but I do insist you hear me out.'

'Okay, but can you make it snappy?'

'What you're doing,' he said. 'It's wrong, Khalil. All wrong.'

I sighed. Should have seen that old chestnut coming. I suddenly had the sucker read. He kept me there so he could try guilt tripping a confession out of me. Sooner or later he'd start harping on about drugs being bad and dealers being the spawn of the devil. Some shit like that at any rate.

'I had a daughter once,' he said.

I could have laughed. To me, it sounded like the blues already: *my woman done gone left me* and all that shit ready to roll in the next verse.

'She's dead, Khalil.'

'And?'

'I think you know what killed her.'

Drugs killed her. Drugs were evil. She could have been clean and got hit by a bus. Would that have made buses evil? All buses or just the one that killed her? It's at the point of human involvement where the errors come along, not before. People who kill themselves with drugs only have themselves to blame.

'She was called Christine.'

Playing me. A good move, coming out with a name. A name made her seem real, a person, someone I should give a shit about and someone I could, perhaps, start to visualise. Probably had blonde, curly hair and blue eyes. An innocent kind of girl, Christine Price.

'And like your father, she was a victim of drugs.'

'No,' I said, a reflex action. 'You're wrong. My dad, he died in hospital. A nurse fucked his treatment up, human error.'

'You don't believe that, Khalil. His death was because of drugs and you know it.'

'Fuck you, man. You didn't know him. You don't know what you're talking about.'

'I apologise. Rude, insensitive of me to talk about someone close to you.'

I got off the bunk and looked at him, trying to grasp his angle but there didn't seem to be one. Price, he spoke the truth and although it should have been a good thing, it made me feel even more uncomfortable than I had been throughout this interrogation. I realised that it said a lot about me, feeling out of place with a man who sounded as if he cared. Conversely, when amongst liars, thieves and cheats, I felt comfortable and at home.

'Where was I?' he asked himself and then seemed to find the thread again. 'Ah yes. When Christine was still young, sixteen – a funny age by all accounts – she started to, well…I suppose rebel might be the word.'

I heard that. Been there myself.

'Don't misunderstand me,' Price continued. 'In my own youth, I was a little wayward as well. We all have our moments, don't we, Khalil?'

'Suppose so.'

'Adolescents,' Price said, staring me out. 'Adolescents have ways of tricking their parents. Biting the hand that feeds them, you might say.'

I sometimes wonder how my own kids will turn out, if I ever have any. Will they be how I used to be or how I am now? Will they hate me, love me or will they perhaps feel nothing? Trouble is, I don't know what I'll want from them and what they'll want from me. I suppose I'll end up like my dad who simply desired offspring he could be proud of. Can't see it happening, though…we sow what we reap. My kids, when and if I have any, will take me for everything I have and they won't feel an ounce of guilt. And the funny thing is, I'll be expecting it all along.

'Just before her nineteenth birthday, Christine died.'

I knew she'd died. Pointless telling me a tale with a happy ending, given the circumstances.

'The coroner said she'd been using heroin, injecting it, for two years at the very least.'

'That's rough.'

I wondered how come he didn't notice her. I mean him, a trained copper and all, Drugs Squad guy no less, missing a junky in his midst? Maybe she hid it well, but still the jury would remain out on that one for a while.

'But it wasn't your fault,' Price said, as if blame rested entirely on my shoulders.

'I know,' I said. 'Nothing to do with me.'

Price looked at me, smiling, but pitying me, not agreeing.

'It's the greatest of burdens to live on after your only child has died.'

Big deal. If his daughter couldn't work out how much became too much, then tough. What did she want? Drugs are all or nothing. No proficiency tests and no second chances for messing up the first time. There's experience and there's common sense. Those who sniff, jack and inhale do so at their own peril and that means knowing the difference between enough and too much. A grain over the limit is as good as suicide in some cases. Even if a user gets lucky with six numbers during rollover week, the limit remains the same. Weight, dosage and consumption are figures that simply cannot be messed with.

'It seems unnatural, somehow,' he added.

'I'm sorry about your daughter,' I said.

'Are you?' he asked. 'Are you really sorry, Khalil?'

'I'm sorry for your loss,' I shrugged. 'What else can I say?'

Not unheard of, the odd user getting dead. And there were plenty of idiots who didn't know when to pack up but hell, these people were adults and they could make their own minds up about how they wanted to kill themselves. Myself, once I'd grudated from the early kid-stuff to become a full-time dealer, I never sold a single thing to an amateur, not even a headache pill, never even gave away a pack of fucking Rizlas. Even back then it was only some second rate weed. None of my shit ever killed anyone and knowing that much alone helped me sleep at night. What kind of businessman would I have been if I made one-shot deals which ended up offing all my customers? That kind of thing defeated the whole idea.

'Do you know how many people die each year thanks to drugs?'

'I don't know and I don't care, either.'

Price raised his eyebrows. He wanted an answer, even a half-hearted guess would do him.

'Have a stab.'

'I dunno…a dozen, maybe?'

Price nodded a couple of times.

'Officially,' said Price, forefinger tugging his lower lip. 'There were nineteen.'

So what? Twelve didn't sound so far away from nineteen. And anyway, what real difference did the number make? Two, twelve or twenty, nothing compared to all those who died from drinking and inhaling every kind of pollution into their bodies.

'Unofficially, however,' Price continued. 'There were one hundred and fifty-four.'

A big number. An epidemic, no less. But how come the press and everyone else never made a fuss? Price talked bollocks, that's how come.

'You know what the best bit is? The reason why no one knows?'

I shook my head. He had me hooked which left him with the easy task of reeling me in to complete the task.

'Only thirteen out of a hundred and fifty-four victims were white people, Khalil. Most were black, Asian or belonged to some other ethnic minority.'

'I never heard about that.'

'You're not meant to. This is not the kind of news that's supposed to make the news.'

Could have been bullshit but it didn't seem like it. He had every reason to lie but no, this seemed like the truth.

'I don't get it. Why? Why not tell the truth?'

'There are reasons why we, the police, decide not to make public these kinds of statistics.'

'Reasons. For example?'

Price sighed.

'Do I have to spell it out?'

I nodded. Price sighed again, shaking his head, disappointed in me for missing what he figured to be the obvious.

'It doesn't matter if your people die. Do you think we, people like me, actually care when you and your kind kill themselves? They use drugs which makes them scum. And nobody cares about scum, no matter what colour it is.'

I didn't answer. No need.

'As long as it's not people like us, then we'll just leave you people to get on with it.'

'That's not right. People can't do that.'

Price cracked up laughing then, the kind of laughter that made me feel like a tit, not being in on the joke.

'What's so funny?'

'What's so *funny*? Don't you see the irony? You're a party to all of this and you're talking as if it's got nothing to do with you. You're the one who's killing your own people. You're far from innocent, here. You do realise that.'

Me killing people? My people? Who the fuck was I all of a sudden? Had someone just made me non-elected leader of Asian and black people without having the decency to have asked first? I had no *people*. I didn't claim to be a politician, nor did I push myself as one of those selfish bastards who claimed to lead the community. I was a drug dealer, and, for all the difference it made, I was happy with it.

'So now it's a race thing?' I said, a wry smile quickly spreading across my face.

'Not necessarily,' Price admitted. 'But such actions do affect certain people more than others.'

'Listen, I'm not the only one who sells,' I said, deciding to at last counter the crazy old goat, deciding to show a little spirit. 'There's hundreds of others out there. Not just me.'

'But you sell all the same, Khalil. How can you live with yourself knowing what you're doing to innocent children?'

Wait a minute, now. This was simply getting out of hand.

'Children? What children? Nobody sells to kids. What do you think we are?'

Price's expression grew stern. He seemed to tense up, losing his cool and ultra friendly demeanour. I'd hit a sore nerve but I spoke the truth. No dealer worth his salt sells to a child. Only those with a death wish go for that.

'Have you ever seen the new born baby of an addict?'

I got it. So now he tried the guilt by association trick. So much easier to blame dealers, rather than all those thick junky slappers getting pregnant and dropping kids.

'Have you seen how an addicted baby breathes, how it cries? Have you?'

'Can't say I have.'

'Well,' smiled Price. 'Permit me to enlighten you.'

The Right Reverend Doctor Price spun his yarn, an education he felt I needed. Most babies are born with only three fundamental needs: to breathe, to be nourished and rest. Simple. Breathe, eat and sleep.

'An addict's baby, however, is different because it has one more need which is just as real as the needs everyone else is born with.'

I didn't need three guesses on that one.

'While a baby is being formed, it takes on everything its mother takes on. All those loves and hates, likes and dislikes are passed on with all the strength of a contagious disease.'

'Yeah I get the picture. I might be a drug dealer, but I'm not stupid.'

'Unlike normal new borns, it's not a blank canvas with its own picture to paint. Already, it's been unfairly sketched upon, chemically conditioned into being what it is.'

'And what is it?'

'Addicted, of course.'

If I could do something for all those nippers who are born hooked, then I swear I would. If I had a magic wand, I'd be waving it all day and all night for as long as it took, but it doesn't work like that. One person on a mission won't make the slightest difference.

'It really is quite distressing,' said Price.

'And how would you know? You're a copper, not a social worker.'

Price didn't take a blind bit of notice. Like a juggernaut, he just motored through any obstacle I put in his way.

'It cries for longer bursts, it hardly sleeps and as well as that, its growth and development is stunted.'

'You're speaking to the wrong person.'

Price smiled at me, like he could spot the lie on its way out.

'Look, what am I supposed to be all of a sudden? Pablo Escobar? I'm not one of those fuck-ups.'

Price nodded, put his forefinger to his lips and then told me that:

'You could say…well, in a way, you could say it's deformed.'

'Come on. Why *is* this bullshit being shovelled my way? Does it have anything to do with me? I don't think so.'

Price raised his eyebrows.

'What are you saying? That new born junkies are down to me?'

I walked up to him and told him, face to face, how things stood.

'I sell my shit to people who are old enough to fuck other people, drink liver rotting liquids, get duped into extortionate HP deals, marry people they don't love, do time for the crimes they're thick enough to commit in the first place and vote for people they know nothing about.'

'Really?'

'Yes fucking *really*. I deal with adults, not kids, and if all those adults are irresponsible about it, then so what? It's got fuckall to do with me. I'm just a channel – a conduit – but I'm not the cause.'

'Deformed, Khalil,' Price insisted. 'Those babies are born deformed.'

I could try denying it but I knew what I'd done in life. The shit he came out with kept me awake at night. Telling myself lies about what I did only worked for so long. I might have convinced myself that only the money mattered, but when it came right down to it, when I mustered the courage to be honest with myself, everything Price implied rang true. It began and ended with me helping to fuck people up.

'It's thinner and it's weaker, compared to normal babies,' he continued as I backed off. 'Of course, treatment helps but only so much. Within the first six months, it's weaned off but by then, it makes little difference. The damage has already been done, Khalil. It will grow and mature differently to normal children, at a slower rate. It won't be as mentally quick, as strong or as skilful as other children. Every single ability it was fortunate enough to have been born with will be lacking. What kind of chance do children like that have in a world as cruel as this, Khalil?'

I turned away from him and sat back down.

'Fine fucking speech. You want a standing ovation?'

He didn't reply.

'Your preaching's all well and good but you don't even know me. You've not seen the shit I've seen, done what I've had to do, just to get here, to where I am now. Fuck you, Price. You're like everyone else making out that you really give a shit. No one really cares about junky babies.'

'And your point?'

'Look, it's the way things are. Supply and demand, and if it means junky babies, then so be it. They're a by-product, maybe even punters for the fucking future.'

'Start them young, eh?' said Price, smiling way too deviously for my liking.

'You got it. I mean look around. There's parents out there who buy their one year old kids Nike fucking trainers when there's millions of starving kids still in the world. All kids are junkies like that, man. They're all hooked on wanting for the sake of wanting.'

'I see, so that makes everything alright, does it?'

'Since when has *anything* been alright, man? I'm not saying it *is* alright. It's just the way it is and that's why it's not my problem. Way of the world so fuck you very much and now, please, just leave me the fuck alone.'

'Tell me something and try to be honest about it, Khalil,' he said, licking his lips. 'Do you sleep well at night?'

How did he know which buttons to press? That's what I wanted to know. Of course I didn't sleep well. I dealt drugs and sleeping well didn't come into it. I hadn't slept properly since the whole thing started. I thought, for the longest time, that restless, nightmare-filled nights went with the job.

'Look,' I said, maybe clutching at straws. 'People use drugs because they want to.'

'People use drugs because people like you sell drugs. Don't tell me you actually think you're a symptom, Khalil, when you know full well that you and all the others like you are the cause.'

'I don't know about that.'

'Well I do. If no one had been around to supply my daughter, my Christine, then she would not have overdosed.'

He turned away and cleared his throat, getting all choked up by the thought of her.

'She'd be alive and well today if it wasn't for the likes of you. If it wasn't…if it wasn't for someone like *you*, Khalil, my daughter would have given birth to a normal, healthy child.'

I stared at him, trying to work it all out. The junky mothers, the junky babies…

'Shit happens,' I shrugged.

Price laid the whole thing out about his daughter. I mean from A to Z. I wished he hadn't because it sounded so terrible, the way he told it. Not a horror story, however. More like a tragedy.

In order to continue getting loaded, his daughter got talked into selling her body for money. In order to stay in that business, she got pimped. In order to stay pimped, her pimp fucked her, got her pregnant but because pregnant chicks are something of a niche market, that son of a bitch he made her work all the while. To cut a long story short, Price's daughter died only minutes after giving birth to an addicted bastard child. That's how Price knew all about babies being born addicted and how bad they got it. Poor bastard. But still, all that shit, not my doing. Not directly, anyway.

'I don't have to listen to this,' I told him. 'I got better things to do than to sit here and listen to this.'

'I've said my piece,' said Price. 'You can make your own mind up.'

'About time too. Can't wait to get out of this shit-hole.'

'We will meet again, though,' he said.

'Can't wait.'

dead wrong

Five o'clock in the morning, driving around with the windows open, speakers kicking heavy bass lines, my head still reeling from Price's preaching. I told myself to forget about him but I couldn't. He had my attention. Had me hooked from the moment I clapped eyes on him.

Didn't fancy going back home. Needed some company, someone to talk through this thing. Only one place and one person fitted the bill. Cowboy, the only honest man I knew.

We'd been in a few scrapes together over the years, Cowboy and me. Nothing serious, but enough for me to trust the guy. A casual customer, originally. Never messed around paying and never complained, not that I gave reason for punters to bitch, but out there, in the big wide world of drugs, there's punters who moan out of habit and others who bitch due to what they perceive to be a sense of duty. Not Cowboy. Always had thought of him as more than just another customer. So after a while, I felt obliged to deal him discount. This resulted in him middle-manning to his friends, making his own habit either cheaper, free or perhaps even profitable. Later on, once we got tighter still, he started pushing weight full time. I showed him the ropes, introduced him to the right people and he did okay. Well, he never complained.

Cowboy lived in Manningham, a pretty quiet part of town, compared to how it used to be a few years before. The locals, mostly fanatical Muslims (words from the press, not me) set up little patrol squads which chased out the prostitutes and dealers back in '96. And when I say *chased*, that's just what I mean: ran them out, with bats, petrol bombs and God knows what else. Punters would come from all over the place: from all the nice little burbs where none of that crooked, seedy and, I guess, unpleasant shit goes off. Residents as well as outsiders got laid or scored drugs but not a lot else. People treated Manningham as if it had become, over the decades, the city's own drug dealing little whore. Sure, it might be all well and good having a red light district, but no one wants it in their own back yard.

His door unlocked, I let myself in. A scratched up old record played on that scratched up old hi-fi of his. A nasty little twangy number. Tammy Wynette. I recognised her voice straight away because I'd heard her wail and scream like a mad old witch plenty of times in the past. One of Cowboy's favourite artists, that old Dolly Parton wannabe. Everyone had upgraded to CD players but not Cowboy. Said he had too much invested in vinyl. Take him years to convert everything over to CD and when he did get through, some smart fucker would invent some newer format so he'd have to start all over again. He had a point.

Lying on the sofa, stripped down to his shorts and boots, he seemed as chilled as a man could get. Absorbed by that shit he loved so much, he didn't even notice me enter.

'Kilo,' he said, noticing me eventually, his hands in his shorts, giving his balls a vigorous little scratch.

'Fuck's wrong with you?'

'Man,' he said, scratching his balls some more. 'I think I got something crawling down there. Crabs or something.'

'Well,' I said. 'You do have this knack for picking classy pieces.'

'Gimme a sec. Go drown these lil bastards.'

He got up and scurried into the bathroom, coming back a few seconds later, his shorts wet, his meat and two veg all shrivelled. He looked like a tit, albeit one with a little cock.

More to Cowboy than met the eye. We called him Cowboy simply because he made fancied himself as one and that alone made him stand out a mile. How many cowboys, apart from builders, plumbers and mechanics, can you see in a place like Bradford? Obsessive about it, though. Especially movies and music. When it came to movies, he watched nothing but westerns. Listened to Tammy Wynette, Dolly Parton, Jim Reeves and a whole host of other country and western knobheads. What he did – his obsession – that wasn't even the point. The man had a goal and fucked up and impossible as it might have been, he never gave up on it.

'Can I turn this shit off?' I asked him. 'Giving me headache.'

'Now why you gotta say that?' he said, all offended. 'Don't be calling it shit like that. This…this is music…this is art.'

Not a bad bone in his body so not really cut out for this line of work. Not that you have to be evil to sell drugs. But Cowboy? Simply put, *too* nice a person. One of the most popular dealers around. Ever ready with the slate and just as generous with the weight.

'How about we compromise and listen to nothing instead?'

'This is my place. My place, my music box and my music so how's *fuck you* sound for a compromise?'

Anyone else would think of him as strange. Dressed funny. Actually, he dressed as he pleased which made a deviant by definition. That cowboy hat – a Stetson no less – hardly off his head. Wore it, so he told me, even when he performed *the buckaroo* with some *hot momma* (who probably carried everything from a common cold to the clap). Blue jeans, denim shirt, invariably fastened to the neck with a boot lace tie. In winter, heavy sheepskin jacket. Pointy, high heeled leather boots. Once or twice, I'd seen the silver spurs shining above his heels, jangling like a pair of tambourines as he walked along. His pièce-de-résistance, however, was his means of transport. Not a vehicle, but *the* ve-hi-kul, a word he pronounced like some mid-west yank sheriff would. Pretty special, that huge red Chevrolet monster. Cream coloured leather interior, soft top and masses of chrome all sitting beautifully on whitewall tyres. Myself, I thought he went a little over the top with the oversized bull horns fitted over the grill.

'So how's things?'

'Things is good. Business been kicking like a mule, man,' he said.

'Yeah?'

'Did double. Just over,' he sniffed. No big thing.

I let out a whistle.

'Glad someone got happy.'

'Happier than a hog in shit,' he laughed.

John Wayne, Clint Eastwood and Jack Palance portraits hanging everywhere. In his cellar, an automated rodeo horse slept, a beast he bought from the Exchange & Mart a few months before. Already, he'd grown bored with it. Childish, sure, but at least the man stood out. At least he did his thing and didn't run after fashion like a mindless sheep.

'You wanna coffee?' he asked, scratching his balls and then wandering into the kitchen.

'I'm alright, man,' I called.

Cowboy came back in, now wearing a denim shirt. On the floor there lay a frame, a photo of his kid, smiling at the camera, or whoever was behind it.

'Damn!' he said, bending down to pick it up. 'How'd that happen?'

'You smashed it?'

'Shit,' he said, and then turned to me, mystified. 'What?'

'The frame,' I said. 'It smashed or what?'

Cowboy didn't answer. Instead, he started picking the shards from the frame.

'Must have trod on it.'

'You been using?'

Cowboy sat down. Already somewhere else. Not with me, least not in mind, not any more.

'What?' he asked again. 'You just say something, man?'

That kid must have been something truly special for Cowboy to lose his mind every time he looked at a photograph of him. Cowboy's wife – the one he married in Morecambe (the closest thing to Vegas) – took the kid with her when she ran off with a guy who sold life insurance for Legal & General.

'Sorry,' he said. 'Just thinking.'

'I know.'

He put the frame down and lit up a smoke.

'So, what's the gig? I mean, I heard you'd done a deal with King. It turn bad?'

'It went bad. But not that bad.'

'But what happened? Gimme some details, man,' he urged.

By the time he'd stubbed out another two Marlboros, he knew the story, except for the bit about Price. For some reason, Price didn't seem relevant where Cowboy was concerned.

'Shit,' said Cowboy, looking at his kid. 'You came out good.'

I got up and walked over to him, taking the picture of the little boy out of his hands. I'd never seen him, not in real life and in all likelihood, I never would. God knows where his mother and the insurance sales-man were.

'Adam, you called him, right?'

'Yeah, Adam.'

I sat down next to him, a hand on his shoulder.

'So what's been said?'

'About you? Usual bullshit. You know, that you're going down, that you're not going down. Rumours, speculation, but…'

'But? But what?'

'Well, not many thought you'd be out, you know. Even I thought this was serious, man.'

'Take more than that to catch me out.'

'What about the chick? That Rose chick? You think she was in on it, then?'

'I don't think so.'

That got me thinking. No doubt about Tony and the two coppers acting as one. But Rose? Why her? There to reassure me or there to be given up? A sacrifice? These thoughts were all good and well, came thick and fast but one thing I never considered was *why*. Why go to such lengths to snare me? Like I told Price, I was no big player.

'You know what?' said Cowboy, staring up at the ceiling. 'One of these days, I'm gonna get out of this fucking place for good.'

'Yeah?'

'Gonna do what I've always wanted to do, man. I'm gonna get me one of those Winnebagos, you know. They're like caravans only they're made of aluminium.'

'I know what a Winnebago is. They use them in films.'

'They look great,' he continued. 'Got everything going. TV, shower, kitchen, the whole works.'

'And that's it? A Winnebago?'

'Hell no! I'm gonna get me a nice four wheel drive and then I'm gonna drive.'

'Beats walking.'

'All across America. Coast to fucking coast.'

'You got to get out of here first.'

The sun coming up outside, a bird chirping its head off; another day born.

'Tell you what, partner,' he said earnestly, close to choking up. 'You don't worry about that son of a bitch Montana.'

Already, Cowboy had thought up a response. His mind made up, he informed me to consider *it*, whatever *it* would turn out to be, a favour.

'Take care of him the old fashioned way,' he insisted.

I didn't know about the old-fashioned way, not exactly, but it probably involved a barrel, some tar and a shit load of feathers. Deciphering that cowboy-speak mode of his wasn't always straight forward.

'This is my problem, Cowboy,' I said.

'This is a problem for all of us, partner,' he insisted. 'Yesterday he gave you up, tomorrow, he could do the same to me. The way I see it, we owe you for keeping your mouth shut.'

I looked at Cowboy and gave him a smile.

'How do you know I did?' I teased.

Cowboy's expression became serious instantly.

'You didn't tell them nothing, did you?'

'Sure I did.'

Cowboy swallowed but said nothing. I could have kept him hanging there forever, had I wanted.

'Like what? What you tell them?'

'I told them they could go fuck themselves.'

The import of what I'd said began to sink in only after I left. Cowboy's willingness to exact some kind of revenge may well have sounded appealing but it could only be taken at face value. An offer, but one I could not take up. I had no doubt that he'd get a posse together and organise a lynching if I asked him, but getting Cowboy to do my dirty work didn't feel right. Tony was my business.

The early morning cold, in the process of being beaten into submission by the rise of an eager sun, matched my mood. Hungry, I pulled up at a petrol station and bought myself a sandwich. I ate as I drove, thinking about Tony and how best to deal with him.

Not even dawn when Rose called. She said she got my number from some dealer I never heard of. Still sounding as cold as last time, she said we needed to talk and I said fine. We met in a caff where we could get half decent coffee and talk with some degree of privacy.

Without asking, she explained the night from her perspective. Just as I thought, Tony had used her as a pawn to add credibility and to authenticate the scenario. She had no idea why he'd given her and me up but she could now hazard a reasonable guess:

'Tony was away last week. For three days. Said it was business.'

'So what's your point?'

'I think he got caught carrying. I think he got squeezed into giving up some names.'

I shook my head. Tony wasn't that stupid.

'Well, if that's true,' I ventured, 'then how come just you and me got done?'

'That's just it,' she enthused. 'Another six just like you were stung.'

Sounded plausible but if he'd really given up so much then he'd have to be gone. I mean out of sight for the rest of his worthless life.

'Tony. You seen him?'

'I've seen him alright,' she said. 'Last night.'

'And?'

'Denied it, of course.'

Didn't seem logical. If Tony had any sense, which I knew he did, then he should've scarpered without trace. Sticking around was stupid.

'So what now?'

'I don't know,' I mused, my mind beginning to wonder. 'Need to think about this.'

Barely in her twenties, slim, clean, pretty. A tidy bit of fanny. Only not fanny as such. She had a sound mind which is always a bonus. Not that women are predisposed to being thick or anything. Matter of fact, my old man always told me women had better minds than men, generally speaking. The trouble with minds is that not many of them, neither male nor female, are particularly well exercised. Most people, my dad would say, were pretty stupid for not realising their full potential. Sad thing is I'd always tell myself that he had room to talk.

'He seem worried?'

'Worried? Shitting himself more like.'

'And why's that?'

Definitely had something about her. A bit miserable, a bit of a sour faced cow but that was front, a put on, I decided. No slack bint, no slapper. Liked to do things on her own terms and in her own time. As I sat there, anticipating her response, my mind hit another channel and started to wonder about her background. I soon decided she had to be wealthy and only ran with crooks for kicks. There are people like that, born with a silver spoon up the arse, who grow up hating their comfortable but boring lives. And so, they start kicking around with the Reggie Krays of the world. Running around with a small time prick like Tony suggested these were early days for Rose. And what about that? Still bugged me, him and her. A guy like Tony, he couldn't possibly keep a woman like Rose. And anyway, not her style to be kept or to sponge off people.

'Why? Why do you think? Sooner or later he'll have to face you and your mates.'

'And what about you? He sold you out as well.'

She didn't reply. The answer perhaps all too obvious. Tony didn't fear her because men aren't supposed to fear women. Rose had nothing to be ashamed of, though. Men all over the world think women are easy to control, scare and intimidate. Nearly all are wrong. Man, woman or beast, you get on the wrong side of a female, and that's it, you're fucked because one day, sooner or later, she will get you back.

'He's a bastard,' she said, then looked me in the eye. 'All men are.'

I shrugged if off. Maybe she was right, maybe she was wrong but this was no time for a crash course in any of that lesbian feminist bollocks.

'Can't believe he did that to me.'

In the same boat as me: placed into the Dustin, Bjork and Kilo scene by Tony for the sake of authenticity and nothing else. Like me, a pawn amongst pawns. Strangely enough, the rage that comes with betrayal didn't make an appearance as it rightly should have.

For a few moments we sat there, contemplating our respective situations, which weren't all that distinct. Rose staring into her mug, me into mine, in silence but minds active in thought. I tried thinking of something to say, but I couldn't come up with a word. After a few more uncomfortable moments, we parted company. I said I'd see her around. She said nothing.

I felt okay, confident, as I pulled up outside Tony's yard. Shaping up to be a nice sort of day. The sun now risen above the horizon, the faintest of breezes brushing against my face as I got out of my car. I switched my phone off and headed up the path.

First and foremost, I wanted it out of him. An admission for my own peace of mind. Couldn't be that hard. Piece of shit like Tony would confess to killing his own mother if pushed hard enough. Not that I walked around like some big hard man, but next to Tony, Michael Jackson came up diamond.

A couple of milk bottles stood on his doorstep. This surprised me for two reasons. Tony was a drug dealer and somehow, the idea of a drug dealer having a milkman didn't seem right. Secondly, I had no idea you could still get the white stuff delivered to your door. Hadn't seen a glass pint bottle of milk for years. The last time must have been in my dad's shop. We used to sell about three crates of it every day. And then, the next thing you knew, some bright spark thought paper cartons were a good idea and then, a while later, plastic bottles had taken over the world of milk packaging. The glass pinta had died and nobody even mourned its passing. But no, not dead after all. Here, half a dozen years later, give or take, a couple of them stood, as happy as shit on Tony's doorstep. I never liked milk so I don't know why I grabbed one of

Tony's pintas, gave it a shake before downing the sucker in one.

Tony took a while answering the door. He had the chain on but one half decent shove and anyone could have been in the place.

'K,' he said, bloodshot, sleep-hungry eyes peering out from the gap between the door and frame, nervy as anything. 'Erm, how's it going, guy?'

'Alright,' I said. 'You gonna keep me standing out here or can I come in?'

He tried smiling but instead, ended up looking like he needed a real big shit all of a sudden.

'Bit early for a visit this, innit?'

I shrugged and once again asked him:

'I come in?'

'Sure.'

He took the chain off. In I walked, following him into the lounge. Not my taste, but not such a bad looking place, really. Plenty of colour for a start. Reds, yellows, blues. Some *Changing Rooms* maniac had obviously been working overtime around these parts.

'So,' he said, feeling a little more secure for some reason. 'How goes it?'

'I was gonna ask you the same thing.'

Tony looked himself up and down.

'Like you can't see? I'm alright,' and then shrugged, 'you know me, right? As cool as.'

'You look tired,' I casually commented. 'You not getting enough sleep?'

Tony must have been wondering about my game, acting all easy like this.

'So this a social call or what, then?'

'Sort of. Come to say thanks for those punters yesterday.'

'Yesterday,' he said, smiling. 'What can I say about yesterday, K?'

'I dunno. You tell me.'

He shrugged which really annoyed me. This reaction, this *shit happens so tough shit attitude* left a hell of a lot to be desired.

'Had to be done, K. You'd have done the same thing, man.'

To say the least, this sudden, unforced and completely unapologetic admission surprised the shit out of me. Didn't expect something so frank and up front from a weasel like Tony. This, I figured, must have been an offensive strategy and, as soon as I acknowledged it to be that, I began to get a little nervous.

'I don't think I would have done that. That was low, man.'

'No,' he said. 'Don't think so. If it had been a mate, then it might have been low. But you, you're not a mate, are you, K? You're just a fucking idiot who thinks he's good.'

I nodded, thinking fair enough. Least that got things in the open.

'Like I said, had to be done.'

Which is when my perception of the world changed. I started to see things in slow motion, only less detailed, blurred. I remember Tony pulling something out of his Adidas tracky bottoms, edging closer to me, while repeating that one stinking line: 'Had to be done.'

A fear rose within me but it had nothing to do with Tony. No one actually feared him, this fucking windbag. No, my fear centred around giving life to violence. Testing myself, seeing how far I'd go, could be a problem.

'You're a sad fucker,' he sneered.

I looked at his hand, a cut-throat razor held a little too tightly for it to be a natural, comfortable grip. No trace of the shakes, though. A new experience to Tony but he did appear to have his shit together; in control. Again, another unexpected turn of events. Tony could not be classed as a tough guy by any stretch of the imagination, but he acted the part well enough to convince himself, maybe even me.

'Had to be done.'

Maybe I'd been wrong about him all along. That first beating of mine I always put down to numbers, to Tony having an army behind him. But what now? He was one and so was I, and yet he still came for me. Still strong and still sure.

'Fucking wanker. Sort you out.'

I had nothing to fear, I told myself. This guy was nothing. Still a boney little fuck who talked the talk, nothing more. A loud mouth idiot who'd been asking for a beating since day one. And now, any second now, I'd be giving him it. Something he'd remember for the rest of his sorry life.

He made his move. A slip of air swam across my throat as I weaved out of his reach. Felt like second nature, dealing with a blade. Didn't have to think about what I was doing, but then, I didn't have time to think of anything. Tony trying to cut me up didn't seem to be such an extraordinary situation, somehow. Felt inevitable, now that the battle had begun. My reactions, which must have been pretty impressive, could only have been instinctive. Pressure forced my instincts to cope. Thinking would have only slowed me down, perhaps got me killed.

'You're out of your league,' he bragged, the blade being tossed from one hand to the other, West Side Story style.

'I'm gonna shove that up your arse.'

Tony swung his blade, one way then the other. The third arc glanced off my elbow. Stung like a motherfucker.

'Fuck!'

Hot and then cold blood trickled down my arm, the palm of my hand wet within seconds.

'Fucking bastard.'

My mind, transfixed by transparent red covering the length of the blade, stalled and then jump-started back into action. My own blood on the blade. Not a sharp piece, no wonder it hurt so much. A blunt, uneven and even slightly rusty blade is much more dangerous than a well oiled and well honed razor. Dodgy blades cut but they also tear skin, leaving wounds which take much longer to heal.

He swung again, this time narrowly missing my face. Once again, instinct guided me out of the way. Ducking, weaving and bobbing seemed so easy, obvious and natural to me. Even so, I don't know how I got the better of him. Don't know if I punched, kicked or wrestled him or what. All I know is one moment Tony flashed his shitty little blade all over the place, and then, I had him held, watching him catch his last few breaths of air.

'You…you fucking cunt,' he gasped, his breaths filled with surprise as opposed to pain, sadness or anything else.

I let go and he fell to the floor. My hand, dripping with his blood, held onto the blade. I looked down and saw blood continue to gush from his neck, spreading into and over the carpet. Like a tide of red, it edged closer to my feet. I dropped his blade and stepped away.

'Fuck.'

The patch of carpet grew darker, like a slab of stone in the rain. Tony, staring up at me, eyes bulging, about to pop from his sockets. Throat gurgling, lungs working ten to the dozen, barely operating but trying all the same. Nothing doing because of all the shit that continued to spew from his mouth and because of the neck I'd just ventilated. Legs shaking, a stain of piss spreading from his groin down to his knees. Blood, spit and snot dribbling out of his mouth and nose. Dying and yet, and yet it seemed obvious that he had so much life left to live.

From in between his weakening fingers that red gloss continued to dribble. He made a noise, his hand trying to stem the flow but that tap just could not be turned off. I put the blade in my pocket. My shirt soaked through to the skin, my jeans and my trainers almost as bad. I looked at him again, not panicked and not worried, not any more. All but dead and dead men ceased to matter. What I'd just done had to happen. A kill or be killed situation, him or me, do unto others…all of the above seemed to apply. I stood there, watching him for at least five more minutes when, eventually, his lights went out.

About to leave the scene, already thinking of planning alibis. I stopped myself in time.

'Calm down, Kilo. Just calm the fuck down. No rush.'

I had myself a little scout around his place, just to see what the man kept stashed away. Well, it wouldn't do him any good now. I expected to find some dope but he had nothing, unless he had it all shoved up his arse. Probing a dead man's shitbox? Not something that interested me, no matter what or how much he had up there. But I did find a shit load of money in a shoebox under his bed. Twenty thousand pounds, most of it in fifties. Talk about a nice bonus. Almost made killing the bastard worthwhile. Actually, it seemed fitting. A form of justice. In one swoop, I paid him back for what he did to me. Although accidental, it still felt a little like revenge. It might sound fucked up but it seemed so right at that time. Like it was meant to happen.

I couldn't be arsed tracing my footsteps and then erasing all forensic evidence so I decided to take the easy option in the end. Not as serious as it sounds as he lived in one of the council maisonettes and he had no neighbours, unless they were living there with all the windows boarded up. A bit of petrol splashed around, a match and bingo, instant house-keeping. Beat the shit out of Mister Muscle.

I got home easy enough. Ran up the stairs, ran the bath, jumped in and spent half an hour scrubbing myself so much that I turned red raw. Didn't matter, nothing mattered as long as I got myself clean. Out of the bath and back into the car heading to see a man called Papa. Papa the Scrapper.

Ten o'clock by the time I got there. Still closed. A German Shepherd seemed to be barking for fun. Half past ten when the lazy old fart rolled along in his recovery wagon, looking shagged out of his head, results of a night out on the cider, no doubt. I jumped out.

'You're late.'

Papa gave me the Vs in exchange.

'What the fuck do you want?' he asked, one hand on the steering wheel, the other now holding a fag to his lips.

I pulled out a wad of notes to shut him up.

'Get a move on you old bugger. Got business.'

Little fat fuck took an age getting out and when he did, he waddled over to the gates, like a little fat duck, walking on the outsides of his feet on account of those veruccas he constantly bitched about. The dog barked even louder when it saw him. Once he got inside, the dog went for him. Not attacked him, but tried shagging him. Probably just as bad.

'Gerroff yer dirty bastard!'

Papa shouted and cursed as he tried getting the randy mutt to cease. His attempts seemed a bit lame, a bit of a put on to me, though. Maybe he didn't want it to get off. The dirty bastards, I thought, the pair of them.

'Ooh yer fuckah…gerroff for fucks sake!'

Eventually the dog either tired or shot its muck before relenting. Papa slapped it a couple of times and gave it a stern look:

'Told you about that before yer dirty bastard,' he said, wagging his finger. 'Any more of that and I'll have veterinary cut yer balls off. Then we'll see.'

The randy mutt whimpered then mooched off somewhere out of sight. Off to contemplate a future without testicles, or whatever dogs call their bollocks.

Papa opened the gates wide open and waved me through, scraping them shut after I'd driven in.

'Rush job,' I told him. 'Not got time to watch you getting buggered by a mutt.'

'Dirty little bastard,' he said, matter of factly. 'Mind yer, who wouldn't be in his shoes? Never had his end away, that one.'

'Poor bastard,' I said and then remarked: 'Yer a right rotten bastard, you are, Papa.'

'Can't be helped,' he said. 'Can't let a dog like that get his end away even once.'

'What?'

'Oh yeah,' he said. 'Well known fact is that.'

'What you on about? Why not?'

'Drives them mad once they've had a taste for fanny. All they fucking think about once they've got the taste for it.'

'Don't think you got much to lose with that one. Looks as if it's got a taste for something already.'

'Good guard dog, that, though,' he commented.

'Good guard dog? How the fuck do you work that out? Bet if you had a break in here, it'd be too busy trying to bugger the first pillock it came across.'

Papa shrugged and took out a handkerchief, all creased to bits. Then he took out his left eye. Pretty real looking, for a glass eye. Real looking or not, it didn't impress anyone, certainly not me, when he pulled it out and started cleaning the thing, something he did whenever and wherever he pleased. I could imagine him polishing the thing as he got an OBE from the monarch for services to The British Scrap Industry and, of course, to Insurance Fraudsters.

'Tell you what about you fuckers,' he said, shoving his eyeball back in, as easy as you like. 'You an' yer fucking insurance jobs never cease to amaze me. Ever thought of selling a car instead of losing it?'

He looked up, blinked a few times and then rubbed with his knuckles. There. All done and dusted.

'All I ever get are pakis wanting their motors lost these days. No fucker wants to buy owt.'

Sure thing, I thought. Pakis are the only ones in the whole world who do that shit. Unheard of for white folks to be bent in any way whatsoever. Stupid fat fuck didn't even realise the shit he talked, nor did he realise his own complicity in this illicit little industry. He chopped, crushed and melted the shit out of cars every day of the week but did I moan on about whitey scrap merchants being bent? Did I fuck like. Anyway, being a criminal isn't about skin colour. Much simpler than that.

'Not insurance. This is serious. I need you to make this thing disappear forever.'

He smiled, hand held out. I put the wad there but I didn't let go.

'And don't even think about knocking it out as spares. Even if a wheel nut gets traced on this thing, then that's it, me and you both screwed.'

'P-i-ss off.'

'Two hundred notes there,' I told him. 'You just make sure everything gets melted, not shelved.'

'You're taking the piss.'

'Don't say I didn't warn you.'

He gently shook his head. If he shook any harder, his glass eye would probably fly out and land in a pile of grease, German Shepherd shit or maybe even spunk.

'What the fuck's this bin involved in? I don't touch owt dangerous. Nowt bar fucking insurance jobs. You know that.'

'You do now, Papa. Two hundred notes. No questions asked.'

Not happy about not knowing, of course not, but two hundred quid, twice the fee for making a car seem stolen and unrecovered, spoke volumes.

I bunged him another hundred notes and drove off with an old banger he had lying around – a Nissan Bluebird estate – a big old thing, ten different shades of blue and twice as many owners in its history. Still, a few days tax, a month's MOT, a gallon of juice in the tank so it did me fine, short term. Falling to bits but pretty comfortable and went like the clappers, once the wind got behind it.

I got home. Once inside, I sank to the floor, partly in relief, partly due to being tired but mostly, just down to shock. For the next three hours, give or take, I sat there, thinking about Tony, his blade and the way his eyes stared and the way they went out, like his brain hit the switch. I saw him – imagined him – being burnt to a crisp and then I imagined his father, then his mother being asked to identify his body. They couldn't because they saw a black, charred and bone dry shell that vaguely resembled a human being. His mother wept and his father tried comforting her. Not guilt I felt. More like responsibility.

keep your head up

I awoke when some stupid fuck decided banging the shit out of the door worked better than pressing the bell. Turned out to be the coppers, carrying out their duties which entailed being inconsiderate, arrogant and above all, the law. A couple of minutes after I opened the door and greeted them, I found myself in the back of a cop car being driven down to the nick in town where all the serious shit, like murder, arson and heavy duty crimes got investigated.

It's a funny looking building that nick in town. Lots of glass and angles. Might have looked all futuristic back in the 70s, when some kid fresh out of school designed it on the back of a fag packet. Always looked like a piece of shit to me. Outside, by the entrance, there's a still shiny brass plaque commemorating the nick's opening way back in 76 by Princess Anne, a year before mother dearest celebrated sitting on the throne for 25 years. Before my time but I heard it all thanks to my dad, who, for some reason, felt a certain sense of pride whenever the place got mentioned.

By the time I got picked up, it must have become common knowledge, even at street level, about Tony having ratted me out and then getting a fair old dose of payback. And the coppers, the ones who made him rat me out in the first place, well, they couldn't just ignore me. Had to be seen to be making an effort.

I got shown into an interview room. A skinny little CID runt by the name of Hopkins asked me if I wanted a solicitor. Fuck knows why because he hadn't arrested me.

'I think I'll be alright. Thanks for offering, though.'

I wondered how a guy his size got into the force. Thought wannabe coppers had to be a certain height, a certain weight before they got the uniform and all the other perks.

'Suit yourself.'

My old friend Price walked in a few minutes later. For a couple of hours they gave me the good cop/bad cop bullshit like they were reading it off a script. The pointing fingers, cigarette smoke in my face, raised then lowered voices, well timed exits and entrances, the dim light bulb and the coffee breath. The full dramatic works. Just like a movie but it didn't work. An exercise and they knew it. After all, they only had to *seem* thorough about investigating some paki drug dealer getting burnt to death. Like Price told me the last time, no one really gave a shit.

Dealing with them wasn't half as hard as it should have been. Didn't take my prints, no blood or anything. The whole thing seemed too easy for it to feel a real, concerted effort to get to the bottom of things. They knew the score as well as me but they couldn't prove a thing, even if they wanted to. I'd been thorough eliminating evidence but that had nothing to do with anything. They weren't even trying.

'So you were at home all night?' Hopkins asked me again.

'That's what I said before. You got a bad memory, man.'

Hopkins leant over my shoulder and breathed my way. I didn't have the heart to tell him his mouth smelt like a compost heap.

'You know what your trouble is?' he said, breathing all over me again.

'Right now it's you. Do us a favour and go suck on a pack of mints.'

'Comedian,' he said, edging back a couple of inches. 'Your trouble is you think you're something special. You've never been caught, that's your trouble.'

Myself, I thought the not getting caught part figured pretty high in terms of priorities when committing any crime. Speaking for myself, experiencing the experience of capture was not on the cards.

'Think you're invincible. Special. Lemme tell you you're not.'

Price turned away. I wondered if he had the problem with me or his sidekick. Didn't matter. Neither one of them really mattered.

'Who is special, these days?'

'You think yer funny, you. Another paki with a big mouth.'

All an act, of course, this little battle. Least that's how it felt until Price decided on asking his buddy to leave us alone. Hopkins didn't like the idea but the dip-shit walked out, although in a bit of a huff.

'So, Khalil,' began Price. 'Proud of yourself?'

'Scuse me? Proud of what?'

'Come on,' oozed Price. 'We can talk freely.'

I laughed. It seemed more than funny, him coming out with this free and easy shit. Any minute now he'd pull out a tube of KY Gel and ask me if I wanted to go first.

'Trust me, Khalil. This is between you and me.'

'Oh?' I said. 'What is?'

Price sat down opposite me and crossed his arms, ready to explain something important, the way parents do when telling children off for smoking, drinking and fucking before their time.

'You felt it was a matter of duty, I take it.'

'What was?'

Price didn't blink.

'Ilyas Musa. Killing Musa was something you had to do.'

I shook my head.

'Are you asking me or telling me?'

'Asking,' said Price after a moment's consideration.

'No comment, man.'

Price scratched his head.

'You do realise I'm responsible for you being here.'

'So?'

'No,' said Price, sitting up, to attention, now. 'I'm the one who's responsible for you being here. *I'm* the one who made Tony give you up.'

Had to be someone. Not such a surprise, it being Price. After all, Price had a point to prove. A man with justice, truth and fairness engraved across his heart. Well, that's what he made out when going on about his dead daughter and accidental junky of a grandchild.

'I feel guilty about that now,' he said. 'I didn't realise you would take it that far. Didn't know who I was dealing with.'

'It was your fault, then? You admit that?'

'I admit I played a part, yes. Do you?'

'Me? Nothing to do with me.'

'There's really no need to play these games, Khalil.'

Silly, me denying it, when he and everyone else with a brain cell knew it could only be me as all the other sting victims were still locked up. Talking freely with the man felt okay, harmless, but if I didn't watch it, I could end up hanging myself with my own tongue.

'Can I ask you something?'

'Of course. Please do.'

'What made you go for me? Why not get Tony to give someone else up instead a little guy? I mean look at me, I'm nothing. Small fry.'

'I don't know about that, Khalil,' he mused. 'Perhaps you're being too modest.'

'Modesty's got nothing to do with this. I'm a street dealer. Maybe you should think about the ones who really control the shit around here.'

'I do think about them. I think about them all the time, Khalil.'

'Really? So why piss me around?'

'Means to an end, Khalil. Means to an end.'

'Means to an end,' I repeated. 'Bullshit.'

'It's my job but it's also my duty. We all have duties.'

'Yeah, I guess we do.'

He smiled, pleased to hear me agreeing with him, perhaps. That didn't mean him and I were friends all of a sudden. Price was a copper, a bit friendlier than the usual breed, but still a copper.

'Tell me something, Khalil,' he asked. 'Who is the most important person in your life?'

'What's that got to do with anything?'

'Please. Just humour me.'

There were a few important people in my life, the most important freshly buried in a grave I'd never visit. My dad, he had nothing to do with this, though. Didn't seem right mentioning him to Price. Felt personal.

Price raised his eyebrows.

'Your dead father, your living mother?'

'Maybe.'

Price nodded to himself, pleased about something.

'Next? The next most important person in your life?'

The face, not the name, popped into my head without any effort whatsoever. Important but bad important. Important as a reason to stay alive but not important in terms of a reason to live. Nothing to do with love, affection or even respect. Important for giving me a sense of purpose. Personal business, nothing to do with Price. Again, didn't seem right, uttering that name to a stranger, giving my weakness and my life's game away.

'No one. There is no one else.'

Price licked his lips, not quite sure what to say next. Didn't matter.

I'd had enough.

'Are we done here?'

Price nodded.

'For now, yes. But please, Khalil. A favour, before you leave?'

'Sorry,' I said. 'I'm a drug dealer. Don't do favours.'

get out

From the nick, I took a cab home and from home I took a cruise in the old banger, deciding I needed to check the scene out. Turned out to be no busier and no quieter than usual. A few dealers, a few working girls but, as usual, never enough punters.

I hung out with Cowboy for a while, talking meaningless talk. Passing time, shooting shit. For the most part, Cowboy ripped the crap out of my new motor, of which I'd grown a little fond. It started first time, was a pleasure to ride in and all the pedals worked OK. Noisy thing, though. Made more racket than a tank being driven by a trigger happy gunner. Had a certain character, that motor. Crap maybe, but definitely not anonymous.

Cowboy and me had been sat in the car arguing over a pizza, one of those special ones with the cheese in the crust. Cowboy had only gone and ordered the thing with a shit load of olives, knowing damn well I hate olives. I thought we'd agreed on having olives on his half, not half as many olives as usual all over the fucking thing. I loved him like a brother but he could be as thick as shit.

As I started picking out the little fuckers from the slice, my mobile went off.

'Hello?'

'Hello?'

Rose.

'How you doing?'

'I'm okay, but…but you know.'

She whined on about Tony for a while, which was to be expected, I guess. And then, quite suddenly, she stopped and asked me, outright, if it was me. I told her it wasn't safe to talk over the phone.

'Was it you?' she insisted.

'All I'm saying is I'm glad it happened. Fuck him, the twat,' I said. 'Serves the bastard right.'

After a short silence I heard her sniff and then she carried on talking. I couldn't understand her problem. How come she seemed so wrecked over that fuck, after what he'd done? She asked me to call round and I said I would, just so we could talk things over, get our stories right in case the coppers came snooping again. I said I'd see her sometime after ten.

I didn't bother working the rest of that day. Deserved time off, after the shit with the coppers, and Tony before that. I hung around doing nothing except talking, and when I got bored with that, I drove around, bigging myself up in front of the others, making out to be some hard fucker who didn't give a shit about anyone or anything, on either side of the law. I had, after all, just killed a man that very morning, a pre-breakfast ritual, something I did all the time. Some of them seemed in awe, others merely respectful. Not one of them disputed my credentials. The facts, or what I said were the facts, spoke for themselves. That was the thing of it. That's what made me stop and think. People actually believed what I said and they also went and believed what they told each other. In no time at all, I would be the baddest bastard on the face of the planet. One small act, I realised, could change everything. This was how rumours grew and rumours made reputations. This was how Sweet became the man we all thought he was. Perhaps I'd be like him, in years to come, but for the life of me, I simply couldn't see it. I didn't know the guy, had never even met him, but Sweet and me, we were beyond comparison.

I left Cowboy at about nine that evening. As I got on to Leeds Road, I noticed a car flashing me to pull over. I slowed down and had a closer look in the rear view mirror. A right piece of shit, almost as bad as mine but I recognised it. Behind the wheel, a pale, gaunt and ghostly face sat, almost transparent. He got out and joined me.

'King,' I said. 'How's it going?'

'Easy, Kilo,' he said, looking around, uneasy. 'How's it going with you, guy?'

'Okay,' I said casually. 'You know, so-so.'

'I hear you've had your little ding-dong with Tony.'

'History, now,' I said. 'Had to be done.'

'Oh yeah,' he agreed with a smile. 'You got that right.'

With the pleasantries over and done with, King got straight down to business. I looked at my watch not because I might have been getting late for Rose, but because I didn't like being around the man any more. Gave me the creeps even though he'd grown so weak. The thought of ending up like him frightened me.

'I been thinking,' he said, wiping sweat off his brow. 'You're a good guy, you know?'

Didn't sound like him at all. Clearly after something.

'You know,' he nodded. 'Me and you, we do good shit together. I mean, if it wasn't for my bag of talc, you'd be inside now, looking at a ten stretch like the others.'

Maybe, maybe not. If not for me, he'd have been a lot poorer too, so I figured we were good for each other. I turned to look at him for a moment. Stupid bastard. Been hammering the pipe again. People like King keep the drugs industry alive because they're so weak and so damned prone to succumb to temptation. I felt like slapping the shit out of him but even that wouldn't have done any good. Nothing short of tying the bastard up in a strait-jacket and throwing him in a padded room would do the trick. Always needing, always craving something to make him feel. It's easier to wish problems away than it is to try solving them.

'I guess we do okay,' I agreed modestly.

King looked even more haggard than he did some 24 hours before. I realised he'd continue to look gradually worse until the day he died, which, the way things were going, couldn't have been too far away. He'd developed a stoop, and he'd grown so thin. Too many veins hard and dead. Blood had a tough time getting around, forcing his other organs to work harder just to keep the sorry bastard alive. He rarely ate, but he drank buckets of cheap Netto rum to help take a nasty edge off all the coarse, bargain basement shit he got for personal consumption. A couple of short years before, the man looked like a prince. Clean complexion and decent looking muscles that functioned fully. A fine frame of a man with a mind to match. Looked after himself, too. Ate all the right food, worked out down the gym three times a week and flossed his teeth morning, noon and night. Used to be one of those twats who went on about his body being his temple. Not any more. Now his body was a crack house. Not even thirty but looked no better than an ageing, prune faced rocker. The man could have passed for a Rolling Stone.

'You know, I've always trusted you, Kilo. Looked out for you, you know?'

Could have been wrong, but he seemed scared about something.

'What's going on, King? Something's fucking with your mind.'

A junky with only himself to blame but still, I couldn't help but to feel bad for him. I'd known the guy since I started and although he'd ripped me off more than enough times, I never took it personally. Ripping people off seemed to be a part of his nature; it's what he did. Didn't seem right, hating a man for being himself.

In recent years he'd suffered a few setbacks, most of which, from what I could tell, were down to his habit. The woman he'd been with for most of his adult life finally left him and took his kid because he spent more free time out of his head than he did with her. Her leaving only made him worse. Since then, a series of slappers shacked up with him, the latest being a dirty lass from Salford called Stella. Stella could suck your arse out from the end of your cock if you asked her.

To make his life seem better, he began using like he had a death-wish. Soon enough, he'd lost that hard business edge of his, an edge that had always seen him right in the past. But now a junk disposal machine sat next to me, a machine due to break down any day now.

'How's that Stella, anyway?'

'A bitch as usual,' he said, shaking his head. 'Major walking mind fuck, that one.'

Most of the time, King buzzed like a dildo on super-speed but only because he had the means to buzz. When clean, he got pissed off at everything because he didn't have the patience to stay high on life. Most days, however, he kept his shit together well enough to stop himself from falling apart. Certainly organised enough to still pass himself off as a medium sized franchise holder. Remained important for King to keep straight enough for long enough to do the deals that mattered to his big daddy supplier: Saleem Choudhuri.

'You can handle her, though,' I commented.

'Handle anyone,' he said, not quite boasting. 'Anyway, I'm not here to talk about that bitch.'

'Oh? What's on your mind, man?'

King sighed.

'You wouldn't believe the shit I have to put up with these days.'

'We all have our ups and downs.'

'Not like mine,' he said, letting out another, deeper sigh.

'Sounds serious.'

'Is. Need a favour.'

King had never done anyone a favour so he had no right asking one off me. Still, I could hardly refuse the man without hearing him out.

'Favour? What kind of favour are we talking about, King?'

'I might need a bit of back up from you that's all. Might need you to vouch for me.'

'Vouch for you? What you on about?'

'Just say you will.'

He passed me a business card: *New Commonwealth Restaurant.*

'Be there. Midnight.'

'Midnight? What for?'

King laughed.

'It's Sal's place. One of his fronts. He's heard about you. Impressed to fuck, he is.'

'Impressed? With what?'

'With what? What the fuck you think, man? You play your cards right and you're set for life, Kilo. This could be good for you. All I'm saying is just remember me when you make it big.'

King buggered off but I stayed in the car, contemplating my next move. I could see Rose a little earlier than agreed and work on getting fucked sometime in the near future. Alternatively, I could now see Saleem Choudhuri and, perhaps, get fucked, but probably a lot sooner and in a way I wasn't too keen on. I had no illusions about Choudhuri. He expressed an interest in me only because he imagined some advantage to be gained. Didn't think he bought into all that personal development shit. The Saleem Choudhuri's of the world were all about the best ways of using people. They didn't get to be such big players by being nice, considerate and sensitive to the needs of their underlings.

The last time I got my end away had been a month ago with Stella when she needed a place to stay for a night or two. She hooked up with and started leeching off King because I told her to get a job or get lost. Since then, I'd been celibate but not by choice. More a case of being restricted in terms of variety. Don't get me wrong. I could get my end away if I wanted but the talent around there didn't really qualify as talent. All I ever noticed were slappers who got off on the prestige, scrubbers who got off for money and junkies riddled with all manner of disease who no longer recalled what it meant to get off. Some of them existed as vessels for men to shoot their muck in and nothing else. Might sound it but I don't intend to sound mean or cruel. That's just the way it is.

But Rose. A different proposition. She signalled hope for one thing. Still a bit cold towards me but a real person with decency, morality and sense. Not a slapper, scrubber and not even a casual user, let alone junky. She seemed so pure compared to everyone else. Rose. Nice name and nice face. Nice tight figure to boot. The kind of woman – yes woman – a man would give his back teeth for. A prospect which, of all things, suggested happiness could be there for the taking. I decided on seeing her first, then dealing with Mister Choudhuri or Sal, as King called him. Choudhuri could be important. My chance to make a big fat career leap.

Dealing drugs, as a business, had changed even during my short time on the streets. Although I started off thinking it was a good way to make lots of money, I was still pushed into it. Sure, at the time I told myself it was my choice, that it was a really cool thing to do but that wasn't the whole truth. I'd always known that dealing drugs was only a means to an end. I'd do it for a while, save a load of money and then quit while I was ahead. It was never a real career, never something I'd be truly proud of.

It couldn't be any different for the newest breed of dealers. Dealing's become one of the best, most appealing and lucrative careers going and it just seems to grow more and more tempting. Why this is so is not such a complicated matter. When you can't get a job and when every drug dealer you see happens to be driving around in a flash set of wheels, then it seems to be the *only* realistic and *sensible* choice to make. That's the logic behind the new guys. Dealing drugs might still be a quick route to money and status but now, it's more or less an acceptable way to earn.

My first deal had been hard. I had no one telling me what to do and there were more, much greater implications at stake when I started out. Some of us lost everything when we began dealing. I lost my father. Funny thing is, these days I see fathers, five-times-a-day people with the beards, the prayer beads and the tickets to Paradise, knowing damned well what their sons are up to and not doing a thing about it. Matter of fact, as long as the sons bring in a few hundred notes every week to go towards the mansions in Pakistan, or the upkeep of the family four wheel drive, there's no problem. When money comes into it, conflicts between religious beliefs and criminal activities are suddenly and quite miraculously overcome.

Maybe it's just me, and maybe it sounds fucked, but I do recall an old time dealer telling me that at one time, most drug dealers had a certain sense of ethics. They weren't tough guys, flash guys and they weren't even overtly loaded guys. Drug dealers were drug dealers, not gangsters who used fear, violence and wars to further their personal causes. I'd watched it grow worse in my time dealing. These days you see young fuckers, some of them barely out of school, swaggering around, more gold draped around their neck than Mister T. Expensive clothes, expensive cars but worse than all that is a complete lack of ethics, decency and even honour. You look at one of these little bastards the wrong way and the next thing you know, there's a dozen of them around you, ready to kick, maybe even slice, ten bells of shit out of your old fashioned self. That kind of thing didn't happen too often in the past. Drug dealers didn't want attention, they just wanted to make some money, not run the whole city like these new wannabe Dons.

Cars. Cars were and still are important in the drugs trade but not just in terms of status. There are certain cars which have become known as stock drug dealer cars. Toyota Corolla Twin Cam Sports jobs used to be the favourite for the low level dealer (I even had one myself) but any dealer worth his salt wouldn't be seen dead in one of those things these days. Dealers have moved up a few notches by riding anything that screams Bling fucking Bling.

It annoyed the hell out of me. Before the thing with Tony, I'd still been driving around in a piece of shit. Not an awful machine but nothing special, either. Shit. Even some of my crappest punters drove better motors. Some sons of bitches seemed to be going places. There was this one weedy, pug-teethed fucker called Bugs and I hated his guts. I was not jealous in the least, but he pissed me and everyone else off simply by being himself. So special, so bad and so fucking invincible, he thought.

I could never understand how the hell a prick like him got so high up. He wasn't a fighter, a looker or even one of those people with a busy brain. Everything about Bugs was crap. When he talked, he sounded like he'd been toking on a helium filled balloon. And his teeth kept getting in the way of his words. As for frame, he looked positively malnourished. The guy not only sounded ill, like he had a problem with his lungs, but he looked it too.

But Bugs had this great big sports car that he'd parade around in, doing his middle manning business deals. Bugs, like King, had a good dozen street dealers working under him. He'd even brought his crooked family in on his business. His brothers, his cousins and even his brown import brothers-in-law were dealing, keeping the profits within the clan, each and every one of them driving a set of wheels bought with money that could in no way be accounted for, other than being obtained through illegal channels. And yet…and yet the coppers, the Inland fucking Revenue and the DS fucking S didn't lift a finger. Sure, the coppers went on and on about having a wonderful record on drug arrests but they only ever arrested the street punks, always staying well away from the bigger, more active and significant dealers. I'm not saying this was a Godfather style arrangement but at times it got pretty close.

On the way over, I considered the idea of having fallen in love with her. Hardly knew her, but love could have happened. Maybe not, though. Maybe I only thought it to be love, this, whatever I felt. But no, not love, couldn't be *love*. Just a case of the hots, that's all. I would not be the first to be smitten with a nice looking woman and I wouldn't be the last. Some people say they know, can recognise love instantly, whereas others say it's a gradual realisation that might take years. All I can say for myself is that I tried to take an open approach. This could have been love but it could have equally been the need for me to score some pussy.

Rose opened the door and suddenly, the world was full of light. She smiled. That's right, she smiled and then she asked me to come in. What the hell had brought all this on? Head held high, more than a little hopeful, I followed her.

'Have you eaten?' she asked. 'We could have a meal. A take away or something, if you like.'

'Oh,' I said, racking my mind for something to explain this strange, but welcome change. 'Erm, yeah…sounds great.'

'You want a drink or something, Kilo?'

'Sure, erm, Rose.'

She smiled back, passed me a glass, her hand touching mine in the process. I swallowed.

'I don't drink,' I said. 'Something soft, if you've got it.'

She looked at me as if she was trying to read something off my forehead. Something drastic had clearly happened to her. Either that, or something had happened to me. She treats me like shit one day and the next, it's like I'm gold. Something was going on.

The subsequent formalities, which included agreeing on food, lasted a couple of minutes, if that. For a long while we just sat there and talked. Actually, that's not quite true because she talked while I listened. Sure, some people are prone to talking but all over the world, there were hundreds of donkeys missing their hind legs – forced to arse around – thanks to this one. In the beginning, her talking seemed fine, interesting even, but then, everything seems fine in the beginning.

'I knew I shouldn't have trusted him,' she said. 'I knew it. Had a funny feeling about him.'

She then told me about this funny feeling of hers, a feeling she'd been getting on and off ever since she'd been old enough to remember. It's like that funny feeling about a kitten she'd been given as a child, a funny feeling which confirmed itself when she witnessed her father run it over one morning while backing out into the road. She also had a funny feeling about anything which happened to turn out bad. She had an accident in a car once, she said and guess what? Yes, that's right, she'd had a funny feeling about that car as soon as she bought it. She also had a funny feeling about Princess Diana, Saddam Hussein, Bill Clinton and she most probably would have had a funny feeling about Adolph Hitler, Idi Amin and Pol fucking Pott, had she been around when they'd been around. I would have asked her if she had a funny feeling about me, but I couldn't get a word in. Myself, I had a funny feeling of my own…I had a funny feeling that I needed to get the fuck out of there and fast. But no. She had her own plans that night, most of which involved her telling me all kinds of shit about her life.

Still, can't say it was all bad as the subjects ranged far and wide. Her childhood, the relationships she'd had and her family. She'd been with two men in her life. The first man she had feelings for was married, a school teacher. Love for him was in fact a crush which had worn off by the time she hit eighteen. The second guy she'd ever been with she'd truly loved. Tragically, she also lost him thanks to a motorbike accident. And yes, she'd had a funny feeling about him, his motorbike and the stretch of road on which he met his end.

She told me about Tony and what he meant to her. He was okay, charming in his own way, she said. She'd met him at a club he'd been dealing at and she thought he was okay, in the beginning. They went out once or twice and after that, she just kind of hung around him and watched the things he did. She said she found it interesting. Myself, I had a funny feeling she was bullshitting me.

king of rock
ladies and gentlemen, the King has left the building

Saleem Choudhuri. A man who'd travelled further in life than anyone could have reasonably expected. Ten years ago a nothing. Barely fresh out of the fields, finding himself on the other side of the world, stepping off a plane onto black, cold and hard Heathrow tarmac. So much, and all of it good, happened to Choudhuri in such a short space of time.

Many were jealous about so many good things happening to a man like him. Ten years ago, a skinny me-no-English-speaking brown import, just about earning his keep washing dishes. Fast forward a decade and he's a pot-bellied millionaire, owning a string of Indian Restaurants and half the *Indian* nation that worked within them. Made it look so simple. Never broke a sweat by all accounts. Like getting big came naturally.

Easy or not, different people reacted in different ways to the life and times of the by then Saleem Choudhuri *Sahib*. Some unconcerned, others passionately appreciative of his success but he had plenty of critics. Like a bunch of bitches, they'd moan about him, getting so big, so rich and successful. Him being an import is what hurt the most. How come an illiterate fuck managed it so well while everyone else couldn't get the breaks? How come he stepped over the rest of the population and made getting big seem so damned easy? As sure as shit smelt of shit, it should not have been him. But it was him and he made it here, in *their* country of birth. Shit, the man had either been blessed or had sold his soul to the devil. Either way, justice had ceased to exist.

Choudhuri's biography, in this side of the world, seemed easy enough to follow, although not so easy to believe. According to popular wisdom, he smuggled a batch of processed heroin into this country when he arrived that first time, late on in the seventies. He packaged his product and then walked around, practically hocking it on the street himself, just so he could screw as much as possible from his investment. After that, through buying off some key players on both sides of the customs industry, he established a few dedicated lines of supply from Afghanistan, via the home country which made the whole thing so much easier. Slowly but surely, the size of his operation grew which meant he, the image, and then the person, also started to fill up nicely. And then, like all criminals who scam too much money, like criminals who do too well, he fell in love with the idea of legitimacy and so, whilst still trading in huge amounts of natural and synthetic chemicals, he started buying up legitimate businesses all over the North of England. Although not an act of supreme genius, doing so covered his back in case the wrong people started asking the right questions. He happened to be a legitimate businessman because he happened to own legitimate businesses…And that, more or less, was what most people knew about him. That, to all intents and purposes, was the truth.

Choudhuri, however, didn't get the respect he would have liked. Sure, nobody could afford to ignore him because yes, the man courted big money, big action and big names, but when it came right down to it, Choudhuri was something of a joke. This one big problem need not have emerged had it not been for his own ideas of what he, a major criminal, should have been perceived to be. Even now, I have no sure answer as to why he tried to be what he tried to be. For the life of me, I couldn't see the need for him to act like he'd become some *Godfather* figure but that's exactly what he did. He could not resist laying on all that Al Capone/Don Corleone shit thicker than treacle and what's more, he was so bad at it. Always making noise about how he'd won and lost fortunes, ran with everyone from thugs to politicians, how he'd led brutal, deadly wars against those who dared rise against him and his organisation. To me, these were the usual fictions that helped make any gangster flick seem authentic. On top of that, words like respect, honour and dignity he banded around like they were his own inventions. When dealing with what he called his *own people*, he played at being Mister Cosa Nostra and those around him, they seemed to buy into and maybe believe it also. How did I know any of this? I started seeing it for myself soon after the first time I met him.

Girlington, location of my interview, if interview is the right word. Not such a bad part of town, although you'd think otherwise if you believe the shit you read in the local paper. Lots of Asians, who, like everybody else, are intent on living their lives, not breaking any major laws and not sticking their noses into anyone else's business. As for the dealers, well, just too many in Girlington but the same could be said for

156

every other part of inner-shitty Bradford. That new, up and coming breed of low level dealer had emerged and started taking over the business as well as the streets. Strutted around like lords, carrying on like gangsters to everyone except their mothers.

The New Commonwealth Restaurant, one of Choudhuri's most prestigious legitimate enterprises. A nice place, as Indian Restaurants, which happen to be owned and run by Pakistanis, go. Without doubt the biggest perk of owning legitimate businesses like this place was the opportunity to disguise the profits of all those illegitimate endeavours Choudhuri headed up. There's a dozen different names for this opportunity including cleaning, brushing, scrubbing, sanitising, processing, polishing, whitening…

Most people call it money laundering. It sounds complicated, intricate and maybe even a little mathematical but in reality it's not all that. Once you see the process in action, it's a simple and obvious concept. Take Choudhuri and the way he did it, as an example. Choudhuri had a few legitimate restaurants but he also dealt in drugs. His restaurant businesses were fine, everything above board. His chefs cooked the curries, chapatti men slapped dough on to the hot plates and tandoors, customers ambled in, scoffed up, paid up and when they got home, a fair number of them probably puked up. At the end of every night, the managers checked the tills and, after skimming some of the takings for themselves, they'd make a deposit in the night safe. Once a year, some fat accountant did a few simple sums to establish the state of business. From the sales, he took away running costs which left a gross profit, only to be pissed all over by the VAT and Inland Revenue people. So far so good.

Not so good with the drugs business. Choudhuri made a mint through drugs but he couldn't go around broadcasting the fact. It's an illegal business and so are the proceeds. Drug money might be as real as any other kind of money – look, smell and feel the same – but sadly, it does not have the legal right to exist. And that's what laundering illicit money is all about. Launder money and you give it a reason, an explanation, for being.

So, to legitimise profits made from drugs, to 'launder' those profits and thereby give those profits a new identity, Choudhuri had to use his restaurants and all his other legitimate businesses as filters or as cleaning agents. He put the drugs money in the tills, making out as if that money had come from curry eating customers only he did it gradually, built the takings up over a period of months or even years. So what he had was a restaurant that, on paper at least, was doing twice as good, maybe even three times better than it was in reality. In reality his restaurant turnover remained the same but that didn't matter because what had been dirty money – the drugs money he'd put in the tills under the pretence of customer spending – was now clean. Those illegal profits could now be traced through his businesses as the results of takings, as spent cash. Not drug money any more but restaurant profits. So as it went through his businesses, it got scrubbed, polished and when it came out the other end, the shit sparkled.

The smell of spices and herbs, mixing in with incense hit me as soon as I walked in. Food was cooking but the place looked empty. A waiter, complete with white shirt and black bow tie, came around from the back and nodded at me before asking me what I wanted. He asked in the plural, a linguistic trick which denoted respect.

'Choudhuri Sahib,' I said. 'Where are they?'

'Who shall I say is asking, janaab?'

'My name is Kilo. Choudhuri Sahib, they're waiting for me.'

He nodded.

'Choudhuri Sahib, they're upstairs. I'll let them know you're here.'

Weird thing about my mother's language, this way of referring to one person in the plural. When the waiter said 'they', he didn't mean a whole bunch of Choudhuris, just the one who happened to be king shit in this little universe. This had nothing to do with arse kissing, either. If your parents brought you up right, then you automatically referred to anyone as if there was more than one of them. Having manners and being polite got to be second nature after a while.

After maybe a minute or so, the waiter came down the stairs and then asked me to follow him back up.

'Upstairs,' he told me, 'is where Choudhuri Sahib dines. It's more private than down here.'

You couldn't get more private than downstairs, considering down-stairs looked deserted. Still, I didn't argue as I trudged up the stairs, following the waiter, along the narrow corridor and then through into Choudhuri's private eating space. The place felt warmer all of a sudden, much warmer than downstairs. Didn't like the look of it, either. Too extravagant and a little too cheesy for my taste with all that tingle and tangle, glitter and gold, polish and wax. An over-the-top kind of room with deep red, maybe blood red, carpet that went half way up the walls. A huge, ornate, yet delicate looking crystal chandelier lighting everything up, including the thick flock wallpaper which must have been nailed in place. Smack bang in the middle of the room there sat this huge and immaculately polished mahogany table. Around it, my welcoming committee awaited. For all its grandeur, for all its swank and class, the place, for my money, needed an overhaul. Either that or demolishing.

There were four but I only really knew King. He seemed to be edgier than a blade, that night. Nothing new there, but an especially unpleasant sight in company. Needed cleaning up and his suit could have done with incinerating. Surprised he'd turned up at all, looking the way he did.

Next to King sat an old, short and meek looking man. Funny looking at first glance. Small in stature, sporting a tightly trimmed, henna dyed beard. A pair of silver rimmed spectacles pushed up right against his eyeballs, emitting reserved, perhaps guarded intellect. Out of place, such a humble, pious looking man. His almost blank expression seemed to magnify his peaceful, modest but studious demeanour.

As for Choudhuri, I'd never seen him before this close up but even so, his appearance did not surprise me at all. Large framed, heavy structured and a deep, but not a dark tone to his complexion. Clean shaven. Probably one of those men who had a barber come over to do him in the privacy of his own home. Crisp white shirt, blue tie, sweat staining his armpits. In all, nothing too flashy but then I noticed his hair. Jet black but so obviously not his. Glints of silver peppered his cheeks and eyebrows. So, not quite jet black hair but certainly an awful jet black toupee that looked like a jet black toupee, a toupee that made no attempt to look like a real head of hair. Surely, he must have known.

Next to him sat a man I had seen before. Clocked him straight away, as soon as I walked in. I chose to ignore him at first, thinking I'd made a mistake, that perhaps he looked familiar and nothing else. But no. Not a mistake. Him. A long time since we'd last met. So long I'd almost forgotten about him and his significance on my life.

Adults seem bigger when you're a kid and, as you grow, they seem to shrink. Not this guy. Huge then, in my childhood, and huge now. Six four, this blood relative of Satan. Long, black hair but no longer pony tailed. Nifty looking rags on his back, still every inch the gangster's side-kick but somehow less than he used to be. He, Tahir the pony tailed fuck, still seemed to be the sidekick, but without his original boss, he was incomplete, lost. Where the hell had Charlie Boy got to? Didn't seem right, one being there without the other.

'You need a picture, man?'

I blinked, realising I'd been staring at him for a while.

'I know you?' he asked.

I stared again and shook my head.

'Don't think so.'

'Look somewhere else, then, innit?'

Same cocky tone in his voice. I wondered what split him and Charlie Boy up.

'Look familiar, though.'

The little guy with the red beard stood up and waved me over.

'Good to see you,' he said. 'Kilo, isn't it?'

I nodded and walked closer to the table. I sensed anxiety on his part as I shook his clammy hand. I almost felt like telling him to calm down, that nothing bad would happen.

'Good to see you,' he repeated.

King stood up next, smiling his tits off. I didn't really give a second thought as to what brought him there and why he appeared to be so pleased to see me. King, I figured, knew something I didn't.

'How you doing, Kilo? Glad you could come,' he said.

'No problem.'

Choudhuri mopped his sweating forehead with a white handker-chief before clasping my hand in his.

'How you doing, kid?'

'I'm alright, thanks. You?'

Choudhuri lit a cigarette and immediately, before he could even in-hale, started coughing like an old man. King asked the boss man if he wanted a glass of water.

'No. I don't want a glass of water,' he replied. 'I want some food.'

'So what's new?' laughed King.

Choudhuri glared.

'Sorry, Sal. Just kidding.'

Choudhuri glared again, causing King to shrink back.

'I mean…' said King.

Choudhuri turned his gaze to Tahir.

'Shut the fuck up, man,' said Tahir.

Choudhuri raised his hand, fingers clicking a couple of times.

'So,' he said, watching the waiter make his way over. 'What you guys want to eat?'

They didn't mess around with starters but opted to jump in, head first, and order good old fashioned masala dishes. I followed suit, one of the boys already. The waiter nodded, said 'Sahib' and left to relay the orders to the kitchen staff. Choudhuri cleared his throat, readying himself to say his piece.

'You should know,' he began. 'I've asked you to come here for a reason.'

'I see,' I said. 'A reason.'

'I'm gonna offer you a proposition,' he said.

A proposition? I didn't think a man like Choudhuri offered propositions. A word like proposition suggested at least two options: accept or decline. Now, from what I'd been led to understand, Choudhuri gave orders, not options. He told people what to do which is just what they did. Without question. Options were not an option.

'I see. What kind of proposition?'

'Might have an opening,' he said, turning and flashing King a quick smile for some reason. 'I hear about the way you work. Have to say I like it. Like the way you don't fuck around.'

'Thanks.'

'A guy like you working with a guy like me…sky's the limit.'

I nodded.

'That thing with the coppers…that thing you did…with the dope and the powder – the talc,' he said, nudging Tahir, then smiling while making a circle with his forefinger and thumb. 'Showed a lot of foresight, that thing.'

161

'Yeah, that was pretty good, boss,' said Tahir, without any sincerity whatsoever.

'Pretty good? That was beautiful.'

The old man with the red beard smiled and nodded wisely, as if showing me his approval as well.

'But the way you handled Tony,' he said, looking up at the ceiling, moving his head from side to side. 'What can I say? You're a class act. I mean, took a lot of balls to do that. So soon, too.'

As I sat there listening to him, only one word came into my head. Fake. An actor, a bad one at that, this man. Should have been playing mafia heads of families in all those cheap Hollywood flicks that go straight to video. He really had missed his vocation in life, giving me all that *you're a class act/you're going a long way kid/big balls* bullshit.

'Well,' I said, playing along. 'Maybe he should have kept his mouth shut.'

The little man cleared his throat. Choudhuri looked at him.

'What?'

'I think you should introduce us all properly, Sal. You know…'

Choudhuri appeared apologetic.

'Shit. You're right, Soof, I should.'

Tahir smiled.

'This is Soofi,' said Choudhuri nodding towards the little guy.

'Pleasure,' I said.

'And this is Spanner.'

I smiled. What a name. What a stupid fucking name.

'Spanner?'

'Nickname, man,' he informed.

Okay, so a nickname but still stupid.

'Oh. And your real name?'

He laughed, looked from one side to the other.

'Why? What's it to you?'

'Just asking.'

'Tahir, it's Tahir,' smiled Soofi. 'You know.'

'Spanner's an associate, a trusted associate,' winked Choudhuri.

'Okay,' I said, deciding to forget thinking about the transition from Tahir to Spanner until later. 'This proposition you mentioned.'

'Good,' he said, happily. 'Glad to see you don't like fucking around. Straight down to it. That's what I like to see.'

I didn't enjoy that mock Italian thing one bit. It works great in the movies but in real life, it's almost comical. Next thing I knew, some Pakistani Bobby De Niro wannabe would come storming up the stairs, with those trademark chin, cheek and forehead expressions and start going on about the moolanyans, the shylocks and all that Effa Bee Eye shit.

'But we talk later. Can't do business on an empty stomach.'

'Whatever you say.'

But talk is just what they did. Low level talk while waiting for the grub to show up. Actually, the only ones doing any talking were Tahir and Choudhuri. Soofi, like myself, sat listening intently, out of politeness more than anything else. But King, that bag of nerves just bit his nails and continued to look edgier by the second.

'So I said to him,' said Tahir. 'There's no fucking way Sal's gonna take a container full of vibrators instead of smokes. It's a bum deal, right?'

Choudhuri nodded.

'Fucking vibrators. What am I supposed to do with them?' he said. 'Shove 'em up my arse?'

'But he says to me,' laughed Tahir. 'But he says: They're Bully Boy vibrators, they're the best ones going. So I said:

'Yeah? How about you bending over and showing me how fucking good they are!'

Choudhuri laughed. The little guy shook his head, offended by the language as well as the theme.

'I mean, what the fuck do these people take us for, Sal?'

'I know,' said Choudhuri. 'Small time pricks think they're something else, something big. And them bastards been owing me a container three months now.'

King cleared his throat.

'Bad payers,' he said with a sigh. 'Tell me about it.'

Choudhuri laughed and then looked to Tahir who smirked as if he and his boss were wise to something. King got all embarrassed about it. Stupid thing for King to say, really, considering his financial debt to Choudhuri had been growing ever greater for a good few months by now. Choudhuri put him out of his misery through talking yet more bollocks with the dildo man.

'Anyway…'

They talked about *deals* mostly. Vague sounding *deals* about cigarettes, electronic equipment, clothes, sex toys and drugs. It meant nothing to anyone, not even them, probably. A hundred grand, quarter mill…Sony, Aiwa…Regal King Size, Silk Cut…Luscious Lucy, Three Hole Tina…Gold Seal, Afghan Horse…just numbers and just names that could have been plucked out from thin air for all the difference it made. In and amongst these discussions, nationalities got mentioned like they were the final ingredients to some strange dish. Jamaicans, Greeks, Turks, Italians and I even heard Choudhuri mention some Australian syndicate. For a moment, a long moment at that, I was tempted to think they were just coming out with all this shit because they thought it sounded impressive.

'You seem like you're really busy.'

King looked away. Soofi looked up at the ceiling. Choudhuri looked at but also through me. Tahir tapped me on the arm and nodded down the room at the two waiters who'd just come in, carrying silver trays over their heads.

'We talk after we eat, okay?'

I nodded and watched the waiters proceed to our table. Choudhuri's face lit up as he breathed in the aromas. Tahir rubbed his great big hands, King bit his nails some more while Soofi appeared to come over all indifferent to the whole thing. Only food, after all. A mountain of thick tandoori rotis, a tray full of salad, two pitchers of clear water. None of that popadom and onion bhaji shit in sight.

'Tuck in,' said Choudhuri, giving us all permission. 'Come on: what're you guys waiting for?'

I found a strange kind of entertainment watching them eat. Choudhuri didn't eat like a normal person eats. Fat bastard devoured food with a vengeance, like he hadn't eaten for days on end, like he had something against that which would sustain him. Teeth attacked every mouthful while fingers prepared and shaped the morsels before being tossed in to his black hole of a slavering, always eager gob. It took him a couple of minutes before he broke into a sweat.

Soofi ate as if bored stiff with the idea of nourishment. He picked at his food and only rarely did he put something in his mouth and once in, it seemed to stay in for ages, being sucked into nothingness, as if he was eating a boiled sweet.

Tahir amused me most. A joke of an eater. The man leant forwards, his face hovering off the dish, and as he placed the food in his mouth, he moved his head around like a dog, nodding to himself as his small, already overworked mind, ran a mental running commentary, a simplistic *like* or *don't like* critique of the flavours his palate encountered.

I found no enjoyment watching King. Perhaps I felt pain for him, I can't be sure. He looked at the food and excused himself a couple of minutes after the rest of us had started. In he went, to the toilets and out he came, less than five minutes later, walking steady, face a fair bit perkier, mind ever so slightly sharper but, sad to say, not sharp enough for what lay ahead.

'You okay?' I asked him.

'Yeah, man,' he said.

Choudhuri burped, shook his toupee topped head and sniffed.

'You got to eat, you know?' he said, pointing at King, chuckling. 'Man can't survive on junk alone.'

Tahir laughed. I didn't think it was too funny and, thankfully, neither did Soofi.

'I'm not that hungry,' said King.

'Have a little something else,' Soofi suggested. 'Have a look at the menu, King.'

'Ah leave him,' said Tahir. 'Not a fucking kid. Man can make up his mind on his own.'

Tahir wiped his mouth with the back of his hand and looked at me. I didn't realise, but I'd been staring at him for ages.

'Good nosh, that,' he said.

'Yeah it was nice,' I agreed.

'You got a good chef here, Sal,' said Tahir, holding his thumb up.

Choudhuri carried on eating, pausing for the occasional breath and wipe of his forehead.

The waiters cleared away and Choudhuri sat there, all tired and looking like a big fat walrus. For ages, his gaze never left King.

'So,' said King. 'Everything's cool, then? Right, Sal?'

Choudhuri shrugged. King looked away. I could tell things were not cool between them. I decided I'd get my business over and done with and then leave them to it. In the back of my mind King's request for back up – for me to vouch for him – was busy being shut away. I didn't want to be a part of this, whatever it was. I didn't ask to be here. King could go fuck himself. Only had himself to blame.

'So, can you tell me some more about this deal you got for me?'

'Oh it's a great deal, Kilo,' said King. 'For a guy like you, this is a great fucking deal.'

'And who the fuck asked you?' said Tahir, leering right back at King.

'I was just saying, you know…'

'You leave the saying to Sal, right?' said Tahir, picking at his teeth with his little fingernail.

'Sure thing,' King replied. 'I mean, you know me, right?'

Choudhuri nodded.

'Please, for me…I'm asking you nicely, here, but just be quiet. Beginning to annoy the shit out of me.'

Choudhuri lit himself a cigarette and blew smoke at King. I had a feeling things were about to get worse. King, the stupid bastard, had got himself into a lot more shit than I thought.

'But this could be good for all of us, right, Sal,' said King.

The guy must have been running on fumes or something. Just couldn't stop himself from butting in and making a spectacle out of himself.

'You know what would be good for me?' suggested Choudhuri as if the thought had just come to him.

'What, Sal?'

'You could start by giving me my money. What is it now? Twenty grand you owe me?'

King looked as if he'd just laid something shit-like in the back of his trousers. Head shaking nervously, face a picture of pain, lips trying not to quiver, words barely audible.

'I thought it was ten, Sal,' he whispered, looking around the room, walls closing in, the beginning of the end of his long, slow and painful death.

'Yeah well, you've got a few late payment penalties to think about. I'd say that takes it up to an easy twenty.'

'I thought you were cool for the money and shit,' said King.

He sounded whipped already. His voice no louder than a whisper, but now an overwhelmingly clear, pleading tone within:

'We never said nothing about penalties and shit, Sal. I mean, we didn't say nothing about being late.'

Choudhuri shifted in his seat a little, not because he'd been sitting uncomfortably but because he needed to adjust posture in order to mete out the real serious shit.

'It's been four months and I haven't seen a penny from you,' he remarked plainly. 'You think I'm fucking stupid or something?'

'No Sal,' replied King, all but defeated. 'I would never think that. You know me, right? I mean come on, Sal. You *know* me.'

Choudhuri didn't lean on King in order to impress me. King's marker getting called in might have hurt to watch but the businessman in me thought high time, too. This dressing down had been on the cards for at least a month and yes, King did deserve it. With any luck, and by the time Choudhuri got through, there'd be enough fear instilled into King for him to start getting his shit together and his finances into the black once again, like they used to be. However, it did surprise me that Choudhuri had been so good about it for so long. Letting anyone get away without paying for such a duration sends out all the wrong signals. Being soft in the all important debt department suggests you're soft in every other department, too.

'Don't give us that shit again,' said Tahir. 'Sick of hearing it, man.'

King seemed ready to burst into tears. He cleared his throat and looked at me with those sad, lost, hungry dog eyes. I looked away, feeling bad for deserting him. He helped me out, started me off, but no one else could be held responsible for all this shit with the man Choudhuri. I could have done nothing anyway, except to watch with cold eyes, without emotion or involvement. To make it in this world, you can't afford to give a shit and if something inside you fights against that, then you have to silence it, at least for the moment.

'I know,' Choudhuri said, lifting a finger, sounding inspired. 'Tell you what…'

'What?' asked King, excited, eager and energised back to life.

'Give me it now and we'll settle on fifteen.'

King's eyes darted all over the room.

'Fifteen? But it was ten, Sal. I mean, there's still a big difference between ten and fifteen.'

Choudhuri sighed, shook his head and then looked at King like he saw a piece of shit on the pavement.

'You know what it is? You're a junky but I like you all the same. Honest to God,' he smiled, sounding quite sincere as he raised his right hand, swearing an oath. 'I like you. If it makes you stop bitching like this, just give me the ten you owe me and we'll say no more about it.'

King let out a huge sigh of relief and then started laughing.

'Thanks, Sal. You had me going there for a while.'

'Sal's such a kidder,' Soofi informed us, happily. 'You know what he's like.'

Choudhuri smiled. I saw something devious in that face. Son of a bitch hadn't finished, not so soon. The ten, fifteen and twenty talk warmed him up for the main event.

'You got a problem?' he asked me.

I shrugged, not sure whether to speak or remain silent.

'Well,' I began, avoiding eye contact with anyone. 'This isn't my business and it's not why I came here. Thought you had some proposition for me.'

'I know that but this won't take long. That alright with you, Kilo?'

Again, I shrugged. Choudhuri turned his attention back to King.

'Now,' he said.

King looked blankly ahead.

'Now,' repeated Choudhuri, tapping the table with his finger.

'Now?'

'Now,' said Tahir. 'You heard the man: now.'

'Sure thing. I mean, no problem. First thing tomorrow I'll have it for you.'

'Now,' Choudhuri insisted, hitting the table with his fist. 'Now you son of a bitch! Now!'

King made a face like he'd just been kicked one in the balls.

'What do you mean, Sal? Gimme a chance to make some calls and shit. I can give you it, you know, first thing when the bank opens.'

'If we leave it 'til morning, then we'll have to call it twenty,' Choudhuri told him.

'Junky punk,' commented Tahir.

'I'm getting some help, Sal,' King said, struggling to sound in control. 'On the method, man. I mean, I go down the chemist for that shit three times a day. Why are you doing this to me, Sal?'

Bullshit. Methadone got prescribed for brown whereas King used anything going. Only one method could possibly work with him and it involved cutting his head open then taking most of his brain out.

'Why, Sal? Why?'

He sniffed and wiped a streak of snot onto his sleeve. That didn't impress Choudhuri, or anyone else, for that matter.

'Your heart's not in the job any more,' said Choudhuri.

'It is Sal. I swear it is,' King whined. 'You got to believe me Sal, I'm clean. I'm getting my shit together. Got the prescriptions and everything.'

'It's about time we ended our little business relationship. Getting sick of waiting for you to pay up. I mean look at you. You're no fucking use to anyone.'

King had had it all. He'd been pretty good at what he did but not now. Nothing lasts forever but hell, some drop he'd experienced. No better than a gutter-snipe.

'Face it, I've been carrying you way too long. I should have got shot of you months ago.'

Choudhuri shook his head regretfully. Perhaps, I hoped, he changed his mind.

'I don't know why I bother,' sighed Choudhuri.

When things looked as if they couldn't get any stranger, or worse, King freaked out. Started slapping and cursing himself like a crazy.

'I'm so fucking stupid. Fucking stupid!' he wailed.

'Have some decency, man. Try having a little fucking respect for yourself, junky bastard,' moaned Tahir, trying to grab his hands.

'What's the matter? What's all this?' said Soofi, with a little shrug, like he didn't understand any of it.

'I'm sorry Sal. I'm sorry. I'm just so fucking pent up with this shit.'

A waiter had been watching all this shit going on but when he saw me spying him, he turned around and left the room. Not for the help, a spectacle of such magnitude, I suppose. Then again, not my cup of tea, neither. Messing King around reminded me of a bunch of kids teasing some dumb animal.

'Just calm down,' Soofi said, sounding genuinely sympathetic. 'We'll sort things out.'

'I'm sorry, Sal.'

I don't know about the others, but for me it was embarrassing being in the same room as him, the way he'd been cowering.

'Now,' said Choudhuri, looking at me. 'I got some questions that need answering.'

'Go ahead,' I smiled, glad that Choudhuri diverted his attention away from King. 'Ask me what you want.'

Tahir sniffed and shuffled closer to the table. I stole a look at King, head down, nodding silently to himself, looking more fucked than he'd ever been.

'The way you work, I hear it's good. Hear you're a pretty loyal kinda guy.'

Choudhuri looked at Soofi who resumed the spiel.

'We have an opening. Right now, yours seems to be the name on everyone's lips and…'

'And?'

'And we thought we'd check you out.'

'Check me out?'

Choudhuri smiled.

'We did some digging. We know some things about you.'

'Like what?'

'Well, you're careful. Never been done for a thing. Not even possession.'

I didn't stop to wonder how he knew any of this but it couldn't have been too hard to get that kind of information. A man like Choudhuri got himself into everyone and everything, including law enforcement.

'I like to keep a low profile.'

'I like that. Hate these guys who flash it all over the place.'

Everybody except for King grinned. Still nodding his head like one of those toy dogs people place on the parcel shelves of their cars.

'So. What exactly do you have in mind?'

'Like I said, there might be an opening.'

'No might about it,' added Soofi. 'If you want in, then say the word.'

'Are we okay?' King asked, suddenly coming back to life, as if surprised to find himself in the room. 'I mean, are we cool and everything, now, Sal?'

'That depends,' said Choudhuri. 'That depends on Kilo, here.'

'On me?'

Choudhuri nodded.

'You want in or no? If you want in, then you're in.'

I didn't get it. Didn't get the connection between me being in, or out, and King being cool, or uncool. The way I figured it, if I said yes to this proposition, then King would be cool once again through redeeming himself by having head hunted me on behalf of his boss. Couldn't have got that one more wrong if I tried.

'Yeah,' I said. 'I'm in.'

Choudhuri looked at Soofi and then Tahir. Choudhuri shrugged, and got to his feet. The next thing I new, he'd pulled out a gun. A gun. I could not believe what I saw. Sure, I know, gangsters had guns but Choudhuri? A *supposed* gangster, a joke, *paper* gangster? A man who play acted? I decided the gun, like everything else, had to be for show. No way he could actually use it, that's if it was real in the first place.

'You have no idea how much I hate you,' said Choudhuri.

'What?' King whispered, standing sharply, his chair falling behind him, hands held aloft. Surrendered.

'Calm down, Sal,' said Soofi.

Choudhuri didn't seem to be listening. Just him and King in the room.

'Sal? Take it easy, Sal,' said King, moving round to the front of the table so he could plead with Choudhuri face to face. 'You're scaring me, Sal.'

Choudhuri shook his head but not too vigorously. Last thing he wanted, at such a moment, was his toupee to make like a frisbee.

'You know the more I think about it, the more I like the idea.'

'Idea? What idea?'

'Yeah, what idea, Sal?' echoed Soofi.

'This one.'

Before I could do anything, speak, move, puke, scream or do whatever, he'd done it. I remember being startled by the noise more than anything else. Deafened me, momentarily, but my eyes continued to work and watch as King back-pedalled, collapsing in a heap a couple of yards away from the table.

A discharged gun has a smell and it's one that stays with you forever. It filled my nostrils and I wanted rid of it. I looked around at the others. Tahir seemed unconcerned as did Soofi, like this kind of thing happened regularly.

'Fuck. Fuck me.'

I didn't want to but I couldn't stop myself from looking at King. Eyes closed, his mind and body approaching, perhaps already arrived at that place called death. But not quite. I saw him move his hand towards his gut, now a glistening, sticky redness. I continued to watch, unable to move, not knowing what to think. And then he opened his eyes. His gaze seared into the very heart of me. In that instant, and with that one look, he succeeded in accusing and proving me of complicity in his murder but at the same time, he offered me mercy. King forgave me. What *could* I have done to save him? Words would never be enough, not to stop Choudhuri from doing the inevitable. I could have taken a bullet and even that would have solved nothing. Instead of one less drug dealer, there'd be two but even that wasn't true. Two dead dealers would be replaced by two new and very much alive ones.

Blood seeped out from between his fingers. His hand, covered in that deep, narcotic-rich glaze seemed to catch the light and sparkle as he fidgeted, trying to find some place that didn't hurt or perhaps wasn't wet.

'Kilo,' he said, the first time in an age that he sounded entirely in control of his faculties.

'What you say his name for?' Choudhuri snapped. 'You're not worthy to say any fucker's name around here.'

'Take it easy, Sal,' said Soofi.

Choudhuri shook his head and shot again. Sickening but amazing, seeing King's whole body lift itself off the floor and float back those few inches. The drama of his death made him a more interesting person now. Much more of a spectacle being around him now – now that he was so close to death – than actually being around him while he lived. King, I realised, had been dead for the last six months at least but he just didn't know it.

King might have been dying but death didn't come so easily or quickly. His chest continued to rise and fall, slowly but regularly. He looked at me again. I wanted to but couldn't look away. Seemed wrong to look away from a dying man.

'Sorry, Kilo,' he sighed.

Choudhuri shot him again, this time in the middle of his forehead. No way could anyone, or anything, come back from that one. My vision panned around the room, still only us. Choudhuri standing, King horizontal, the rest of us seated. Tahir shrugged and appeared satisfied with the outcome. Similarly, Soofi didn't look at all phased. In fact, the old fuck, he looked pleased.

'You okay, Sal?' he asked.

I wondered why the hell he'd asked him that. Not like he'd lost someone close or anything. The whole thing, the restaurant, the gangster shit, the food and now King's demise, it all felt so wrong, so illogical, irrational and, from a moral kind of standpoint, so illegitimate. But I'd been a part of it because they wanted me to be a part of it. Only God knew what else they were lining up for me.

'Yeah. I'm okay,' said Choudhuri. 'Thanks, Soof.'

'Don't worry,' said Soofi. 'We'll make up for it.'

Choudhuri did seem to be pissed off at this loss which he himself had incurred. Soofi, however, was looking at the big picture and knew they'd got off cheap.

'Ten grand? Neither here nor there,' he said. 'We can handle it.'

Soofi smiled and gave me a nod as if order had been established in the world once more. Choudhuri sat back down, shoved the gun into his coat pocket and then cleared his throat.

'Now, I think we can do business together, me and you.'

'Erm…business?' I asked, not able to move my gaze away from King.

A couple of waiters came in, carrying a roll of carpet on their shoulders and then, when they got close to King, placed the carpet on the floor and started rolling it out. A nice, thick, heavy bedroom type of carpet, beige to boot. One of the waiters grabbed the arms and the other the legs. Everyone carried on as if this was no big deal, as if these two guys were mopping up a spillage, which, I suppose, is pretty near the truth.

From the blotch in the middle of his forehead, a fair bit of blood had dribbled, onto his hair, face and then down his chin. The waiters, on the count of three, lifted him up, shuffled sidewards but dropped him onto the middle of the carpet, headfirst with a loud thud. Suddenly, and like a small red fountain, blood flew upwards from his head while his body convulsed and yet more blood with much greater force started pissing everywhere. One of the waiters quickly grabbed an end of the carpet and threw it over his still moving body.

'One minute,' he said. 'Will stop in one minute.'

I looked at Choudhuri, willing him to spend another bullet but he was seated already, toking like mad on his inhaler, done exerting himself, for the time being.

'That opening I mentioned,' he said, not bothered about King's disruption. 'I've just made it for you. That's if you think you can handle it.'

Soofi looked down at the carpet, cool as you like and then told me:

'You said you wanted in. So now you're in, if you want to be in.'

I looked around and wondered about this, about what I'd got involved with. Whether I liked it or not, I had indeed played a part in King's death. Choudhuri would have killed him no matter what I said but even so, I felt responsible.

'How do I know I won't end up like King?'

'That's up to you, isn't it? If you wanna be a junky, then you better walk out of here right now. If you wanna make some money, then join the club.'

On the verge of asking for time to think it over, I noticed Tahir eyeing me, jealously. In some way he felt threatened and that's what decided it for me. I hated him and I owed him revenge. I'd be mad to miss a chance which allowed me to get so close to that son of a bitch.

'Maybe he should think about it,' said Tahir.

'It's okay,' I said. 'This feels good. I'm in.'

Tahir got all pissed off but not the other two. Soofi, and then Choudhuri shook my hand. One big happy family. So happy I could shit.

4. death of a salesman

The memory of my dad always lurked at the back of my mind. Always in there, flitting around, mostly the faintest of echoes, other times as good as, or even stronger than the sound of my own voice. It had been too long since I'd seen either of my parents in person. My dad, of course, under the ground but my mum near to him. I could picture her, in that village in Pakistan, her native sun restoring health while she tended to his grave, said prayers, read holy verses. It's what we do that defines us. People like my mother are not made, but born. Life now revolved around the soul of her dead husband. All she could do was her bit to help him get an easier ride to wherever he was destined to head.

We hardly kept in touch, my mum and I. To her credit, she managed to track down my phone number somehow. She'd phone me, once every couple of weeks but I never exchanged a word with her. Too ashamed, too scared, too used to my ways by then to respond to the first meaningful voice my ears ever heard. As always, I'd leave the ansaphone running, listen to her messages, over and over again, just so I could hear the sound, the music that was her voice. I'd become a coward at heart, perhaps always been that way. Didn't have guts enough to confront her or even tell her of this detour my life had taken. Just another fuck-up without reason for being.

Still. Taking comfort from recorded messages might sound a bit heartless, but it worked. She'd always call me *Son* and on its own, that small word gave me more hope than I could have asked for. One day, when all this shit got done, she'd get the surprise of her life. I'd wander into her village, like one of Cowboy's heroes, and for the rest of our lives, I'd set about making things right.

Pakistan's a terrible place, so they say. Corruption, military dictatorships, poverty, acid attacks on women. A man's world with little or no regard for sisters, mothers and daughters. I even heard about this one guy, a serial killer, who murdered a hundred runaway kids and no one even noticed. A hundred kids got strangled and no one gave a rat's arse. Here, in England, a teacher slaps some little shit with a chip on his shoulder and there's hell to pay.

I'm sure the glorification of Pakistan by Pakistanis abroad is little else than a case of absence making the heart grow fonder. Going on about its aromas, sights and how their blood and its soil are mixed. It's all sentimental bullshit. Pakistan, for most people, is a graveyard. For others it's still a place to find some cock-eyed son or daughter-in-law for their any westernised runts they've spawned here. Pakistan, like anywhere else, is as good or as bad as you make it but there's one variable you have no control over and that's people.

According to my old man, Pakistan had a disproportionate amount of bad people. That's why he never returned while he lived. He told me there are two types of people in the world. Sounds obvious, but there are good people and bad people with no in betweens. Sure, sometimes good people do bad things but that's got nothing to do with nature, nothing to do with the essence of people. The trouble, my dad added, is the good are not necessarily rewarded in this, the earthly existence which is one reason why good people sometimes do bad things. The bad people, however, are drawn towards places like Pakistan because that's their element. Only in a lawless, corrupt place can the lawless and corrupt feel truly at home. Just a child when he told me and perhaps too young to fully understand something so simple. But I understand his point now. Of course, he was wrong about Pakistan because it's just like any other part of the world. Once people get together, there's a tendency for things to get fucked.

I know the way it goes, better than him. He wanted me to be the same as him. A good, upright and honest son. I saw his real worth but it came too late in the game to make a difference. For the longest time, and to my undying shame, I believed my dad to be the biggest loser, the lamest person to have ever walked the earth. And then, he went and proved my point by kicking me out of his house. He didn't have the strength to sort me out, to make a decent person out of me. Instead, he took the easy way out and got rid of me.

For years he fought for everything. And for years, little by little, he continued to lose what he held dear. Eventually, he lost me. He might have held me, looked into my eyes when I was born, but he never really had me. I realised I had stopped blaming him for failing. Not as if he failed with me and me alone.

My dad the shopkeeper. Never, it seemed to me, truly happy in his work. Memory has not become pleasantly tinted with the rose hue of time. I try to find an image of him or even a sound which expresses sincere pleasure. There's nothing that comes close. I dig deeper still and I can see a truth I've been keeping from myself all along. Could it be, perhaps, that he never wanted to be happy? Miserable, but not always… The only people he made an effort for were his customers. His precious punters. For them, yes, he would smile. Always, he'd smile, and I'd wonder whether he suffered from some psychological condition. One day, the wind changed, and his smile became permanently etched on his face.

People must have thought he raked it in, smiling like that. Jesus, they'd say to themselves, that paki in the paki shop must be fucking loaded, smiling his head off. Creaming it in. They didn't have a clue.

My dad, like all those other smiling one-man shows, didn't have it easy as one of Thatcher's small businessmen, the backbone of the then Booming British Economy. Up at five in the a.m. and on his feet 'til eleven at night, standing there like a machine, giving people what they wanted. Serving customers and taking their shit in return. Could anyone be happy doing something so desperately mundane? Lesser mortals would have died of boredom, exhaustion, or perhaps, taken plain old suicide as a way out. Could anyone stand fifteen, sixteen hours behind a counter, smiling for all those pricks and actually be content? Fuck no. Not happy, not loaded and not even himself, by the end. The sorriest state to be in. Just making do. Doing O-fucking-right. People would ask him and he'd tell them:

'O-right.'

That's right. O-right. Sounded like fruit juice in a carton. He could've at least lied and said he did great. Business could have been booming. Of course, he couldn't do that. No, not lie. He survived, he'd say, although barely. And that's where it all stood. Surviving was enough because surviving wasn't just about him, it was about my mother, me and him. Supporting us, the family, meant more than anything else. And if it meant sacrificing his own life, his own peace of fucking mind, then maybe it didn't feel like such a price to pay. Maybe it would all be worthwhile. His reward would be delivered upon my maturity but like most things, he got that one wrong too.

But that smile of his…really started getting to me after a few years. He'd smile all the time. Even when Tahir came in for his master's dues, that grin never left his face. He'd smile when customers gave him abuse for being the wrong colour and he'd smile when the postman made him sign for another red letter. When the bailiffs came for money, he'd positively beam about it. When he turned customers away because he didn't have what they wanted, then he'd turn them away with apologies streaming out, the smile intact. It must be his facial muscles, I'd tell myself, that were frozen in a strange state of spasm. And even when he died, he'd look the same. The funeral directors would try to push, pull and smash it away for the sombre occasion of his internment, but they'd have little joy. So instead they'd suggest a closed coffin and my mum, reading between the lines, would concur.

He couldn't have always been so wretched, though. Living, loving and working made him that way. He must have known for years that both he and his stinking paper-shop business were just one day closer to folding for good. Seeing his brow furrowed permanently, seeing him take shit from customers gave me all the impetus I needed. That shop, that hole he'd dug himself into had been killing him since day one. Not a job but a life sentence. And me, I did the only thing I could. I reacted, made a vow, although subconsciously, that nothing so lame, nothing so weak, would ever get the better of me. I'd sooner kill myself than go out like that.

My dad would tell me things that I could not possibly understand. At the age of four, maybe five, he carefully explained the workings of the internal combustion engine. I remember him telling me about explosions, sparks and horses. A while later, he told me about dreams, where they came from, what they meant, how they differed. Something of an expert on that particular discipline he made himself out to be. Only it wasn't such a discipline, I now know. Apart from having a rudimentary understanding of people, his interpretations were based on religious references, common sense as well as a reasonable measure of good old calculated guesswork. He talked about symbols, hidden meanings and also how the dead had a way of coding their messages. It all sounded impressive enough but I was at a very impressionable age. Right now, all that dream interpretation stuff sounds a little too much like astrology to be credible: open a newspaper and somewhere inside it, there's some smart bastard telling a twelfth of the population what'll happen to them today.

After he died, my dad would often come to me in my dreams. It seemed somehow fitting that he paid me a visit the night I thought I'd made it into the big time.

The surroundings weren't particularly eerie like I still expect them to be and he was not shrouded in an intense pool of light. It was a dream, nothing more and I allowed myself to go with it, to accept and live it.

Home, my childhood bedroom. Lying on that bed I'd had since I'd been old enough to climb out of a cot. What did the setting mean? Had he been alive and had I asked him, my dad would have no doubt told me that it suggested a desire to find that happier person with a simpler, uncomplicated life ahead of him; a desire to find an innocent child but more than that, perhaps it symbolised the regrets I carried, the losses I'd cut, the guilt I still felt.

My dad's smile, the one that so annoyed me had gone and instead, his eyes now presented happiness to the world. For once, a content man, nothing dull about him, no sadness, no mistakes written on his face. The nylon shop coat he wore for every day of my life? Gone and replaced with the last thing he ever wore, the one item that accompanied him to the grave: a length of white cloth, his *kuffan*.

He kissed me on the cheek. Before I could ask forgiveness, he sat down on the bed and stroked my face as if I was still his young and precious son. In my dream and in the real world also, I found myself smiling at his tender but somehow strong touch. Dreams are wonderful. They might be make-believe, but the real beauty is the strength they give a person. Dreams are where sins are forgiven, cowards find courage, beggars own the world and as for victims, well, victims get justice.

'I'm worried about you.'

Worried? Dead people worrying? Well there was a turn up. Once you're dead, what does it matter what happens back in the world of the living?

'I'll be alright, Dad. I'll be fine.'

'I worry.'

Not like the usual dream I had with him. Usually, he didn't say much and he didn't stick around for too long, either. He'd forgive me, I'd forgive him we'd both be happy and on our respective ways. But not this time. Felt like he had a mind of his own this time.

'Forgive me.'

'There's nothing to forgive. Not your fault.'

He got up and walked off. I wanted to call him but my voice, already deserting me, could only croak one syllable. I closed my eyes, willing myself somewhere else.

The New Commonwealth. Empty, not even a waiter to greet me. I walked up the stairs to Choudhuri's private room. There, on the very seat where he'd been killed, sat King.

'You? What the fuck are you doing in my dream?'

King stood, dusting himself off at the shoulders.

'I'm fine, thanks. How're you, Kilo?'

'This is a dream, man. You shouldn't be here.'

'A dream?'

'*My* dream,' I asserted.

King looked around and then moved toward me. He didn't smell bad, like you'd expect a dead person to. He smelt okay, actually. Smelt like he used to when I first met him.

'Then maybe you *want* me to be here, Kilo.'

'I don't think so. I think I'd know if I wanted you to be here. I think I'd know that much at least.'

'Well, not like I wanna be here by choice. Your dream, mate.'

'I know it is. So do me a favour?'

'You want me to go?'

If only it could be so easy in real life.

'No need to be like that, is there?' said King. 'Thought you'd be glad to see me. Some friend you've turned out to be.'

'Friend? Since when did you have friends?'

'And there was me, thinking I could trust you,' he said, ignoring anything I had to say, shaking his head.

Some nerve, coming out with that one. Sure, he might have been okay with a few quid now and then but if it came to serious shit, King would run a mile.

'Trust? What did I ever do to you, man?'

'You could have backed me up. But all you did was sit there and slaver over Choudhuri. Couldn't wait to get in with him.'

'It wasn't like that. Just wasn't my place to speak.'

'You were just waiting for him to get rid of me.'

'Didn't even know he was gonna sack you.'

'Sack me? Fucking *sack* me?! In case you didn't notice, he only went and fucking killed me!'

'You know what I mean.'

'Tell it to the judge. You knew what was going on. Could see it in your eyes.'

'I don't have to take this. You're no saint. You can't try to put this guilt on me.'

'I don't have to do a thing to make you feel guilty. You got the guilts anyway.'

'You see a troubled soul before you, King?'

'You've always been troubled, Kilo,' he sniggered. 'Knew that the first time I saw you.'

Maybe he did, maybe he didn't. The man was dead so he could argue all he wanted. Funny thing is, as a dead person, he looked better than he did while he lived.

'You look really good, though.'

King shrugged the compliment off.

'Yeah, well.'

'Haven't seen you looking this fit for ages.'

'I'm fucking dead, you idiot,' said King. 'And guess what? I'm not happy about it. Being dead is so…being dead is so shit, Kilo.'

'I suppose you wouldn't be happy, would you?'

'Not much to look forward to once you're in my shoes.'

It was my mind, not King, delivering these messages to me. King was dead but he was no ghost. He wasn't in my dream in the way he appeared to be. Seeing King was my own way of dealing with what could grow to become an increasingly fucked situation. I was on the up and up, working for Sal Choudhuri no less, a huge step in the right direction, a bright future ahead of me. Good things were happening but, and this was the fucker of it, these good things were kind of bad things at the same time. I'd seen Sal Choudhuri kill someone without so much as batting an eyelid. And this apparition, this 'King' of my own making was telling me to watch myself. If I didn't, then sooner rather than later, I'd be right next to the real King, dead, bored shitless and in Limbo or wherever the hell his essence happened to come from.

waiting for my man

I'd become an insomniac. Over a period of three days, I couldn't have slept more than ten hours max. Thing was, doing without slumber didn't seem to matter. I felt fine. Hell, I felt better than fine. Alert, fresh and as keen as I'd ever been. The visions I'd encountered in my sleep had startled me and then pushed me into a strange state; one which comprised of both paranoia and a newer, incessant and annoying guilt.

Without sleep to worry over, I became a man of almost complete leisure. I spent my nights either at, on my way to, or on my way from trendy night clubs, illegal blues joints and various dives which, to all intents and purposes, functioned as opium dens, crack houses and ganja cellars. That was business but for pleasure, I'd sit in my car and I'd think about where this life of mine was taking me.

The trading zones weren't the hive of activity they are before midnight. Pushers all over town, including myself, sat in their cars, counting their money. Meanwhile, junkies were either tucked up in bed, their bodies shivering to the tune of a junky dance number called *Do The Cold Turkey* or were getting as high as their budgets would still allow. As for plod, a few were out cruising but most were sat in the nick, busy looking at the clock, urging the shift to end. There were a few exceptional coppers out that night. Exceptional because they had a mission. Coppers like Grizzly.

Apart from being a fat and ugly example of the human form, D C Adams, the most righteous of crusaders, had the appearance of a big old bear hence the tag *Grizzly*. A funny copper because of his police job. What you might call 'a copper but not a really copper', perhaps a 'nearly', 'pretend' or 'used to be' copper. Employed by the West Yorkshire Met as the approachable, sensible, caring and sharing mouthpiece they'd wheel out during times of distress. Grizzly played the part like a pro which meant he was concerned, proactive and positive whenever the locals got restless or started kicking up a fuss about whatever happened to take their collective fancy. Anything heavy went off and Grizzly would appear, sirens screaming, lights blazing, his mates from the local press ready, eager and willing to regurgitate whatever shit he cared to come out with. Grizzly seemed to enjoy sticking his nose in and becoming a part of the whole community affairs loop, a part of that fantasy world where nothing sounded too real, meaningful or even remotely sensible.

Grizzly might have been an *almost copper* but he was no pussy. Never that. Fact is, of all the coppers I met Grizzly was probably the worst. A fucking animal. Partly, this was because he seemed to be stupid, perhaps ignorant enough to have conviction in the shit he spouted. An overt, self confessed and proud racist is one thing – a harmless thing in a way – but a racist who manages to convince the rest of the world that he's something else, a racist who somehow disguises his world view to perfection, well, that fucker's got a talent big enough to make anyone wary.

I figured he'd come to give me the usual concerned community relations copper shit. He'd lean on me whilst showing concern for his patch, his town, his world.

'So,' he said, as he jumped in next to me. 'Making trouble, are we, lad?'

All throat, his voice, like he'd chewed a couple of pounds of gravel for breakfast, a pint of disinfectant washing it down.

'I don't know,' I said. 'Are we?'

Grizzly looked around my vehicle while I thought about his ride. Even now, I often wonder if there's any point in coppers using unmarked police cars as they're all so easy to spot.

'You can do better than this.'

I shrugged.

'It'll do me. It's legal.'

'Dunt look it. Looks ready for scrappin.'

'It's got character. Least it's different.'

Grizzly laughed.

'That's a good un.'

Nearly always the same model and colour, undercover cop motors, and if that doesn't defeat the object of being undercover, then the registration plate often has just one character that's different to the plate of every other undercover car. Not that I ever had cause to complain because it worked to my advantage. Except the time I got set up with that black Lexus. Pity those boys didn't get lumbered with a run of the mill shit-box like Grizzly.

'You know something?' he sighed. 'I often wonder about your lot.'

'Really?' I asked. 'What makes you wonder about *my lot*?'

Grizzly sighed again.

'I can't understand it,' he began. 'I mean, I can see it as a way out with the niggers and the council estate trash, but not for you lot. Not for you pakis.'

'Oh,' I said, like I really gave a shit.

'Nearly every paki peddler I know,' he said, raising, somewhat pre-emptively, an apologetic hand, 'has come from a good, solid background. Might not be rich and that, but the parents, you know, they've got their heads screwed on right.'

'Oh…'

'Ninety-nine times out of a hundred, they're good, law abiding folk. Talking about folk who know about values, discipline, right from wrong.'

'I see,' I said.

'For the life of me I can't see where they mess up.'

Might have gone on the race awareness training days, might have known all the hip, politically correct language but Grizzly would always be ignorant when it came to humans and why we do what we do.

'What makes you fellers get into this business?'

'How about this,' I said with a wink. 'Maybe it's got something to do with the money.'

Grizzly looked at me like I'd made a joke at his expense.

'Bollocks. I'm not having that.'

'You think we do this for the prestige alone? You think we do this for health reasons?'

'Now you're just being clever, now, Son.'

Grizzly didn't understand me and I didn't really get him, an arrangement I could easily live with for the rest of my life. Grizzly, however, he didn't want to let it go. The man needed to know, needed satisfying, needed answers to what he perceived to be some huge mystery.

'Appreciate the conversation but I've things to do.'

'Just thought I'd see how you're doing, you know.'

'That's considerate of you.'

'I hear things are looking up. Heard you've had a bit of a promo, like.'

'You must have me confused with someone else.'

'Don't get funny.'

'Up yours.'

I didn't get it but that's a reflection on the way I was, even then. Although I'd moved up considerably, I still didn't know a thing about these people and how they all linked up in this chain of association. I was still thinking of me and the small space I occupied when I should have been looking at the bigger picture. I should have been asking myself why the fuck Grizzly had come to see me. Instead I played the hard man who had nothing to fear. It seemed like the right thing to do.

'Do you know who you're talking to?'

I shook my head, sick of this shit.

'Are we through?'

'Look, lad,' he said. 'No need to be like that. Me and your guvnor, we've got a little relationship, like.'

'What?'

'You heard. Anyone gives you any hassle, and you let me know. Got that?'

I allowed it to sink in – the fact that he was telling me he was bent – before replying.

'Sure. I'll let you know.'

'I'll be around. And don't think I've just gone and given you license to start tearing up the town like it's your own.'

'Course not.'

'Good,' he said. 'Now give us your mobile number.'

'What? What for?'

'Cos I fancy you. Why do you think?'

Tip offs. Shit. This was a big thing. Choudhuri, like the rumours had always maintained, was keyed in after all. To the hilt. I wondered how much higher it went.

'Right,' he said, now that it was all sorted out. 'I'll be around. You need me, then all you have to do is give me a missed call and I'll get back to you.'

Mike called and said he was needing. Mike's a junky but he's not a junky, not in the classical sense of the word. Contrary to popular belief, junkies are not all of the same type. There are innocent, unwitting or accidental junkies whereas there are others who know all about the risks, both long and short term, that are involved in taking such important lifestyle decisions. These people are usually financially sound, economically active and have some measure of control in their lives. For them, the beast is all but tamed. Nevertheless, they cannot do without their weekend, *social*, *recreational* use and so, like it or not, by virtue of their consistent and habitual use, they qualify as junkies. Trouble is, when you hear the word *junky* you immediately think *low life desperate case* but these people are not that. These people seem normal and I suppose they are. Except they're junkies.

Meanwhile, there's the other junkies, the real *junkies*. The ones who get sucked into the whole sorry mess only realising what the hell's happened when it's too late. These people are not especially stupid but they make two fundamental mistakes, have two things all out of proportion. They overestimate themselves but underestimate the nature of addictive and illegal drugs. And yes, they do choose to be junkies, even if it is a choice by default. Sure, they might start off with an open mind. They might say they're *trying* it to *see what it's like* but the next thing they know, they're sucking dick, mugging old age pensioners and getting fucked in the arse. Junkies who are owned and controlled by the addiction only become this way because they're overconfident. They think they're special but no one is special when it comes to drugs. Thousands, maybe millions have become slaves to crack, coke and brown but along come these pricks, thinking they got a handle on it, thinking they're something different when the only thing they'll ever be are victims.

Some have it worse than others. I've seen people who, over a couple of years, become totally unrecognizable. People like King. There is, however, a tiny minority who actually need to be junkies. Technically, these people aren't junkies even though they are. These are people who include a guy I knew called Mike.

When Mike first rang me I din't know the man from Adam but he said he'd been referred on to me. A couple of minutes after the first how-do-you-do over the phone, he'd convinced me that his credentials were as he said they were. So I asked him what he wanted and he told me weed. Hardly seemed worth the effort but this was a new punter and new punters don't come along every day.

191

'So, you wanna come collect?' I asked.

'No. Can't do that.'

I figured him for a junky straight away. Sounded too much like a junky to be anything radically different. Sounded unsure of himself, tired, intoxicated but if that was the case, then he'd have been hurting for serious junky fodder, not weed. Weed's no pushover but in itself, it never makes hardcore addicts. Weed, comparatively speaking, is kind of safe. Hardcore addicts, however, they like the feel – the sensation – of needles piercing into skin, of foil being smoothed before the dragon is chased, of pipes being gripped by teeth, in some cases gums. Rizlas and roaches are not where it's at.

'Oh?'

'Got mobility problems.'

So I drove up to his gaff. He lived over in West Bowling, in one of those crumby little council maisonettes. I knocked on the door and someone, Mike I presumed, called from within:

'Turn the handle and push!'

So I did.

Didn't like the look of the place at all. Bits of crap all over the floor, walls a combination of dirt, graffiti and flaking matt lilac paint. And I could smell something worse than cow shit drifting towards me. Definitely something wrong in here. Should have been a government health warning on the door.

'Through here,' he called. 'First on your right.'

In I went, holding my breath. In the middle of the room, by the fire, lying on the floor I saw him. A skinny, scruffy little white guy. Maybe in his thirties. He looked weak, like one of those old men, needing plenty of rest and buckets of vitamin pills to see him right.

'You okay, man?'

'Yeah,' he said. 'Just gimme it. Order book's on the fireplace.'

He didn't look at me, not because he didn't want to but because he couldn't. Fuck knows how long he'd been there, lying on the floor. Could have been a day, could have been a week for all I knew. I asked him again:

'You okay, or what?'

'Since when does a pusher give a shit?'

192

'You don't look too good, man.'

Turned out the poor bastard had cancer and he'd been keeping a handle on it with a joint every few hours or so. His regular pusher, Dominic Deacon, had been ignoring his phone messages for days on end but in truth, Double D had been doing no such thing. DD was on remand, awaiting trial for fucking some fifteen year old scrubber (fifteen going on twenty). Least that's what he planned on telling the beak.

I cleared the shit away and then helped Cancer Mike to his feet. He could barely stand. He looked hungry so I went into his kitchen and had a rummage through his cupboards where I found nothing but mould. I could give him his dope and then leave but he'd play on my conscience forever, especially if the bastard went and died, his rotting body only to be discovered a month later by neighbours concerned about a stink coming from next door. I might have been a pusher and I might have been a bad person, but I just didn't have it in me to leave a guy to die like that.

So, while he lay there and skinned up, I opened up a few windows to get rid of the stink. Poor bastard had been shitting in a cardboard box which he kept close to himself, in his lounge. He had a home-help woman but she'd been skimming his money so he told her to go fuck herself the week before. He'd been there, in that lounge, on that stinked up floor, with only a packet of Bourbon Creams for sustenance, for three whole days and nights. I made a phone call and got this old dear called Irene to come round with some food and to clean the gaff up some. I left Mike with a week's supply on tick because I didn't mess around with Giros and money books like some of my colleagues. As for Irene, for a few quid, she agreed to visit him once a week to keep the place looking reasonable.

As it goes, Mike became one of my most regular and favourite customers. He'd spend maybe fifty notes a week but it wasn't the money. I felt like I did some good in the world when I dealt Mike his weed. He deserved it for free but I always charged him the going rate. My scales weighed the same for every fucker, dying of cancer or not.

After dropping off at Mike's, I caught up with Cowboy in a blues club where we often hung out. He'd knocked back plenty and didn't make too much sense, rambling on about his kid, about women and stuff I couldn't be bothered listening to. I walked him out to the car park to get some air, to wake him up some but no, still talking shit and walking crooked lines. I ended up having to take him home, where I put him to bed. I spent the night on his sofa, watching TV fit for only doleites and daysleepers: Jerry Springer, Trisha and the good old Open University.

I drove the shitbox Bluebird over to Mister Shah's garage the next morning. In his sixties but still hard at it, still buying and selling motors, repairing insurance write-offs, creaming as much as he could for as long as he had left. Funny sort of bloke, Mister Shah. I could never work him out, really. The way he spoke, his manners, his almost complete acceptance of working class Englishness seemed strange, considering he was a first generation migrant, from the homeland and all that, just like my dad. When you heard Shah talk, you couldn't help but to be confused. He looked like us – same colour – but he spoke nothing like us. Well, nothing like my old man at any rate.

My dad bought that Mazda off Mister Shah before I was born. My dad liked Mister Shah, although Mister Shah had clearly been a bit on the wide side, especially in his younger days. According to my old man, Mister Shah once knocked a copper flat on his back for barging into his house uninvited. I never found out why the copper barged into Mister Shah's house in the first place and I didn't ask. It's the only time my dad sounded amused, proud even, when a man broke the same law he'd always lived by.

My mum gave that old Mazda right back to Mister Shah soon after my dad died. Mister Shah, being an essentially decent sort I suppose, offered my mum six hundred notes, the price my dad paid for it. My mum didn't accept it, wouldn't accept it, of course. She didn't really want the money and with no one else to leave it to, she thought she might as well give it to someone who'd taken care of it for so long. I figured Shah sold it on to someone who ran it into the ground. A car like that, for some people, is only good for being abused.

I had a quick glance around his yard, all fenced in with barbed wire over the top. Nothing lit my wick. From left to right: a couple of Transit vans, a Mondeo, an old Sunny Coupe, a Vectra, an Almera, a Micra, and in the corner, there stood a piece of shit Renault something or other. In the other corner, a couple of Rottweilers sniffed and padded around, the kind of rabid mutts that send themselves berserk every time someone walked in. During the day, he had them on short chains but at night, those beasts got the freedom of the yard, protecting his investments as well as slavering, shitting and pissing all over them.

I walked into his workshop, ignoring his crazy mutts, busy barking for dear life, it seemed. I saw him, head under the bonnet of an old red 2.8i Toyota Supra.

'Try it now!' he yelled.

The driver cranked the engine which cycled for a good ten seconds before spluttering, coughing and then finally firing up in earnest. The guy in the driver's seat started revving the arse off it. It sounded good, loud but strong. Potent like a big lump of engine should. Threatening, even.

'Whoah! Whoah! What the fuckin' 'ell y'think yer playin' at yer great dosey bastid!'

The driver's foot came off the accelerator; the engine slowed down quickly and settled to a gentle tick over. Could barely hear it hum.

'Fuckin' idiot,' muttered Mister Shah, shaking his head and wiping his hands on an oily old rag. 'Just spent best part of three hours putting a new fucking head gasket on this bastid! Don't you go blowing it again!'

A rather large but young apprentice got out and smiled at him like an idiot.

'Don't you gimme that daft fucking goggle eyed look-a-yours, pal. Had it up to 'ere wi' you and your stupid fucking attitude.'

Mister Shah shook his head and turned around.

'Daft bastid,' he said and then, when he copped for me, smirked. 'Well, well, well. Look who it is.'

'Uncle,' I said. 'How's things?'

'Alright,' he nodded, looking me up and down.

'How's your health?'

'Yer health's yer wealth,' he grinned. 'That's what I allus say.'

'Yeah,' I said, following him into a little office situated around the side of the workshop. 'Suppose it is.'

'Sit down, then. You wanna brew or summat, lad?'

'No. I'm fine, thanks.'

He sat down behind his mess of a desk, all kinds of paperwork strewn around. He didn't seem to mind it looking as if a whirlwind had just passed through. Maybe he had a system.

'So what brings yer down 'ere, then?'

'You do. What else?'

'Don't come the sweet talk with me, lad. Not born yesterday, y'know.'

'I need a car,' I told him, sitting down on a dirty plastic chair.

'And 'ow's yer mum? Hear from 'er from back home, do yer?'

'Yeah. Once in a while she calls. You know.'

'That's good. No one loves yer like yer mam does, lad. Don't forget that.'

I couldn't help smiling. Not just his accent, which would put most natives of Yorkshire to shame, but the shit he came out with, the values he expressed, and the way he expressed them felt so odd. Born in Pakistan, arrived here a young man, a twenty something year old, according to my dad. Nothing left to see of that side of Mister Shah, not unless you looked real hard and knew where to look in the first place.

'Have you got anything going?'

'Depends,' he said. 'Depends what kinda brass we're talking.'

'Money's not such a problem.'

He sniffed, sat back and folded his arms. Didn't like my attitude. Neither did I, but it just…well, it just slipped out.

'Sound like yer loaded, lad. What you bin up to, then?'

'I've been saving,' I said. 'You know, for something special.'

'Not what I hear,' he said. 'I hear different.'

'Oh. And what do you hear?'

'Rumours.'

'Rumours don't mean anything, Uncle.'

'Some do. Depends if they're true or not, duntit?'

I didn't need this shit from him or from anyone else. The world would be a much nicer place if people minded their own business.

'So what does that mean? Do I have to go somewhere else to spend my money?'

'Money's always gonna be money, lad. It's how you get it that makes all the difference.'

I just wanted a decent set of wheels, not to clash morality swords with him. I did enough of that with myself.

'Outside, is that all you've got, then?'

'More or less.'

'Right,' I said. 'I best be off then. Need a car. Something special.'

'Wait on, though,' he said. 'Might have this one motor you might tek a fancy to.'

'Oh?'

'Bit pricey, though. One of those big fuckers, one of those Jap jobs.'

'Oh yeah?'

'You know, one of those fancy things – a Lexiss.'

I have to admit, my heart did skip a beat at the thought of owning such a marque.

'Sounds interesting. Where is it?'

'Not an *it*, lad. Car like that's a *she*. Gorgeous, she is.'

'Good nick? Straight?'

'Perfect. Thinking of keepin' her for meself, matter of fact.'

'Oh,' I said.

'If I get good money, for it, though…'

'Thought it was a she.'

Mister Shah smiled.

'Yerra sharp one you are.'

I followed him to the back of the garage. Like a conjurer doing the thing with the table and the vase of flowers, he whipped away a dirty old dust sheet. And there she stood, an early but spotless model. Sold, except for a few details like:

'How much?'

'To you? Well, seein' as it's you…'

We went through the motions. He started at nine thousand pounds, but only because he knew me, otherwise he'd be asking closer to ten, so he said. Eventually, a good ten minutes later, we'd finished at eight and a half but he did get the Bluebird in exchange. I wasn't sure who gained and who lost with that one.

I drove into town and bought some new clothes including a couple of designer suits, two pairs of shoes, some shirts and a new timepiece. Now that I'd become something of a mover, it seemed like the right

197

thing to do, this make-over shit. Clothes maketh the man. I suppose there's some truth there. As I stepped out of some clothes shop with a name I couldn't pronounce, I suddenly felt quite different, at ease with who I'd become and where I fitted in with the scheme of things. The reflection in the paintwork of my new car was the real me. Kilo Khan, drug dealer extraordinaire. I had no idea, of course, that my rapid upward mobility was due to efforts other than my own.

big pimpin

Cowboy, stretched out in his American monster of a ve-hi-kul, the roof down, listening to Kenny Rogers croak, was dealing. A couple of those scruffy but strangely pretty students nodded while Cowboy tried pulling, which he did through talking politics or whatever he thought they were into or would be impressed with. I crept up by the side of him after they moved off, further educated, sorted and happy. He tilted his hat back and smiled.

'Well fuck me.'

'You like?'

He jumped out and joined me in mine.

'Nice wheels, partner,' he said, then let out a whistle as he cast his eye around the back. 'Lotsa room.'

'Suppose,' I said.

'Nice threads, too,' he said, his approval delivered. 'Your boss's idea?'

I didn't ask how he found out about Choudhuri and me. Figured it must have already filtered down to the lower levels, the way these things do.

For a few minutes, we talked nothing talk including the state of local politics, local prices and then we moved on to the subject of local pussy.

'Your woman,' he told me. 'She's been looking for you.'

'My woman? She's not my woman, man.'

'No? I thought you and her...you know...'

'You thought wrong. She's not my type. She's a nutter, that one.'

'So what? Least she's clean...I know I'd give her one.'

'Coming from a guy who'd fuck a hole in the ground, that doesn't exactly inspire me to change my mind.'

'Have to admit, she is nice. Tight body, nice looking...what more do you want?'

'You don't know what you're talking about. Right mouth on her. Proper does your head in.'

'Anyhow, said she had some things she wanted to talk about.'

Not such a surprise, considering all she ever did, when she got the chance, was yak on better than a parrot.

'Fuck.'

'Sounded serious. Something about the coppers talking to her.'

I got over to her place a while later. Sadly, since the night before, a crazed oral surgeon had not broken into her house, sedated her and then removed her tongue to add to his collection.

'I have to admit,' she said, looking me up and down as I walked in. 'I didn't think you'd do this well. What are you thinking of next? New house out in the Burbs?'

'Doubt that. Inner-city kid through and through, me.'

She smiled but not just an ordinary smile. One of those sly little fuckers that told me she knew more than she let on.

'So,' I started. 'You been looking for me.'

She shrugged.

'I was wondering about you, you know.'

'No…I don't know,' I said with a smile, thinking she was about to start telling me about another one of her funny feelings.

'Well, yes. I was looking for you, actually.'

'So now you've found me.'

'You've come here. You've found me.'

She moved close and kissed me but it didn't seem real, an act, rehearsed. A duty.

'Can I ask you something, Kilo?'

'Sure,' I sighed. 'Ask me.'

'You sure?'

I nodded.

'Don't you have a problem selling drugs?'

I laughed not because she amused me, but because I could think of no other reaction. An absurd question. Did I have a problem? Of course I had a problem. My problem, in a nutshell, was refusing to acknowledge and then succumb to the fact that I had a problem. That was my problem. Well, one of my problems.

'Go down the road and ask the guy with the off-licence if he's got a problem selling booze.'

'That's not the same. What you sell is dangerous,' she said plainly.

'Please. Let's not go there.'

'It's not even about the drugs. It's about the money, Kilo. That's what'll kill you.'

'And what makes you an expert all of a sudden?'

She shook her head.

'You don't have to be an expert. It's common sense.'

Her hand touched then held onto mine. Soft, slender, milky white fingers. She moved closer still, her very slight pot belly pressing against me, her hands now on my stomach, squeezing them in between her and the fabric of my shirt. Then slowly, so slow that I hardly noticed her doing it, she moved them further up, yet still insisting on giving me something else to think about. Maybe Cowboy was right. Maybe she was worth fucking after all. Actually, I told myself, she owed me a fuck with all the talking she made me put up with. Besides, a girl like Rose on my arm would complete the image I'd been shaping for myself. Primo rags, an even tighter ride…only thing I needed was the bitch and here she was. Perfect, if I played it right.

'What was it?' she asked.

'What was what?'

'What made you start this? Selling drugs, I mean.'

'Oh,' I smiled. 'That.'

'Yes, that.'

Gently and slowly, she stroked the contours of my chest.

'Lots of things.'

A nag in the making, maybe, but she was beautiful, Rose. And she had quite beautiful hands, soft and white with totally symmetrical and beautifully polished fingernails. I wondered if she did them herself or whether she got some tarty manicurist called Shirley to go over them once a week.

'Kilo.'

Her hand started to move lower down, acting with a mind of its own. About time.

'What's your game, Rose? What are you after?'

She stopped moving her hand and simply let it hover there, over my crotch, for a few moments. She reminded me of a doctor, perhaps a nurse, feeling for a pulse.

'You think this is a game, Kilo?'

'No,' I said. 'I'm asking you.'

She moved her hand up and down. Slowly. Real slow and so gentle that she hardly touched me at all. Her face, close to mine, lost definition and then, at a certain point, became a blur and little else. Centimetres, millimetres, a hair's breadth away until I could smell her sweet breath as she talked into me, her fragrance brushing over my lips and face, her own lips moving over mine until, at long last, they touched.

I caught the local news on the telly later on, after I'd left her to sleep. The man from Look North, some guy in a suit and tie, sat behind a desk with an ugly co-presenter bird to his side, made a grim face when he told of a gruesome discovery by one of Bradford's bin men. Body parts of a white male had been discovered in the early hours of the morning. Some pieces wrapped in carpet, others in carrier bags. The police, so he said, were treating the death with suspicion. Good to hear that the boys in blue were as sharp as ever.

Coppers, whether they're on the ball or spend most of their time watching it, have no respect for the dead. Sure, King's *suspicious* death made the local news, but it didn't get another mention, not ever. A bunch of guys in baggy white jumpsuits (the ones with hoods) – a forensics crew – sealed off the whole crime area. For a few days after, they sat around drinking tea, talking politics, football and telly. Even after King's body had been tossed inside a rubber bag and carted off to the mortuary, they pissed around at the scene some more, still looking for clues.

Meanwhile, King's body lay on a cold, stainless steel examination table for days before some old guy who'd been examining stiffs for more years than he cared to remember did his thing. This involved cutting King open, examining his insides with all the subtlety of a butcher equipped with a blunt cleaver, and then, once satisfied that bullets had actually killed him, he'd stitch old King back up, ready for the next and last journey King would ever make. Under ground.

King had always maintained that he had no one to call family. He said his parents were dead, were losers when alive so I have no idea how the authorities actually dealt with him or who took responsibility for his corpse. Could have burnt him or shoved his rotting shell in a cheap wooden box, buried it and have done with the fucker, left the rotten son of a bitch to the worms of West Bowling Cemetery. Coppers, to be fair, saw the King the same way most people saw him. King, nasty little purveyor of death, a social pariah, actually deserved to die. Even the most generous hearted of people didn't think of his death as such a big loss. If anything, his murder did the world a favour, saved the coppers a job.

Soon after it happened, I allowed myself to believe that King deserved what he got. After all, Choudhuri had been more than generous by giving him countless chances to make good on his debts. The more I thought about it, the more uncomfortable it made me. First of all, the debt he owed Choudhuri was not as big as Choudhuri said it was. Secondly, I figured Choudhuri had allowed King's debts to spiral out of control, so indirectly he was just as responsible for them. Choudhuri wasn't being careless, however. Lenders are not interested in people who pay up on time because those people present smaller profits. This is not just about loan sharks and back street heavies who loan money to untrustworthy people. This is how every high street bank under the sun maximises its profits. Fines and trumped up interest charges are pure profit. In the world of operators like Choudhuri, bad payers are gifts from above because all they ever seem to be paying off are penalties and interest which, more or less, makes them tied for the rest of their lives. Killing King simply because he owed was not an astute thing to do. No, King was killed for a different reason but I was damned if I could see it. Of course, this also meant I could be dealt with in the same way for whatever reason Choudhuri saw fit. I didn't really care, though. I figured he'd only resort to fucking me over if I went and fucked up. A guy like me, with my track record, could not and would not do that.

As I pondered King, his death and whether or not a similar or worse fate awaited me, I got the most unexpected of phone calls. It had been a while since I'd heard from my mum. I'd been expecting her, perhaps willing her to pick up the phone and remember her son.

Her health, she said, could have been worse. Then, same as always, she started crying, calling me *Son* over and over again, as if that would somehow make up for all that happened, for what I'd done, for what I'd put her through. I sat down and listened to her every word, breath and sob. I should have picked up the handset and talked back to her but I couldn't, didn't have it in myself. She hung up after a minute or so but not before telling me to remember God. I ejected the tape and put it in the drawer with all the others.

The bag my mother handed me at the airport contained a prayer cap and a copy of The Qur'an with an English translation. It was her way of keeping some kind of hope alive, I guess. It had been years, over a decade easily since I'd even looked at something like that, but I needed to revisit it. I have no idea why but I thought it would help me make sense of the situation, perhaps give me guidance.

And so, after bathing, I came back downstairs, sat on the floor, cross-legged, opened the book at random and I read. One line in Arabic followed by a line of interpretation. I never understood any of it as a kid. I'd go to mosque, read a few pages and then I'd go home like all the other kids. Like them, I knew how to read, how to pronounce, where to pause and where not to, but I never understood like I should have understood. Just a load of words in Arabic; could have been Russian, for all the difference it made. Something felt wrong about the whole thing. Either a wrong time for me to learn or a wrong way to be taught. I could have been a monkey, mimicking and learning by rote, being conditioned into reading for the sake of it but not for the *sake* of it. But that day, as I sat there, reading in one tongue then another, I did get a certain sense of relevance. Sounds weird, sounds like a lie coming from someone like me, but I did get a sense of meaning, a sense of place in the universe, and yes, I even felt a sense of purpose that day. First time for everything.

And so, on the day my conversion to big time dealer was all but complete, a reconversion stopped it, not quite dead in its tracks, but as good as. I must have read for a good couple of hours at least before giving my eyes a break and when I did, I started laughing. Not the giggles of a crazy man, but the kind of laughter that comes with sudden but all too obvious realisation. One minute I'm there, another punk thinking about money, cars and bitches, and the next, I'd turned my mind to something much more important. I'm not saying I felt the urge to grow a beard and become a five-times-a-day-er but I did get a sense of perspective. I was not evil. I was a good person who happened to do a few bad things. Through that badness, goodness would ultimately prevail. So far, I realised, the things I'd done were a means to an end. Trouble was, I didn't really know what the end looked like or when it would come.

I opened the door to leave the house. Two visitors, without intimidation, greeted my would-be exit. A strange duo. One a beauty, the other a beast. The devil was black but by his side stood the whitest of angels.

Blonde hair, big blue eyes and lips you could kiss forever. A beautiful, unblemished sheet of skin stretched over the most exquisite mass of bone. Sharp looking, angular, but perfect. Amazed me how such a technically beautiful woman managed to stomach such an ugly dog of a man. Maybe he had a wonderful personality. Women love personality.

'Something I can do for you?'

He smiled and walked past me, pushed the door open and went right on in. His woman followed, also smiling but turning around, giving me this *fuck me* look. I wondered why she would do that.

'Come in. Make yourselves at home…'

She didn't dress like normal people. Neither one of them dressed normal, for that matter. She had a thing about black. Not that stupid Goth-look black, but that slick, serious, power-dressed-up-to-the-eyeballs black. And it did look good on her. A bit 1980s but she pulled it off well. Mini-skirt, boots going up past her thighs and a black leather jacket over a cute little crop top with her belly button. A young Madonna, only not as slutty.

Sweet was not a good looking man but every inch the gangster. Only he was not a gangster in the Al Capone mode, but a bad bastard gyangsta in the bling mfuckin bling, 20 inch blade, bitches, blunts and bullets mode. Short hair but neat, cut with scissors, not an electric razor. Clean shaven, a gold pirate's earring in one ear, a lobe missing off the other. Four tattooed tear drops falling from his left eye, each one symbolising a life cut short. It was there, in his eyes where all the anger, hate and desire to inflict pain lay. Brown eyes but surrounded by seas of red. This guy, I figured, lived life like each day was his last, like every drug known to man had to be sampled before each night crept into day. As for his clothes, he was a bit more formally attired than the woman. Italian designer suit with the label on the cuff, ultra-shiny shoes, also Italian, and glimmers of gold and precious white rock on his fingers, neck and wrists. A walking jewellery store, his body sparkling brighter than fireworks, the kind that came with free sunglasses. Not reserved. Not like Choudhuri. The loudest gangster this town had ever seen and he didn't give a shit who knew it. No wonder he and Choudhuri had parted company. They were opposites. Sweet was too loud, too proud and too sure of himself to complement Choudhuri's desire to become absorbed by straight society.

And me, I felt like a bit of a tit, doing nothing as they strolled in, ideas of ownership and territory gently floating away. I walked into my lounge where Sweet had already made himself at home on my sofa, his woman straddled across his knee but moving backwards and forwards like she was riding it. Fucking it. Wanted to see me nervous, scared or even filled with awe, these two. They could have saved themselves the trouble of simulating sex as the very sight of them, particularly Sweet, had me shitting bricks.

'Kilo, right?'

He looked around the room, nodding to himself, perhaps appreciating something, perhaps not.

'Nice yard you got here.'

He stopped looking at the walls and then, smiling a diamond toothed smile, faced me once more.

'Nice wheels you got out there, too.'

Lost for words, I just nodded.

'Thinking of moving up to a Lexus myself,' he said. 'Nice machines them things. Reliable, too, so I hear.'

'Yeah,' I managed. 'Starts first thing.'

I didn't bother sitting down. Didn't seem to be the right thing to do. Besides, too busy thinking of something appropriate to say to worry about anything else.

'You're thinking what am I doing here, right?'

'Thought's crossed my mind.'

'Wondering what a man like you can do for a man like me.'

'Yeah. I am.'

'It's what I can do for you that matters.'

'I see.'

'I don't like to waste time, Kilo. I heard about you and that prick, Tony.'

'It was no big deal,' I began modestly and then decided to forget all about being modest. 'Had to be done, you know.'

I wondered if I'd ever get one of those tear drop tattoos. I did have the right; I had earned one. Didn't seem me, though. Then again, there were lots of things that didn't seem to be me.

'That was cool, sorting that pussy for bitching you out. Had to be done, like you said. Like your style, man. You got style.'

'Had to be done,' I repeated. 'Style's nothing to do with it.'

'I think you've got potential,' he said, his woman now turned around, facing him.

I got it. He wanted me to be with him. That's the reason why he was being such a nice guy, for coming out with the *had to be done, that was cool, like your style* bullshit.

He smiled and then decided on kissing his woman real long and real hard. I coughed three times before they broke.

'I've come to make you an offer,' he said, she now off him, walking around the room, heading towards my CDs.

'Oh,' I smiled. 'An offer I can't refuse?'

He smiled back, clearly warming to me now, smiling, appreciating the reference.

'I like that. Godfather, right?'

I nodded.

'Okay,' he said. 'Let's cut the shit. Why do you think I'm here, Kilo?'

'I don't know,' I said. 'No idea.'

Sweet smiled.

'Cos of you. Why else?'

'Me? What can a guy like me do for a guy like you?'

'I told you before: it's the other way around.'

His woman was nodding to herself as she finger-flicked through my music.

'Well,' asked Sweet, addressing her.

'Alright,' she nodded back. 'Some old shit, but some good shit.'

I didn't get it.

'Cool.'

She got up and came over to me. I cleared my throat, ready to speak but my mind went blank. She edged closer and closer until she got right next to me. Real close but not personal, least not yet. Her chest touched mine. I moved away. I've no shame in admitting it, but it felt like someone had put a couple of electrodes to my balls and right then, a hand hovered over the switch while I braced myself for the moment it got pulled.

'You got some nice tunes, there, Kilo.'

'Glad you like them.'

'Can tell a lot about a man by considering his musical taste,' informed Sweet.

Which is, of course, a total bag of shite.

'It's varied,' she said. 'But there is a consistency, a certain pattern to it. It's mostly safe, apolitical and popular.'

Maybe there was something to that after all. My taste in music reflected the way my mind worked. Sweet didn't want no Public Enemy listening politically aware activist working with him because that person could be unpredictable, intelligent and, I suppose, a potential threat. Someone who listened to any old meaningless pop shit, now that presented a different proposition. Someone like that was too busy thinking about meaningless things to ever present a threat.

'No serious rhymes, then?' he asked.

'Usual,' she called back, still looking into me, looking for some sign of weakness, perhaps. 'You know, Public Enemy, Tupac, some Jungle, some House. All that shit.'

'I don't get this,' I said. 'What is this?'

'Relax, man,' said Sweet. 'Like I said, you can know a lot about a man by looking at the CDs he has.

'Listen,' I said, looking over her shoulder, at Sweet. 'This is all interesting enough but what's the gig here?'

'Chill out, man,' called Sweet and made a peace sign with his fingers. 'I come in peace.'

'I like this guy,' she said, saying it as if she meant it.

'Good,' said Sweet. 'I think I might like him too.'

'That's nice.'

I let out one of those little nervous laughs, the ones that tried to hide a lie but didn't. Still, did seem a bit silly, all this *weird/freaky gangster* bullshit. Straight out of a fucked up movie about super villains and their super fucked up broads. That's the part she seemed to be playing. A weird, melodramatic but entirely fictive broad.

'You should feel flattered,' said his woman. 'There's not many people we both like.'

She grabbed my head, turned it and forced me to look at her.

'Do you think you could grow to like someone like me?'

'Sure,' I said.

'Do you think,' she smiled, 'do you think you could handle me?'

I didn't reply. In truth, I didn't think I could handle the thought of her, let alone anything else. You'd have to be a sex dynamo to take on this kind of woman. That ruled out 99% of the male population, then.

'Okay,' said Sweet. 'That's enough kidding around.'

And just like that, she did an about turn and walked back. Sweet laughed as she practically jumped in his lap.

'So, Kilo,' said Sweet again. 'How about you and me working together, bro?'

Bro? Bro?! Fucking *bro*? This was not right. No way could it be that a person with such a bad bastard rep could be so chilled, so easy and so…so fucking nice. This had to be a trap. Something was rotten in the state of Kilo's pad and that's all there was to it.

'Erm…'

'Erm? That's not the answer I want to hear,' he smiled.

'I don't know. I need to think about it.'

'Think about it? What's to think about? Why work for that fat fuck?'

'Choudhuri? Why not work for him?'

'Are you trying to hurt my feelings, Kilo? Is that what it is?'

'Course not.'

'You don't know him. You don't know what he's capable of.'

But I did. I knew he killed King, and I knew he did it in cold blood. The worst thing of all? King was a victim of Choudhuri's making.

'Maybe you should tell me,' I replied.

So here's the low down. The making, if you like, of Sweet. Real name Shahid Hussain. Like myself, the second generation son of a first generation migrant. Unlike myself, Shahid had been a bad boy since the beginning. In and out of trouble since his early teens. Undertaken robberies, muggings, car crime before finally settling on the most lucrative criminal industry going. Didn't take long for Choudhuri to notice this guy, the way he took care of business, got things done. A natural. Within no time at all, Choudhuri had taken Sweet under his wing and made him a wholesale supplier; another one of several Kings but this guy was the best but also the worst. His ruthlessness made him stand out. Sweet ran a tight ship and couldn't bring himself to cut his customers an inch of slack. And those who tried to take advantage, or simply rip him off, would find a butcher's cleaver heading their way which meant Sweet would simply have to make another visit to the tattoo parlour. So far, he'd killed four people. Rumour had it that he'd killed even more for strictly personal reasons, whatever they would be. Clearly, I had to tread carefully with this guy, no matter how nice he appeared to be.

'Threat?' I asked. 'What kind of threat?'

'Thing is, bro, Choudhuri don't understand the likes of me. For that matter, he don't understand the likes of you, either. Actually expected me to be one of his wholesalers and stay that way for the rest of my life. Like he owned me or something.'

We're all dealers, I told myself and as such, we think we own our punters. Trouble is, once you start climbing, a thing called pride starts fucking with you. But then, maybe pride's always there. Certainly had been when Vinny made out that I ran for him. Seemed like such a long time ago and I guess it was. So much had happened. So much had changed. King was still alive and so were lots of other people. Like my father. It felt fucked up, but I couldn't help thinking how things had moved along since he died. Maybe it was just coincidence or maybe it was something about me, something subconscious making things happen.

'Thing is, bro,' continued Sweet. 'Choudhuri never could handle the fact that I was as good as him. I wanted to be at the top. I wanted to be where he was at.'

'His position.'

'That's not what I said. That's not what I said at all. There's lots of room up there, at the top. Plenty of profits to go round but it's those fucks like Choudhuri who wanna keep it all to themselves. I don't know about you, but that ain't right. Where's the spirit of capitalism in that?'

'Maybe this is meant to be a closed market. A monopoly.'

'Maybe it is but that don't make it right. I'm not happy with it and I don't see why a man like you should be happy with it, either.'

'But Choudhuri's Choudhuri. No offence, but like you said, he's the one at the top. He's the one with all the juice. I go with you, and who knows what he'll do.'

'Fuck him,' he dismissed. 'Fuck him, bro. You and me, we can beat that fuck and his joke gorilla.'

'Spanner?'

'Yeah, Spanner. Fuck him. They're nothing and their time's over. Old news – yesterday's news – man. I'm the next big thing. I mean look at me.'

He pushed her off his lap, stood up and turned around for me, flexing his muscles, posing like one of those Mister Universe fellers. One bad bastard. Maybe, I wondered, there was scope for something here.

'Choudhuri's days are numbered. He's growing weaker and I'm grow-ing stronger. The shit I got, I can sell ten times over. I just need a partner to help me source it and move it. You cannot lose. I got people scream-ing for everything under the sun.'

'I dunno,' I said. 'I'd still like to think about it.'

'When are you gonna realise?'

'What?'

'I don't know you but I can tell you one thing.'

'What's that?'

'You and me, we're the same.'

'The same?'

'Slick, talented and we both know the scene. I can sense it in you. You have this desire, this ambition to get what you want and you know what?'

'What?'

'I'm your ticket to it. Work with me and everything you've ever wanted is yours.'

'This sounds familiar,' I said, half smirking, thinking that perhaps Choudhuri and Sweet had been listening to the same Motivational Speaker tapes.

'Nah,' he said. 'What Choudhuri gave you was bullshit. What I'm giving you is the real deal. Why be a slave when you can be your own master?'

I shrugged.

'I don't have to sell you this offer because it sells itself. We're young, gifted and we're hungry. Besides, what's that fat fuck got in common with you? What's he got *for* you? Nothing 'cept a fucked up sidekick who'll do his best to hold you back and fuck you up. And if he doesn't, then Choudhuri will. I know how them people work because I worked under them.'

I understood what he meant and, as it goes, I agreed with him. The only way to get the better of drug dealers like Choudhuri was to simply get rid of them. Deport them, imprison them, kill them. Take them out of the picture. Nothing else cut it.

'You know what I'm talking about. You know what this means and you know you want in on it. Choudhuri and you? Chalk and fucking cheese. You and me? Two peas in the same fucking pod, bro. Two peas.'

Decisions, decisions. Sweet or Choudhuri? Was there a choice? Of course not. No contest, really. Work with Sweet and, sooner or later, take care of Tahir. Work with Choudhuri and be right next to him.

'I'll think about it,' I said after a while.

Sweet shook his head.

'No you won't, but that's cool. Don't say I never gave you the chance.'

With that, they left. For a while, I sat there, going over the meeting moment by moment, analysing Sweet's demeanour from memory. He seemed earnest and, in a fucked up way, he seemed to be on the level with the offer. Maybe I fucked up. Maybe I should have bit his hand off and got to work on Tahir. But no, didn't seem right and I now understand why I thought that way. Sweet was a form of temptation that would have diverted me from doing the things I needed to do. Sure, if I went and worked with Sweet, I might well have got my own back on Tahir but then what? I'd have become wrapped in that whole bad boy drug dealing lifestyle forever and although tempting for some, it no longer appealed to me.

Your options are limited in the rougher ends of town. You can be a junky, a dealer, a resident or, for the especially talented like King, all three. As I drove through, seemed I'd put some distance between myself and those three broad categories. Never had been a junky in the first place, so much more than a dealer and as for resident, I'd been passing through, that's all. A transient.

Things change, some quicker than others. Within no less than a day the world was different and so was I. What I took to be looks and nods of admiration could have actually been resentment from my former peers. If they did begrudge me, then it didn't matter because they were petty and so were their jealousies. They could piss on each other, hurt each other and if they wanted, they could even go kill each other. I didn't care because I'd finally crawled out, made it beyond that festering bucket of lobsters. Out and not enveloped in material possessions but I felt strangely unsure. I was beginning to suffer from a lack of confidence but not in myself. No, this lack of confidence stemmed from the system, not from the people who worked within it.

Dealers, like companies on the stock exchange, need one thing above all else. Not product, not money, not demand or supply but confidence. Confidence can make an industry or it can break the crap out of it. When it comes to dealing in anything of value, confidences rears its pretty little head at least three times:

1). Are you confident that this new invention will sell and therefore make you money? If not, then walk away and stick to working for someone else.

2). Does your customer feel confident enough to actually buy this product? If your customer is unsure, then either think of something else or go back to stacking shelves.

3). Does your product inspire confidence in others to compete? Competition is good and is proof that you are doing something right. Absence of competition indicates absence of confidence.

Confidence, on an individual and then collective basis is really what it all comes down to. If dealers don't have the confidence to trade, then drugs don't get dealt, money does not change hands and, most importantly, profit ceases to be made. This has nothing to do with the consumer, but everything to do with their immediate line of supply. Dealers to you and I.

When King got himself killed, the system experienced an adverse, unintended knock-on effect which resulted in the scarcity of that all important street dealer confidence. Sure, we all knew King had it coming, but no one really expected a guy like Choudhuri to actually go and pull the trigger. What happened next? Well, Choudhuri's other debtors started coughing up in case they were next on his hit list. Choudhuri's public image, his bank balance and his ego got a nice fat boost but, in the long run, Choudhuri stood to lose tens of thousands in shrinking loan sharking profits: the quicker debtors pay up, the smaller the profits. Meanwhile, the dealers on the street got it up the arse harder than ever. Not only did they feel obliged to pay the fat man, they weren't selling a thing. All of this because they lacked the *confidence* to carry. It would pass, though. These things always passed.

I pulled up in an alleyway overlooking Valley Parade. I sat there for a while, listening to some crazy little bastard singing about how crazy and fucked up he was, telling the world how *M'fuckas had forgot about Dre*. Bored with his bitching, I went through my phone messages. The first, from Deaf Jeff, I could barely make out because he spoke the way some of those half-deaf people speak. I got another one, from this desperate sounding turd called Edward, public school loser, who wanted me to help him out 'til his old man sorted his allowance out. I got a message from this woman called Joan who said she wanted to suck my cock, which she would, so long as she got a couple of rocks for her efforts. After that, there were the usual people I dealt to.

I heard the sound of tyres on cobbles and in the rear view mirror, I saw the front of a Mercedes, one of those long vehicles, with the extra doors, the fancy aerial on the boot and the private plate. This kind of vehicle belonged to Wall Street Scumbags, Politician Scumbags and Saudi Arab Millionaire Scumbags. Every now and then, a Gangster Scumbag like Choudhuri would find himself sat in the back of one, from where he'd plan the growth of his empire.

The headlights flashed a couple of times and then a couple of times more. I didn't get out, but I did decide to comply, although in my own time. Then the horn went, the driver's door swung open and out climbed the tall but heavy frame of that shit-eater Tahir.

'Kilo,' said Mister Memory.

'That's me.'

'It's Sal,' he said, nodding at the Merc. 'Sal wants a word.'

'Oh.'

'He's in the back. Just get a move on, right. Haven't got all fuckin' day.'

I took a step but he stood before me, stopping me from moving any further.

'Problem?'

He sucked his lips and then turned away before moving over to the Merc. I joined Choudhuri in the back of the car, cosseted by plush leather and walnut trim.

'How's it going?'

My new boss didn't seem to be in such a good mood. Seemed miserable about something or other.

'Okay,' he began. 'So you wanna tell me?'

'Tell you? Tell you what?'

'What's going on?'

'Going on?'

'There an echo in here?'

'I don't follow.'

Choudhuri edged forwards and tapped his driver heavy on the shoulder.

'Drive. You know where.'

On the way to wherever we were going, Choudhuri seemed lost in thought for a while, perhaps wondering how best to give form to his grievance.

We drove through town and then out, up Leeds Road towards Thornbury, ending in a street just on the outskirts of another one of those council estates with identical houses, except for a few with white, UPVC double glazed windows and matching doors. The street, like all inner city streets, was packed with cars. Kids were running around like a bunch of headless chickens, but when they saw Choudhuri's motor creep into their turf they promptly stopped, suddenly overcome with awe, and stared.

A load of them ran up, smiles on their faces, gawping up at us, a welcome that reminded me of commoners greeting royalty. These kids, however, they saw big men who drove around in big cars which is just what they wanted to see. Most of them would forget us within an hour or so, but some, one or two at the very least, would remember this scene and this experience for the rest of their lives. As fucked up as this may sound, our presence would serve as inspiration. By thirteen, at least a trio of these bright sparks would be moving five pound deals, on the road to greater things. At sixteen, one of the three would be in a young offender's institution, possibly jail proper, whilst another would be cruising around town in a prestige motor of his own. And the third one, well, he'd be snuggled up, nice and tight, in a wooden overcoat, six foot under.

Tahir and Choudhuri walked away from the car, a gang of kids following, like curious but hopeful, awe filled beggars. I wondered if I'd ever been like that and for a while, I convinced myself that I couldn't have been. Brought up better than that. Never had been in awe of anyone, nor had I been so impressed by one single person as to lose sense of myself. I sighed as I acknowledged the truth of the matter, something I'd been suppressing for years. That truth had a name and this was it: Charlie Boy. Charlie Boy Swain. No, not exactly in awe of him, like these young kids, but certainly impressed by his presence. Scared, definitely. Not for nothing that I pissed myself that night in the shop. I hated him, always will hate him. And yet, something similar to but not exactly the same as admiration for the man had been formed within me that day. A terrible thing to admit after so long but perhaps healthier than denying it for the rest of my life.

As I watched those wide eyed kids hover around Choudhuri, Tahir and even myself, I wondered if I'd ever have children of my own. Not a morally good thing to do, I told myself. What balls it would take to think the innocent can be protected in a world where danger lurks at every corner. Men in parks with fictitious puppy dogs, teenage Grand Prix racers on the streets not to mention the hundreds of kids who are sicker than the parents who are supposedly responsible for their misdeeds. And if that's not bad enough, there's all those sickos, just waiting for the right moment to snatch some young kid clean off the street and do what a twisted mind does.

'Make sure you work hard, you kids,' preached Choudhuri, attracting my attention in the process. 'You hear me? Work hard and you'll have a car like this when you grow up.'

Hypocrite. Where did he get off telling these kids what to do? Could have been worse. Sure beat telling them to sell drugs. Irrelevant what he told them because in a few years, these kids would have fathomed Choudhuri's definition of 'work hard' for themselves.

'Yeah,' his goon added. 'Work hard.'

I walked towards them.

'What's here, then?' I asked.

'You'll see,' said Choudhuri.

He put his hand in his pocket and pulled out a stackette of ten pound notes, each one brand new, crisp and still pure. Without giving it a second thought, he started handing out notes to the kids, who by now had gone mental at the prospect of so much money from a stranger. All for doing nothing except being young and impressionable kids. Maybe he saw potential dealers in them. Seeing the money triggered a memory…the shop, my dad, his ethics and his money. That was different; a heaven and earth's worth of difference. His money had been earned. Clean and honest money and yet its influence and meaning diminished to nothing once I'd witnessed the power of Charlie Boy. I'd been wrong about myself, I realised. Kilo might have been born when King came along, saying a dealer needed to be someone else to the person he used to be but Kilo had actually been conceived years before. The seeds of Kilo, I realised, were sowed by Charlie Boy.

'There's enough for everyone,' said Choudhuri, beaming. 'Wait your turn and you'll all get one.'

The kids didn't stop with the fuss but Choudhuri didn't mind. Matter of fact, he seemed to be relishing so much attention. It could have been some new teen idol and a load of his teenybopper fans, not King Choudhuri and a selection of potentially loyal subjects. That's what it meant for him. This whole thing was a public relations exercise but instead of kissing the babies, he pulled out his wad and one by one, he bought them. A much easier and much more effective strategy.

Like a healer, Choudhuri started to move among them, one by one, placing the healing paper in hands that would, in time, be handing that money right back, but thousands of times over.

'See? If you wait, you'll get some.'

I felt sickened but not entirely surprised that a man would do such a thing. He was, after all, a ruthless man and by nature ruthless men did ruthless things including recruiting and corrupting the innocent. Morality didn't enter into these things because profit, whether illicit or not, towers above everything.

'Kids,' he said, turning to Tahir. 'I love 'em.'

More kids had suddenly appeared and got in line, holding their hands up, needing to be felt, blessed and graced by his touch. One kid, however, stopped himself and appeared thoughtful. Too shy, perhaps too embarrassed to hold his hand up and make like the rest of his little friends. As I watched him, he looked up at me and for a while we held each other's gaze. Seeing something of ourselves, reflections, of sorts.

'C'mere.'

He looked around and then trundled over, not looking too happy about something. I crouched down, my eyes and his at the same level.

'You want some of that money?'

He shrugged.

'You do, don't you?'

He shrugged again.

'I'll tell you a little secret,' I half smiled. 'That isn't real money.'

'It is.'

'It's not. It's like joke money. You know, like pretend money.'

His forehead tightened in concentration.

'How would you know?'

'Because that man,' I said, flicking my head at Choudhuri, 'he likes to play these jokes on people.'

'It looks real to me,' he said, not believing this bollocks of mine for one second.

I felt bad for the kid, who must have been torn between asking and not asking for money. Still, at least this one seemed to have stopped and thought about it which was some consolation. Perhaps he was naturally paranoid and suspicious. Or maybe his parents, like my own, had brought him up not to accept a single thing from strangers.

Choudhuri looked at me, at the kid, and then walked over.

'What have we here?' he said, smiling at him.

'Just talking,' I said.

Choudhuri revealed his hands first to me and then the kid. Empty.

'Missed out, kid. Sorry but I got nothing left.'

The kid smiled bravely.

'It's okay,' he said. 'Didn't want it anyway.'

'You didn't? And why's that?'

'Not real money.'

I found myself smiling. That told the fat fuck.

'It's not?'

Choudhuri looked down the street, at the other kids who were now running, most likely towards the shops.

'Well, your friends seem to think it is.'

Sick bastard, getting off giving a kid this kind of grief. I could have knocked his fat fucking block off for that. Instead, and I don't know why, I pulled out my own wad and peeled off a twenty.

'Here you go, kid,' I said. 'Don't spend it all at once.'

He stayed still, not even looking at it but instead staring at me.

'Seems like we got a kid who doesn't understand the value of money,' said Choudhuri.

He understood, better than Choudhuri or me. The way I read it, that kid didn't sell himself out to anyone and who knows, maybe he never would.

'I think we're the ones who don't understand.'

The kid smiled, only at me, and then ran off. I figured him to be either one of those gifted, blessed kids or one of those weird kids who had no idea of the world around him. Whichever way round he was, I hoped he stayed that way.

'Look at the balls on that kid,' said Choudhuri.

'Balls?'

'Yeah. Takes balls to snub a twenty like that.'

Could have been intuition, just knowing the difference between right and wrong. If a kid can get it right, I told myself, then what the fuck had been stopping me for so long?

'So? What's here?'

Choudhuri flicked his head at a door on which the number 15 had been aerosol-ed. High class neighbourhood.

'Come on in,' he said, walking towards the door. 'Something you shouldn't miss.'

In we went, Tahir first, Choudhuri next and finally me. Just as rough on the inside as the outside intimated. No carpet down on the dirty, rough and scrappy wooden floor. A horrible, scratched up coffee table in the middle, a settee against one wall, pile of red bricks against another and a small chest of drawers by the window. Where the fireplace should have been, there sat a scummy old portable gas fire. I looked around, trying to find something pleasant to view but no dice. The walls covered in graffiti, piss, shit and fuck knows what else, a dirty old light-bulb dangling from the ceiling, the cord all covered in a sticky combination of cobwebs, dust and nicotine. The cleanest thing in the room, however, turned out to be an aluminium ladder, twelve rungs in all, maybe ten foot high.

On the settee, there lay a living being. Asian, skinny, small and the seediest man I've seen in my life. About forty years of age and, like his surroundings, rougher than this own stubble. String vest, tatty old checked trousers, nothing on his feet except dirt. Needed a shave, a comb and something drastic to be done about those huge toenails. Obviously, personal hygiene wasn't the highest priority for this guy.

Choudhuri clapped his hands together, startling the string vested carrier of disease into action. At the same time, I heard a sound come from underneath us, from under the floorboards. To me, it sounded like the rattling of a chain. A dog in the cellar, I presumed.

He greeted Choudhuri with an almost Japanese bow and called him *Janaab*, Mister Big Deal, in other words. Choudhuri didn't shake his hand but he did smile.

'So,' said Choudhuri. 'Tell me, *Raakhee Kuthaa*, what's happening?'

The handle translates as Guard Dog, an insult as far as most people are concerned, but that fucking creep in the vest, he seemed to get off by being called it.

'Janaab,' he said. 'I'm here, doing as you ask.'

'And how is our guest?'

'Alive,' smiled R K. 'Last time I looked he was living.'

Choudhuri nodded.

'Where's the torch?'

R K nodded eagerly, before mooching over to the chest of drawers. He took out a heavy duty torch, switched it on and then, like a jackass, smiled at us all.

'Working.'

'Show us,' said Choudhuri, plainly.

R K appeared a little disappointed with that.

'Some tea? Something to drink first?' he offered.

Choudhuri looked around the room and shook his head.

'You think I'm mad? Hurry up. Just show us. Quickly pen chode.'

R K nodded eagerly and then briskly padded into the middle of the room and lifted up a trap door. He pointed the torch down, into the cellar. Choudhuri peered in and then looked at me. He smiled.

'I said I had something to show you.'

I looked into the hole. There, at the bottom, directly beneath us, cowered a fully grown man. In that strange, unnatural but frank electric torchlight, he seemed to be shivering but that, I reasoned, was due to being naked. He lifted his head up, at the light and then shielded his eyes, his shackles rattling uncomfortably. I felt sick.

'What the fuck…'

'Some people,' Choudhuri said. 'They need to be shown a thing or two, you know?'

The captive groaned. Well, not groaned, but cried. This wasn't just about the guy in the cellar, but about me also. This had implications on me, on my life. This was Choudhuri's way of showing me his consistency, that killing King was not a one off. Choudhuri was a bad bastard full time.

I swallowed.

'What is this? Who is that guy?'

'That's not important right now.'

'This isn't right. This is sick.'

Choudhuri seemed pleased with himself.

'And there was me, thinking you were a tough one.'

What kind of maniac had I got myself mixed up with? I thought I knew but I was wrong. Way off the mark.

'Look, why are you showing me this? What's this got to do with me?'

'I don't like to fuck around,' said Choudhuri, the big hard man. 'People like you, you need to see before you believe.'

'Like I need convincing? After what you did to King?'

'That was nothing. That was business. This is pleasure.'

Tahir laughed and nodded knowingly.

'But,' I began. 'But you can't keep a man down there like that. It's inhuman, it's sick.'

Maybe it was me who got it wrong. Maybe I wasn't ready for this kind of thing because for these three fucks – Choudhuri, Tahir and R K – there was absolutely no problem here. Nothing to make a fuss about. Just a way of dealing with people. Another aspect of life you lived with once you got into the gangster business.

'Well,' said Choudhuri, nudging Tahir. 'Maybe it's about to get sicker.'

The guy in the cellar let out another pained, pathetic little cry.

'I don't want to be a part of this,' I found myself saying, the smell of excrement and urine having drifted upward, slowly filling R K's room.

'I hear you had visitors last night.'

Sweet and his woman.

'I didn't think it was important,' I began.

Choudhuri nodded.

'So what did he want?'

'He…he offered me a job…you know.'

'And? What did you say?'

I caught Tahir watching me like a hawk.

'What do you think I said? Told him I work for you.'

'That's good to hear.'

Choudhuri seemed assured but he wasn't. A man like him wouldn't trust his own mother, let alone some dirtbag he'd known for a few days.

'But let me tell you,' he continued. 'If you're lying and you think you can get away with it, then you're mistaken. I will find out. I didn't get where I am by getting duped by guys like you. I catch wind of anything funny – and I mean any-fucking-thing – then it'll be you in that hole down there. You understand me, Kilo?'

'I understand,' I said, wondering how long the guy in the dungeon had been shackled and what he'd done to get there in the first place.

Choudhuri nodded.

'Good,' he said and then set about telling me the real deal with the guy in the cellar. 'See that guy down there?'

I looked down again. I saw him, just about. On his haunches, hugging himself to keep warm, the smell of shit not mattering to him one jot. I wondered what crime could he have committed to deserve this. What low life son of a bitch child molesting pervert got this sort of treatment as punishment?

'I see him,' I said. 'What's he done?'

'Done? You wanna know what he's done?'

I decided I didn't want to know after all. Choudhuri must have sensed it because he smiled and then told me. The man in the cellar was rumoured, only rumoured mind, to have given up some information to the filth.

'I hope that's the difference between you and him, Kilo. You kept your mouth shut but he didn't. And now look where we are. One's standing next to me and the other's living in a hole.'

I looked at Choudhuri in disbelief.

'What if it's not true? What if it's some other cunt?'

Choudhuri shrugged.

'Better safe than sorry.'

'I don't believe this.'

'You know what your trouble is, Kilo,' Choudhuri said, then took aim and spat down the hole. 'You're too confused.'

'Too confused?'

'Sure,' he said. 'Now everybody needs some confusion. A little bit of confusion is good – healthy – but guys like you, you take it to the extreme. You're never prepared to simply accept that things like decency and morality have different meanings to guys like us. Now you might think what I'm doing is wrong, morally speaking, but that's where you'd be mistaken and you wanna know why?'

I said nothing but he continued.

'I'll tell you why: it's because the idea of wrong has a much narrower definition as far as we're concerned. For guys like me and you, it's much harder to be wrong, but when someone does do something wrong, then it's *really* fucking wrong. You understand that much and you'll do fine.'

I remembered King advising me in a similar vein, about becoming someone else in order to succeed. Well, I had changed. And lo and behold, I'd moved up the ladder but was there a causal link? Did my changing facilitate any upward mobility? Even if it didn't, it still felt wrong, being here, in this place where I now stood.

Choudhuri turned away from me and told his guard dog to seal the door back up. R K said he needed to feed the prisoner to which Choudhuri nodded assent. R K padded into another room and came out a few seconds later. In one hand, he had two slices of stale, bone dry bread, and in the other, a small plastic bottle, half filled with dirty looking water. He threw it all down, into the hole. The captive yelped because the bottle hit him on the head. R K, the sick old bastard, laughed and then called:

'Room service, pen chode!'

Choudhuri laughed as did Tahir. R K slammed the door down and repeated his curse. Animals weren't treated this bad. Choudhuri the sick fuck, I felt sure he'd burn in hell for this. Not that I was some saint, far from it. Peddling drugs out of a car might have been one thing but this shit was on a completely different level. Still, distasteful as it may have been, I was not about to let it get to me. I was not about to give everything up because of some poor fuck stuck in the dungeon.

Tahir breathed a huge sigh of relief when Choudhuri handed over the book of names he'd taken from King. Just about the only thing that will part a wholesaler from his book of names is death, not money and certainly not a generous nature.

The terms Choudhuri offered were good and bad. The profit margins were immense but the downside was of a non-negotiable nature: one week's grace for payment and fuck you very much for your trouble. Once again, he insisted on lacing the deal with a clear and simple threat. If I did something funny, even if I thought about doing something funny, then he would track me down and kill me. Before he killed me, he'd stick me in a cellar and get his guard dog to feed me two slices of bread and half a bottle of dirty water once a day. Only when he got substantially bored with that would he put me out of my misery. I did believe him which is why I quickly dropped the idea of selling his dope and then running like a bastard.

They said they'd be in touch soon. I couldn't wait.

double barrel

I saw a ghost that night. Wiped from memory, made dead and to all intents and purposes, he might as well have been. But he lived. He'd been resting, asleep, a dormant part of my lie. Like Tahir, he'd always been in there but I'd closed him off, shut him away so that his significance – his being – no longer fucked with my mind. If he hadn't turned up, then in truth, I do believe I'd have lived the rest of my life without thinking of him again. That night, however, destiny presented him. Charlie Boy Swain. Once again I failed to deal with him. No matter. He was on the scene and it was just a question of time.

Tahir called.

'Manningham Park,' he said. 'Side entrance, by the tennis courts. Half hour.'

That first delivery came as something of a shock. From the boot of Choudhuri's Merc, Tahir took out a couple of pizza boxes and handed them over to me. I sat in my car, and then, with Tahir watching, I checked them out. Six bags of cocaine, each weighing a round five hundred grams. At fifty quid a gram, I had damned near a hundred and fifty thousand notes in my hands. And then there was the heroin which amounted to the same figure, more or less. This was the surplus that had built up during the lean spell which Choudhuri himself had inadvertently enforced after offing King. Not that it mattered where it came from because I couldn't get rid of it in a week even if I started sprinkling it on my cornflakes. This much product could not be moved in Bradford.

'So? So what's the score?'

'Score? No score: you got a week,' he said as he walked back to Choudhuri's wheels.

I started the car up.

'Nearly forgot,' said Tahir, stopping and then turning back to face me. 'Sal's throwing a party. Tonight. He wants you to be there.'

'I'm not into parties, man.'

'Wanna bet?'

'What am I supposed to do? Sell this shit or party?'

'You do as Sal says. Understand?'

'Fuck.'

'Bring some friends, if you got any.'

Cowboy was no genius, but then it didn't take one to say:

'You're fucked, partner.'

No way could he see anyone shifting so much gear in the space of seven days. Seven days? Seven weeks was more like it. He sounded keen about the party, though. I wish I hadn't invited him. At the time, I thought the change of scenery would do him good.

I realised I needed a female hanging off my arm. Could not attend a party with another male, could I? That would be just so...suspicious. So who better than Rose? I mentioned it to her soon after I left Cowboy to his dealings. I wished I never mentioned it because she practically wet her knickers over the prospect, going on and on and fucking *on* about what to wear, how to wear it and whether or not a visit to her beauty salon was in order. I told her she could do what she wanted but she had to be ready in time for me to pick her up. Cowboy, thankfully, said he'd make his own way over.

Choudhuri held his parties in a large function room of one of his less busy restaurants. Choudhuri's parties, without doubt, were of the shittest kind, and long may they rest in peace with him. Choudhuri threw parties that became legendary because they were so bad. Turned out he had a party in honour of himself or some other jumped up wanker almost every week. The same people always in attendance, the same food, drinks and the same vibes. Such details didn't matter one iota, neither to him nor his lousy guests. Parties were important because they gave him the opportunity to show all his cronies how big and powerful he felt and, I guess, they also gave him the illusion of being loved, or at the very least liked.

As we walked in, Rose and I heard the music playing. It sounded like music, but not a soul had been emotionally moved enough to dance. Strictly for the less active, Choudhuri's parties. Slower, quieter and a whole lot more reserved than the parties I'd been to in the past. In a corner, he had one of those lounge bands which consisted of four guys in hired-out tuxedos, performing easy listening loungey versions of songs like *Crocodile Rock*, *Let's Dance*, *Don't You Want Me Baby* and even hip-hop classics like *The Message* and *Fuck The Police*. Radical was not the word. For that matter, neither was bearable.

As for the guests…well, they were no better, just as shit if not shitter. No other word seems to cut it, sadly. I looked around and saw people who were simply shit at being party guests. The men wore tacky Burton's suits, polished up shoes and crept around like a park full of flashers. Not many came with their wives because this kind of thing wasn't really for the little lady indoors. The women that had been dragged along were young, invariably blonde with nice tits and even better legs. Bits-on-the-side, those women. LBDs, too much make-up and cheap fake jewellery. The men talked with other men, about business and about money. The slappers cackled about the married man; how best to get him off and how best to bleed him dry.

On the tables in the middle of the room, there stood bottles of wine, juice and a range of expensive Czechoslovakian beers with unpronounceable names. People filed by, filled up and fucked off along to the next table where nasty looking morsels sat on silver platters, which, by and large, were ignored because they looked like various forms of animal shit, and, I assume, tasted even worse.

'Well,' said Rose. 'You sure know how to show a girl a good time. When you said party, I had no idea it was something so wild.'

'We can go somewhere else, if you want,' I said.

'We'll stay for a while. Shame coming all this way just to leave.'

I picked my way through the sea of fat businessmen and their dumb blondes and got to Choudhuri. Fat boy seemed happy. I smiled, only because it looked like he'd soaked his toupee in lacquer; all shiny and shit.

'Kilo,' he said. 'Didn't think you'd make it.'

Without doubt this man was either cursed or blessed with a split personality. Earlier on the son of a bitch came across like he hated the sight of me but now he was so different, practically the opposite. Anyone would have thought we were a couple of old mates the way he carried on.

'I was told I had to come.'

He winked at me and said:

'That's just Spanner being a prick. Pay no attention to him.'

'That include the one week turnaround?'

He nodded and then wagged a forefinger at my face.

'A week's enough time. You'll just have to widen your horizons and be innovative. Sell out of town, make some new contacts or something. You can do it. A guy like you with your talent is sure to come up with something special.'

That's when it hit me. Choudhuri was fucking with me. Not fucking with me as in winding me up but just seeing how far he could screw me. A hundred and fifty grand's worth of dope in a week? Why give me that kind of deal when he knew damn well it was an impossible deal to fulfill? There simply weren't enough hours in the day for me to move that much, not so soon, not without an already well established network. The answer, then, was obvious. He was setting me up to take a fall. The question, of course, was why? Maybe, I reasoned, he was simply being a cunt for the sake of being a cunt. Maybe this is what a split personality does to people.

'You see him there?' he said, his eyes fixed on this grey haired but not too old guy, one of those refined looking types. 'He's a lawyer, a barrister. A QC if you really wanna know. Works down south.'

He went through his elites like a roll call. All sorts of high powered movers including lawyers, doctors, professors, judges and yes, I even caught sight of a politician or two, no doubt spreading the word about some new way or other that was in fact a rehashed old way with a new name. Rose seemed to be getting on okay, mingling with strangers. Choudhuri couldn't take his eyes off her.

'See you brought some company,' he said with a nudge. 'Looks tasty.'

'Rose?'

'Yeah,' he said. 'You and her…?'

Choudhuri pursed his lips, raised his eyebrows a couple of times and then wiggled his tongue.

'You screwing her?'

'What if I am?'

Choudhuri nodded.

'She's nice. Good enough to screw.'

Choudhuri might have wanted her but she wasn't his type…her eyes worked just fine – 20/20 vision – which put a big fat ugly old turd

229

like Choudhuri out of the picture fairly quickly.

He lifted a glass of red wine to his lips and took a small drink, looking around as he did so.

'Who's that guy? I never invited him,' he said, catching sight of Cowboy who'd just ambled in.

'He's with me. Spanner said I could bring some guests. Is that a problem?'

'Oh no,' said Choudhuri. 'I just wondered who the guy is, that's all. He a friend of yours, then?'

'Yeah. A friend.'

'He looks funny. Them clothes…that hat, I mean.'

'I know but that's just the way he is.'

'Looks like a weirdo…'

'He's alright.'

The fat man shrugged and then, in order to keep this already dying conversation resuscitated, told me that:

'Soofi's here,' with a flick of his head. 'There, over there.'

I looked and in a corner and alone sat the little guy.

'He don't like these things. It's the booze and the women. Has a moral… what you might call a philosophical problem with that. Soofi's one of those religious types, you know.'

'Oh,' I said, beginning to wonder whether or not this was indeed a philosophical problem. 'I see. I'll say hello maybe.'

'Yeah, go ahead. Miserable prick could do with the company.'

Before getting to the little guy, I copped for Cowboy who was not impressed with this little shindig. Well he was and he wasn't. He digged Choudhuri's opulent surroundings and he certainly enjoyed the women who seemed to enjoy the novelty of him. Like myself, Cowboy thought the party was too slow even for snails.

'Seen more life at a fucking funeral, partner,' he complained.

'We don't have to stick around too long.'

'I don't know,' he mused. 'Kinda interesting, though. You know…'

Cowboy headed off to a corner where he saw two women standing next to each other, in conversation but giving him the eye all the while. I headed off towards the little guy who only seemed to notice me when I'd sat down right next to him.

'So you don't like these things.'

'These things,' he began. 'They're not right.'

I understood, sort of. For a guy like him, being around booze and loose women is a major no-no. Being part of a drugs gang, however, well, that's a different story.

'So you've never drank.'

Soofi touched his ear lobes and shook his head.

'God willing, I never will.'

'What about drugs?' I asked, thinking that perhaps he might have been a bit of a rogue in his younger days. 'You ever done any drugs?'

Again, he touched his lobes, shook his head. Life and soul of the party. What a mistake, a tragic one at that, this so called party was turning out to be.

I looked around some more and, because I had nothing better to do, found myself sizing up the company once again. All those other crooked people present were unlike me because they were not open with themselves about their criminality. These fuckers? More bent than a U-turn but they just couldn't bring themselves to admit it. Businessmen who set light to their buildings for the insurance pay off. Others specialising in setting up bogus firms only to draw funds and then go bankrupt as soon as they'd screwed the arse off a worthwhile overdraft facility. Some took out a load of juicy fat loans, never to be repaid. Slum kings rented bedsits that weren't fit for dogs. And these were the very same people who made themselves out to be purer than pure, whiter than white, the best of the best when in truth, they were no better than me. Fuck it, though. We've all got our own graves to worry about.

Surrounded by people, I felt, however, alone. But Rose and especially Cowboy appeared to be getting into it in a big way. A bunch of women had crowded around him and were laughing at his cheesy jokes. Their body language, their facial expressions and even the way they looked at him indicated better, perhaps much more intimate things to come. Likewise, Rose seemed to be enjoying herself, doing okay, not getting bored as she talked to this really tall black guy. About forty, maybe even fifty. He looked pretty fit and healthy for an older man. He saw me approach and smiled to reveal a couple of gold gnashers in amongst the ivory.

'Having fun?'

Rose smiled and turned to face the man.

'This is Doctor Fehintola,' she said. 'He's a plastic surgeon.'

He offered me his hand and I shook it. Didn't feel plastic.

'Pleasure,' I said.

'How are you?' the good doctor smiled. 'Kilo, isn't it?'

I turned to Rose and gave her a cold look.

'Khalil,' I said. 'My name's Khalil.'

'I apologise,' he said, the glint of light reflecting off his teeth damn near blinding me.

'My mistake,' said Rose.

The man with the gift for making plastic look human turned to me.

'You've never had plastic surgery, I take it?'

'You think I need it?'

He laughed politely.

'Nobody needs plastic surgery, my friend. Beauty is a constructed concept.'

And with that, Rose suddenly got interested, like this was some wise old bastard she happened to chance upon.

'Beauty is in the eye of the beholder.'

Myself, I know all about that. No such thing as beauty. Like the man said, beauty is engineered by all those bastards who work in the advertising and fashion industries.

'In my country,' he said, 'a slender woman used to be seen as less desirable than a fat woman. In my country, the aspiration that all young girls would desire was based on size, on fat.'

'And now?'

'Not so now. Sad to say this is yet one more side-effect of globalisation. Now, they all listen to the Pop Group Boy Bands and they all wear the Nike Swoosh sportswear and they are all dieting even though half of them are already under-weight.'

'That's very interesting,' said Rose.

'And where do you fit in?' I asked.

'Over there? In my home country I do very little work. Only the very rich – the extremely rich – can afford to indulge in the services I offer. My personal and philosophical belief is,' he said seriously, as if making some grand declaration. 'That it is only the ugly people – the spiritually ugly people – who wish to make themselves beautiful on the outside.'

'Be careful, doctor,' said Rose. 'That kind of talk could lose you business.'

At last I had her read. She was greasing up to him because she wanted something out of him. The more I heard, the more patently obvious it became that she was hanging on to his every word. I realised why. She was hoping to get the good Doctor Fehintola to work on some part of her; a part which she thought needed working upon. Physically speaking she was faultless and by going under a scalpel, she'd ruin herself. Not my decision, though. If she wanted to get all butchered up, then that was up to her.

'Oh I doubt that, my dear,' he said. 'As long as there are people with ugly insides and plenty of money, I'll stay in business for a long time yet.'

He excused himself and went off to mingle. I turned to Rose.

'Interesting man,' I said. 'That doctor.'

'Yeah. Isn't he just? He's so deep. Some of the things he said…about the people he makes beautiful.'

'Deep,' I repeated, thinking his cuts were anything but.

'I bet he's expensive.'

'Maybe you should have asked him how much it costs.'

'Do you think? I didn't want to seem rude.'

I watched Fehintola get to the other end of the room where Choudhuri greeted him warmly. They shook hands, laughed at something and then nodded their heads at each other. I continued to watch as the doctor whispered something in Choudhuri's ear.

'Maybe we should go,' I said. 'This place is dead.'

I turned and saw her smiling back at Choudhuri and Fehintola. She didn't even know I was there.

'Rose?'

'What?'

She turned to me, still smiling, and put her hand on my arm.

'I like this,' she said. 'It's a bit slow, but I could get used to this sort of thing… given time.'

'Good. I'm glad.'

And off she went, a-mingling, but clearly heading in Fehintola and Choudhuri's direction. I scratched my head, turned and walked towards Cowboy's corner. As I got closer to him, I noticed a new guest enter the room. For a few seconds my mind went blank, just emptied. The next thing I knew, he was within earshot and I could hear him exchanging pleasantries with some old fart with white hair, a red nose and a grey, three piece suit.

The seasons are kind to some and miserable towards others. To him, they'd been more than kind. His face had barely changed, save for the odd wrinkle and worry line. Older, sure, but looking healthier than he did all those years ago. Still the same taut facial structure defined by angles that even a supermodel would envy. Hair neatly trimmed, a departure from the thug-like suede-head look of his youth. A pointed, Roman kind of nose, just a slit for lips and light, but piercing blue eyes. All of this combined to create a face that could be a template in a math's set. As for his attire, he wore a crisp, well-defined suit. Not flashy but not modest.

Two questions entered my mind, one straight after the other. What the hell was he doing here and what was I going to do about it? Being so close to him made me feel uncomfortable, physically sick, so I moved away, back towards Choudhuri, who was now flanked by both Tahir and Soofi. Choudhuri surveyed the room for the fiftieth time, a universe of which he alone was master. Perhaps the Three Stooges would shed some light on the most recent party guest.

'You don't know who that is?' Soofi asked, mystified by my ignorance.

'Gerroutofere,' sneered Tahir. 'What planet have you been on for the last five years?'

'Why? Who is he?'

'Only Colin Padgett.'

'Who?'

'You know, Colin Padgett – fucking MP.'

'Padgett?' I found myself asking. 'MP?'

'There an echo in here?' quipped Tahir.

I didn't get it, not right then but it didn't take too long to seep through. Charlie Boy Swain and Colin Padgett were not a couple of dead ringers for each other. Swain, in order to start a new life, changed his name. How the rest had happened – the MP shit – that was anyone's guess. Still, people do change. Happens all the time. That's what life's all about when it comes right down to it. We grow physically, spiritually and mentally and we call it life.

How fucked was this, I suddenly thought. I'd been a good kid, Swain had been a bastard and now look where we were. I'd gone one way but Charlie Boy, he'd gone the other. I became a drug dealer – a criminal – but Charlie Boy, for some unknown reason, decided to abandon his ways and become a citizen, a decent one at that. One of the best, come to think of it. For all the violence he'd done in his young, despicable life, not one charge was ever brought against him.

No mean feat, such a drastic transformation of character. The first thing, perhaps the most important thing, was to change his name. This he did by deed poll which he left in the hands of a solicitor. Next came the important details. He tidied himself up some, grew his hair to a respectable length, got a surgeon to remove the tattoos, allowed a few months to seal the pierced ears and, of course, spent a fortune on a new wardrobe. Easy enough so far. But next came the tricky part, the changes which involved Charlie Boy's mind and manner. First, a job which he got through a cousin, perhaps a friend of the family. The job involved doing all sorts of menial tasks in a local, family owned DIY store. It seemed right, a fitting and humble beginning for a man destined to go far in life. I could imagine his day. Up and shaved at the crack of dawn, another man at C & A wearing his sports-casual attire. Everywhere he went, he went by bus, always allowing plenty of time in order to arrive on time. Always willing to give a hundred and ten per cent to his employer, his customers; the epitome of conscientiousness, a paragon of virtue. He gave up *The Sun* and instead took to *The Express* or failing that, *The Mail*. Charlie Boy Swain was on his way to becoming Colin Padgett and the funny thing is, nobody of any significance had taken a blind bit of notice.

He started seeing one of the girls who worked the checkout at a local supermarket. Within a year, he'd married her. The happy couple started along their path towards happiness. Kids, security and a half decent knee trembler once every fortnight, twice every time he got a bonus in his pay packet. They got a mortgage with flexible repayment options, lease purchased a Ford Mondeo, had barbies on the patio, caravanning holidays in Skegness and shopping trips to out-of-town complexes which, at that time, were only beginning to sprawl up out-of-(every)town in the land. After a couple of years, during which time key members of staff had been the victims of the most unfortunate of accidents and attacks, he found himself in his first position of real, but honest power. General manager, McMahon's DIY. With the extra money, he bought himself another house which he rented out to students. And then he bought another, then another and another. Fast becoming a respectable businessman, an upstanding member of the community, he eventually bought out the store that had helped him get so far in the first place. And that was it, more or less done: the image he wanted to present complete.

A few years down the line, Colin Padgett could afford to relax. The numerous businesses he now owned were practically running themselves and so, the time to instigate a new phase in his life seemed to have arrived. With more time on his hands, he decided to become civic minded. He put himself forward as a parent governor at the school his two children attended. Next, after considerable pressure from friends, he gave in and joined the Conservative Party of Great Britain. A year later, he stood at the local elections and, without too much ceremony or surprise, he got in. No one suspected a thing because there was nothing to suspect. He was the local boy done good and everyone who knew him loved him for it.

The leap from councillor to MP was just as easy only he made it in another town. Maybe it's because Bradford's a shithole or maybe it's because such a high profile position was too risky a proposition to undertake for someone with such a colourful past. Either way, and with the blessing of Tory Central Office, he relocated to some place in Surrey which, as it goes, suited a man of his stature right down to the ground. As fate would have it he turned out to be one of the few success stories for the Tories in the 1997 General Election. Colin Padgett, however, took all this without fanfare and insisted his success was more of a reflection on his party, not himself. He had not decided to devote himself to the field of politics for his own selfish reasons. As a successful businessman, he felt he owed something to the British Nation, of which he was so proud.

Pure bollocks, of course. Power manifests itself in a whole host of different ways, but the seed of it, the desire for it, is only within certain abnormal people. If such desire is within us all, then we'd all be at it, trying to be politicians, ultimately aspiring to be leaders of other leaders. Think about it. You've got to have some seriously scrambled eggs, an ego the size of an elephant, to actually think you're wise, competent and charismatic enough to be trusted by people you've never even met. Politicians, they might like to think they're virtuous, civic minded and morally sound people. Truth is they're egomaniacs. Choudhuri thought something similar, too.

'Politicians are the worst kind of people in the world,' he said.

'Oh?'

'Not Colin, though,' said Tahir, not able or perhaps not willing to stop himself from sticking up for his old running mate.

'Especially Colin.'

'Why's that?' I ventured.

Before Choudhuri could answer, I noticed Swain, Padgett, or whatever the fuck he wanted to call himself, heading our way. I didn't feel like sticking around. Who knows what I'd do once I started dwelling on him and what he'd done to me.

'I'll be off,' I said.

'No,' Choudhuri insisted. 'Stick around. I'll introduce you to Padgett.'

Swain shook hands with the others while I looked the other way, pretending to be distracted, dreading the moment his hand touched mine through the ritual of greeting.

'Kilo,' I heard Choudhuri call.

I turned around. Swain holding his hand out for me to shake seemed so wrong. I looked at it for a long while, recalling how it stank of tobacco smoke back then.

'Hello?' I heard a voice say.

I shook myself out of it and then gripped his hand.

'How you doing, Son? You alright?'

Son. He called me Son. That felt absurd as well as wrong. I managed to stop myself from looking at him even though hate began to swell inside of me. It took a lot for me to stay there, quiet, biting my tongue in half. It wasn't a question of wanting to be someplace else any more. I *needed* to be gone from here, for my own sake as much as Swain's.

'I have to be going,' I tried again.

'Oh dear,' said Swain. 'Hope it wasn't something I said.'

'I got work to do.'

'Nightshift, eh?' he laughed. 'Must be in the blood.'

''Scuse me?'

'You know, working nights…comes natural to your people.'

Tahir smiled but neither Choudhuri nor Soofi seemed to find the joke to their taste.

'You mean like not working at all seems to be natural for your people? Is that what you mean?'

He took a step back, partly offended, partly apologetic.

'No need to be like that.'

'Yeah,' said Tahir. 'Col's only joking like.'

Rose had been working her way over to our end of the room. I wanted her stay the fuck where she was but she had a mind of her own, that one. I really wished I'd come alone and had fucked off five minutes after arriving. Seeing and then crossing swords with this blast from the past was the last thing I needed. I could have been doing a hundred other things better than this. For a start, I could have been making that mountain of Choudhuri's dope a little smaller.

'Stick around, Kilo,' said Choudhuri.

'Yeah,' agreed Tahir, watching Rose as she got closer. 'You could introduce us to this piece of yours.'

Rose smiled at them but her gaze settled on Swain.

'This is Rose,' I told them all.

Choudhuri looked at me and made a couple of expressions, prompting me to fill in the blanks.

'This is Saleem Choudhuri.'

'Call me Sal,' said the fat fuck, taking her hand, slavering all over it.

'This is Tahir.'

'Spanner,' he corrected as he shook her hand.

'And this,' I began, suddenly needing to clear my throat. 'This is…'

'Oh, I know who you are,' she interrupted, giving him that same fuck me look she'd given me a few days before.

'Do you now?'

'You're an MP. Sorry, but I don't know your name.'

'Padgett,' he said. 'Colin Padgett. Call me Colin.'

'Pleasure,' she cooed and gave him one of those silly, dippy-bird curtsies. 'Colin.'

'The pleasure's all mine, Rose.'

And then he did it. He held on to her hand with both his and I could see her melt. It wasn't the smell of his aftershave, it wasn't his looks and hell, it wasn't even personality that did it. In a word, it was power. That's what really lit Rose's wick; the one thing that made her juices flow. He guided her along, asking her if she wanted him to introduce her to some interesting people. I felt like an idiot, standing there, watching my woman get hijacked.

'That guy,' Tahir moaned. 'That guy knows how to impress the women.'

'And the men,' said Choudhuri with a laugh.

'Thought you wanted to go,' said Tahir, rubbing it in.

I caught up with Rose. By now, Swain had his arm around her waist, squeezing, feeling and slightly massaging it. She didn't mind one little bit, the dirty, power hungry bitch. I suppose that ended our relationship, what there'd been of it. I wasn't upset about losing her because I never really had her in the first place. But I was on the verge of being driven insane by the whole fucked-up-ness of it all.

'Rose?'

Too engrossed with whatever Swain was saying to notice me. I tapped her on the back.

'Rose?'

She turned around and so did Swain.

'I'm leaving…'

'The party's just begun,' Swain said, now speaking for her, doing what he was supposed to do, being her representative. Should have saved that shit for Parliament.

'I'm talking to her.'

'Erm,' she began. 'I think I'll stay for a while. I'll get a cab home…I'll call you.'

I got in my car and just sat there, a barrage of emotions and desires washing over me: anger, confusion, hatred, jealousy, revenge and on the list went. This was so wrong and so was my calm, rather English reaction to it. What else could I have done in that situation? Tried choking him with one of those Ferrero Rocher chocolate balls? Could I have stood up to him and told him to stay the fuck away from her? No. I couldn't do a thing because I was a coward. Not only that, and just like my old man, I was a failure.

Thing is, like many times before, I'd been deluding myself. I'd imagined him to be dead, or just gone, wiped from existence, for so many years but here he was, back in my life. I always told myself that if and when I ever saw him again, I'd end his time on earth; with my bare hands if nothing else. And what had I done? Bottled it. But as I sat in my car, mulling it all over, I realised I still wanted to do something to make things right which meant I hadn't failed at all. Seeing him there – still alive and still in my universe – was not a bad thing or even a thing to be feared. This was a good thing. A chance to make everything alright again.

When I knew no better, when still young and relatively innocent, much of my life revolved around him, the father who by rights should still be alive. When I was young, my dad and that shop of his meant as much to me as it did to him. As an adolescent I started to deny it but there'd been times when I allowed myself to dream of standing behind a counter full of sweets, ringing the till open and shut every single minute of that sixteen-hour shift. As stupid as it sounds, I wanted to be like him in every respect and that includes taking shit from ignorant arseholes, convinced they were being robbed blind. I wanted to drive a knackered old Mazda estate, wear a grey nylon work coat and I wanted to make deals with shady looking travelling salesmen who'd nearly always end up ripping me off. Before too much wisdom filtered into my life, the father I grew to resent was my hero. The only one I've ever had.

My father. A nobody who struggled all his life. But so what? There was a certain honour, a certain strength to him and the way he chose to live his life. Always putting everything he had on the mere hope that one day happiness would find him.

After leaving Choudhuri's party, I drove straight home and lay on top of my bed, just getting my thoughts together, working things out, allowing my mind to run free. It was about then when Cowboy rang. Must have been some time around eleven. He filled me in with the bits I'd missed.

As I suspected, I didn't see much of him because he scored some pussy. One of the women he got to know sneaked off with him and spent a bit of time in the back of his car. However, as he and his short term lover shared a post-fuck cigarette, he saw Rose leave the party. Only she wasn't alone. Not such a big surprise with the way she'd been carrying on.

'What?' said Cowboy. 'That's not how it looked to me.'

'Oh?' I asked. 'How'd it look?'

'Well, she wasn't willing, you know?'

'Willing? Willing about what?'

'Spanner was dragging her into the back of this big motor.'

'Choudhuri's?'

'Nah. Might have been a Bentley or a Rolls; all look the same to me those things. So anyway, I got out and asked her if she was alright. Spanner, he tells me to go fuck myself.'

'You do not wanna get on the wrong side of that bastard.'

'Say that again.'

So Cowboy watched as the car screeched off. I said I'd ring Rose to make sure everything was alright but on second thoughts, I decided not to: she should not have thrown herself around like that.

Cowboy, meanwhile, had left the party and was heading back into the neighbourhood to make himself some money. I said I'd see him later.

At some point, I must have nodded off. I only know that because I dreamt that night.

I found myself shopping in a supermarket. Totally alone, not even a shelf stacker cared to make an appearance. I wandered around, looking at items, occasionally reading ingredients and getting bored.

The dream switched to another location. In a hospital. I could hear mothers screaming their throats off as they gave birth and then there came much fresher, much stranger and healthier rasps that belonged to new born infants.

A baby lay in my arms. New born, naked and blue. It shivered, I held it close yet it felt warm. I looked into its eyes but got no response. Still blind to world, to the horrors that await. So beautiful this child, a he, I decided.

In my dream, I continued staring into him, a smile on my face which was strange considering I'd never actually held a child in real life.

The dream moved on, forward in time and to another place. The child had grown older and stood a couple of inches above my waist. We were walking, to where I don't know, and he held onto my hand, just as tightly as the first time he felt the instinct. He looked up at me and asked the strangest thing:

'What's my name?'

His name? How did I know?

I woke up, rubbing my eyes but thinking about the dream all the while. The light sneaking in hurt my eyes. I looked at the clock which showed half past five, the same time my dad used to get up for the shop.

For an instant, fear overcame me as I heard a noise in the hall. I got up, grabbed my trusty baseball bat from under the bed and sneaked towards the door. In he walked, the child from my dream. He rubbed his eyes and crawled onto the bed.

'I had a dream,' he said, half putting it on, the way kids do.

He sat next to me. I smiled, looked him in the eyes and through those two beautiful gateways, further yet in time I travelled.

He'd grown up so fast. Young, handsome and happy. Movie star looks but so modest with it. Before I could ask his name, and whether he was who I thought he was, the scene changed yet again.

Must have been midday, with the sun being so high above the house. A good, well built house that I'd spent the best part of my forty-eighth year working on. I'd bought a plot of land in Cottingley, employed an architect to design the house and then employed a firm of builders to do as the architect had planned. And this was the result: a house in which I'd been living for the last twenty-three years.

I'd been released from prison at the age of thirty-nine, a reformed murderer. I sold my story to newspapers and then to a biographer who sold enough books and screenplays for us to both live in relative comfort. So as I sat there, in the expanse of my lawn, the sun out, warming me to the bone, I pondered over my life and how so much had changed. Born innocent but destined to die with the stain of blood on my hands and soul.

I'd developed a slight stoop over the decades and I'd been using a stick to aid my movement for the last three years or so. Pains in my chest had become regular and more intense so I had no doubt that death approached. I felt strangely satisfied but didn't realise why until I looked further down the lawn where I saw him once again. Fast approaching his fortieth year, losing hair but he still looked good, this son of mine. Decency in every bone, muscle and sinew. Following him, like a small army, I saw his own tribe.

Was I his father? I don't know. To this day, that dream continues to give me hope. I like to think part of it could be true. Is a son, a family what lies ahead? Are those the people I'll leave behind? If so, then it's more than enough for the life of one person.

police and thieves

The dream ended and I awoke, my eyes focussing on my watch, the minute hand glancing past midnight. I'd slept for less than an hour. Just as well, really. I needed to get out and start dealing. First stop, Little Pakistan, the place my life began.

I passed my dad's shop but I didn't bother looking in. Too many things on my mind to worry about or even relive a few memories. I called Cowboy but his phone was switched off. Not like him to be out of action at such a peak hour.

I met up with a Pathan lad called Shak around the back of a petrol station just off Manningham Lane. I heard he moved a lot of product for a street guy and after not too much sweet talk on my part, I managed to work him a decent deal, which included him giving me a few names who'd also be interested in what I had on offer. Before I approached anyone I didn't know, I drove around some more, looking for all those other faces that were always up for a bargain.

I copped for Ivan fairly soon after I left Shak to get busy. Ivan was a weird looking fuck on account of this thing he had about piercings and tattoos. One of those scruffy looking hippies but he did okay and once you got over the way he presented himself, he turned out to be a reasonably okay sort. He limped over to my car and told me he'd just had a great big ring put through his bell-end, which is why he walked the way he did. Like I gave a fuck.

Ivan, however, proved to be a bit harder to convince than Shak because he said he got his wares from some other dealer. What did that matter? I asked him. After going through the motions by debating concepts such as loyalty, ethics and even civility, he got to the nitty gritty: profit. I gave him some bullshit discounts and he took what he said he could. Like Shak, I left him my number and offered to top him up whenever he wanted. Between them these two did a pretty good advertising job because after that, anyone who happened to be interested in making better than usual profits came looking for me. Within four hours, I'd sold cheap but good cocaine to anyone who wanted it. Sadly, I still had most of it left.

So, faced with no choice, I headed out of town, into unchartered but relatively safe waters like Leeds, followed by Huddersfield and finally, I drove further up the M62 into Rochdale. Any closer to Manchester, and I'd be heading straight into crazy-bastards-with-shooters territory. Thanks but no thanks. Leeds is a booming town in lots of senses but because it's booming, everything is much more valuable and that includes drug distribution networks. I played it carefully and didn't ruffle any feathers. By the time the big men in Leeds realised that someone had been fucking with their lines of supply, I was long gone. Huddersfield and Rochdale, however, were dead cities; worse than Bradford. The one dealer who did show some interest turned out to be a wanker, also. He ended up telling me that he *wasn't sure*, that he'd have to *ask his supplier*, and that he was also in the middle of *renovating his kitchen* and how he didn't *really* have the money to invest in the first place. Waste of time.

By the time I got back into town, it had grown dark again. A full eighteen hours on the go, non-stop. Physically I was fucked but mentally, I still felt alert and with it enough to deal some more. So I drove around, looking for any action I might have missed the first time round but, as expected, nothing doing. Before I headed home, I decided to go check out Cowboy. He'd probably give me all the gory details about last night; from how he'd yee-hawed the arse off that bint he met at Choudhuri's do to how close he came to getting a good kicking from Spanner.

He was home. Sitting on the sofa, in the front, his back to me and his head tilted back. Every time I slept like that, I ended up waking up with a sore neck. Still, must have been one hell of a night for him to flake out without lying down. I called his name three times in all. He didn't respond.

'Hey, you lazy fucker,' I said, wandering into the kitchen, heading for his fridge, hoping he had something to munch on. 'Wake the fuck up, man!'

Again, nothing. Only one thing for it: a glass of cold water over his face.

He bought that sofa, so he told me, at one of those *Final Closing Down Bank Holiday Half Price Everything Must Go* sales. A nice, but above all comfortable piece of furniture. It had been a creamy, off white colour for the longest time. Now, as I stood there, wondering what to do next, it seemed as if some kid with a paintbrush had been busy flicking a tin of red paint all over it.

From ear to ear, his throat had been slashed. The structures of his neck, the inner workings which should remain hidden beneath skin, now exposed, obscenely uncovered for all to see. Veins and arteries cut but so cleanly cut. What might have been his Adam's apple along with muscle tissue and even fat, coated in a layer of already congealed, slowly scabbing blood. A mass of wires covered in a multicoloured jelly, glistening like something solid and inanimate, like a painting with all the highlights in all the right places. His face, the parts that were still untouched by the stain of his blood, along with his hands, had changed from that Italian shade of light brown to death's dirty, blue-grey hue.

I felt tempted to close his eye-lids, like they do in the movies, but I assumed it wiser to leave things be. And that's exactly what I did. I left him there and drove home, all the time wondering why I wasn't freaking out, why I wasn't mourning the man who had been my only real friend for so long. Had I become one of those cold hardened criminals? I don't know about that but I did feel a sense of loss. No pain, though. This, people getting dead, seemed to be something that came with the turf.

I stopped at a phone box and called for an ambulance. Not that it would do him any good but it didn't feel right, leaving him there, dead but alone. Figuring the coppers would want to interview me, I went to the New Commonwealth to stash the dope and the money I'd made. I was in two minds about telling them about Cowboy but remembered what he'd said about Rose. Maybe something had happened to her last night, too. I called her mobile. No reply. Dead line. Fuck.

Choudhuri apologised for my loss. Two things struck me about that. Firstly, it reinforced my belief that Choudhuri was indeed a schizophrenic son of a bitch. Secondly, and much more important, how come he knew I had suffered a loss when there was no way of him knowing? I played dumb, thinking I'd make my move, speak my accusations when I had the proof. As it turned out, I didn't need to wait too long.

'God's Will, Kilo,' said Soofi, to which I responded with a nod.

'Ah fuck him,' said Tahir. 'He was a fucking weirdo, anyway.'

I didn't see Tahir. Didn't see his form. All I knew was this: there existed an entity called Tahir, sometimes Spanner and it became clear to me that this being could not exist within the same vicinity as me. Some people say they see a red mist descend over their complete field of vision when moments of extreme rage overcome them but that's not how it was with me. With me, it was black and where Tahir was, it was even blacker.

I picked up a fork and lunged at his face, the implement skewering his left eye. I'm not a fighting man and I'm not strong or even agile so the explanation I have is that I must have caught him off guard. Within no time at all, Choudhuri, Soofi and a handful of waiters had leapt onto me and dragged me off. The black lifted and that's when I saw the red: most of it over Tahir's face. I'd just half blinded him but he carried on, kicking and screaming as if it was nothing; a flesh wound, hardly noticeable. Lucky for me, the people who'd saved him from me were now saving me from him.

'I'll kill you!' he yelled. 'Motherfucker, I'll kill you!'

I said nothing which seemed to work him up even more.

'You are so fucking dead you cock sucking, cunt eating, arse licking son of a bitch! Gonna take you out just like I took your weird fucking bum chum out! You hear that? That's right! Gonna cut your fucking neck like I cut his and I'll do it with the same fucking blade! You hear that Mister fucking Kilo? Gonna do you like I did him!'

I don't really remember how it happened, how I did it. Can't even recall if the world went black, red or pink with blue fucking dots, to be frank. He just knocked me into a different plane. Nothing existed anymore except for one thought which seemed to have lodged itself in my head, looping itself over and over again: *first my dad and now Cowboy…first my dad and now Cowboy…first my dad and now Cowboy…* Choudhuri told me later that he'd never seen anything like it in his whole life; this from a man who paid good money to watch illegal fist fights whenever it took his fancy. Apparently, I was that fast they barely saw it. One minute they were holding the great big fucking giant back, the next they were watching me, straddled across his chest, my knees pinning his arms to the floor, the fork a millimetre away from the cornea of his one seeing eye.

Suddenly, the noise of Choudhuri, Soofi and a number of others yelling and panicking hit me. Suddenly I came to, a little surprised to find myself with the upper hand.

'I'll blind you first, then I'll kill you,' I whispered.

'Gerrimoffme! Sal! Sal! Gerrimoffme!!'

Without looking over my shoulder at any of them, I warned:

'You come anywhere near me – any of you – and I'll take his other eye out and I'll eat the fucking thing.'

Tahir licked his desert dry lips.

'You go fuck,' he protested. 'I – I swear – I swear I'll fucking kill you.'

'I'll kill you first.'

I felt a thud on the back of my head. A piece of wood, a baseball bat or maybe even a pick axe handle could have done the job.

I must have been out for hours because when I came to, it was beginning to grow light outside. Choudhuri, Soofi and yes, even Tahir (now with one eye patched) were sat on the other side of a table which also served as a boundary between them and me. I wasn't tied up and I hadn't been roughed up in any way. My head, however, hurt like hell. I didn't feel like venting anything else towards Tahir any more. I considered myself fortunate not to have killed him, or totally blinded him. It would have served no purpose, maiming him any more, or going all the way and killing him. I did not feel any better about what he'd done to my old man but maybe revenge isn't about making you feel good. Maybe, if done right, revenge is about feeling purified, liberated or even relieved.

'So,' I said, cold as ice, not giving a shit.

Choudhuri stood and walked to my side of the table.

'You calmed down, now?'

I nodded.

'You're a nasty piece of work, you know that?'

I shook my head, surprised at his choice of words…the pot calling the kettle black and all that.

'I'm not the one who goes around killing innocent people,' I said, staring Tahir in his one good eye.

This was a just thing, I told myself. Somehow seemed fitting for a man who'd instilled fear into the innocent for so long to be seeing the world through only one eye.

'Now,' said Choudhuri. 'I want to know if you're still a part of the team. If you wanna walk away, then walk the fuck away.'

'Why would I wanna do that?'

'So you're cool? You and Spanner here are friends again?'

I smiled.

'Friends? Since when have people like us had friends? We sell drugs. We don't need no fucking friends.'

Choudhuri slapped me on the back and said:

'That's what I wanna hear.'

He stared at me for a while and I stared back. Fear had gone. There's a certain point beyond which fear ceases to have significance. And me, I'd moved past that point years ago, as a kid, the day Charlie Boy took me to the edge of death.

'Nasty piece of work, you are.'

'Just tell him to stay out of my way.'

'Stay out of each others' way,' said Choudhuri, addressing Tahir.

'But I wanna know one thing,' I said. 'Why Cowboy?'

Choudhuri sniffed and looked around.

'Now's not the time to explain.'

'I want to know. What the fuck he ever do to you? You didn't even know him.'

'Now you're getting excited again. I thought we were past that.'

Smart. Not smart but sly. Devious. Trying to twist things around and make me feel all fucked up, the one to blame for anything bad that had or would happen. I figured the best way was to stay calm and not allow myself to rise to his bullshit.

'So,' I started again. 'Why?'

'You're not gonna let this go, are you, Kilo?'

Choudhuri paced, obviously thinking up some bullshit story to cover his back…some shit like a voice from the telly made him do it.

'Your friend – the Cowboy – he wasn't a nice guy,' he began, rubbing his chin. 'He was out of order last night.'

'How? What he do that was so bad?'

'Okay,' nodded Choudhuri. 'If you wanna know, then how's rape for starters?'

'Rape? You're taking the piss…No. Not Cowboy.'

'I got proof.'

'Proof?'

'You want me to prove it?'

I didn't respond. I had this situation read. Any fool could find some scrubber to regurgitate any old bullshit story that happened to be needed: rape, sexual deviance, alien abduction – any fucking thing.

Choudhuri nodded to a waiter standing by the door who promptly did an about turn and left the room. We waited. A few minutes later, he re-entered, a scrubber, one that Cowboy had been with last night, walking in with him.

'This is Tracey,' said Choudhuri. 'Tracey's a friend of a friend.'

'And she was raped, was she?' I first asked him, then looked at her. 'Were you?'

Tracey, like a good little slapper, tried to nod convincingly. I got up and told them I was leaving. Choudhuri asked me if I was satisfied.

'Yeah,' I said. 'I'm satisfied.'

The coppers were already outside Cowboy's house. They'd come in droves. I took it all in my stride, of course, watching from the hallway as everywhere else was out of bounds. They scurried around, taping up rooms, dusting surfaces and moving furniture, their clinical whites in touch with everything but corrupting nothing. I left them to it and sat in my car, thinking a few winks would do me no harm. I must have actually nodded off by the time Price got around to tapping on my window, causing me to jump out of my short but not altogether fruitless slumber.

'Hello Khalil,' he said solemnly.

I nodded.

'I'd like you to come down to the station with me.'

'I can't be arsed.'

D S Hopkins mosey-ed up and whispered something into Price's ear. Price shook the suggestion off, whatever it was.

'We're not asking, lad,' stated Hopkins. 'We're telling you: a statement…down the nick…now.'

I didn't like Hopkins but I couldn't feel the same way about Price. Seemed more human, more weak and fallible than the usual, run of the mill copper.

Hopkins continued to stare.

'Well?'

'Make me,' I said. 'Arrest me cos I'm not going anywhere otherwise.'

Before Hopkins could stick his hooter in it once again, Price – the voice of reason – butted in.

'It won't take long, Khalil.'

I looked at Price. I hardly knew him, but I could tell he had a good brain in there, perhaps even a half decent heart beating in his chest; an essentially good soul occupying his body. He might not have known exactly what had gone on over at Cowboy's but, as I stared, his expression gave too much away. He seemed sympathetic. And how did I feel? Obviously hurt, my best mate killed, but when it came down to it, I was in no mood to play twenty questions *down the bloody nick* and I had that prick Tahir to worry about. Didn't have to be a genius to work out his next move. It concerned inflicting a slow, painful death on me. Killing Cowboy was nothing more than a job he'd been asked to do, perhaps told to do but now, he simply had to take care of me – teach me a lesson – for what I'd done to him. I needed help, someone to watch my back. With Cowboy gone, who was left?

'Won't ask you again,' said Hopkins.

'Just hurry up about it,' I told him. 'Got things to do.'

I found it amusing, the potential of the situation. A few years down the line, I'd be a regular, down the nick more often than the plods themselves. There'd come a time when I'd be that familiar, that they'd start inviting me to their weddings, birthday parties and general knees-ups. I'd almost be one of the lads, with all the work I'd create for them. I could see it, daydream it, as I rode in the back of the cop car, coppers like Price introducing me to their wives by saying:

This is Kilo, he's a drug dealer.

Their wives would smile and say:

Really? That's nice. Do you enjoy your work?

And I'd say:

Yes, very much. How about you? Do you enjoy sleeping with swine every night?

I wondered about them, the three little pigs, Bradford's finest. Adams, Hopkins and Price, three stages of a nice little model of evolution. Grizzly Adams, a crude, nasty, jealous and vindictive man. Blinded by ignorance and hatred for all he misunderstood. An old blood and guts type copper who didn't give a rat's arse about anything except looking good for the press. At the same time, a crooked, dishonest copper. On many a payroll for many a year. Turned out that everyone knew, even his superiors but they let it slide because in some way, shape or form, they too were on the take. Grizzly had it down to a fine art and always succeeded in making himself look squeaky clean. Even so, this one, without doubt, happened to be the most primitive of examples. A breed driven to the edges of extinction but still resilient, hardy and resourceful enough to come through all the same.

Hopkins, a fairly close relative of Adams, but nowhere near as intense, nor extreme and, strange as it sounds, not as capable of taking everything so damned personally. Not a crook but an honest, professional copper. In it for the career, the perks and the prestige. A weak, powerless and insecure man in ordinary life but those two initials in front of his name made all the difference, did his ego the world of good. *D C* Hopkins, he'd nod to himself every morning as he looked in the bathroom mirror. D C Nigel Hopkins, WYMPF (West Yorkshire Metropolitan Police Force). At school, the other kids would laugh when he told them he wanted to be a copper when he grew up but now who was laughing? Who had the clout now? Whose dreams had come true? His dreams, however, had grown to ridiculous proportions over the years. Now, fast approaching his forties, he had visions of cracking cases, presiding over press conferences and then, upon retirement, he'd create yet another Perfect TV Detective, based loosely, he'd always say, on his own police experiences.

Price. The oldest of the three but the most evolved. The youngest, healthiest and freshest in terms of outlook. A man who always remained himself, never allowed the job to change him in the slightest. A decent, honest and reliable man. One of those men who believed in doing not only the right thing, but the well considered right thing. Intelligent, compassionate and, he often thought, much too moral to be an officer of the law. As such, a minority and often thought of as a bit of a Miss Marple by his colleagues, including that up and coming nosoul loser called Hopkins. For Price, Hopkins represented everything bad about the force. These people were about systems, policies and consistency; about the machine, not the components that made the machine what it was, or could be. No room for independent thought, no room for the *right thing*, a principle Price was still prepared to sacrifice his career for.

Price showed me into his corner of a huge, open plan office. Other coppers remained at their desks, some on the phone, others sitting in front of computer screens, no doubt tapping bullshit sentences into their bullshit reports.

'Statement,' I said. 'You want a statement, then.'

Price flicked his head at Hopkins.

'You got five minutes,' said Hopkins then buggered off.

'Your friend,' said Price, referring to Cowboy. 'I'm sorry about what happened.'

'Me too.'

'I've been told he was a decent sort, for a dealer.'

'He was a good guy. Didn't deserve that. Motherfuckers.'

'Who? Who, Khalil?'

'I don't know,' I said, feeling the beginnings of a prickly sweat come through on my forehead.

'Well, certain professions do have risks built into them.'

'Tell me about it,' I said.

'You tell me.'

I shook my head. Price sighed and then said:

'I hear one of your other colleagues has had something of an accident.'

I didn't follow.

'An eye,' he said. 'An eye for an eye? Or was it something else?'

Tahir. But how the hell would Price know? Maybe, I considered, maybe this fucker was as corrupt as Grizzly.

'And it's not what you think,' he said. 'The hospital informs us of all suspicious injuries.'

'I see. Had nothing to do with me.'

'Oh please, Khalil. Who are you trying to kid? I'm not stupid and neither are you.'

'I thought you wanted a statement.'

'It'll wait. But you do realise you're in danger now. He's after you.'

253

'Who? Spanner? Fuck him and the horse he rode in on. I'm ready for him.'

'Fighting talk. Admirable but foolish. There's no way he'll be beaten twice. Unless…'

'Unless what?!' I snapped.

Price tutted to himself and then shrugged.

'Have it your own way. But I'm afraid I've some other bad news for you, Khalil.'

'Bad news? You have no idea how lame that sounds to me right now.'

'Sit down, Khalil. I think you should sit down for this.'

So I sat and waited for him to deliver this shellshock, or not, as the case may be.

'It's bad news, then. Let me guess…'

'I'm being serious.'

Again, another shrug. Given recent events, how bad could it be?

'It's that young lady friend of yours. Rose,' he said and then added, 'It's about Rose.'

I looked at him, wondering what he was playing at, mentioning her name. Why so grave? Why so sympathetic?

'What? What about her?'

I knew it before I even asked. It made sense. Cowboy got killed and now I knew why. Rose.

'She – her body – I'm afraid it was found this morning.'

Dead. That's what he meant, but couldn't bring himself to say the word for so long. I wondered how many similar situations he'd been in. Maybe this was the hardest part of the job.

'Dead,' I repeated out loud. 'Dead.'

'She'd been raped, Khalil, mutilated…'

I shook my head.

'I'm sorry Khalil. I truly am sorry.'

And I believed him. Truth is, and it might sound like the lousiest thing in the world, but he was a damned sight more sorry about her than me. I had no sympathy for her. What the fuck had possessed her? That's what got me. Why the fuck did she have to be such a fucking slut that night and flirt with all those sick fucking men? What did she expect?

These people were fucking animals, not gentlemen who took a month's worth of dinner dates, boxes of chocolates and flowers before venturing a peck on the cheek: you got these bastards excited then you paid the price. She had it coming. Of course, it wasn't right but hell, you play with fire then you get burnt.

'Are you okay, Khalil? Would you like a cup of tea?'

I looked up at him and felt trails of salty wetness on my cheeks. I might have been lying to myself for half my life but I still hadn't managed to become an expert. My lies never worked completely.

'No,' I said. 'I'm fine. Do you still want a statement? About Cowboy, I mean?'

'For official purposes, yes. That would be good.'

So I gave them a cock and bull story about not knowing anything about anything. I did know it all, though. The picture was so clear, now that I had all the pieces: Swain or Tahir – perhaps the pair of them – had raped and then killed her. Tahir got rid of Cowboy because he was the only person, save for the one dippy tart, who could, perhaps would put them in the picture. The green Roller that Cowboy had mentioned, I realised, was Swain's.

When we got back, Price got out and followed me over to my car. I got in and so did he. I wasn't in the mood for listening to any more of his spiel but I didn't have it in me to be uncivil to the man. Not after the respect he'd shown me.

'I should warn you, Khalil,' said Price, initiating one final angle. 'We're still very concerned about your activities.'

'That's a new way of putting it.'

'We know you're dealing large quantities, now. You're much more important now. But then, you've much more to lose.'

'No comment.'

'Let's be honest with each other, Khalil.'

'No, let's lie.'

'Trouble is,' he continued, ignoring my flippancy. 'You've no buyers left, have you?'

'No *comment*, man. I don't know what you're talking about.'

'This is off the record, Khalil. Relax.'

'What is this? How come everything's always off the record?'

255

'I'm trying to cut you some slack here, that's all.'

'Sure you are.'

'I'm right about your market, though. Saturation point has already been reached.'

'What if it has? I can deal with it. I'll think of something.'

'Whatever you do, don't even consider dealing to Sweet. He's a dangerous man, Khalil.'

'Why would I do that?'

'That's a good question,' he said and then got out. 'You take care of yourself, Khalil.'

Why *would* I do that? If I sold to Sweet, who could probably do with the gear – he did say he could sell his shit ten times over – then I'd be undermining Choudhuri. Professionally, that was a very bad thing to do. Strategically – tactically – however, that could be a brilliant thing to do. But like Price had warned, it could also present a shit load of danger.

Sweet, obviously, was more than pleased with this idea that had been sparked by a natural but rather friendly enemy, Price. We met at a service station, just outside Bradford and laid what little there was all out and in the open.

'This is good,' he smiled, loading up the back of his car with everything I had. 'Show that fat fucker a thing or two.'

'We'll just keep doing it like this for a while. No waves. Okay?'

'See about that,' he smirked. 'Now that I got you with me, but with him, just a matter of time before we kick up a real fuss. I want what he's got.'

Which is not what I wanted. Too messy and too greedy, such a plan.

'What? No.'

'No?'

'No. We'll keep things like this for a while. We can move later, when we've built up a decent client base.'

'I already got one of those, man.'

'A better one.'

'Sooner's better than later, guy. Anyway, he won't be expecting it.'

'Expecting what, exactly?'

He didn't seem to be getting upset, crazy or dangerous, even though this little discussion felt like a back and forth *oh yes it is/oh no it isn't* pantomime deal. He had to get it through his head, though. I didn't need him doing something silly. At least, not yet. I had other ideas and they'd only work if the sea was calm, not being rocked by storms of Sweet's making.

'Just relax, guy,' he said, shoving a case of notes into my arms. 'You just tell him you been busy selling out of town for now.'

'Don't do anything stupid, Sweet.'

'I know what I'm doing. I'll sort him out my way. Deal with him once and for all.'

I clocked it because of his tone and because of what he didn't say. Everything about him now was *I* whereas before it had been *we*. And there was something in his voice, perhaps contempt, for anyone who challenged him. Sweet was planning something and, for some reason, me covertly supplying him was important. All that shit about me and him being two peas in the same pod was bullshit, spiel to rope me in and make me feel like one of the family. And all the while, same as everyone else, Sweet was using me. It would be a miracle if it turned out any other way. In hindsight, it wasn't that complicated. In hindsight, I realise it was nothing more than Sweet being himself: a crazy, power mad maniac.

sometimes

I caught Choudhuri and his crew at The N C. Sat, but this time, down-stairs. They stopped talking as I entered. I spied Tahir, still a fuck-up only now resigned to seeing the world in monovision. He cyclopsed me back, his strength regained, at least part of it. Then, all eyes turned to the main man. I dumped a bag full of money on the table, counted up and stacked. Choudhuri's drugs? Sold like a motherfucker.

'What's this?' Choudhuri asked.

'What do you think it is?'

Choudhuri looked inside and shook his head.

'Problem?'

Choudhuri giggled to himself and then wagged his forefinger at me.

'I don't believe it,' he said. 'I don't fucking believe it.'

Now this surprised me but I didn't let it show. It's what he wanted, wasn't it? He told me I had a week and now, lo and behold, well within that span – within four short days no less – I'd got rid of every single speck. He couldn't ask for more. He should have been happy, should have been on his knees, showing me his gratitude by sucking my dick. This, so I thought, appeared to be a dose of the highest calibre dealing known to man. No, scrub that because technically speaking, this was without doubt the finest example of drug salesmanship in history. What, exactly what, was this fat fuck's problem?

'What? What's so bad?'

'I knew you were supposed to be good, but this is something else.'

As Choudhuri's initial shock subsided, and was replaced with glee, Tahir's expression grew more grave.

'I don't understand. Who'd you sell to?' said Tahir, his voice loaded with suspicious, overtones.

'Mind your own fucking business. I sold it and it's staying sold. You got a problem with that, man?'

'I smell a rat, Sal.'

'Yeah?' nodded Choudhuri. 'Got to admit, that was a lot of shit for one man to move so quick.'

'You're kidding me,' I protested. 'See, I was under the impression

258

that I was supposed to get innovative and sell that shit, you know?'

Choudhuri shook his head. Again, it would have to be that one eyed prick Tahir who spoke.

No fucker could sell that much shit.'

I figured I could now afford to talk the tough guy talk. Well, I'd only half blinded this bastard. Wouldn't seem right not continuing to act accordingly.

'If that's the case, fuck-head, why give me so much?'

'We wanted to see you sweat,' said Soofi. 'We wanted to see how you'd cope under pressure.'

'Well, tough shit on that count,' I smirked. 'Cos I got pressure covered easy.'

'Real sharp piece of work, you are,' beamed Choudhuri. 'Only I think you're fucking me around, here.'

'Tell you what: fuck you all,' I moaned. 'I'm gone and from now on, I'll choose my own terms.'

I turned around and started heading for the door. Another sterling performance, worthy of a BAFTA, even.

'Wait,' said Choudhuri. 'Where do you think you're going?'

'Anywhere's better than here with you dead beats.'

Choudhuri sighed.

'Okay. Relax. But I want you to explain.'

'What, exactly, do you want me to explain?'

'Who'd you sell to?' sneered Tahir.

'Your dad,' I snapped.

He got up and came towards me. Choudhuri got in his way and told him to sit the fuck down.

'Out of town. No choice. No way I could move that much in this fucking place.'

'How far?'

'Been all over, man. What's it matter? I got rid and I made money. It's the idea, isn't it? I mean, fuck me…what I do that was so wrong?'

'What about the coppers?'

'What about them? They don't know nothing. I'm careful.'

'That's not what I meant. Why were you down the station? I heard you were interviewed.'

'And? So what? I see those fucks more than I see you. They're just fishing.'

The interrogation didn't last much longer. During that time, I learnt one lesson: Choudhuri had a way of being played. If I showed him a bit of strength and if I also threatened to walk away from him, then he almost felt compelled to believe me. It was almost as if only an innocent man would be hurt enough to risk losing everything by leaving his organisation. For him, only liars and disloyal fucks stuck around and tried proving him wrong by either begging or greasing.

'You're gonna go far. I better watch myself,' he said, eventually.

I sat down and then waited for a while, collecting my thoughts.

'Now it's my turn,' I found myself suddenly saying.

'For what?'

'I wanna know what happened to her, I wanna know what happened to Rose.'

Choudhuri looked at Tahir who in turn looked to Soofi. Soofi cleared his throat and said:

'Erm…who?'

'Don't gimme that shit. What happened to her?'

Again, the looks and the silence.

'The coppers told me about her,' I said. 'I know what happened to her. She's dead.'

'Everyone dies,' muttered Tahir.

'She'd been raped.'

'Raped?' quizzed Choudhuri, sounding genuinely surprised. 'Not raped, Kilo.'

'Oh? Then what? She just happen to fall on a dick a couple of hundred times? She was raped and then she was killed.'

'That's not how it happened, Kilo. I swear it's not.'

'Bullshit. I know that Padgett guy's got something to do with this,' I said, looking at Tahir.

'You can't prove that,' blurted Tahir, sounding as guilty and as involved as hell.

Choudhuri looked surprised and offended by Tahir's interruption.

'You just shut the fuck up and let me take care of this shit. I'll explain this.'

And that's just what he set out to do. I didn't buy it for a second.

'She got a little out of hand after you left, Kilo. Said she was in the mood for a party, you know?'

'No, I don't know.'

'A *proper* party,' he said.

'And what the hell's that supposed to mean?'

He said she got loaded. Up to the eyeballs with booze and dope. She was all over the place, carrying on, touching people up, offering them her pussy. She did want to leave with Padgett but a guy like him, being an MP and all, had to be careful so he asked the one eyed wonder to drive her over to his pad. This much, in part, I could buy because I'd seen her crawling all over him and, I suppose, because it tied in with Cowboy's version. So once he got her home, she just went wild and gave him the fuck of his life. In the morning, Padgett woke up and saw her lying next to him: dead as a fucking dodo. A heart attack, most likely due to all that dope she'd done. Padgett, a man in his position, panicked and could think of nothing else apart from calling Choudhuri in to help clean the situation up some. End of story, almost.

'So you carve her up a bit and make it look like a murder.'

'That's about the sum of it, yeah,' admitted Tahir, proud of his quick thinking.

I didn't believe it because there were too many flaws in the story. I hadn't really fallen for her, but she was clean. Veins pure and as yet uncontaminated. As for the excessive sexual behaviour, that's not how Cowboy told it. But why had she acted like a slut at that party? Maybe I missed something, or needed to know more about her. One thing for sure, I knew Choudhuri's version was bullshit.

I worked out a better, so much simpler version. Tahir took her to Swain's gaff where one or both men raped her. Then one or both men killed her. Why they'd do such a thing was anyone's guess but Swain was a politician and maybe that was enough. One way of making sure a potential scandal stays hidden was to bury the source of it.

'You okay with that, Kilo?' Choudhuri asked.

'Fine,' I lied. 'I'm just fine.'

I tried putting her out of my mind. I didn't love her, I knew that, but she and Cowboy were the two reasonably decent things in my life.

Both died – been killed – because of me and the people I knew. What was I? Some kind of jinx? Her, Cowboy, King, Tony…my dad. And who was next on the list? I had no problem suggesting my own name. The way things had been moving, it seemed obvious.

I went to see a mullah at the mosque. He told me how a couple of thousand pounds would pay for the plot of land in the cemetery, the wooden box to go in it and the hearse to get it there. For the first time in over fifteen years, I stepped foot in a mosque and it felt strange, like I shouldn't have been in there.

Cowboy's Janazah went without a hitch. Just after Jummah so there was a good turn out. Shame, but the congregation was full with people who didn't even know him but that's not important when it comes to these things. When it was all done, the mullah made an announcement: if anyone was owed anything by Cowboy – only he called him Pervaiz, the name he was born with – then they were to see me about it. Dying in debt is a bad thing, a curse on the soul. No one ventured anything because people owed Cowboy money, not the other way around. Not that it would do him any good now, but still, it would have been a nice surprise if a few junkies offered to give up their debts to charity or something.

The burial was a strange affair because there were only two people involved: the driver of the hearse – a middle aged guy called Khadim – and me. He had a very nice, quiet manner about him. Somehow, we managed to lift his coffin to the grave site and slowly, we lowered him in, me in silence, the driver reciting something holy with every breath.

Shagged out, I sat down next to Khadim after shovelling a grave's worth of soil from a mound into a hole. Khadim got up and went over to the grave, cupped his hands and offered a prayer for a man he'd never seen, let alone knew. After he left, I stood over Cowboy's grave and prayed but not just for him: I prayed for everyone, including me. I stayed there for a good half hour more, by his graveside, thinking how easily it could be me.

let forever be

4:00pm, Leeds. Sat behind the steering wheel, round the back of a Turkish Kebab House which happened to be owned by a pair of Greek brothers. I didn't ask any questions about them being Greek and their kebab house being Turkish.

'Wees…wees don' likes to fucks arounds, you knows,' the older one said.

'Hey, same here,' I replied.

We transferred goods for cash. It was a sweet deal because they were paying ten grand for two grand's worth of dope. Why would they want to do such a thing? Well, they were paying me with funny money, but we were talking about dud notes of the highest quality. I planned to mix in the dud ten grand with all the other money and gain eight grand's worth of pure profit in the process when I tallied up with Choudhuri later on. I had nothing to lose. Even if Choudhuri did spot the fake money, then so what? It was those fucking punters of mine, thinking they could palm off dud notes. We were about to shake hands until next time when my phone rang. It was Choudhuri. He needed to see me. Something urgent had come up.

Downstairs was chock-a-block that night, but that's Friday nights in the Indian restaurant business for you. Like the tides and the moon, piss-heads with bloated egos and bellies share some strange rhythm with curry houses up and down the land. Piss-heads and their relationship with Indian restaurants are now a part of the landscape, a fact of life. What never ceases to amaze me is how drunks dole out shit to waiters and still expect the same waiters not to piss, shit and spit in their food.

I went up the stairs to meet them. Out of sight, out of mind. Choudhuri and his dynamic duo awaited me in the company of another guest. Grizzly Adams talked his shit while the others listened.

'Starving millions? There might be millions going without but it's all a game, all politics. Left wing-right wing, capitalists-anti capitalists, rich-poor. All about sides.'

Choudhuri waved me in impatiently. Adams stopped with his nonsense, turning to smile also.

263

'Come on, Kilo. What's the matter with you?' Choudhuri asked.

Tahir looked as miserable as usual, Soofi seemed to have sunk into think mode but Grizzly looked pleased with himself. Maybe he'd been on the rounds, collecting his fees.

'Doing alright, are you?' he enquired.

'Well enough,' I said, giving Choudhuri a large envelope full of money. 'You?'

'Mustn't grumble,' he said, tearing off a piece of chapatti, dipping it into his curry then shoving it all into his gob, the way people like him do. 'Gotta take the rough with the smooth, I suppose.'

Choudhuri peeked inside the envelope and smiled appreciatively.

'You're something else, you know that?'

I shrugged off the compliment.

'So,' I said, turning my attention to Choudhuri's phone call. 'What's so urgent, then?'

'Mister Adams has some information that might be useful.'

'Oh?'

'Yeah. Thought you might make some use of it, you know.'

'Make use of what?'

'That lass,' he said. 'The one you were shagging.'

'Rose,' I said. 'What about her?'

'Well, I only just found out,' he smirked and then broke off.

'Well?'

'Just as well she had that accident, like.'

I stood up, ready to storm off in a huff. I didn't want to sit there, listening to this shit.

'She was plod, Kilo,' said Choudhuri. 'Undercover plod. Drugs.'

Now this, although shocking, was believable. I sat down and considered the revelation, ran its credentials through my head. Her existence in my world suddenly made a lot more sense. Her limited time on the scene, the way she got roped in and then released by Price and, of course, how she suddenly grew attracted to me when I started making it big could only mean one thing. That's why she was giving me the questions about life, death and the deeds in between. Now that I knew who she really was, it seemed so obvious. Still, I should have known, should have worked it out. Maybe I would have done if wasn't so keen on her.

'How do you know? I mean, how come you never knew before?'

'Price.'

'Price?'

'Yeah. What do you know about him?'

'Not like you,' I said. 'He's straight.'

Grizzly paused, gave me a look then continued.

'She was working with him and, with him being the way he is, not many others knew. Even his own partner, that wanker called Hopkins, even he wasn't in on it. So anyway, Price puts in a report about her death and I happen to catch sight of it. All in there. She'd transferred from Manchester Met over a year ago. A slow and long burn.'

'What?'

'You know, she was in for the long run. Or not, as it turned out.'

'So what now?'

'What now? What do you think? You think Price is gonna let this go?'

I looked at the others.

'So? What the fuck's this got to do with me?'

'He knows about you and her. Knows, well, you can imagine what he knows. Got you down as prime suspect, mate.'

Me? Surely he didn't believe I had anything to do with her death. Of course he didn't. If I knew Price, this was just him sowing seeds of misinformation.

'What? You're kidding!'

'Just watch yourselves, that's all. All of you.'

'And you?'

'Don't worry about me, lad. I can look after myself.'

Choudhuri didn't seem to be too bothered about all this. I suppose he could afford to be unconcerned. If anyone was going down, it was the people he surrounded himself with, never him.

Rose, a copper. Would I have worked it out? I doubted it. Even though she was lying all the time, she had this decency about her. She was doing what she was doing because it was right, not because it was a career thing or because she'd be famed in police circles if she managed to come through. This, of course, made me feel like a right fucking heel, thinking of her as a crazy, nagging bitch when all she did was play a part, act the way she thought a dealer's chick ought to act. In some ways, she and I were the same.

Grizzly carried on eating. Before I could make my excuses, Choudhuri stood up and looked over my shoulder as someone entered the room. Tahir stood then so did Soofi. Grizzly looked around, smiled and then, just like the others, got to his feet. I didn't get up but by the time I turned around, he was more or less standing over me.

'About time,' joked Choudhuri.

A cold shiver ran down my spine and yes, what I saw frightened the shit out of me. The man towered above me. I felt so small. This was just like that day in the shop. All he had to do now was speak.

'Evening,' he smiled. 'Said I'd be back.'

Swain shook their hands as I slowly stood. I held out my hand, feeling obliged to follow protocol even though it made me sick to the stomach. Eventually, he turned to me.

'So, we meet again.'

'So we do.'

They all sat down again and, as bad fortune would have it, Swain took up a place next to me.

'How's the eye?' he asked Tahir but for some reason stared coldly at Choudhuri.

Tahir shrugged then stared at me with his good eye by way of response.

'Looks nasty,' commented Grizzly.

'Maybe he could do with another one. Make a matching pair,' I suggested.

'Now, now,' schmoozed Swain. 'No need for that, is there, lads?'

I got up.

'I have to go. Work to do.'

'Don't be like that, lad,' complained Swain. 'We're all friends, here.'

'I have to go,' I repeated.

'Stop being a misery guts,' added Grizzly.

Choudhuri in silence, an onlooker, almost.

'Let's not be children,' added Swain.

Tahir giggled to himself. I looked at Choudhuri who seemed to be staring at Swain with a look of intense hostility. I didn't know what problem he had and I didn't really care. Still, it was clear they wanted me to stick around. What was the big deal, anyway? I could take another ten or fifteen minutes more of being here, Swain or not.

'Okay,' I said. 'I can hang around for a while.'

'Ah,' smiled Swain. 'I feel quite privileged to be graced with your presence.'

'Look, er, Mister Padgett. I have work to do. You know, I have people to see, business to conduct.'

'Oh,' he nodded. 'I like that. Nothing beats conscientiousness, does it? I hear you're as keen as mustard. But not as thick, eh?'

'Oh, Kilo's a fast mover,' said Soofi. 'You better watch yourself, Charlie.'

Charlie? I pretended not to notice Soofi's slip. I looked at the little guy who looked back serenely as if nothing was at all wrong. I didn't know these people too well, but something wasn't quite right here. Choudhuri was taking a back seat in the presence of Swain and I couldn't understand why that would be. I thought Choudhuri loved mixing with the knobs. This was not like him at all.

'Could be too much for you,' Soofi said, teasing him.

'Doubt it somehow. Had all sorts work for me in the past: camel-jockeys, yids, the micks, and you lot, of course. Can't forget your good selves, can we?'

Although I didn't understand what he meant, I actually felt relieved upon hearing him come out with all that bigoted shit. It confirmed the fact that nothing had changed about him. Still the same old Charlie Boy. Colin Padgett MP maybe, but a man who remained rooted to a certain time and place.

'Kilo's one of the best. Moves more product than all the others put together,' said Choudhuri, at last.

'That a fact, Sal?'

Choudhuri nodded. Again, it was as if Choudhuri was a junior, here. As if he'd suddenly lost all power in the presence of Swain.

'That's just what I like to hear.'

It had almost slipped through, what Choudhuri had just said: moves more product than all the others put together. *Product*? Was I hearing things?

'What?'

Swain smiled.

'What? What you mean, *What*?' said Tahir.

'What are we talking about, here? What product?'

Grizzly burped and then said:

'Excuse me.'

'Oh,' said Soofi. 'You know, the usual kind of products we deal with. Illegal products; drugs to be blunt.'

I turned to look at Swain, a picture of calm.

'You seem surprised, Kilo.'

'You know about all this?'

'We thought it was about time you got to know how things stand,' added Soofi.

Things are never how they seem. A man can change on the outside but inside, there'll always be residue of what was before. In Swain's case, the residue outweighed anything else.

It was, in every sense of the word, a revelation. I'd been selling drugs for almost ten years but I was still naïve about some things. Choudhuri and Swain had never parted company. They'd been together for years and even when Swain became Padgett the MP, he saw no reason to relinquish a thing. Swain dressed better and he sounded smoother but he was still a crook, still interested in making lots of money in relatively little time. Whereas before he loved the practice of using force, he now used words to ease his way through life. The real killer, though, the one line that stole the whole fucking show was where the power lay. The big man was not Choudhuri, as everyone thought, but it had always been, since the beginning, Charlie Boy Swain.

Without having to ask, Swain told his history and I was fascinated by it. I sat in silence while Swain relived their collective past, with Soofi and occasionally Grizzly throwing in a detail for good measure. Choudhuri, again, hardly spoke. I was right. Something was wrong in the camp and, although we could all taste the unease, no one dared mention it.

Swain talked and talked. He always had loved the action. So what if people misunderstood the hierarchy? He remembered the early days when he and his 'old mate' Spanner would hit the streets, whilst

Choudhuri would sit around, count the money and seem to be the one who pulled the strings. He also confessed about the change of name. Colin was his father's name and Padgett was his mother's maiden name. To Tahir, Soofi and to Choudhuri, however, he'd always been Charlie Boy Swain. I smiled but inside I felt nothing but hate.

'Now I know what's on your mind,' Swain said. 'Why would a man like me even consider going into politics?'

Tahir smiled.

'Someone like Sal going into all that you can understand but not me.'

'So why, then?' I asked.

The answer was as simple as it was absurd.

'Well,' said Swain, somewhat sheepishly. 'It all started with a bet.'

'A what? A bet?'

Tahir laughed.

'It's true, Kilo. These two,' Soofi said, meaning Swain and Tahir. 'They had this thing.'

I remembered how they'd betted in the shop and how Tahir had lost, miserably. I wondered who'd bet on which outcome this time around.

'So who won?'

Swain's eyes lit up.

'Do you know,' he said, clapping his hands together. 'I don't think I've ever collected on that one.'

Tahir pulled out a wallet and handed over a tenner.

'Very nice doing business with you,' said Swain.

'Jammy,' said Tahir.

'Mind you,' said Soofi. 'This is a useful place to be. A man in your position makes many friends.'

'And from all walks of life,' added Swain, nodding at Grizzly.

Swain was no longer the thug I'd first thought. He used his position in order to make some huge financial and political gains. He'd invest in anything going and it would all seem above board. Swain, due to the success of his DIY stores and his housing empire, was now a million-aire so investing in anything that he took a fancy to was not a suspicious thing to do. Thing is, the only money he sank into such endeavours were the surplus profits from the drugs industry which neither he, nor Choudhuri, could otherwise legitimise. Swain, in essence, had become the launderette.

Bringing me into all this was only one reason why he'd shown up that night. A man in Swain's shoes could not be in the habit of turning up every time Choudhuri recruited, or promoted one of his soldiers. Even at the best of times, his relationship with Choudhuri was of a remote nature; only meeting in person when serious shit happened to be going off.

Cue Sweet.

I'd dealt Choudhuri's dope to his mortal enemy only the day before. I thought he and I had an agreement, that we were to do nothing untoward and carry on with this little deal until…well, until as long as was necessary. And what did Sweet do? Sweet did what he always did: whatever the fuck he wanted.

I left Sweet at about eleven that morning. I didn't have anything for him but I needed to see him to make sure he was still happy with the way things were going. I'd get him next week's batch a day or two early. I asked him if he was cool. He said:

'Never been cooler.'

Ten minutes after I left (11:20am), Sweet started whatever plan his mind had hatched by calling Choudhuri on his phone and asking for a sit down. Choudhuri said he didn't think that was necessary and put the phone down on him.

Sweet and his woman picked the first guy up half an hour later, just before midday (11:57am).

The second guy was lifted a half an hour or so after that (12:31pm). Cleanly done but in broad daylight, for one and all to see.

Give or take an hour later (1:35pm), Choudhuri got word that two of our street guys had gone missing. An effective but rarely used strategy for getting the wrong kind of attention.

And then, less than two hours later (3:20pm), The N C received a delivery of two items: one cardboard box and one sealed envelope marked for the attention of a certain Saleem Choudhuri. The envelope contained a note spelling out the contents of the box: one penis, one heart and one right hand. These still warm body parts belonged to the same guy, who was, not surprisingly, pretty fucking dead. As if I needed convincing, Sweet did not believe in half measures. No *sleeps with the fishes* bullshit for this guy.

3:30pm, Choudhuri rings Sweet and this time, it's he who asks for the sit down. Sweet, being the gentleman he is, accepts the invitation but, because it's such short notice, can only do it late on tomorrow evening. Choudhuri, already put out by all this, agrees.

4:30pm, I roll into The N C, completely unaware about any of this and instead hear Grizzly Adams talk shit about the Starving Millions and also explain how Rose was an undercover copper. Less than an hour later, I'm still sitting there, so much more information in my head but none the wiser.

'Don't worry about it, though,' Tahir informed us all, as if he actually believed it. 'Sal and me, we're gonna take care of him.'

Swain looked at Choudhuri.

'That's good to hear. And what do you intend to do?' he asked, a slightly malicious tone to his voice.

'Thinking about it,' he said.

'What's to think about?' said Tahir. 'He takes two of ours, we take four of his. That's the way.'

Tahir had obviously seen way too many American gangster flicks for his own good. Sweet didn't have men like Choudhuri had men. Then again, truth of the matter was, neither did Choudhuri. There was no damned organisational pyramid like I always imagined. There were the people who brought the shit in and then there were the people who sold it. Simple as that. No Mister Big and no armies of foot soldiers. Just people like me, some of whom were good at selling drugs and others who were a lot better.

'Show that bastard a thing or two,' Tahir said, giving Swain a wink.

Swain responded with surprising insight and tact.

'We have to think about this situation carefully. The question is, of course, why has he decided to start annoying us now? What's he got up his sleeve? What's he know that we don't?'

'I don't know,' began Choudhuri. 'I'll find out when I see him.'

I left The N C shortly after that, my head filled with concerns about my options and my place in the world. Working for Swain. What a sick joke that was. Practically had dinner with him, too. I did nothing about him and it pissed me off. The least I could have done was walk out, not giving a fuck about protocol. But no. Like a good little soldier ant, I sat there, obedient, complicit, ready to take orders. Not totally true, of course. I was, I optimistically reassured myself, merely gathering intelligence. I stuck around for my own reasons. Matter of fact, all I needed was to use my imagination in order to fuck things up for all concerned. Misinformation, I believe they call it.

On the way home that night, I made a seriously long detour…to Manchester. I decided, with hardly any thought at all, that I was drastically under resourced in the self-preservation, or personal protection department. I'm not talking about personal alarms or Mace spray.

Buying a gun is not the hardest thing in the world. You need two things in order to buy such a weapon. You need money, obviously, and you need a phone. In my case, it took two calls to get the name of a guy and another one phone call to set up an immediate, high priority meet with him. Ten minute's worth of research. Pretty good going for a drug dealer.

Mojo lived Manchester way. I didn't know him, never met the guy before, but he did intrigue me somewhat. Young, but like Soofi, a righteous brother. The weird thing – the thing that had me intrigued – was how he could justify selling extremely illegal items, including stolen cigarettes, clothes and alcoholic beverages, whilst hitting the prayer mat five times a day. None of my business what people decide to do with their lives but still, people like that always make me wonder. I mean, they must have an idea that…well, that what they're doing is fucked up.

By nature, I've never been a fussy person and nor have I ever been one of those shoppers who needs to be hard sold. I bought the first thing he showed me. He held it up and looked at it, like it was something wonderful, something quite amazing but in a good way.

'It's made by Taurus Armaments. American company. Making weapons is one thing those Americans are good at.'

'Pretty good at selling them, too.'

'This particular item is the Taurus PT-92. Semi-Automatic weapon. Nine millimetre ammunition. Very effective and very versatile. In the wrong hands, this could be a very dangerous piece of metal, my friend.'

'Oh,' I said, like it was news to me. 'Right. Well, I'll try to be careful with it, then.'

'Forged alloy frame, five inch barrel. Adjustable rear sight, full safety firing pin block, chambered warning indicator. Fifteen rounds in the cartridge and one more in the hole. This, my dear brother, is one of the best value guns in the world.'

'Value? I don't care about value. I just want something that fires when you press the trigger.'

'This is a good, quality piece of weaponry you see before you. Reliable, accurate and it suits most defensive purposes. It's one weapon I've never had a complaint with.'

He spent a good half hour giving me yet more bullshit. This gun was a celebrity in the world of guns, considering all the awards it had won. He even had one for himself, so he said. He laid it on thicker than treacle. This bullshit spiel of his he gave to everyone no matter what they bought:

'This is a good, quality piece of equipment you see before you. It is reliable, accurate and it suits most…erm mopping purposes. This mop bucket, my dear brother, is one of the best value mop buckets in the world. Made by Taurus Mops. American company. Making mop buckets is one thing those Americans are good at...'

Sure, for all I knew, it could have been the crappest weapon in the world, the Renault of guns.

Next he walked me through all the procedures he thought I ought to know. Told me how to load the ammunition into the cartridge, how to 'install' the cartridge into the gun, how the safety mechanism was engaged, what the little red dot meant, where the oil went to keep the moving parts moving sweetly. All reasonably straight forward enough to understand. At the end of each little stage of the demonstration, he handed it over and said:

'Now you try.'

It felt heavy, *really* heavy for something so small. I always thought guns were heavier than they looked but that thing felt lead heavy. I wondered how people held the bloody things steady.

'Thirty-four ounces unloaded,' he told me. 'A good weight.'

'Feels heavy.'

'Heavy? No. I've handled guns weighing twice as much.'

All in all, including ammunition and cartridges, he ended up taking twelve hundred quid off me but I didn't mind. Well, what was there to mind when I'd just paid with money that wasn't even mine to begin with?

Although no one could be sure if it really was Sweet, the next person to get picked up and disappear was Tahir, which happened early the next day. Unlike the other pick-ups, no one had seen Sweet in action but who else could or would do such a thing? Choudhuri took it well, considering he'd personally made the call to Sweet, asking for the sit down to be moved forward. Picking up Tahir was not a snub, however. It was a declaration of war.

Choudhuri didn't seem to mind too much and that bugged me. I expected him to be all cut up about it but he wasn't. To me, it was obvious what had happened. Sweet picked up Tahir and was presently putting him through a meat grinder. Why? If this was war, then you killed your enemies. But like I said, Choudhuri didn't seem to give a fuck and I asked him why that was.

'That's because I don't give a fuck,' he told me, without too much pressing from me. 'You were there, you saw who's boy he is.'

'I don't follow,' I said, because I didn't, not completely. 'He's Swain's eyes, not mine. Spanner's never been with me.'

'You call him Swain, still?'

'What's the difference? He's still the same person.'

Swain had dropped off the face of the earth but Spanner/Pony Tail/Tahir remained to do his bidding. As far as activities went, nothing much had changed, except, maybe, for the scale of their operations.

'Ah fuck 'em. Fuck 'em all. Especially Swain,' moaned Choudhuri.

And what about that? What was the story between Choudhuri and Swain. How come Swain came out with all that cold shit towards Choudhuri? What was the source of friction between these two? Swain was the boss and Choudhuri was just a front man, a face who took the shit and the praise.

Choudhuri did need to be told that it made sense to use the sit down to get rid of Sweet. After all, Sweet was probably planning on doing the same thing. And without any real back up, especially now that Spanner had been disappeared, Choudhuri was left with no choice but to ask me to watch his back, to be his eyes. Well, Soofi didn't seem to be up to the job and in fact had decided he needed some time alone to think things through.

We had a few hours to get ready but there was not a great deal to do, in preparation for the meeting. We walked down into the kitchen, then into the cellar. On the wall, he had a large metal tool cupboard which he unlocked with a key he kept around his neck. One side was stacked with notes. The other contained a small arsenal: hand guns, ammunition, a couple of hand grenades and yes, even a machine gun. I could not believe my eyes.

'Take your pick,' he said, no big deal.

'What?'

'Choose one. Hurry up. I'd go for one of these,' he said, selecting a gun identical to the one I'd bought from Mojo.

'These are supposed to be good. Made by an American company. Making weapons is one thing those fucking yanks are good at.'

'Pretty good at selling them, too.'

'Yeah,' he agreed. 'That's a good one, that.'

Back upstairs, waiting for the hours to pass, Choudhuri started yakking at me. It wasn't nagging or nothing, just telling me stuff because he thought it was interesting. And I guess it was, sort of.

Choudhuri came here less than thirty years ago with next to nothing. One of the original brown imports, he giggled to himself. A founder member of that not so exclusive Mangaythur Club, a Boy from the Barns, another Sufaari from Chakswari.

His father worked in Chakswari wheat fields all his life, sowing and reaping for a farmer who specialised in screwing the shit out of the little guy. Choudhuri, however, had an uncle by the name of Asghar. Asghar didn't fancy the idea of hanging around and getting similarly shafted. So instead, he borrowed some money and made his way over here, to England. He travelled around and eventually settled in little old Bradford. Walked off the street and straight into a job in one of the city's many mills. That was 1960. A few years later on, uncle Asghar had brought his young family over and that side of the clan settled and allowed themselves to take root in what was sometimes unsuitable soil. Sometime in the late 1970s, Asghar's eldest daughter needed wedding and so, he got in touch with his brother back in Pakistan and offered him the deal: your son for my daughter kind of thing. Done.

If I had to blame anyone for the way Choudhuri had turned out, then it had to be his uncle Asghar who also doubled up as his father-in-law. For over ten years Choudhuri's existence was no better than that of a slave. Come pay day, his wage packet, without even being opened, got handed over. I asked him why he hadn't taken off, got his own place, took his wife with him. How come he hadn't showed a bit of spirit? Not the done thing, Choudhuri told me. Would have killed his old man back in Pakistan. Even so, through such adversity, Choudhuri found strength, a sense of purpose, something to live for. Strange, but as he talked of what drove him to success, he reminded me of me, of that kid called Khalil who at one time, more than anything else in the world, wanted revenge.

He didn't mean to sound awful, but Choudhuri said he found freedom with the death of his father. After burying him in Pakistan, he came back but not empty handed. Fifty grand's worth of brown shit hidden in his luggage and amongst his person. A brown import bringing in an altogether more valuable commodity than himself and getting away with it was a pretty big deal back then. Choudhuri's next move, however, was the smartest, but the simplest thing he ever did. Instead of bringing the shit in himself or even using people who were prepared to act as knowing mules, he got *innocent* and unwitting people to do it for him. How did he do that? First of all, he set up a network of scouts. Whenever one of these scouts got wind of a brown import about to make the journey to England, be it a he or a she, the system would kick in. The scout would approach and then ask the travelling party to take a small package of something or other (herbs, wild tobacco or a course of fakir's cure) to a relative over in England. Sometimes, a whole family would take bits and bats without suspecting anything even remotely untoward was going off.

After a while, he'd got to a stage where everything was in place and all he had to do was be there just to collect the package. By now, of course, he wasn't working alone. While he busied himself bringing the shit in,

Charlie Boy and Tahir set themselves the task of refining a distribution network. The rest, what little there was of it, I could work out for myself.

The line wasn't so clear but I still recognised his voice with the first sound he uttered. What the hell did he want with me?

'We need to talk,' he said. 'Somewhere private.'

I was suspicious, naturally, but I had some long unfinished business with him. A meeting presented an opportunity that I could not afford to miss.

'Where?'

'The park. Side entrance. Now would be good.'

I checked my watch and figured I still had plenty of time. I got up and told Choudhuri I'd be back within the hour. Choudhuri was not having it and instantly lost his mind: brandishing two guns, one in each hand, accusing me of everything under the sun, threatening me with even more. When he stopped, I calmly told him the truth. Choudhuri sank into thought, perhaps realising something beyond my comprehension.

'Okay,' he said. 'You go and see him but you be careful with that son of a bitch. He's up to something.'

It wasn't for my sake that Choudhuri gave the warning, but his own. Anything happened to me, then he'd have to face Sweet alone. Not that he was afraid – crazy people are rarely afraid, I imagine – but he did believe in the strength that came with numbers. Choudhuri stood a much better chance of survival with me than without me. Maybe he was right but I was not going to risk my own existence for the sake of his. If it came down to it, I would not take a bullet for him or for any of these bastards for that matter.

'Tell me something I don't know.'

I drove over, as agreed, to the side entrance to the park. Time was tight but it wouldn't last long, I hoped. He turned up in his Bentley – not Roller – but still the same car Rose had taken her last journey in. He parked it in front of my Lexus. I got out and approached the passenger side of his car.

'Get in,' he said.

Even though it made no sense, Swain decided to extend his stay in town until things cleared up with this Sweet thing. He said he had too much to lose and really couldn't bring himself to leave it all in the hands of Choudhuri, a satisfactory but uninspired, perhaps weak second in command. Swain was keen on telling me all this because, according to him:

'The whole thing could go pear shaped.'

'Because of Sweet?'

'Because of Choudhuri. He should never have let this get so out of hand.'

I nodded.

'And then there's Price. I think he knows too much.'

'What makes you say that?'

'I have sources of my own. I hear things.'

Sources singular. Sources Grizzly.

'Everything's a mess.'

So what? Did I give a fuck?

'And then there's you.'

My heart sank as I watched his hand slip into his pocket.

'What about me?'

He pulled out a white handkerchief and mopped his brow.

'You're good. Too good to be true, really.'

'Meaning?'

'I know what you're after.'

I cleared my throat and carefully located the weapon in my jacket pocket.

'And what's that? What am I after?'

'Choudhuri. You want his spot. You do, don't you?'

I didn't answer, mostly because I was too relieved to talk. For a minute, I thought he was onto me.

'I don't blame you. Choudhuri's been slipping for years, now.'

How wrong could one person be? I almost laughed.

'I've got a bad feeling about this situation and that's why I'm here, risking my career, talking to you.'

'Why are you talking to me?'

He cleared his throat, then turned and looked me in the eye. I looked back and did my best not to blink.

'Well?'

He seemed to be in a trance, just looking at me, perhaps seeing something familiar, perhaps not.

'Well,' I asked again. 'What do you want from me?'

He blinked and then rubbed his eyes, mumbling something to himself before, once again, he cleared his throat and said:

'I need someone I can trust. I need someone to take his place.'

'Take his place?'

'In case anything happens to him with this meeting he's having with Sweet.'

Sounded to me as if Swain actually wanted Choudhuri out of the picture.

'There's no *in case*,' I said. 'One of them's gonna get killed.'

'All you have to do is not turn up. Let Sweet finish things off.'

'And then what?'

'And then you finish Sweet, of course.'

And how the fuck would I do that? Never mind how? Why? I was not like these people. I wanted out, not to sink deeper still.

'I have to think about it. Sleep on it, maybe.'

He said he'd call me within a day, two at the most. Funny thing is, I had a feeling he would, too.

On the way back to The N C, I noticed a set of lights glow to life and then continue to follow me for half a mile at least. Only Price would follow me with the intention of getting caught. He was like one of those friends who keeps popping up all over the place. I didn't really mind but he could be a pain in the arse, at times.

I checked my watch for time. Three quarters of an hour left before Sweet showed up at The N C. Price flashed me to pull over.

'So,' he said as he got in next to me. 'Things are moving, I see.'

I didn't respond.

'Padgett,' he said. 'What's he doing mixing with people like you and Choudhuri?'

'I wouldn't like to guess. Far as I know, Choudhuri invited him over for a meal.'

'And why would he do that?'

'You know what Choudhuri's like.'

'I see. But why the secret meeting with you? What was all that about?'

280

'I thought you were a copper.'

He didn't get it and said:

'But I am a copper.'

'So how about you doing your job instead of me doing it for you.'

He smiled.

'What's going on with you and Padgett, Khalil?'

I sighed and told him:

'He wanted some money.'

'What? Money? What money?'

'He was fundraising. I gave him a grand.'

'Did he give you a receipt?'

'I didn't ask.'

'You're lying. I can tell when you lie.'

'What do you want? I don't need this questions and answer bullshit right now.'

He nodded sympathetically.

'Okay, Khalil. Have it your own way.'

Maybe I was going about this all wrong. Perhaps I should have included Price in my game plan. It felt like a good idea but it was too risky. Could I trust him? Could I fuck. This was the same bastard, the same righteous fuck who didn't tell me about Rose being undercover when he had the chance. No one, not even myself, could be trusted any more.

'How've you been, Khalil?' he asked, starting over, hoping it would make a difference.

'Fuck how I've been. How come you never told me about Rose, man?'

'Are you over her, yet? You seem to be over her.'

Truth is I wasn't over her at all. I treated her the same way I treated everything else that ever meant anything to me. All I did was block her out because doing that was the easier thing to do.

'How come? How come I had to find out from that fucking mate of yours?'

'Adams?'

'No, your dad. Who else would know?'

'Were you surprised when he told you?'

'Course I was surprised.'

'How do you think it would have looked if you weren't surprised, Khalil?'

I sulked. He was right, of course, as usual. Wise old man Price. I hated that.

'She was a good girl, Khalil and, for what it's worth, she thought you were a good person.'

'You should never have put her in that situation, man.'

'It was her job. She knew what she was doing. She knew the risks. No one's to blame for what happened to her.'

'Maybe everyone's to blame.'

He lit up a cigarette and inhaled deeply. I opened a window.

'So,' he exhaled. 'Were you there when it happened?'

I shook my head.

'What do you take me for? Do you think I'd have let that happen?'

'I'm sorry. I meant something else.'

'Sure you did.'

'Do you know who did it?'

I thought about it. Thinking over a response to such a straightforward yes/no question is a mistake, a dead giveaway.

'No.'

'I don't believe you.'

'Don't believe me. I don't care.'

I then told him about Sweet and the sit down with Choudhuri.

'Interesting,' he remarked.

'You know about Tahir, then,' I stated.

'The Spanner. Yes. I hear he's been detained.'

'Detained? That's a new way of putting it.'

Price smiled and started to tell me there was something else he thought I might need to know. I didn't have time, I said. I was running late. I turned the volume up which hinted Price to get out. He started saying something again but I couldn't be arsed with his crap any more.

Choudhuri seemed anxious. With the evening's business already planned out, he needed something to help pass the time. What better than food?

As he ate and as the seconds ticked by, I could sense his nervousness grow stronger, more urgent. Although not entirely strange, this was still a little puzzling. This was supposed to be Saleem Choudhuri, the self made man who came to this country with nothing and beat everything it could throw at him. He was not supposed to suffer from nerves.

'How come he's got you so worried?' I asked.

Choudhuri swallowed his food, stared at me and then said.

'He's like you. That's why.'

What followed is the only real conversation I ever had with Choudhuri. Everything else was either posturing, argument or nothing more than general chit chat. What happened that day turned out to be the one interesting, perhaps human memory I have of Choudhuri.

'What?'

'He's like you.'

'Me? How do you work that one out?'

'He's a new breed, this guy.'

It just came to me. I have no other explanation as to why I would say:

'You trust me?'

Choudhuri cocked his head, as if puzzled or in thought.

'I don't know. I really don't know about you. With some people you can tell straight away with what you see. Some people are either arseholes or geniuses, citizens or crooks, dogs or snakes.'

'Dogs?'

'Yeah, dogs. Dogs you can trust, snakes you can't.'

'Oh.'

He scooped some food into his mouth and as he started to chew, he continued.

'You wanna know what I see when I see you?'

I shrugged.

'Sure. What?

'I see too much. Sometimes I see the smartest son of a bitch I've ever seen and other times I don't. Other times I see a kid who can't even wipe his own nose. Sometimes I see a killer, sometimes a priest. I just don't know with you, Kilo. Maybe you should tell me.'

'Tell you what?'

'If I can trust you.'

'In that case no,' I smiled. 'No, you probably can't.'

Choudhuri laughed.

'See what I mean? I don't know who's the bigger threat: you or Sweet.'

Surely not me. I was not like Sweet. Sweet was a land mine: indiscriminate, bloody and unfeeling. I saw myself as something much more clinical and exact: a bullet, one of those smart bombs, perhaps.

'When I first heard about him, the way he was, I thought he'd fizzle out and settle down in no time. That was maybe four or five years ago.'

'So he's always been this dangerous?'

'That's putting it mildly. He used to do all sorts to guys he didn't like. Beat 'em up, mug 'em, move 'em on. After a while, I got really pissed off with it but I thought I'd give the man a chance. So I set up a sit down with him, just like now. We talked and he seemed okay about it. We agreed not to fuck with each other. I mean, who wants war, right?'

I nodded and then looked at my watch. Ten minutes before the fireworks were scheduled to begin.

'So, a month later, it starts happening again. This time, I've no patience to talk with this fucking idiot. I make a few calls, get a few names and then set the wheels in motion. First of all, I send these three guys to take care of this matter. These three crazy Pathans. Brothers they were. Fought against the Russians: Mujahidins, you know?'

'Sounds serious.'

'Oh yeah,' he commented. 'Real serious. But guess what happened?'

'What?'

'Coppers found 'em a week later in that river, the Aire.'

Choudhuri shook his head.

'That's not the half of it. Two months after, I got these crazy fucking idiots, these stupid fucking nazis from down south, from Chelsea,' he nodded. 'A whole army of the bald bastards.'

Choudhuri paused and didn't seem to want to continue.

'And?'

'And? The ones he didn't kill ended up in a lunatic asylum.'

This did not sound anything like the Sweet I'd spoken to. Choudhuri was not the most honest soul around but I could tell he was not making this shit up. People don't get scared by their own bogey man tales.

'He's a maniac,' he sighed. 'An out and out maniac. No other word for him.'

I shook my head. I didn't want to be there any more. Too late to run, hide or make excuses.

'You know what I did in the end? I got this guy from the States. Got him to come over specially. Paid for his flight, for his keep, paid for everything.'

'Go on.'

'Now this guy, a Mafia guy no less, guaranteed a result for his fee.'

'How much?'

'Hundred grand: sterling. Payable upon completion.'

'And?'

'What do you mean *and*? In case you haven't noticed, that cocksucker Sweet still happens to be very much alive.'

Cometh the hour, cometh the man. Only not. With each minute that ticked by, Choudhuri grew more desperate. A nervous breakdown was imminent.

'Without Spanner,' he kept saying, 'we're screwed…screwed.'

I was tempted to get up and slap him, like heroes do to hysterical women in the old black and white flicks. Instead, I simply said:

'Chill out.'

I didn't feel any less worried but it seemed to calm him down. Actually, worried is the wrong word: shit scared pretty much summed it up.

Five minutes before the hour I went downstairs and waited, readying myself for Sweet and his woman. I was half tempted to leg it but it seemed wrong even though it meant being dishonest with the dishonest, dishonourable with the dishonourable. They parked up outside and in they came, not saying a word, just nods all round.

Sweet was in casual gear: a pair of Nike Air Something Or Other shod his feet, some other brand name tracky covering his body. This time he had more gold around his neck than a rich Pakistani bitch on her wedding day. Sweet's woman, however, she was in her stock black attire. She smelt nice as she drifted past.

They followed me upstairs and as soon as Choudhuri copped for them, he began with the coughing shit, his now dulled toupee almost but not quite working itself loose. He pulled out his inhaler and toked until he got some colour back in his cheeks. I sat down next to Choudhuri. Without saying a word, they sat opposite us.

'Glad you could come,' wheezed the fat man.

'So,' said Sweet, crossing his legs, cool as a cucumber. 'You think we need to talk.'

'I think so,' said Choudhuri.

Choudhuri started huffing and puffing like the Big Bad Wolf after a marathon. I cleared my throat.

'So,' I began, feeling a little like a peace maker. 'Who wants to start off?'

Choudhuri sniffed and then said:

'Spanner. He alive?'

'Spanner?' asked Sweet. 'How the fuck would I know, guy?'

'I thought you wanted to talk,' said Choudhuri. 'Why the games?'

'I ain't no kid and I don't play no games. I don't have that fool.'

Choudhuri sighed and took a sip of water.

'Okay,' continued Choudhuri, pausing to dab his lips with a napkin. 'How long you been working for him?'

I looked at Choudhuri, then at Sweet, wondering who he was talking about now.

'Not working for no one. That's not what I do.'

Choudhuri nodded.

'Okay…I'll put it another way: how long you been getting advised by him?'

Sweet smiled.

'Oh,' he said. 'Is that what it's called?'

'What is this? Who are you talking about?'

It was as if I wasn't even there. One thing that no one likes is not being in on the joke. More than anything else, it's just plain rude.

'Call it whatever you like,' replied Choudhuri.

'Well, not long if you must know,' Sweet said. 'Few weeks, if that.'

'And I suppose he's promised you my spot.'

'What's going on here?' I asked, only to be ignored again.

'Amongst other things, yeah,' said Sweet. 'Not that I wouldn't get it sooner or later anyway.'

'Just wait a minute here,' I said. 'What the fuck are you people talking about?'

Choudhuri smiled at me.

'See what I mean? When I said I couldn't tell about you, this is what I meant. Sometimes you're really smart, Kilo. Other times you're as thick as shit.'

I looked to Sweet, hoping he'd put me out of my misery.

'Don't tell me you've not clicked. Like everything else, this is all about politics and power. Having the product to sell is one thing, having the distribution is another.'

One by one, the pennies dropped.

In the beginning there was Choudhuri who brought the shit in and then got rid of it. A long, slow and arduous process. Then along came Swain. Now Swain had a distribution network which consisted of hundreds and hundreds of dealers. Without the product, the dealers had nothing to sell. Without the dealers, Choudhuri had no one to sell it through. It seemed Choudhuri and Swain were destined to be together.

Over the years, Swain grew tired and greedy with this equal but different relationship. His side, the movement of product, after all, was the real money spinner. These days, any fool can bring the shit into the country but a solid distribution network is another matter. And so, Swain figured he could do without Choudhuri in the chain. But he still needed a puppet to be there in place of the fat man.

And this is where we'd got. What better way for Swain to get rid of Choudhuri than this? Promise Sweet an uncontested spot at the top and leave the rest to work itself out. As to why Sweet had courted me, that was obvious. With me on Sweet's side, Choudhuri was weakened from within. His product still went out, but only now it appeared as if Sweet was controlling it. Choudhuri, so the guys on the street were beginning to think, really was old news.

'Swain's using you,' I found myself saying.

'Oh,' said Sweet. 'Like I don't know? You think I'm stupid, guy?'

'It's just…'

'It's just business,' said Sweet. 'The way these things go.'

No one spoke for a moment. His woman, who hadn't said anything at all starting gently humming a tune to herself. I looked at her and she smiled at me, not a fuck me smile like before, but something much friendlier. I smiled back.

'So what now?' asked Choudhuri.

Sweet shrugged and then said:

'I'd have thought that was obvious.'

In a single blink, the scene and the situation had changed so much. I was a part of it and I didn't even notice.

It could only ever be this way, I suppose. Everyone was holding everyone else to ransom. Sweet was pointing a gun at Choudhuri. Choudhuri was pointing a gun at Sweet's woman. Sweet's woman was pointing a gun at me. And me, I found myself pointing my gun at Sweet. I suddenly realised it didn't matter who I pointed my gun at because these people, all of them, didn't really deserve to live. I looked at his woman and told her:

'We need to chill out, here.'

'This looks complicated,' she said.

'I know. But how about you put the gun down…'

She raised her eyebrows.

'You put yours down and I'll put mine down.'

Sweet smiled.

'While you're at it, suck my dick!'

And with that I closed my eyes, said a few words of prayer, and expected the worst. He didn't pull the trigger, though. Neither did any-one else.

'Chill the fuck out,' I said again. 'Okay?'

I looked at them all, one by one, gently nodding all the time. Choudhuri was sweating his fat arse off but the other two were still looking cool. Me, I was ready for a heart attack.

'Look,' I began again. 'This is fucked up.'

'Don't you say another fucking thing, Kilo,' urged Choudhuri. 'Don't you say a thing.'

'Maybe we should all lower our guns. On three?'

'Shut the fuck up, Kilo,' said Choudhuri.

'One,'

Sweet nodded and so did his woman.

'No way,' said Choudhuri. 'No fucking way.'

'Come on, Sal,' I said. 'Stop being a fucking pain in the arse.'

'Two,' counted Sweet.

Choudhuri sighed and with that, it seemed he accepted a truce.

'Three.'

Sweet's woman lowered her gun and so did I. Choudhuri licked his lips and placed his piece on the table. Sweet smiled.

'There,' he said. 'All friends again.'

'Lower your piece,' I said. 'We said on three.'

'Oh yeah,' nodded Sweet and lowered his gun. 'Forgot.'

I sighed with relief but it wasn't over. I closed my eyes and shook my head, thinking this was a mistake.

I heard two gun shots and then I heard nothing. The blast had deafened me. I looked and saw Choudhuri and Sweet's woman with their faces on the table. Both dead. Sweet was staring at the gun in Choudhuri's hand; another Taurus, just like the piece he carried.

'Good guns, them,' I managed.

Sweet shot Choudhuri three more times and then reached for his dead woman.

I never thought I'd live to see a man like Sweet cry, especially over a woman.

'Shit,' I said.

'Is that all you can say?' he complained, real tears flowing over the ones that had been inked in. 'This is my woman, guy. And now she's dead. Cos of you. You fucking cocksucker.'

He turned on me but faced the rectangular barrel of the weapon I'd bought off Mojo.

'This shit was your own doing, man,' I told him.

He went back to sobbing over his woman. I was torn between shooting him – and resolving a future problem – and walking away. In the end, I allowed him to have a say in his fate.

'I'm gonna just walk away. But understand this, I can finish this now. I want you to know that.'

He nodded.

I thought about this, whether I was doing the right thing. Leave him living and risk his wrath or kill the motherfucker and look forward to a relatively peaceful time of it?

'Are we cool?' I asked.

He said nothing. I walked closer to him and touched his head with the gun.

'Are we fucking cool?'

'We're cool,' he said. 'We can live in peace.'

I backed myself out of the room and then ran down the stairs, feeling a weight lift off my shoulders.

As soon as I stepped outside The N C, I breathed a huge sigh of relief; half expecting to hear the sound of Sweet come bounding down the stairs after me. I closed my eyes and leant against a wall, telling myself I'd made it, survived. When I opened my eyes, I saw Soofi approach and stop by my side.

'You're Ayub Khan's son,' a smile forming on his face.

'What?'

'I've known about you. I remember seeing you as a boy. In your father's shop.'

He looked at me fondly, as if he was remembering something pleasant.

'I don't understand. Why are you telling me this now?'

'Seems like the right thing to do. It's better to do some things while you still can.'

'Things are bad,' I said.

Seemed Soofi had his own concerns right then.

'I knew him quite well, you know; your father. A good, honest man. I thought you should know. I thought you should know that I know about what happened.'

'What do you mean?'

'I'm talking about Swain, Kilo. I know what happened and I know what you're going to do. I can see it in your eyes.'

I stepped up to him but he didn't back off.

'Don't worry. No one else knows about it. I'm sorry, Kilo. It was disgraceful, the way he died, how he died.'

'God's Will, though, right?'

'Ultimately, yes but even so, sometimes men create just as much pain.'

He was right. The first time I saw him I remember thinking he was a wise one, this funny little guy with the red beard. Still waters run deep and all that.

'Sal's dead,' I said.

To look at him, you wouldn't think he had it in him. He took my gun and in he went, not giving a shit, ready to end his own life, if that's what it took to avenge the life of the only friend he'd ever had.

'It's okay,' he said. 'It's okay, Kilo. I know what I have to do. This is my duty.'

And right then, for the first time ever, I was truly prepared to face mine.

white man's got a god complex

I remember getting in my car, starting it up and then driving around aimlessly. I wasn't expecting him to call but in hindsight, it was obvious that he would.

'I've heard about what happened. What a fucking fiasco,' he said.

'I got away. How come you heard so soon?'

'Contacts. Inside info's expensive but it's always worthwhile.'

Inside info my arse.

'We should meet,' he said, with a calm but slightly urgent tone.

'Should we?'

'We *need* to meet.'

And so, we met up. He ended up giving me a little tour of the town. I, amongst other things, took the opportunity to sort my life out once and for all.

After getting a shave and a fresh change of clothes, I drove back to The N C. I figured someone must have heard the ruckus and then called the coppers, one of whom blocked my way in. I told him I had some information that might be useful:

'Piss off,' he said. 'That's what they all say.'

Not wanting to create a fuss, I backed off but stuck around. Soon enough, I saw Price and Hopkins walk out and then, for a couple of minutes, stand around, twiddling their thumbs, trying to make themselves look useful. I approached the copper again.

'Tell Price I wanna see him.'

'Who the fuck are you supposed to be?'

Was it any wonder young gangstas decided to embark on gangsta careers? Coppers like this guy needed a crash course in manners, never mind any of that community relations cobblers.

'Me? I'm your dad,' I said, giving him the coolest stare I could.

He nodded a couple of times, saying something about *fuckin' pakis* under his breath, and then walked over to Price. Fighting fire with fire is the best way, sometimes.

Seemed Price and his boys had been busy over the last couple of hours. They'd cordoned off The N C by slapping that yellow and black chevron-ed police tape all over the place. They'd also blocked the road off, keeping reporters and members of the public at bay. About time they started earning their pay.

'Well, well, well,' Hopkins started. 'Look who it is.'

You could still smell the gun smoke which had seeped out, onto the road.

'Looks like there's a new boss in town, then,' he added.

'And who would that be?' I said with a smirk. 'Your dad?'

Hopkins moved forwards, only to be stopped by Price.

'Don't know whether to offer you sympathy or congratulations,' Price said.

'Don't bother with either.'

'You were here, were you?' Hopkins asked. 'When all this shit went off?'

'I've been busy. Just got here. I'd have thought you'd have noticed that much at least.'

'What is it about you?' he asked. 'Ever since you've been around, people have been dropping like flies.'

'Must be a gift I have.'

'That's not funny. Three people are dead.'

'Oh? And who might those be?'

'Soofi's alive,' Price said. 'But he's in intensive care. Shot in the neck. Looks like he got caught in the crossfire.'

'Fuck 'em. Maybe they deserved it.'

Price cleared his throat and asked me for a few minutes in private which I granted with a nod. We walked towards his car. I sat on the bonnet. He faced me.

'We're not through with you,' he said.

'Well, I'm through with you. I've had enough. I just wanna go home. It's over.'

'Don't lie to me, Khalil. You never were any good at lying.'

'Leave me alone. The big boys are dead. What more do you want?'

'A statement.'

I gave him a look.

'A statement spelling everything out; naming names.'

This was not such a surprise. Every other time we'd met, he'd men-

293

tioned the big names but never the biggest. I realised he'd known all along about Swain but never had any proof. Least not until I came along.

'I staked everything on you.'

What was he talking about? Why was he making it out as if I'd been a part of his plans? Did he ever have any plans?

'If it wasn't for me, you wouldn't be here now,' he said. 'This has taken me years.'

'Bullshit. You just took your chances same as everyone else. Same as me.'

Price laughed.

'Why else do you think I singled you out when Tony gave me every name going? Why did I speak to you and not King? Why you and not Tony for that matter? I needed you, Kilo. I needed someone like you.'

'What's that supposed to mean?'

'I needed someone with a purpose in life.'

What was he saying? He was saying he played me like a fucking fiddle, that's what. It didn't seem right, but then, it didn't seem too wrong, either.

'Now I need you more than ever, Khalil. Think about Rose, think about your friend Cowboy. Think about what happened to them and who was responsible.'

'Swain. All down to Swain,' I found myself saying.

'Think about your father. He was ruined by the same man. You've always known that. Don't deny it now. Don't start thinking otherwise now. Not now when you need it most.'

Price was right. That's all I'd ever thought and even if I wanted to, I couldn't somehow not stop thinking it now. One thing that spurred me on, no matter what I did or where I was in the food chain, was Charlie Boy Swain and his impact on the life of my father and then me. He'd always been there, always an itch I couldn't scratch.

'There's nothing more to do,' I said. 'Everything's done. Taken care of.'

'You're wrong, Khalil. You're so wrong.'

'About what?'

'I know everything. I know what you've done.'

I looked at him with a cold, hard stare but I had him all wrong. He was not threatening me. Congratulating me was more like it.

'I'll deny everything,' I stated.

'You don't have to. I know where you've been, Khalil. I know what's happened and it's okay.'

'Say that again? Where I've been? What's that supposed to mean?'

Price did the strangest thing. He gently held my face and then whispered in my ear.

'Sweet never had Spanner.'

I looked at him in disbelief. I felt dizzy. So much so that I had to open a door and sit down before I fainted. The skin across my whole body broke into a cold sweat.

'You,' I said. 'This is about you. You and your fucking daughter. That's what all this was about.'

'You make it sound as if it was something bad. As if it's meant nothing to you. You got what you wanted.'

'I don't know what this is. Not any more.'

'Don't worry, Khalil. You did the right thing.'

'How can you say that?'

He sighed, frustrated about something.

'Don't worry,' he said. 'It's okay. It'll all work out.'

'What?'

'I know,' he said. 'I know all about it. I know what's happened. Don't worry, Khalil,' he said again. 'You did the right thing.'

'I don't think you understand.'

'Of course I understand,' he said. 'If it wasn't for me, you wouldn't have done it.'

'You're confused. You don't understand.'

'The car park. The little trip around town. You should know, Khalil, that I've never let you out of my sight.'

'Does that mean you're not going to arrest me?'

'Now why would I do that, Khalil? You did a good thing.'

'What? A good thing? How ...'

'Don't ever forget this, Khalil. What you've done today is a good thing.'

'A good thing?'

'Yes. A good thing even though it was bad.'

'Fuck.'

'Don't ever forget this, Khalil. What you've done today frees you from your sins.'

'A good thing…A good thing even though it was bad.'

We met on the top floor of the Kirkgate Centre car park in town. It had just gone eight . I transferred into his car, the five year old, light green and austere looking Bentley, which he proceeded to drive like an old man. We drove down Sunbridge Road until he took an illegal right at the lights. Even when we got on to the nice wide expanse that is Thornton Road, the speedo didn't whisper above thirty.

'Suppose I should offer you my condolences,' he said.

'Should you?'

'It's the civil thing to do.'

'Shame, though,' I said. 'Shame it didn't work out how you wanted.'

'How do you know it didn't?'

At least he didn't try denying it. Saved time, if nothing else.

'Maybe I wanted a new start. Choudhuri was weak but that Sweet lad, he was just insane. Each as bad as the other and now they're both gone. Which leaves a vacant position and from where I stand, there's only one person to fill it.'

'Sounds interesting,' I said, a touch of nonchalance for effect.

'I won't bother wasting time, then. A deal,' he sniffed.

Swain cut a tight right by the old car tyre warehouse. From there, he took a left onto White Abbey Road. At one time, some smart arse sprayed BLACK over the WHITE in White Abbey because that's what it was: one of those *Spot the White Man* parts of the world.

'More a proposition than a deal,' informed Swain.

A voice. No, not a voice, but a thought entered my head. This was it, I told myself. This was the moment I'd been waiting for. In my pocket I had a gun and all I had to do was point it in his general direction and press the trigger. How hard could it be? Not like I needed another reason. This was it, the perfect opportunity.

'I think I know what you're going to say.'

Whetley Hill. Swain looked out of the window and smiled at the people we passed by.

296

'I'm like you – a businessman first – a damned good one at that.'

He could also add drug baron, rapist and murderer to his list of talents. Maybe he'd grown modest over the years.

'So I heard,' I said.

Swain stopped at the lights and looked out of the window again. Now was a good time to do it. I wouldn't even have to take the thing out. Just shoot it through my pocket, open the door then walk away. I cleared my throat.

'I know him,' remarked Swain, waving at an old Pakistani bloke on the other side of the road. 'Right piece of work, that feller. Got four houses on rent, all on his kids names, and he's on disability! Talk about your lot being sharp characters.'

The old man smiled and waved back. He didn't seem too disabled, nor did he look like the sharpest tool in the shed.

'My lot.'

'You know what I mean.'

'Oh yeah,' I said, my fingers caressing the barrel. 'I know what you mean.'

The lights went green and Swain swung a right, onto Carlisle Road. Sugar Cane Club on the left and Manningham Sports Centre on the right.

'You known him long, that old bloke? The sharp one?'

'Not really. Tried doing a bit of business with him a while back but he just wouldn't have it.'

A smile came to my face because that was my old man's attitude, at first. The smile lost itself when I remembered Swain's subsequent offers of business. The baseball bat, the skinhead hair cut and the tattooed arms. And me, watching it all, shitting myself but in a sick way, allowing my young self to be impressed by it all.

'I dabble in a bit of all sorts, really,' he said for no reason in particular. 'Property, investment, insurance, retailing.'

Property doubtless referred to his land-lording interests, insurance meant protection and investment was all about extortion. As for retailing, that was anyone's guess. He could have been selling arms to Saddam Hussein for all anyone knows.

'And with him? The old guy?'

'You know how it is with some of your lot,' he explained. 'Want everything for nothing.'

How the tides turned and then some. Everything for nothing? I couldn't have scripted that one any better myself. I didn't know whether to laugh or to…shoot him there and then. That's what I wanted to do. I wanted to shoot but I just didn't have it in me. Like I'd known all along, I never had it in me to do such a thing, not after so many years. Tony? Tony was nothing; self defence, an instinctive and reflexive act. Not like this. Too many years had passed for that youthful, angry and above all, innocent passion to still burn inside me with the ferocity it had started with. I wished that kid was still alive but maybe his essence, his nature, started to die the moment I left home.

'There's a bit of that in all of you,' he said. 'Something about your people that makes them like that. Now with someone like myself, what you see is what you get. Straight shooting, straight speaking business-man.'

'That's good to hear,' I said. 'People like you, few and far between.'

He nodded, proud and as sure of the fact as he could be.

'The only way to get anything in this life is to earn it.'

How could he say this shit with a straight face? After all he'd done in his life, he had the nerve to spew this. I decided not to answer any more of this sanctimonious bollocks, at least not verbally. Instead, I thought it wiser, perhaps easier, to sit there patiently until we got back into town. I couldn't bear being in the same space as him.

'You try telling that to kids these days and they laugh at you.'

Another set of lights. A row of shops on our left and a social services office to our right. Swain indicated to turn left, along Church Street. Still the same turf he ran like clockwork a lifetime ago.

'Shame about Choudhuri but you could see I had no choice.'

'Course you didn't.'

'Not that I didn't like him. Not that at all,' he said, then patted me on the thigh. 'Good man, he was.'

'I know.'

'He ever tell you how far we went back?'

'He mentioned it, yeah.'

'You know,' said Swain, smiling to himself. 'You know that I was one of the first friends he ever had in this country. Didn't know a thing until he met me.'

'Lucky him.'

'Hard but happy days. Me, Spanner and Sal, doing the business. You should have seen us.'

St. Mary's Road lights. Too many traffic lights in Bradford, slowing people down, breaking their rhythms. An auction house on the left where all the local landlords buy cheap, shit and second hand furniture that most people would either burn or commit to a skip. Opposite lay the scattered, and still smouldering remains of a relatively new BMW showroom. It had only been up three or four years. I used to love that building. Through the glass – and there was lots of glass – there sat a nice range of brand spanking Beemers, slowly rotating on turntables, polished brighter than new money. I could never work out exactly what a BMW showroom was doing in a relatively poor patch like Oak Lane. Like seeing Netto in the middle of Mayfair, it just doesn't seem right. Still, won't have to worry about that any more. Like the building it replaced, a load of rioting locals decided to torch it one summer. Bradford and riots kind of go hand in hand.

Swain took a left up Oak Lane. The Hill. That one road has everything you can care to think of in terms of retailers. Supermarket, newsagents, fruit and veg, butchers, curry houses, mortgage advisors, chippies, clothing, massage parlour…the lot. A centre of many a thriving business but it became notorious throughout Bradford after the riots of 1995. As Swain and I drove up we saw young punks, all of them Asian, standing on corners, ready to kick up a fuss for no reason in particular. When the mood takes them, these fuckers will hurl abuse and bricks at anyone, thinking they and the next big thing are one and the same. A bunch of trouble causers, a bunch of cowards with an ever ready supply of petrol bombs for that special, or not so special, occasion. That's what this town, along with the rest of the world, happens to think because that's what gets told. Doesn't mean it's the truth.

'So what did your little gang get up to, then?'

'Ah,' he complained. 'It was never that big a deal. We were just kids in those days and, you know: just kid things.'

'What kind of things? Anything serious?'

Straight through the lights at the top, onto Lilycroft Road, passing Lister's Mill on the right. On the left, facing that decrepit, derelict and dog-eared Taj Mahal to textiles, had appeared an even more impressive building: Lawcroft House. The newest and biggest nick in town. A fortress. Behind the bomb proof walls, it housed more coppers than you could shake a stick at. Handy being here, though. Unlike the BMW showroom, it had reason. With all the young punks causing trouble down the road whenever the urge took them, it made sense to have a supply of riot quellers on tap.

'We did all sorts but mainly it was, you know, a bit of the old paki stuff.'

'Paki stuff?'

'No offence,' he said, amiably enough. 'But that's what we used to call hashish. You know…'

'Oh. So you were just a bunch of pushers, then.'

Swain shook his head slowly.

'Bunch of pushers? Us? Bunch of pushers? You'd have got a slap for that if you'd have said that at the time. We were never just a bunch of *pushers*. Me and the others, we ran this whole town fifteen, twenty years ago.'

'I'm impressed.'

'Should have seen us,' he pondered. 'We were something else back then.'

Thing is, I did see them. He, more than anyone else, made me what I am. The perfect son until he came along. Everything in my world was ruined because of him. I felt like telling him but it didn't seem the right moment. I knew all too well that the right moment would never come at this rate but still, I could try to force it.

'What else did you lot do, then?'

We stopped at the skittle shape roundabout at the end of Lilycroft Road. Swain seemed to take a few moments, considering his options. If we took a left, we'd hit Toller Lane, which would take us back on to Whetley Hill, then into town. Next exit: Duckworth Lane, which would take us past the hospital and then into Allerton. The third exit didn't seem likely as we'd be going Uptown, deeper into Heaton. Full of middle class whites at one time, most of them aspiring to move up a notch to upper middle. But then Asians happened.

Not that a huge horde of them swamped the place overnight. Took decades. Little by little, house by house, the Asians moved in and the whites moved out. The trouble with Asians, especially pakis, is they're different. Different clothes, different language, food, skin, and, of course, we got a different God. That's why the whites move out. They see these different beings, with their different ways and they don't like what they see. So what do they do? They bitch, moan – sometimes panic – and then, sooner or later, they move the fuck out because that's the only thing they think they can do. After that, the only ones who'll move in are more pakis because whites don't want to know, not once the place has become polluted. And on and on it goes until you get these little enclaves, some would say ghettoes, sprawling up all over the town. And then, when the young punks start kicking up a fuss for whatever reason, in comes some smart fucker who tells the world that a place like Bradford suffers from self segregation. No fucking shit Einstein. The whole world is segregated in a million different ways so why should Bradford be any different?

We'd taken the left, then took another left onto Carlisle Road before hitting a right onto Lumb Lane.

'We did all sorts,' he reflected. 'Good days, though. Got up to some right old capers, I can tell you.'

'For example?'

'You know,' he said, a combination of modesty and embarrassment sneaking out with his words. 'Just harmless kid stuff, really.'

I bit my tongue and gripped the gun by its handle.

'You ever hurt anyone? Were you a bad boy, back then?'

'Put it like this: you wouldn't want to come up against me if I was in a bad mood,' he laughed.

I laughed, too.

'You ever get done for anything?'

'Me? No. Far too careful and besides, I don't think anyone would have dared say a word.'

'All that's changed now, though.'

'Oh yes. Saw the error of my ways years ago,' he winked.

'I was right,' I enthused. 'You were a bit on the handy side.'

301

'You could say that, sure. Only now and then did we have to do a bit of strong arm stuff, but it never really got out of hand. Never was a need for things to get out of hand because everyone knew who they were dealing with.'

I nodded and then enquired:

'Everyone? Must have had some idiots who didn't know.'

We got back to the car park. Swain's Bentley crawled up and around the bends like a snail. For a guy who was such a bad bastard in his youth, his driving left a lot to be desired. I'd seen little old grannies drive better than this.

'Oh yeah,' he smiled. 'There were a few we had to, you know, persuade.'

That was it. Rather than the actual meaning, it was his choice of words that triggered a mental, and then verbal response.

'Baseball bats?'

He smiled, not riled in the least, perhaps even enjoying the chance to relive his glory days.

'What?'

'You know,' I said, still trying to remain calm. 'You ever use baseball bats?'

'Well, course we did,' he said. 'Me and Spanner were famed for our batting skills.'

The chocolate unit, the shelves and then my dad's hand. He made a sound, my old man, but he didn't cry and he didn't beg for mercy. I remember that. If anything, being hurt actually made him stronger.

'How do you know?'

'You know, just heard. Like you said: you were famed.'

He shrugged and then, after a moment's consideration asked:

'What else have you heard?'

'This and that, you know.'

Swain parked up and then turned the engine off.

'I heard you were into the odd paki-bashing session when you were younger, that's all. Nothing to be ashamed of. We're all young once.'

'I'm not a racist or anything...but yes, that did happen. I was a bit younger...'

'Oh yeah,' I laughed. 'Sure you were.'

302

He rubbed his chin.

'You're a bad motherfucker,' I smiled. 'You know that?'

He smiled back.

'I know.'

I pulled out the gun.

'I've been wanting to do this for a long, long time.'

I expected him to be surprised but his reaction caught me off guard. He grabbed his chest and started panting like a knackered greyhound.

'What? What…what is this? What's going on?'

I took a breath, thinking I needed it to help calm me down.

'My name is Khalil Khan,' I began, my voice steady, strong: unfaltering. 'My father's name was Ayub Khan. He ran a shop for a long, long time. He would have run that shop until the day he died.'

His face became serious, his eyes relaying my features to the banks of his memory, recalling me. The heart problem suddenly relegated to secondary significance.

'What? What *are* you on about?'

Meal time. That was the best part of my day, without fail. My dad used to love eating and he used to love talking about his day afterwards, almost like a dessert that ritual of his. And me and my mum would sit and listen. Every now and then, I'd chip in and my dad would listen with a great big smile on his face. Dead proud of me and me proud of him. My mum proud of us both.

'You really don't remember me, do you?'

'Remember you? From where? What is going on here? Is this some kind of joke?'

'It's not a joke. But I do remember you, Charlie. And I remember Spanner, coming in every week, telling us to cough up the taxes. I remember seeing my old man die a little bit more every week that happened.'

And then there was the work. It wasn't hard but it was tiring. Pricing things up, stacking shelves, disposing of the packaging, sweeping the floor, dusting shelves and, of course, the most important thing of all: serving the customers. My dad would smile and so would I. Most times people would smile back but there was the odd person who appeared blessed with the gift of a miserable attitude. They were nothing to worry about, my dad would tell me. Just *jahlia loke*: ignorant people. Even so, my dad wouldn't have swapped his shop for anything else in the world.

'What?' he said, 'I…I don't quite…'

Swain licked his lips and swallowed. In his eyes, the faintest light of recognition flickered, slowly glowing brighter.

'You,' he said. 'I remember you now.'

'Good.'

'But listen…'

'Listen?' I shook my head. 'Too late for that. I just thought you should know why I'm about to kill you.'

He held his hands up, but he remained calm. As if that would be enough.

the next episode

The next time I saw Price was soon after they'd released me. Price said it would be a formality and that's exactly how it turned out to be. A couple of high up coppers, ones from out of town, asked me a shit load of questions but they were all very nice and professional about it. I told them what I wanted to tell them. Seeing no reason why corrupt fat fucks ought to be spared, the first act of informing involved me delivering a more than adequate character assassination of Grizzly Adams. Next on the list was revealing Padgett's former name and also explaining how he'd been intricately linked with known criminals for most of his life. As for Spanner, turns out he spilled the beans as soon as they told him about his old running mates getting themselves killed. I'd have been happier with him dead but the thought of him spending the rest of his life behind bars came a close second choice.

And me, I was happy because they had nothing on me. I was being socially responsible and volunteering all this information because it seemed like the right thing to do. I felt morally obliged to share what I knew. I had, after all, turned over a new leaf.

Price could, if he so chose, tell them the real truth. But if he ever decided to tell them how things had really happened, then he'd be forced to impart his own involvement and therefore complicity in a series of highly criminal acts: accessory to murder sitting comfortably at the top of the list. This, needless to say, was out of the question because Price was still that good soul I always thought him to be. Every end he'd achieved he'd achieved for the cause of good. Just so happened that he used bad means. No one's perfect.

So the higher up, anonymous but thoroughly professional looking coppers let me go and off I went. I had one thing left to do and by the time I got there, my heart was racing.

Price must have spotted my car, parked outside on the double yellows, hazard warning lights flashing.

The shop hadn't changed much, if at all. New flooring, a coat of paint but other than that, the same old layout and that included the same till being in the same place, the same newspaper rack sitting on the same part of the floor and the same shelves against the same walls. I looked around for ages before acknowledging the owner.

Like my father, Mister Satnam Singh knew his place and could live with the idea of being a person without a history, a past and a life other than the one he lived in the shop. He stood, same as he always stood, behind the counter, always eager, prepared and raring to serve the next punter that walked through the door. Like my father, and like a million other shopkeepers, he smiled his ethnic arse off. With one look I had him sussed. Here stood a kind of man who did his taxes honestly and then spent a month worrying over them. Paid his bills on time, did his utmost to remain fair and competitive with his prices, never strayed from his wife, prayed to God, believed in hard, honest work and wanted to bring his kids up right. A father, a husband and a believer. So much more than shopkeeper can ever seem.

'Some gum,' I said, selecting a pack from his counter top display.

'Anything else, Youngblood?'

I nodded and smiled at the handle he used.

'Just one thing,' I said. 'Just a favour, really.'

He looked unsure. My father would look this way when people asked for something on the slate.

'Don't worry,' I said. 'It's no big deal.'

He narrowed his gaze, still suspicious but curious all the same.

'Go on. What is it, then, Youngblood?'

So I told him what I wanted to do. After a couple of moment's worth of consideration he said he understood.

'I knew your father very well. He was a very good man,' he shrugged and then added. 'I know it's been a long time but God's Will about him, you know. God's Will, we say.'

And so, Satnam Singh allowed me to stand behind his counter. I ran my fingers over the keys on the till, most of the numbers and symbols worn away over the years but I knew them all. Spent hours studying them and even more hours dreaming about pressing them, about working them, the way my old man would.

'It's a bit slow, this time of night, Youngblood,' explained Satnam Singh.

The door opened and I smiled, eager and at the ready.

'Thought that was your car out there,' he said. 'It's parked illegally.'

I nodded.

'So give me a ticket.'

Price looked around, at the selection of crisps, then the drinks and finally settled on the chocolate unit.

'Okay,' he said. 'I'll have a packet of those Werther's Originals.'

He handed me a pound coin. I keyed in the amount, let the machine do the maths and then I hit the TL (total) button, just like my father would. The money tray sprung open, I dropped the pound in and then selected the change. I don't know how long I took to serve Price but I do know it was a long, long time. Satnam Singh, the consummate shop-keeper who knew the value of rapid but pleasant service, even he could not bring himself to interrupt. He could sense something other than what he saw. I needed to savour it, make it last for as long as was humanly possible. Similarly, Price waited for me in silence, as if he knew the significance of this one moment that had, after all, taken the longest time in coming.

Discography

dil walla dhukra - Mohammed Alam Lohar, Tribute, Oriental Star Recordings, (year indiscernible)

1. witness
dream a lie - UB40, Signing Off, Graduate, (1980)
charlie don't surf - The Clash, Sandinista, Epic, (1980)
rock bottom – Eminem, Slim Shady LP, Aftermath/Interscope, (1999)
legalise it – Peter Tosh, Legalise It, Columbia, (1976)

2. glengarry glen ross
jugni – Mohammed Alam Lohar, Tribute, Oriental Star Recordings, (year indiscernible)
journey - Asian Dub Foundation, Facts and Fictions, Nation Records, (1995)
scorpio – Grand Master Flash And The Furious Five, 12 inch, Sugar Hill Records, (1982)
the negotiation limerick – Beastie Boys, Hello Nasty, Capitol, (1999)

3. how to get ahead in advertising
magic's wand – Whodini, 12 inch single, Jive/Zomba, (1982)
slave driver – Bob Marley and The Wailers, Tuff Gong, (1973)
let the music play – Shannon, Let The Music Play, Mirage, (1984)
dead wrong – Notorious BIG ft Eminem, Born Again, Bad Boy, (1999)
battleflag – Lo Fidelity All Stars ft Pigeonhead, How to Operate With a Blown Mind, Skint/Columbia, (1998)
keep your head up – Tupac Shakur, Strictly For My N.I.G.G.A.Z., Interscope, (1993)
get out – Busta Rhymes, Anarchy, Elektra Entertainment, (2000)
king of rock – Run DMC, King Of Rock, Def Jam Records, (1985)

4. death of a salesman

boyz n the hood – N.W.A. (Eazy E), N.W.A. and The Posse, Ruthless Records, (1987)

waiting for my man, The Velvet Underground and Nico, Polydor Records, (1967)

big pimpin – Jay Z, Volume 3... Life and Times of S. Carter, Roc-A-Fella Records, (1999)

trash – Suede, Coming Up, Nude Records, (1996)

double barrel - Dave and Ansell Collins, Big Tree Records, (1971)

police and thief – Junior Murvin, Mango, (1977)

sometimes – James, Laid, Polygram Records, (1993)

let forever be – The Chemical Brothers, Surrender, Astralwerks/ MMD, (1999)

a message to you rudy – The Specials, Specials, Two Tone Records, (1979)

white man's got a god complex – Last Poets, Last Poets, Douglas Records, (1970)

the next episode – Dr Dre ft Snoop Doggy Dogg, The Chronic 2001, Interscope Records, (1999).

Annie Potts is Dead

M Y Alam's first novel

It's not easy to write when you work in a shop. Customers
can tend to break your concentration.

It's not easy to deal with rejection from an editor either,
especially when he reminds you of that little fat bloke
from the film *Deliverance*.

It's not easy listening to rumours from people who don't
know the difference between fact and fiction.

No wonder all his stories are all about killers.

Ammy is a writer and he writes. And now, he's going for
it - the big time. The problem is, no one is interested.
Things have to change. And they do.
The police are outside, giving it the Ringo Starr with his
door. Annie Potts, they tell him, is dead and what's more,
they think he did it.

ISBN 1901927032 | Published 1998 £6.95

Route Subscription

Route's subscription scheme is the easiest way for readers to keep in touch with new work from the best of new young writers. Subscribers receive a minimum of four books per year, which could take the form of a novel, an anthology of short stories, a novella, a poetry collection or mix and match titles. Any additional publications and future issues of the route paper will also be mailed direct to subscribers, as well as information on route events and digital projects.

Route constantly strives to promote the best in under represented voices, outside of the mainstream, and will give support to develop promising new talent. By subscribing to route, you too will be supporting these artists.

The fee is modest.

UK £15
Europe £20 (35€ approx)
Rest of World £25(US$40 approx)

Subscribe online now at www.route-online.com

To receive a postal subscription form email your details to books@route-online.com or send your details to:
route, school lane, glasshoughton, wf10 4qh, uk

Kilo is a title on the route subscription scheme.

The Blackstuff

Val Cale

ISBN 1-901927 14 8

'The mind is like a creamy pint of Guinness…The head is the engine that drives you through the day…the fuel however lies in the blackstuff, in the darkness, in the depths of the unexplored cave which is your subconscious mind…this is the story of my journey through the blackstuff.'

The Blackstuff is a true story of a road-trip that sees Val Cale in trouble in Japan, impaled in Nepal, ripped off at a vaginal freak show in Bangkok, nearly saturated by a masturbating Himalayan bear in the most southerly town of India and culminates in a mad tramp across the world looking for the ultimate blowjob and the meaning of life.

The Blackstuff is *not* just a book. It is *not* just the opinion of an individual who feels that he has something important to say. This is a story which every last one of us can relate to, a story about the incessant battle between our internal angels and our demented demons. This is an odyssey to the liquefied centre of the brain, a magic carpet ride surfing on grass and pills, seas of booze, and the enormous strength of the human soul.

The Blackstuff takes you beyond the beach, deeper into the ocean of darkness that is the pint of stout in your head…

Weatherman

Anthony Cropper

ISBN 1-901927 16 4

Ken sits out the back, in the flatlands that surround Old Goole, and watches the weather. That's what he was doing with poor Lucy, that fateful day, sat on the roof of his house, lifting her up to the sky. Lucy's friend, Florrie, she knew what would happen.

All this is picked up by Alfie de Losinge's machine, which he had designed to control the weather. Instead, amongst the tiny atoms of cloud formations, he receives fragmentary images of events that slowly unfold to reveal a tender, and ultimately tragic, love story.

In this beautifully crafted first novel, Anthony Cropper skilfully draws a picture of life inextricably linked to the environment, the elements, and the ever changing weather.

Very Acme
Adrian Wilson
ISBN: 1 901927 12 1 £6.95

New Nomad, nappy expert, small town man and ultimately a hologram – these are the life roles of Adrian Wilson, hero and author of this book, which when he began writing it, was to become the world's first novel about two and a half streets. He figured that all you ever needed to know could be discovered within a square mile of his room, an easy claim to make by a man who's family hadn't moved an inch in nearly seven centuries.

All this changes when a new job sends him all around the world, stories of Slaughter and the Dogs and Acme Terrace give way to Procter and Gamble and the Russian Mafia. He starts feeling nostalgic for the beginning of the book before he gets to the end.

Very Acme is two books within one, it is about small town life in the global age and trying to keep a sense of identity in a world of multi-corporations and information overload.

Like A Dog To Its Vomit
Daithidh MacEochaidh
ISBN: 1 901927 07 5 £6.95

Somewhere between the text, the intertext and the testosterone find Ron Smith, illiterate book lover, philosopher of non-thought and the head honcho's left-arm man. Watch Ron as he oversees the begging franchise on Gunnarsgate, shares a room with a mouse of the Lacota Sioux and makes love to Tracy back from the dead and still eager to get into his dungarees. There's a virgin giving birth under the stairs, putsch at the taxi rank and Kali, Goddess of Death, is calling. Only Arturo can sort it, but Arturo is travelling. In part two find out how to live in a sock and select sweets from a shop that time forgot and meet a no-holds barred state registered girlfriend. In part three, an author promises truth, but the author is dead - isn't she?

In this complex, stylish and downright dirty novel, Daithidh MacEochaidh belts through underclass underachieving, postponed-modern sacrilege and the more pungent bodily orifices.

Crazy Horse
Susan Everett
ISBN 1 901927 06 7 £6.95

Jenny Barker, like many young women, has a few problems. She is trying to get on with her life, but it isn't easy. She was once buried underneath the sand and it had stopped her growing up, plus she had killed the milkman. Her beloved horse has been stolen while the vicious *Savager* is on the loose cutting up animals in fields. She's neither doing well in college nor in love and fears she may die a virgin.

Crazy Horse is a wacky ride.

Half a Pint of Tristram Shandy

Jo Pearson, Daithidh MacEochaidh, Peter Knaggs

ISBN 1 901927 15 6 £6.95

A three-in-one peotry collection from the best in young poets. Between the leaves of this book lies the mad boundless energy of the globe cracking-up under our very noses; it is a world which is harnessed in images of jazz, sex, drugs, aliens, abuse; in effective colloquial language and manic syntax; but the themes are always treated with gravity, unsettling candour and humour.

I Am

Michelle Scally-Clarke

ISBN 1 901927 08 3 £10 Including free CD

At thirty years old, Michelle is the same age as the mother who gave her up into care as a baby. In the quest to find her birth parents, her roots and her own identity, this book traces the journey from care, to adoption, to motherhood, to performer. Using the fragments of her own memory, her poetry and extracts from her adoption files, Michelle rebuilds the picture of 'self' that allows her to transcend adversity and move forward to become the woman she was born to be.

You can hear the beat and song of Michelle Scally-Clarke on the CD that accompanies this book and, on the inside pages, read the story that is the source of that song.

Moveable Type

Rommi Smith

ISBN 1 901927 11 3 £10 Including free CD

It is the theme of discovery that is at the heart of *Moveable Type*. Rommi Smith takes the reader on a journey through identity, language and memory, via England and America, with sharp observation, wit and wry comment en route. The insights and revelations invite us not only to look beneath the surface of the places we live in, but also ourselves. *Moveable Type* and its accompanying CD offer the reader the opportunity to listen or read, read and listen. Either way, you are witnessing a sound that is uniquely Rommi Smith.